NAMESAKE

OTHER WORKS BY KATE STRADLING

A Boy Called Hawk (2010)
A Rumor of Real Irish Tea (2011)

The Ruses Series
Kingdom of Ruses (2012)
Tournament of Ruses (2014)

Goldmayne: A Fairy Tale (2013)

The Legendary Inge (2015)

NAMESAKE

Kate Stradling

Eulalia Skye Press
MESA, ARIZONA

Namesake

Copyright © 2017 by Kate Stradling
katestradling.com

All rights reserved. No part of this book may be reproduced or transmitted in any form or by any means, electronic or mechanical, including photocopying, recording, or by any information storage and retrieval system, without written consent of the author.

Published by
Eulalia Skye Press
PO Box 2203, Mesa, AZ 85214
eulaliaskye.com

ISBN: 978-1-947495-00-5
Library of Congress Control Number: 2017949588

For Rachel and Jill,
who wouldn't let me have my
mediocre way

CHAPTER ONE

I WAS A MISTAKE.

My mother always says this as a joke. "Oh, Jen was our little mistake, but she's turned out well enough so far." And then she squeezes my arm and shares a laugh with my dad, and I force a smile at whichever dignitary they're schmoozing. They were once young and in love and faced with a difficult choice that threatened careers and ambitions alike. Owning up to it outright demonstrates their integrity and self-sacrifice.

Except, from what I can tell, the only reason they didn't terminate me was because they dithered over the decision until it was no longer legal to make.

I arrived a month early, squalling and puny, probably over-eager to escape what was almost the stage of my execution. My parents decided to keep me after all, but that didn't change my origins: I was a mistake.

My sister, only fifteen months younger than me, was not a mistake. Mom always wanted a sibling, so once they were saddled with me, they decided to have another child right away. She came happy and perfect and they coddled her to a degree that I never remembered receiving, probably because I was too young to remember it when they transferred the behavior to her.

They named us Anjeni and Aitana, from our country's most famous legend, only I am called Jen and she is Tana, and I am common and she is extraordinary.

Tana excels in everything: school, sports, music, and magic. I struggle with all of these, as though my body slogs through molasses while hers cuts like a knife through the air.

"You could do it too if you'd try harder, Jen."

How many times have I heard those words? I have tried, but things always fizzle in a cloud of wasted effort. Magic in particular has never come to me. I can't even light a spark on a candlewick, while Tana dances around the room with fireworks shooting from her fingertips and a thousand tapers lit in an instant.

But really, who needs magic to light a candle when you live in an age of electricity? I can flip the switch on the wall with the best of them.

My magic tutors hate when I mention this. They sigh and shake their heads, and then they utter that second dreaded phrase:

"Why can't you be more like your sister?"

Believe me, I wish I could. Tana is confident and popular and loved. And I am simply the mistake.

Pitiful, uncoordinated, untalented, ungraceful.

I hate myself for it.

Over time, that self-hatred has seeded bitterness and cynicism. At some point I stopped trying. I go through the motions, attend all my classes, and pull in average grades for everything except magic. Magic is supplementary, but my parents require me to take it, and I fail, year after year after year. I can recite the theories off by heart, but I have not even the slightest budding of abilities, and every class conducts the exams in the same order: practical first, followed by theory.

Every year, I fail the practical. So every year, I scrawl pictures all over my theory exam. I carry a lighter in my pocket so I can flip it open when my tutors present their dreaded candle test. I sleep through magic classes, or stare out the window. I check out of life.

My tutors have asked my parents—begged my parents—not to enroll me anymore.

My dad always has the same response. "She tested positive. She's just being stubborn."

I did test positive for magic, right after Tana started setting fire to her crib sheets by accident. In this day and age, they don't test by making the suspected magician produce sparks. No, they scan the part of the brain that governs magic use. Tana's tests were off the charts for a one-year-old. Mine were just below average, but I'm pretty sure it was a fluke that I registered at all. False positives have occurred.

Really, if anyone is stubborn, it's my parents. They aren't worried about me so much as their own reputations. Magic skipped over both of them, so it would look better to have two daughters as magicians instead of only one—even if that one is the wondrous Tana.

"Jen, I know you can do this." My latest tutor, Miss Corlan, regards me with steady eyes. I can practically read her thoughts: she's going to crack this tough nut. She's going to get through to the recalcitrant elder daughter of Rayvi and Jerika Sigourna. She has the patience, the knowledge, the compassion to coax me from my shell.

Amateur.

"I can't. Some people can't, you know."

"You just don't want to."

The accusation strikes a nerve. "I'm not my sister. What will it take to get that through everyone's stupid head? I'm *not* Tana."

Her mouth twists into a practiced smile. "But you're so like her. You have the same black eyes, the same profile, the same long, dark hair. You two are more alike than you want to admit. If you would only recognize your similarities, maybe you could finally overcome this mental block of yours. You may pretend you don't care, but I can see as plain as day how much you want to be like her."

Five years ago she may have been right. Five years ago, I still held out hope. I don't have any left, though, and being told—again—that my failures are somehow my own fault rankles me in a way that only Tana has ever accomplished. I can't change my profile or the color of my eyes, so instead, I go home and hack my hair off to the nape of my neck. Then I bleach it blond just because I can.

Only I fail at that, too. When the water rinses away all the peroxide and the steam on the mirror clears up, I am left staring at a fiery orange mess.

CHAPTER TWO

MOM STRUGGLES TO BREATHE, her throat tight, her eyes huge and fixed on my head. I hold it high despite the butcher-job I've accomplished.

"What... have... you... done?" She forces the words through gritted teeth, making a valiant endeavor to keep her temper under control. She determined long ago not to let my antics or failures get to her, but this one really pushes the limit.

Next to her, Perfect Tana struggles over whether to gawk or jeer. "Jen, what were you thinking?"

"Did I have to be thinking something?" I round on the stair post, headed for the front door.

Mom lunges. "No!" Her hand clamps around my arm and she drags me back. She holds me fast as she punches in a number on her phone—her stylist, Renado, whom she keeps on speed dial. He answers, and she gibbers into the receiver. "I'm so sorry to call you on such short notice, but it's an emergency. Yes, come to the house, as soon as you possibly can.

"Thank the stars!" she cries as she hangs up, and she finally releases her hold. "He'll be here in half an hour. Go to your room until then, Jen, and if you sneak out, you'll be grounded until you're thirty-five. Tana, make sure she goes."

"I don't need her help getting back up the stairs," I sneer. Tana, the insufferable brat, follows me anyway.

When we're out of earshot, she hisses, "Kind of a drastic cry for attention, don't you think, *Anjeni*?"

"Shut it, golden child," I say. Then I close my bedroom door in her face.

The truth is, Tana is good and kind and perfect to everyone but me. When we are alone, she can be downright nasty, and I'm nasty back to her. For as long as I can remember, she has shoved her accomplishments in my face and taken every opportunity to needle me on my failures. In front of our parents she affects loving concern, but her words always twist the knife deeper.

"I wish that Jen could work a spark. It would be so much fun if we were both magicians, instead of me being the only one." It sounds like sisterly love, but the way she speaks and the sly glances she slides my direction testify of how much she relishes her advantage over me.

Even if I do spark something someday, I will never be her equal, and that will only give her more cause to gloat.

I stew in my room, my fingers toying with my newly shortened hair. The garish orange is growing on me. I mean, I could always run away and join a troupe of clowns. I'd fit right in. By the time my mother's knock taps on the door, I've nearly convinced myself to climb out the window and have a go at it.

"Oh, dear," Renado says from behind her. His shrewd eyes survey the mess. "Come to the bathroom. I'll set it to rights in no time at all."

"Back to its original color," my mother says. "There's nothing to be done about the length, but that orange has got to go. You can use Tana's hair as a reference."

My sister is in the hall, a triumphant smirk on her lips. Renado must see the mutinous expression that flashes across my face—or maybe it's professional pride that prompts him to say, "I think I can manage the color well enough. Come on, Little Anjeni."

Sullenly I follow him. He shuts the bathroom door tight and pulls the necessary supplies from his well-stocked bag. "Caught in the throes of teen angst?"

"I just got tired of long hair," I say.

"Sure you did. Why bleach it, then?"

I speak not a word to this, my nose high in the air.

He ignores my attitude and begins mixing dyes. His voice turns pensive. "You know, I have an older brother. People used to compare us all the time, until I finally snapped and dyed my hair blue. I thought it would help, but it didn't. It was only a cosmetic change, and comparisons tend to run a lot deeper."

He's trying to relate to me. How cute.

"Is your brother better than you in every little thing?" I ask, sarcasm thick on my voice. "Did you fall short in every single comparison?"

Renado chuckles. "No. But I did eventually learn that the comparisons bothered him as much as they bothered me."

"Tana likes it," I say, my words clipped. "She always comes out smelling like roses."

Silence settles between us. He works the solution through my hair with expert fingers, only the slight rustling of his gloves to interrupt my surly thoughts. It's hard to stay surly with someone massaging my scalp, but I do my very best. At long last he sculpts the hair together and sits back to let the dye process.

"You know, it can't be easy for your sister either," he tells me. I glare, but he remains undeterred. "The goddess Anjeni and the mere mortal Aitana? Not much comparison between those two."

"That's only a legend," I say. "It has nothing to do with real life."

"It's the founding of our country. The goddess Anjeni walked through the Eternity Gate and defeated a shadow-army. She restored magic to our people. She's a hero: everyone loves her."

My voice turns sarcastically sweet. "Everyone except Demetrios. He ran away with Aitana, remember?"

"And everyone hates Aitana for it, remember?" Renado replies, answering my sass in kind. "Face it, Little Jen. Your parents gave Tana the short shrift where names are concerned."

"They didn't do me much of a favor either. With a namesake like mine, I was bound to fail. Besides, Anjeni's pathetic enough in her own right. For everything she accomplished, to fall in love with a philanderer? And then, after he leaves, she just disappears back through the Eternity Gate, broken-hearted? What a legacy."

He smiles, though. "It's romantic and poetic. She's supposed to come back someday in a flash of glory, once her heart mends. No, it's definitely better to be named after her. Your sister probably thinks so too. The Aitana of legends was selfish and self-serving."

"Well, the Aitana of today is perfect in every possible way as far as everyone's concerned."

He pats my knee and winks. "Except for her namesake. You win that comparison any day of the week."

CHAPTER THREE

THE SHORT HAIR SURPRISINGLY SUITS ME. Renado has smoothed out my jagged cut and given it a sharp angle to frame my face. He's cut me some bangs, too. The dark color matches Tana's to a shade, but it seems less offensive in its new, sleek style.

Mom still grounds me, of course. "Our family has a reputation to uphold, Jen. What would the media say about your father if you had appeared in public with that mangled head of hair?"

"They probably would have pitied him having to deal with a moody teenaged daughter. I don't see what the big deal is. Lots of girls experiment with their looks."

The vein just above her right eyebrow pulses. "Lots of girls are not the president's daughter, Anjeni."

And there lies the crux of the matter. Everything in our family life revolves around my father's political career. He is not the youngest president our country has ever had, but in its seven-hundred-year history, precious few leaders have been younger. The very youngest was also the very first: Etricos, the older brother of the inconstant Demetrios who broke the goddess Anjeni's heart. We have relics of his life preserved in the National Archives, some of the scant proof that the legends are more than just mere stories. Etricos shouldered the unenviable task of leading the fragile nation, first through its fight for freedom from the armies of darkness that sought to destroy it, and then afterward as it established its foothold upon the world.

Dad, twenty or more generations removed, still claims the same purpose as that first leader: to protect and to serve the nation of Helenia. He rose to the position when I was fourteen and Tana twelve, and from then on, our whole family has lived life under a magnifying glass. I hate politics. I hate the façade required to keep the people happy. Someone judging my father based on me cutting and bleaching my hair is the most ridiculous thing I've ever heard.

But that is simply the way of the world. Good thing the garish orange is gone, right?

I'm still in my room when my dad comes home. The front door opens and shuts downstairs. I'm guessing Mom intercepts him in the entryway, because two minutes later he taps on my door.

"Jen, I want curry tonight. Want to come with me?"

I open the door and spear him with a skeptical glare. Everyone in my family, myself excepted, hates spicy food. Mom and Tana avoid it like poison. Dad eats it only in its mildest forms, and only because curry is a national, ancestral dish. When he wants curry, it means that he wants to garner favor with either the media or with me.

I can eat spicy foods like a true champion. The spicier, the better. It's my one strength.

"Cute hair," he says with a half-cocked smile. "It looks good on you."

"I'm grounded for three weeks," I reply.

"That doesn't mean you're not allowed to eat. Come on."

I follow him, curious about what lecture he'll pitch my way, more curious about how much effort he intends to expend on my behalf. He pauses at the bottom of the stairs to poke his head into the living room, where Mom and Tana both are.

"I'm taking Jen out for dinner. Do you want us to bring you anything back?"

Mom declines. Tana looks as though someone has shoved a spoonful of fish oil into her mouth. I can't exactly blame her: my act of rebellion has earned me special treatment. Even I expected at best a disappointed shake of the head, a fatherly pat on the shoulder, and an admonition not to drive my mother crazy.

Instead, here Dad is, phoning a restaurant for reservations and sending part of his security attachment ahead. He glances my way, assessing my clothes to make sure they're suitable for a public outing. Casual as they are, they pass inspection. He discards his tie and unbuttons his collar, and off we go into the city.

"Shouldn't we just order takeout?" I ask, suddenly nervous. Eating at the restaurant means onlookers and photographs and possibly a blurb in the news.

"Can't let the new haircut go to waste," he says.

Realization dawns. "Oh. I'm being punished." He knows I hate public attention. He knows I had to be in a foul mood to have hacked off my hair. He knows I'll have to put on a happy face for his sake.

"Where did you get the bleach?" he asks.

"I bought it on my way home from school. Don't worry. Everyone was following Tana. No one even noticed me going into the shop."

"Not even the clerk?"

"I used a self-checkout. And cash."

He pats my arm. "Good girl."

I had considered our family's situation, even in the midst of my afternoon anger. The peroxide was an impulse, one I hadn't even been sure I would use, but I didn't want some report of my buying it to reach my mother's ears before I got the chance. In general, President Sigourna's children are off-limits to the media unless we're in the company of one or both of our parents. They aren't allowed to ask about our academic records or take pictures of us on our way to and from school, but that doesn't mean no one tries. Luckily for me, the few dirtbags that ignore this restriction always hone in on Tana. She's more interesting. I've been branded "the shy one."

In that respect, there are benefits to being the common child.

"So what was it this time?" Dad asks. "What made you do something so drastic?"

The question chafes. He knows I reacted to something else, that I didn't simply choose to lop off nearly two feet of hair after careful deliberation. I'm not about to tell him that one of my magic tutors got under my skin. That would only encourage him to think they're making headway with me. So, I blame my usual scapegoat.

"I'm tired of being Tana's less-accomplished shadow. I'm not her, and I don't want to be her, and I don't even want to look like her. All right?"

His brows shoot up as I speak, but he maintains his composure otherwise. "You're sisters, Jen. You're going to look like each other whether you like it or not."

He's not helping. My restraints explode.

"You don't get it! It's not just about looks! It's everything! She's good at everything, and then everyone looks at me and wonders what's wrong with me!"

"It's not Tana's fault she's good at things. Would you have her pretend to be bad, just to make you feel better?"

"No! I just want to do my own things, to have my own interests instead of everyone expecting me to excel where she does!"

His expression shutters. Tana excels in things he values: academics, magic, social skills. As his child, I'm supposed to value all of that as well. But I don't. It's yet another one of my failures.

"What are your interests, then?" he finally asks.

My breath leaves my lungs in a whoosh of air. I slump against the car door in defeat. "I don't even know." I don't, either. My whole life I've been exposed to the pursuits my parents value, but I've always been the odd one out in all of them, never excelling, never even interested.

We arrive at the restaurant. The driver crosses around to open the door. I straighten in my seat and fix my expression to something neutral, in case there are photographers out on the sidewalk.

My dad climbs out first, but as he steps to the curb I grab the cuff of his sleeve. He looks down at me in alarm.

"I want to quit magic," I tell him.

From beyond the door, a camera flashes. He schools away his momentary surprise and fakes a smile. "We'll talk about it when you're eighteen."

"That's only two months away. What does it matter if I quit now?"

He shifts his hand to clasp mine, fluidly assisting me from the car as though that was his original intent in pausing there.

"You're not quitting," he whispers in my ear as a dozen more flashes explode in my periphery. "Now smile and pretend to be happy."

He has to know that both those commands are impossible for me to obey. Somehow I manage not to scowl, but at the moment, the only point of happiness I have in my life is the fiery bowl of curry I'm about to eat.

CHAPTER FOUR

WE LIVE IN THE PRESIDENTIAL RESIDENCE on Monument Hill, overlooking the city. A whole complex of government buildings are scattered across the sides and the back of the hill, facing the ocean on the horizon, but the front is covered in lawn and gardens, with one major focal point: the Eternity Gate. Older than time itself, so the legends say, it stands like a beacon, a stone arch weathered with age, patterns of a dead and forgotten language etched deep into its surface.

The legends claim that the Eternity Gate can connect to the realm of the gods. More contemporary theories suggest that it once opened a portal from another world. My opinion? It's a decorative hunk of stonework. Aside from the legend of the goddess Anjeni, there is no record of it ever having opened to anything at all.

Even so, it's my favorite haunt.

In my younger years I obsessed over the tales, collections from centuries ago. My namesake shaped our world; she changed everything. Helenia wouldn't exist without her, if the stories are true. Plenty of scholars argue that they aren't, that

Anjeni is a figment or an allegory, that Etricos was a genius general who united the tribes on his own merits.

I took those arguments as personal attacks when I was younger, as though, when people said the goddess Anjeni didn't exist they were saying that *I* didn't exist either. The very day my family moved into the president's house on Monument Hill, I begged my dad to take us into the National Archives, to see the remnants and relics from that time in hopes of finding definitive proof.

There was none. They have Etricos's sword and pieces of his armor. They have fragments of his handwriting in some tattered letters to his wife, Tora. Nothing much more has survived the generations. A fire in the archives two hundred years after his time destroyed records and battle accounts from that era, and the legends we know now all cropped up afterwards, when people tried to recreate what had been lost to the blaze.

In short, the naysaying scholars are probably right. The goddess Anjeni is a romanticized myth. The Eternity Gate is the only relic left that she might have ever touched, and it's more likely proof that the whole set of tales is rubbish.

I run my fingers over the Eternity Gate's weather-worn stones, relishing the cold of night that still possesses them. The sun will warm the arch soon enough, but I like it best in these early morning hours when the world is mostly silent.

Monument Hill pitches down at a precarious angle, the Eternity Gate perched near the top and the city sprawled out in the valley below. Only a black wrought-iron fence separates the green hillside from the street at the base of it. Traffic there is restricted, thankfully. From further beyond, the faint sounds of engines and horns punctuate the morning air.

Sunrise through the Gate always soothes my harrowed soul. I have school still to navigate and a magic tutor's confidence to destroy. My new look is going to garner me more attention than I want. In this moment at the Gate, though, none of that matters.

My soul drinks in the sight until the sun's rays begin to warm the stones beneath my fingers. I steel myself to leave, to orient myself toward the academy. Unfortunately, I don't hear the footsteps behind me until it's too late.

A pair of hands shoves me through the arch. With a yelp I pitch forward, tumbling down the hillside as Tana's triumphant voice calls out a jeer after me.

"Off you go on your spiritual journey, Goddess Anjeni!"

That hill, as I've said, is *steep*. I cry out in panic as my shoulder jars into the soft lawn, but my self-preservation instincts kick in. I know from experience that I won't be able to stop my momentum until I hit the bottom. Tana has pulled this trick a dozen or more times over the years we've lived here. It's a wonder I've never broken my neck.

"Tana!" I screech when I finally sprawl out at the base of the hill, my uniform grass-stained and several bruises starting on my skin.

She only favors me with a nasty laugh and darts away again, the brat. She could have killed me.

And no one would believe a word of it.

Gradually I cobble together my wits, allowing time for my racing heart to slow and my breath to resume its steady rhythm. My joints ache as I sit up from the lawn, but nothing seems to be broken.

Getting back up the hill is a chore on its own. I could follow the fence along the base, but my wounded pride won't allow for the heightened chance that someone might see me in such a disheveled state. I have to change uniforms, bind up a scrape on my elbow, and still somehow make it to school on time.

Tana has already left when I trudge in from the garden. My mother, sipping her breakfast tea, takes one look at me and slams the cup down on its saucer.

"What on earth?"

"Tana pushed me down the hill," I report, bitterness in my voice.

"Tana left ten minutes ago," Mom argues, following behind me.

Of course. Her precious baby would *never* harm a hair on anyone's head. Especially not right before she leaves for school.

"Fine, then, I fell. I'm going to change and then I'll get out of your way."

"Be more careful, Jen," she calls up the stairs after me. "You might have broken your neck."

Tana might have broken my neck, I long to say, but I hold my tongue. Short of catching my sister in the act, no one would believe her capable of any malicious pranks. She's a perfect angel in the eyes of the world.

I bind my battered arm and my wounded pride both. Much as I might want revenge against my little sister, with my luck, she'd end up dead at the bottom of the hill, and I'd be off to prison for pre-meditated murder.

Keeping my school tardiness record in mind, Mom sends me in her car instead of on foot. I feel the stares upon me the moment I step out onto the curb. I tip my nose in the air and ignore them all. The bell rings, signifying how close I might have come to missing my first hour. I saunter into class without a word, eager for the day to be over before it's really even begun.

By lunchtime, I loathe Tana more than I knew was humanly possible.

"She tried to do something with it herself first, the poor thing. You should have seen the state her hair was in, but luckily our mom's stylist came to the rescue."

That's what she's telling all her friends, as though my stint with hair shears and peroxide was an optimistic fool's attempt at fashion rather than an outright act of rebellion. My haircut *is* fashionable, you see, and Tana can't handle anyone complimenting me on it.

Throttling her in the middle of school would cause a public relations disaster for my parents.

"It looks good on you though, Jen," one of my classmates tells me after hearing Tana's account. He spoils the compliment by adding, "Tana would look good with that haircut."

"Tana doesn't have the nerve to cut off her hair," I say, my voice a thorn of ice. It doesn't matter if I drive him away. Boys never talk to me except as a way of getting closer to my sister.

When I show up for magic supplementals after regular classes, Miss Corlan observes me with thinning lips. "I see we've made a little change." A note of triumph tinges her voice, as though this is the outcome she was aiming for all along. "Now, how else will you distinguish yourself from your sister?"

She produces from beneath the table a fat, white candle.

I produce my lighter from my pocket and flick it open with an expert wrist.

"No, Jen." From behind me, the Dean of Magic confiscates the lighter right out of my hand.

"Hey!"

"You know the rules. You can have it back after class."

Across the room, in the advanced section, Tana smirks at me. I plop down at my remedial table and perch my chin on one palm.

Miss Corlan starts into the most rudimentary of explanations. "The first fundamental of magic is that—"

"'—it flows like a river,'" I interrupt. I've heard the recitation hundreds of times, every time they produce that stupid candle, in fact. "'The energy gathers from a source beyond sight and, like water in its riverbed, courses to its destination. You are the riverbed, Jen.' Only I'm not, Miss Corlan, or if I am, this riverbed is as dry as a bleached bone."

"You know the first fundamental," she allows.

My patience wears thin. "I know all of the fundamentals. I know all of the intermediates, and all of the superlatives. Tana wanders around the house reading them at the top of her lungs while she tries to memorize them. I'm stuck in remedial because I have no sparks to light a candle. And why we equate something that starts fires to flowing water, I'll never understand. Give it up, Miss Corlan. I'm a lost cause."

She tempers her instinctive irritation into a pleasant smile. "If you know all of the fundamentals, it's simply a matter of practice."

I lean closer, my voice a low whisper. "I think the dean must not like you very much. He usually assigns me to tutors he wants to get rid of."

All's fair in love and war, and this is definitely war.

"I asked for the assignment," she replies with a smirk.

Of course she did, the insufferable over-achiever. I ramp up my innocent curiosity. "You're the one looking for an excuse to quit? How can I help?"

"Why do you resist so much? Jen, if you would just put in a little effort—"

"Don't give me that garbage."

Yet, she persists. "I've seen your tests. You never even try."

"What's the point? I have no magic."

"You do. I've seen those tests too. Why do you fight so much against it?"

I cut off all my hair yesterday because of her. I'm determined not to let her get the best of me today. With practiced calm I look her straight in the eyes and say, enunciating every single word, *"I don't need it."*

And I fully believe my words. Magic is a frivolous pursuit in a world of technology. It's an ego-stroke, a means of elevating one's self above others. I don't need it. No one does. It's gratuitous and divisive, and at this point, I want nothing to do with it.

That afternoon, after I go home, Miss Corlan asks the dean to switch her assignment. The following day, I'm met with the more-than-welcome sight of a new tutor to break.

CHAPTER FIVE

THE WEEKS PASS AT A SNAIL'S PACE. Dad has said I can quit magic when I turn eighteen, and I intend to hold him to it.

(He didn't really say it, of course, but he said we could discuss it, and if I pretend the decision is already made, I'm that much closer to success.)

In this respect at least the Dean of Magic is my ally. He can't wait for me to be gone and has finally awarded my recalcitrance with self-study at the remedial table. Miss Corlan has shifted her tutelage to Tana's benefit. Every so often, I catch her peeking in my direction as though to assess whether her change of favor gets under my skin.

What a paltry woman. All of the magic tutors favor Tana over me. It's nothing new.

The week of my birthday arrives. I'm almost giddy with anticipation. After years of abject failure I can finally quit. My parents will fight me on it, but eighteen has its privileges. I'll be legal to live on my own, to drop out of school all together and get a full-time job. That goes against the path they envision for me—and that I envision for myself, truth be told—but if they want me to cooperate, they'll have to return the courtesy.

I'm so close to freedom that I can practically taste it.

The Dean of Magic knows it's on the horizon too. He sets me in a corner with a stack of workbooks, but he leaves a fat non-magical history book on the top of the pile.

I love history. My childhood obsession with the goddess Anjeni led to that more general love. I can't count how many times the dean has caught me reading history books instead of my magic manuals. I consider his indulgence now as a sign of solidarity with my cause.

Tana glances suspiciously my direction throughout the lesson, as though it's any of her business what I'm reading. If the wonder-child dares to say anything, I'll chastise her for neglecting her own studies.

Life is good.

The night before my birthday—my Birthday Eve—that walk home is the sweetest, most liberating experience. I fiddle with the lighter in my pocket as I go. Tana, up ahead with a group of friends, keeps looking back over her shoulder as though she suspects I'm going to slink away into the falling shadows.

Starting tomorrow, I won't even have to carry the stupid lighter anymore. There will be no more candle tests, no more pointless hours wasted trying to create a spark of energy, no more scrawling rude pictures on theory exams.

"You're such a quitter," Tana mutters as we pass through the door into the house.

She knows I'm at the end of my road too. Is she worried she won't shine as bright without a dud of a sister beside her?

That's her issue. I refuse to lose any sleep over it.

And then all my joyful anticipation crashes in shambles around me.

"I enrolled both of you in summer classes today," my mother announces over dinner. "The Dean of Magic called to say his spots were filling up, so I went ahead."

I can't believe my ears. Did she not get the memo? "I'm not going to magic classes over the summer. I'm not going back ever again. I'm eighteen."

"You're not eighteen yet." Dad lifts his wine glass to take a sip, as if he's weighing in on the most insignificant of subjects.

My indignation swells. "I might as well be! It's *literally* hours away!"

"Jen, keep your temper," says my mother from the other end of the table. Across from me, Tana smirks, a spectator to my humiliation.

I suppress my emotions in favor of deathly calm. "Keep my temper? You enrolled me, against my will, for classes that I am old enough to refuse to attend."

"As long as you live under our roof, you abide by our rules," Mom says.

I shove away from the table, my chair scraping across the tile floor. "Then maybe I won't live under your roof anymore." I don't ask to be excused. Right now, they don't deserve that courtesy.

Dad mops his napkin across his mouth with every intention of coming after me in my retreat, but he's not quick enough. I'm up the stairs before he even reaches the threshold from the dining room.

My mom's voice floats up after me. "It's just an idle threat, dear. She's not foolish enough to run away."

I slam my bedroom door and pace to the window and back. It's not an idle threat. With eighteen looming over me, I have options. I just have to figure out what they are, exactly.

If I don't finish this year of school, I won't have much of a future, except as a spectacle in the eyes of the nation: President

Sigourna's failure of an older daughter, who couldn't even graduate from high school. Running away is a fool's option, but honestly, at the moment, I want to be that fool. At this point, if I stay, it's tacit agreement to abide by their dictates.

I'm done abiding. I'm done.

Fifteen minutes of pacing doesn't relieve any of my stress. They knew I wanted to quit, that I've wanted to quit for years, and they re-enrolled me anyway. And Tana's smirking face from across the table keeps flashing into my mind.

I need open space, away from the oppressive "roof" that holds me down. I grab my coat and leave my room. Dad is halfway up the stairs, with Mom two steps behind him. The staircase is wide enough for me to skirt by them.

"Where are you—"

"Jen, what are you—"

My mom tries to catch my arm, but I twist out of her reach. "I'm going for a walk."

"No you're not. We need to talk." They're both following me now.

"No. I'm going for a walk."

"Anjeni Sigourna, stop right there."

I'm at the door to the garden. "Make me," I hiss, and I wrench it open. A cool breeze hits me as I slip through to the night. Mom catches the door before it can shut.

"Jen! Where do you think you're going?"

"For a walk, I said."

"It's late! You have homework to do."

I turn and point one finger to the sky. "Not under your roof right now. Don't have to follow your rules."

Mom's mouth opens and shuts. Anger builds on her face in a heavy blush, but what is she going to do? Ground me for a whole six hours? She starts to say something, but my dad lays a forestalling hand on her shoulder.

"Don't go past the garden," he tells me. "Even if you're an adult, you're still the president's daughter, and you still have a security detail that will follow you beyond the grounds."

He's going to let me walk off my anger, in other words. Dad always was sensible like that.

I give him a salute and continue on my way, down the path through the rose bushes and out to the bare side of Monument Hill. In the dark of night, the Eternity Gate looms like a shadow-guardian against the backdrop of city lights and sounds. On holidays it's illuminated, but tonight is a normal night.

And I'm glad. I couldn't lurk around the hillside otherwise.

I descend ten or more steps past the Gate and flop onto the grass, my body angled on the hill and my head tilted up for perfect star-gazing. Except that you can't see any stars in the middle of the city. A handful twinkle through the light pollution that obscures their weaker denizens. The cityscape below me, with its street lamps and cars, seems like a blight on the world.

I haven't seen the stars properly in years, not since before my dad was president. Our family went camping once when Tana and I were kids, and it was awful. The sprawl of stars above was the only positive memory I have from that adventure.

As the night deepens, cold sets into my bones and decisions elude me. I have to finish high school. It would be stupid to run away before the end of the school year. That's still three months away, though.

Can I endure the pointless magic classes for another three months? After twelve years of fruitless training, three months seems like nothing. And yet, it's an eternity to me right now. I had my hopes set on today being my last day.

I'm pretty sure the Dean of Magic had his hopes set on the same thing.

Maybe I could just ditch class between now and graduation. He probably wouldn't report me. He'd probably thank me, truth be told.

There's just the matter of that pesky security detail that keeps within a hundred feet of me whenever I leave the executive residence.

But I have to finish high school. And I'm already accepted to the sister college, more on my parent's reputation than my mediocre grades. One school feeds into the other. I have to take that opportunity into account as well.

With a heavy sigh, I finally heave myself up from the grassy hillside. I will not—*will not*—go to magic classes over the summer. Whether I go from tomorrow onward remains to be seen, but this is not a simple submission to my parents' wishes.

As I cross back into the house, Tana emerges from the dining room. She stops short upon seeing me.

"Hey, quitter," she says. "Finally come back to your senses and realize you have nowhere else to go? I thought maybe you'd started off on your spiritual journey."

"At least I have a spiritual journey, Aitana," I reply. "Shouldn't you be off stealing someone's boyfriend or something?"

Her face crimsons. Her legendary namesake was supposed to be an accomplished magician, but all anyone really remembers is how she stole a goddess's lover. Tana, for all her many talents, often gets this man-stealer label thrown in her face, however jokingly, and she hates it.

She also knows that I'm not really joking.

"You don't have to worry about me stealing any boyfriend of yours," she says, her mouth twisted in a sneer. "You couldn't even get one worth stealing."

The truth of her words skewers me inside. I cover my hurt with a sarcastic tip to my mouth and walk away, shoulders back, head held high as though she didn't just pierce me through the metaphorical gut.

I mean, what can I even say? Guys don't look twice at me when Tana's anywhere in the vicinity, unless they're trying to pique her interest or make her jealous. I learned that lesson a long time ago the hard way and have taken a general disinterest in boyfriend-girlfriend relationships ever since.

And Tana knows it.

I'm back in my room for only two or three minutes before there's a knock on the door. "Jen?" My dad's voice muffles through the wood.

Mom has turned over my re-education to him. She always does.

I open the door to meet his reproving face. "I'm not going to magic classes over the summer. You can't make me. I *will* move out. I'm applying to the dorms on the college campus, and I'm pretty sure they'll admit me early, if needs be."

"We've never discussed the dorms," says my dad with a frown.

"I'm done here," I tell him. "I can't do it anymore. I need to get away, to be my own person instead of this shadow you all want me to play."

"Your mom and I only want what's best for you."

Right. I'm sure.

"You only want what's best for yourselves. If you wanted what's best for me, you would have let me abandon things I suck at so I could find something I was good at instead."

A storm cloud descends across his face. I move to shut the door, but he catches it. "You want to know something you're good at? Defying anyone and everyone who should command your respect, insisting on having everything your way, on your timetable, and refusing to cooperate with anyone who tries to help you. You're as stubborn as a mule, Anjeni, and you have been from the day you were born!"

He finishes this tirade with a huff. The accusations shoot through me like a cluster of poisoned darts, painful and corrosive.

"Now if you would just listen, for once in your life—" he continues, but I've crossed the threshold on what I can bear.

"I'm going to bed," I interrupt. "I am of legal age as of midnight. I'll tell you in the morning what I've decided to do with my future, but you and Mom have no say whatsoever, do you understand? And since I'm *as stubborn as a mule*, there's no point in arguing with me."

Something in my tone gives him pause. He steps back, allowing me the opportunity to shut the door and twist the lock. I stare at the barrier between us, numb from his outburst. Beyond, in the hall, he shifts his weight from one foot to the other. I can see his shadow in the ribbon of light at my feet.

He's debating whether to renew the conversation or to give me my space for the night.

His better senses triumph. The shadow shuffles sideways out of my view as he retreats down the stairs.

CHAPTER SIX

I CAN'T SLEEP. AS I LIE in the darkness of my room, my father's words play over and over again in my mind.

Stubborn. Defiant. Refusing to cooperate. Forcing my own way on my own timetable.

And I have been this way since the day I was born. Before that, even. I forced my own timetable on my parents even in my conception, against their family planning and future expectations.

I am a mistake.

I had resigned myself to compromise, at least until the end of the school year. His outburst rings in my ears, though, and my soul chafes with rebellion. I can't compromise now. And yet that will prove him right.

I don't want him to be right.

But compromise will make him right as much as rebellion will. Compromise means I was wrong to object in the first place.

Beleaguered with frustration, I shove aside my bed covers and pace my room. The house is quiet. Everyone's gone to sleep, and I'm stuck awake as the seconds and minutes and hours tick by. I'm too restless to stay in bed and too harrowed to read. I have to walk off this nervous energy.

Out of habit, I grab my lighter from the dresser top as I pass to the door. I slip it into the pocket of my pajama pants and tap quietly down the stairs. I pull a light sweater from a hook by the back door and cross the threshold into the cool night.

The grass is wet against my feet. A noise to my right alerts me of someone approaching.

"Miss Anjeni?"

It's one of the night security guards. He waves a flashlight my direction, though he's polite enough not to aim it into my eyes.

"I'm just walking around the garden," I say. "I won't go any farther than the Gate."

His flashlight briefly flits across my bare feet, but he doesn't comment on my lack of footwear. "Keep inside the fence."

I nod my understanding. As I start down my chosen path, he calls after me, his voice hushed.

"Happy Birthday, ma'am."

As if I were eighty instead of eighteen. The "ma'am" delights me, though. "Thank you," I whisper to his retreating back. He lifts one arm in acknowledgement as he continues on his rounds.

Midnight has come and gone hours ago, and I am officially an adult.

The first glimmerings of dawn begin so slowly that I barely even recognize them. I sit between the two pillars of the Eternity Gate, my back against stone and my head rolled to the side to watch the glittering cityscape that sprawls across the valley. Absently I flip my lighter open and shut, open and shut. The tiny flame probably looks like some strange, alien beacon to anyone who happens to glance up at the monument.

Not that many people are awake. The restricted-access road below is as deserted as always, though I can see the occasional security guard pass beneath its street lamps. The word has spread among them that I'm here. No one else bothers me for the hour and longer that I sit.

What am I going to do? The perpetual calm around the Eternity Gate quiets my troubled mind, but it offers me no answers.

I doze off as the burgeoning gray along the horizon lightens into the pale yellows that herald the rising sun. I'm only asleep for a few minutes. That transition from darkness to light, so long in coming, speeds up as the sun crests the distant mountain peaks, but I miss that moment when the first rays spear across the land.

Instead, a far-off thudding jars me from my sleep. I jerk awake, and my first thought, nonsensically, is that a high school marching band is holding early morning practice for their drum line.

My hand is empty. I feel around the dewy grass for the lighter I dropped when I nodded off. It glimmers nearby. Absently I pick it up as that far-off drumming beats a steady pulse. The air in front of me shimmers, the stark sunlight obscuring the carpet of buildings below. I lift one hand to shadow my face, and for an instant, a trick of the eyes seems to mask the teeming city with the image of a barren valley instead.

I blink away the mirage. The chorus of drums beats again, a heavy sound that reverberates through my chest.

And again, that barren valley flashes into view.

I scramble backward, the hair at the base of my skull standing on end. Something is wrong. The city shifts into view, but the gap between the two pillars of the Eternity Gate ripples, more akin to water than air.

The drum beat is coming from that second, barren scene.

Absently I stash my lighter in my pocket as I stand, my gaze fixed on the ripples. It's as if my eyes themselves are shuddering, though, causing the illusion in their fatigue. Am I that exhausted, that delirious? Is this all a dream?

The atmosphere around the Gate is foreign, no longer one of calm tranquility, but now possessed with the first vibrations of a coming storm.

Either my sleepless night has driven me insane, or this ancient, decorative stonework is trying to fulfill its rumored purpose.

I step closer, both cautious and fascinated. The space within the arch pulses with the beating drum. If I squint, I can see the barren field overlaid upon the cityscape.

It's not barren, though. At the edges, to the north and south, a dark line extends and I know rather than see that there are people there, so far distant that I might as well be looking out upon ants.

Still in the grip of curiosity, I lift one hand to touch the roiling air. An electric shock rips up my arm, and I jerk back, my preservation instincts flaring.

What am I doing? The last thing I need right now is to cross over into some alien world—or to have some alien creature cross over into mine, which seems the likelier possibility. I need to get help, to tell the security guards or my father. But will the disturbance disappear if I look away? Will it still be there when I come back? Will everyone think I've gone crazy? I step backward up the hill, loath to tear my eyes from the sight. The ripples dance in the full dawning sunlight, two landscapes crisscrossing one another.

Behind me, familiar, quickening footsteps dart across the grass.

I panic. "No, Tana! Don't—"

But she's already upon me, shoving my half-turned body. My protest mingles with her crowing jeer.

"Off on your spiritual journey, Goddess Anjeni!"

And I swear she pushes me harder than she ever has before. Light and flame erupt around me as my body flies beneath the arch. A high-pitched scream fills my ears. Is it mine or someone else's? My shoulder jars into stony ground, and I bounce once, twice, three times and then roll boneless down the hill.

I'm in shock as I come to rest at the base. The sky above, a perfect blue, extends like a canopy over the grass. There's no wrought-iron fence, no street or civilization beyond. My fall has knocked the wind out of me. The air, hot and dry, crackles into my lungs as I force an inhale.

The beating drums increase their tempo, and behind them, the gathered host afar on my right raises a chorus of voices in a blood-chilling cry.

The host to my left remains silent. Even their drums are still.

The pain from my tumble is too real for a dream, and my disoriented horror would be more than enough to jolt me from any nightmare, were I asleep.

No, I have passed through to another world.

The Gate looms above me at the top of the hill, so close, and yet so distant. I have to get back to it. My body aches as I heave myself up from the dry, scrubby grass.

My shoulder is bleeding, my sweater torn and stained where I first hit the ground. Above me, the gap within the Gate shows crystal blue skies and no sign of rippling energy.

It's already closed, my instincts warn me.

A desperate sob tears from my throat. The screaming host grows louder, their voices magnified in the harsh, dry air. I scramble barefoot up the steep hill, halfway to the Gate when a chilling sound echoes from behind.

The screech of a monster.

I whirl, only to be met with a horrific sight. A warrior has emerged from the host, a massive hunk of black armor and needle-sharp spikes astride the most hideous creature I've ever seen. It's like someone bred a horse with a giant lizard, all scales and claws and hulking muscles.

The monstrous steed screeches again as it gallops across the barren valley, headed straight for me. Its rider holds aloft a gleaming morning star.

Great. Not only have I crashed into an alien world, but its inhabitants are going to kill me.

The mutant horse launches onto the hillside with sickening agility. In my attempt to flee, I roll my ankle and pitch back down the incline.

Graceful, that's what I am. Meeting my impending doom with dignity and poise.

I tumble past my attacker. Claws scrabble against the stones above. Adrenaline courses through my blood as my body stops at the bottom of the hill. I spring to my feet and bolt.

As if I could possibly outrun my killer.

The creature shrieks behind me. On instinct more than anything else I fling myself out of the way. A whoosh passes too near, the spikes of the morning star dangerously close. The army on the right jeers and catcalls, their derision unmistakable. Still the army on the left does nothing.

I catch myself and thrust from the ground, but the warrior is already upon me.

His aim is better this time, too.

Pain bursts upon my back as the morning star connects, shredding through my clothes and raking up my ribcage. The force of the blow sends me airborne. I collide with rough earth, my limbs in a heap, my mind gripped in mingled agony and shock.

I'm on my side, facing the jeering host. A buzzing in my ears drowns out their frenzied roars.

The monster passes above my head. Its rider holds aloft his weapon, victorious, fomenting support from his rabid minions. My shallow breath puffs along the dirt in front of me.

He's building up their excitement for the final blow.

I'm going to die here, worlds away from my home, from my parents and everything I know and love.

Why didn't I just accept the magic classes? I've sat through them for twelve years, so what was a few more months? Why didn't I just accept them?

It might seem nonsensical, but this is the thought that floats across my mind in these my final moments.

I'm going to die, and it all would have been preventable if I had humbled myself to my parents' wishes, if I had gone to sleep in my own bed instead of wandering through the night in search of an alternative.

My life pulses through my veins, as sluggish as the blood that coats my back.

Death is not acceptable. I can't die, not when my last words to my own family were full of bitterness and hate. I can't die when I've never even figured out what I want to live for.

I can't die.

The buzzing in my ears amplifies, and with it, a pressure builds. My sheer will to live screams like a caged animal, feral and desperate to be free. I push away from the dry grass, slowly, staggering first to my knees and then to my feet.

My attacker is too busy with his audience to notice me right away. I can barely keep my balance, my head pointed downward as my vision blurs in and out of focus. The frenzy of his army shifts its tone, and he glances my direction. I watch in my periphery as he circles his monstrous steed around to face me. His weapon, mottled with blood and torn fibers, angles out toward the ground.

The ruthless crowd behind him screams for a finishing blow.

He takes his time approaching, relishing the end.

The first fundamental of magic is that it flows like a river. The energy gathers from a source beyond sight and, like water in its riverbed, courses to its destination. You are the riverbed, Anjeni.

The feral animal within howls for release. I raise my hands, pitifully weak and shaking, palms facing outward, as though I can block the oncoming attack. The rider swings his weapon aloft. His mount picks up speed for this final blow.

You are the riverbed, Anjeni.

The animal within screams.

And I... I set it free.

If I ever find the moron who wrote the first fundamental of magic, I swear I will throttle them until they die. Magic is nothing like a river. It's a volcano: searing, explosive, and capable of obliterating everything in its destructive path.

CHAPTER SEVEN

SOMEONE IS TALKING. My brain seems to think it should understand the words, but aside from the cadences of spoken language, nothing is intelligible. A man and a woman are speaking gibberish to one another, and I lie flat on my stomach, with only a fuzzy awareness beyond the steady, throbbing pain of my back.

My eyes remain closed. Vaguely I wonder if I'm in my own room, if that could possibly be my parents talking to one another, but the more my mind focuses, the more alien the discussion becomes. Their voices lilt in a way that is completely foreign to my native tongue. So, too, are the smells of this place unique. Smoke and acrid earth meet my every inhale. This is not my home, or anywhere I've ever been before.

I am in another world.

Miraculously, I have survived my initiation into this place. I don't think the same can be said of my monstrous attacker. Or his mutant horse. Perhaps not even of the jeering hordes that lined the hill behind him.

My memory is fuzzy, but the recollection of that last, desperate moment is crystal clear. That caged and raging beast within me, once loosed, tore open the world in a burst of energy that shredded everything in its furious path. I'm not entirely sure at what point I lost consciousness, only that the terrible power nearly consumed me whole.

Now, as I lie in darkness, I can sense its presence still. It has returned to its cage, where it sleeps in sheer and utter contentment.

This is magic? A beast in a cage?

Never in any of the fundamentals, intermediates, or superlatives does anyone refer to magic as sentient. It's peaceful, flowing, tranquil, something one accesses with a calm mind and a serene heart.

Neither of which I have ever possessed. Chart this up as yet another failure. I couldn't even spark a candlewick until faced with imminent death. (And honestly, any candle would have been toast under the impact of what erupted from my hands.)

That creature, seemingly content for the moment… can I ever possibly control it?

The garbled voices end their conversation. My awareness of the inner beast recedes as footsteps approach me. My mind, on a tipping point between wakefulness and sleep, leans towards wakefulness.

The pain on my back flares. A cool cloth has been removed, enflaming my injury. A woman utters something—pitying? Observational? A splash of water follows and the cloth is restored to my back, wet and icy.

I drag my eyes open to view the smoky interior of a dimly lit tent.

Ugh. Camping.

The woman has turned away from me, her attention fixed upon a bowl of water, where she dunks and wrings out a cloth. She snaps the excess moisture from it and hangs it across a small line above her basin. Her quiet, methodical movements give me opportunity to observe her: small of frame, black hair in a knot at the nape of her neck. Her sleeves are pinned up above her elbows, her skin the color of cinnamon.

She is responsible for my care, I assume.

The furnishings inside the tent are worn and rudimentary. At the edge of my vision, I can make out an opening, but it seems to lead into another tent room rather than to the outside. The smoke that permeates the air is thicker in that direction. Its acrid vapors sting my senses.

The woman turns from her work. Her dark eyes connect with mine and she stops short. Terror—panic—crosses her face, and immediately she bolts for that opening flap.

"Kosi! Kosi, kosi!"

I don't know what "kosi" means, but this repetition precedes another string of unintelligible words. I muster my strength to push myself up from the cot upon which I lie, despite the screaming agony of my injured ribcage, but I pause no more than half an inch off the blanket beneath me before dropping back against it.

I'm lying shirtless. Any movement on my part will expose my upper body.

(Of course I'm shirtless. How else could that cold cloth be sitting against my skin?)

Footsteps sound in the doorway behind me. The man has returned. He hangs upon that door flap, staring first at the woman and then at me. She whispers something in a questioning voice. He crosses the threshold slowly.

My brows knit together in annoyance and embarrassment. I understand that treatment of my injury necessitates my shirtlessness, but couldn't they have bound me up in bandages before I woke? Here I am, half-naked and flat on my stomach as a strange man approaches my bedside.

He is black-haired and bearded, but younger than I took him at first glance. His brown eyes lock upon me. He actually kneels so that we are at eye level.

Then he ducks his head further, as though praying. A string of words tumbles from his lips.

Annoyance surges through me anew. On impulse, I gather the blanket beneath me with one hand and hold it to my chest as I sit up.

My back is on fire. The wet cloth falls away. I'm guessing I have a few broken ribs to compliment the mangled flesh, but for the sake of my tattered dignity, I contain my reaction to a pained grimace.

My movement alarms the man and woman both. The woman lunges, and the man, startled from his prayer, reaches for me instinctively, only to check himself before he makes any contact.

The woman is bowing and ducking her head as she speaks, her expression one of fear and apology. She extends her hands, as though she'd like to help me lie down again but can't bring herself to touch me.

I'm grateful they're keeping their distance, but they're acting like I'm made of glass.

"I can't understand a word you're saying," I interrupt her speech. My voice rasps in my throat. My tongue is dry, like sandpaper. I look around for something to drink. Is the water here even safe?

The pair stares at me with their mouths open. I know they can't understand me any better than I can them, but it feels good to talk, even with a dry mouth.

"Thank you for taking care of me while I slept. I could really use a drink, if you have anything." I pantomime raising a cup to my lips.

The man and woman exchange an uncertain glance.

"Do you drink things in this world?" I ask, and I make the motion again.

He mutters something to her. She looks around, her head movements jerky, before her eyes settle on a small leather bag on a chair. This she snatches up, and then she proffers it to me at full arm's length, as though she expects me to claw her fingers off if she comes too close. She drops her gaze away from me when I reach my free hand up to take the bag.

It's a water satchel… or a something satchel. Its innards slosh against their container. The bag tips up to a narrow corner, which is stopped by a plug of cork.

I can't open it without letting go of my sheet.

I look down at the cork and then up again. The woman still won't meet my eyes.

"Open it, please," I say to her, but she only flinches. I shift my attention to the man. "Open it," I say, and I thrust the satchel at him.

A nervous confusion skitters across his face, but he takes the sloshing item. After a questioning glance to the woman, he pries the cork free and holds the satchel aloft. Uncertainty lingers on his face.

"Thank you." I receive it again and sniff at the opening. Sourness emanates from the liquid depths.

My sandpaper tongue doesn't care if it's sour as long as it's wet. Throwing caution to the wind, I take a swig.

And wince. Whatever is in that bag is fermented.

"Thank you," I say again, my face twisted with tempered disgust as I hand the satchel back to the man.

The fear in his eyes has gone, replaced by curiosity and amusement. He replaces the cork. A question crosses his lips, but I cannot tell if it's directed at me or at the woman.

This whole lack of communication is ruining everything.

But, if I'm stuck in this world, I might as well try to pick up a few things.

"My name is Anjeni," I say, and I pat my free hand over my heart. "Anjeni."

The man frowns. The woman gives up trying to avoid my notice and stares at my hand, a furrow between her brows.

"Anjeni," I say again, a little louder.

The man, in his confusion, places one hand over his heart and repeats the word. "Anjeni."

"No." I shake my head. Again I pat my hand to my heart. "I am Anjeni. Who are you?" I point to him.

Understanding flashes through his eyes. He points his finger back at me. "Anjeni," he says.

I nod. "Yes. Who are you?" I point again.

He looks wide-eyed to the woman. Again he repeats my name, pointing to me. "Anjeni." Then, to my utmost relief, he puts his fist to his own heart and says, "Kosi."

So Kosi was his name. That makes sense. I look to the woman, and he does the same.

Reluctantly, she brings her closed fist to hover over her heart. "Tolla," she says, and she thumps her chest once, lightly.

"Tolla," I repeat. "Kosi. Kosi and Tolla. Anjeni. Thank you."

"Sankyu," the man echoes, but he has no clue what he's saying.

Silence falls between us. I consider what else I might possibly say to the pair until a movement at the door draws both their attention. Kosi jumps to his feet, while Tolla backs away toward the wall. An old woman passes quietly through the door flap, her face an intricate pattern of wrinkles and her gray-streaked hair pulled back in a harsh bun. She halts upon seeing the two. Her attention shifts to me, and her weathered brows draw together as she looks back at them.

"Ehhhhh," she says, drawing out the noise in a menacing tone. There's no mistaking her meaning. Apparently a rebuke sounds the same in any language, in any world. Kosi has his hands in the air and already skirts around her to the door, some glib excuse cascading off his tongue. Tolla tries to protest as well, but the old woman silences her with a simple hiss. She chastises Kosi as he ducks from the room, even going so far as to poke her head out of the flap to follow his retreat, so that she can finish her reprimand in full.

Once she's said her piece, she turns back to Tolla and me. In one hand she carries a small earthen pot. She lifts her index finger and gestures at me, pot and all, as more gibberish tumbles from her lips.

Why am I getting scolded, exactly?

Tolla interjects something that causes the old woman to pause. She peers at me as though inspecting a bejeweled gnat—half disbelief, half curiosity.

"Hinahmus Anjeni," says Tolla. I assume it's an introduction.

"Anjeni," the old woman repeats.

I decide to join the conversation. "Anjeni," I confirm, patting my hand to my chest.

The old woman rears back in mock appreciation. "Anjeni?" she says again, and then she launches into a quick-tongued harangue, gesturing with her pot hand and her free hand both, lecturing me. I gather from her gesticulations that she takes offense at my sitting up. Instantly, I lay flat upon the cot again.

Tolla tries to interject something more, but that only turns the lecture her direction. The old woman, fully a head shorter, shakes a finger in her face and then points toward the door flap as she continues her tirade.

I'm going to hazard a guess that Kosi was not supposed to be in the sick room.

Tolla apologizes—that looks the same in any language, in any world too, apparently. She bobs her head and pleads until the old woman finally abandons the long-winded rebuke. The harridan turns back to me and, with a sullen voice, pronounces some instruction I can't understand.

Then, she pulls the cloth cover off the pot she's holding and scoops out a handful of pungent brown goop. Before I can react, she slaps the mess onto my back, right across my injury.

I gasp. She chides me as she fishes out more goop and spreads it liberally from my shoulder blade down to my waist.

Her pungent brown concoction is medicine that burns and freezes at the same time. It smells of cloves and garlic and a dozen other spices mixed together.

And all I can think is, if I don't die of infection, I'm going to have a wicked-ugly scar.

After she applies the medicine, though, she gestures for me to sit up. Tolla produces a roll of linen—the bandages I was wishing for back when Kosi entered the room. I swallow my embarrassment and allow them to wrap my torso. By the time they finish, I'm more covered than I would be on a trip to the beach.

Beneath the fresh bandages, the pungent goop has numbed my injury. Perhaps the old medicine woman knows what she's doing after all.

She issues some curt orders to Tolla, who darts out of the room. I watch, curious, as the old woman shifts her attention to the wash basin across from me. She empties the dirty water into an earthenware container on the floor and refills the basin with fresh water from an urn beside it, just enough to wash her hands.

Tolla returns with a bowl of soup and a hunk of rough bread. She proffers these items to the old woman, who is busy drying her hands.

The old woman, with a string of disapproving words, gestures towards me. Tolla looks hesitant.

I haven't eaten since before abandoning my parents at the dinner table yesterday—or, what I assume was only yesterday. My stomach twists in knots as the soup's savory, smoky aroma fills the air.

"Is that for me?" I ask, hoping to overcome Tolla's aversion towards approaching me. I reach my hands out to receive it.

A hint of approval glimmers in the old woman's eyes. Tolla, still skittish, hands me the warm bowl and the piece of bread. There's no spoon. I sip from the bowl's edge.

Somehow, it's the most delicious thing I've ever tasted. It lacks salt and spices, yet my shock-ridden mind finds comfort in its faint, savory flavor. I swallow it with eager gulps.

The bread is coarse, its edges blackened from the heat of the fire that cooked it. I don't even care. It sops up the broth nicely and makes the meal more filling.

"Thank you," I say to Tolla and the old woman. They exchange a glance, uncomprehending.

From beyond the door, Kosi's voice sounds. A hand thrusts through the flap, holding a bundle of cloth. He continues speaking from the other side of the flap, shaking the cloth up and down. Tolla retrieves it from him and looks to the old woman for instruction.

The crone mutters as she tips her head toward me.

Tolla smooths the folded bundle as she approaches. The words she speaks are quiet, somewhat apologetic, as she offers the bundle to me.

I set aside my bowl, my confusion mounting. The cloth is soft and silken, a buttery color. I unfold it to discover that it's a dress with a line of embroidery around its collar and around the cuffs of its long bell sleeves.

Kosi has brought me some clothes. How kind of him.

The dress is handmade, but I can tell at a glance that its workmanship is fine. The details on the sleeves and collar remind me of the traditional costumes from my own people's history. I look up at Tolla and the old woman. Their clothing is darker in color and rougher in weave, a more commonplace feel to it.

This dress is special.

"Is it all right?" I ask.

The old woman takes the garment from my hands and moves to put it on me. She thinks I was asking for help.

"I can do it," I protest, but she's already undertaken the task. On goes the dress, over my short hair and my bandaged body. It pools around my hips where I'm sitting. Wary of another scolding from the old woman, I venture to stand. The length of fabric falls to the ground. The dress with its high-waisted bodice is loose on my skinny frame. The sleeves fall to my knuckles, and the hem trails along the floor.

Tolla watches me with a strange look in her eyes, as though she's about to cry. Her stance is protective, one hand encircling her waist while the other picks at her lower lip.

Is this her special dress? Her limbs are longer than mine, so it would fit her better. The communication barrier prevents me from asking. I can't discard the garment, either, unless I want to go naked.

From without the flap Kosi calls an inquiry. The old woman answers with long-suffering in her voice. He enters, taking in the sight of me on my feet and Tolla's distressed stance. In two steps he is at her side, one arm around her shoulder as he kisses her cheek. She smiles gratefully, ignoring a grunt of displeasure from the old woman.

That interaction speaks volumes to me. Kosi and Tolla are lovers, and the old woman doesn't approve. Is she Tolla's mother? Her grandmother, more like.

Commotion travels from the smoky room next door, followed by the unceremonious entrance of a second man.

"Kosi—" he begins, but he stops short upon seeing me.

I stare back at him. He's tall and, unlike Kosi, clean-shaven. His astonished eyes flit from my head to my feet and back again. I give him a similar inspection. He has every appearance of a warrior, right down to the sword that hangs at his waist.

"Dima?" says Kosi, drawing his attention. Is that his name, Dima?

The question jolts him from his stupor. He rattles off a string of unintelligible words, but his message ends with something that pricks my attention: he says my sister's name.

"Aitana?" I repeat sharply. My mind flares. She's here? Did she come through the Gate after me? If anyone could open it, Tana could. I'm half hope and half disgust. Is she off in another room, safe and sound while I'm recovering from my encounter with a monster? Knowing her, she's probably already mastered the language and enthralled a score of admirers with her beauty.

But she'd also be a familiar face among strangers.

"Aitana is here?" I say. "Where is she?"

My onlookers exchange uncertain glances with one another. The newcomer studies me, a deep frown upon his face.

Kosi issues him a command. He immediately ducks back out of the room. Kosi turns his attention to me and says something that includes the words "Dima" and "Aitana."

I point to the door. "That was Dima?"

He frowns, as though contemplating what I mean. Then, tentatively, he pats his chest and points to the door. "Dima."

The newcomer's name is confirmed.

CHAPTER EIGHT

I CANNOT CONTAIN MY NERVES. If Tana's here, when did she come? Did she see my graceless tumble down the hill, twice? Did she see me on that battlefield, facing off against that monster astride his mutant horse?

Was it possibly *her* magic that blasted into that enemy host, and not mine at all?

The beast within awakens from its slumber, incensed that I could think of such a possibility. It exists, and it won't allow my self-doubt to rob it of its victory.

Kosi and Tolla stand on the other side of the room with the old woman, speaking in low voices—an unnecessary precaution, given that I can't understand a word they say anyway—and I sit upon my cot. My hands cannot keep still, pent up with nerves as I wait for the warrior, Dima, to return with Tana. I twist my fingers around and against one another, my anxiety burgeoning.

Can I really work magic? Will I be able to prove it to her, or to anyone else?

I raise one finger in the air, level with my eyes. Even a spark would be enough. It would prove I wasn't making things up.

Magic flows like a river—

The start of the first fundamental courses through my mind, but I shove it away. Rubbish theory. *Magic bursts like a volcano,* I think instead. I only need a tiny eruption, minuscule, just a flame on my fingertip.

I will it.

Light and fire engulfs my whole hand from the wrist up.

"Ahh!" I yelp, shaking off the effect like snuffing a match. It winks out as quickly as it came. My hand has not a singe upon it.

A gurgle from the other side of the room draws my attention. Kosi, Tolla, and the old woman huddle together, silent as death, staring at me with huge eyes.

"Whoops. Sorry." I try to laugh it off.

Kosi, in his fright, has pulled Tolla into a protective embrace. The old woman, regaining her wits, notices this and swats at his hands.

I can't help it. I laugh outright. They are terrified of magic, it seems, but the old woman's first instinct is essentially, "Get your hands off of her, you rogue."

She chatters something to Kosi and gestures to the door. He argues under his breath, glancing askance in my direction. She wants him to go, and he is afraid of leaving the two women alone with me.

"I won't do anything," I say, and I hold up my hands defensively.

Belatedly I recall that the last time I held my hands up like that, I blasted away half of a demon army. Kosi, Tolla, and the old woman remember as well, it seems, because they cringe together again as though they expect immediate death.

I drop my hands behind my back and say nothing.

Upon this scene, the door flap parts. Dima reenters, leading a woman by the hand. Her blond hair falls in waves almost down to her waist, and her pale blue eyes regard me with apprehension.

I sit up straight. Dima and this newcomer tip into obsequious bows before me, and he speaks a string of words that end with my sister's name, "Aitana."

But this is not my sister. Someone else in another world has her same name? What are the chances?

Confusion snakes through me, followed by a terrifying epiphany.

Someone else does bear my sister's name—not someone in another world, but in another *time*.

"Aitana," I say as the puzzle pieces in my mind click together. She looks up from her bow, uncertainty playing upon her pretty face.

My gaze shifts to the others as my epiphany takes root. Tolla should have been my first clue, but the pronunciation is different than I've ever heard.

"Tora," I say. She tips her head, a frown between her brows. I move on to the man beside her, who still has his arm around her waist. If Kosi is only a nickname, then logically, he must be… "Etricos."

His eyes bulge. He looks to Tora in growing alarm, and her expression mirrors his.

My gaze moves on to the second man, my heart quickly sinking in my chest. "Demetrios?"

He straightens, the blood draining from his face.

"Sek-nu-es-mi-nam-uh?" he says.

"She knows my name?"

The vowels are wrong, the consonants are off, but my brain latches onto the familiar and everything shifts into place.

The "gibberish" is not some otherworldly tongue. It's my own, seven hundred years removed from its modern form. Shock thrums through me with a sickening realization.

The players of our country's founding legends stand assembled before me: Etricos, Tora, Demetrios, Aitana. Only the goddess Anjeni is missing.

Except that Anjeni is also here.

Either I have unwittingly supplanted my own namesake or I am her.

And both of these options are a complete disaster.

Heedless of my injuries, I tear from the cot and through the door flap. A fire smolders at the center of a circular room beyond, the top of the tent open to allow the smoke an escape. There are two other flaps that lead out of this central room. I bolt for the larger one to my left, uncaring of the protests that sound behind me.

An earthy nighttime scent assaults me as I emerge beneath an endless canopy of stars. Campfires and circular tents dot the field around me, like mushrooms and fairy lights beneath a huge, gibbous moon. I whip my head around, assessing the scene before plunging toward the nearest rim of darkness, the edge of the encampment. Footsteps follow me. The dry grass beneath my bare feet harbors treacherous sharp stones. I hike up my skirts, the better to see the ground as I pick my way up the swell of a hill.

"Goddess Anjeni!"

I glance back. Etricos and Demetrios have both followed me. Further down, by the mouth of the tent, Tora and Aitana stare up in wonder. I continue on my way, to the top of the hill.

At its crest, I stop. The valley before me bears the scars of a wildfire. Even in the dark of night I can see the wedge of black that cuts through the grass and spreads across the opposite hill. To my right, on another jutting hill, a familiar, ancient stone arch reflects the moonlight.

I knew, in the back of my mind, that the second army had taken me in after I lost consciousness. When I thought them backward aliens from another world, I did not question their inaction prior to that. But these are not aliens. These are my people. These are the heroes I worshipped from my earliest years. They are supposed to be brave and stalwart, forging the way to a new and glorious nation.

Instead, like sniveling cowards, they watched from afar as I battled a monster.

Etricos and Demetrios have stopped three or four steps behind me. They think I'm a goddess. They won't touch me without my permission.

"Why did you do nothing?" I ask, my attention fixed upon the battlefield. The terror of those first moments through the Gate rips across my mind. "Why did you just stand here watching? *Why did you do nothing*?"

My voice rises to a yell, fury upon me as I turn to them. They stare, uncomprehending.

Of course they don't comprehend. I speak with a modern accent, with modern vocabulary. It might as well be another language.

I don't even care at this point. I fling one hand toward the scarred field. "You left me down there *to die*! What kind of heroes are you?"

Etricos raises his hands, a placatory tone in his voice. I only catch about half of his words. "Goddess Anjeni... people saved..."

"I almost *died*. Do you understand that? If this smug, sentient magic in me hadn't finally decided to wake up, I would be dead." My mind races with thoughts of what might have been, with what almost was. I'm going to be sick. Our legends claim that the goddess Anjeni appeared through the Eternity Gate and saved our people from a demon horde. No one ever said she tumbled through, or that she was nearly slaughtered by an over-muscled demon and its genetically mutated horse.

Or maybe I've altered history. Maybe the legends will say as much when I return home.

If I return.

A sob catches in my throat. According to legend, Anjeni disappears through the Eternity Gate again, but no one knows where she goes from here. If the Gate chooses the destination, I might be wandering through time for the rest of my life. In sudden panic, I pick up my skirts and bolt for the distant stone arch.

I get no more than five steps before a strong hand snags my elbow and jerks me backward. I tumble off-balance into a pair of ready arms.

Demetrios has dared to catch hold of his goddess.

I look up into his dark eyes—eyes full of concern, of apprehension, eyes set in a handsome face with a straight nose and a chiseled jaw.

No way am I getting caught in a love triangle with this beefcake.

"Get off me!" I fling myself away. He lets go, and I nearly lose my balance again, but I right myself on the hillside. Realizing how undignified I must look, I glare first at him and then at his brother. "So what, you and your army thought it would be fun to stand up here and watch a teenaged girl get slaughtered? Couldn't lift a finger to help me? Worried you might strain a muscle or something?"

They both stare back at me, bewildered. It doesn't matter. I'm only venting my frustration.

Maybe they thought from the beginning that I was a goddess, that I didn't need their help, that I was sent from ethereal realms beyond to save them.

And oh, they'll get their goddess. The fickle Eternity Gate can wait. I pick up my skirts and march back down the hill. The two brothers gape at me as I pass. I hear them fall into line behind me. The encampment, with its mushroom tents and specks of firelight, looks pitiful against the expanse of fields beyond.

Beside the flap from where I emerged, Tora and Aitana have stepped back. In their stead, the old woman stands with her hands on her hips, ready to scold me. Others have gathered, warriors and women from the nearby tents. I stalk forward, my mind calculating with every step. As I approach the cluster of gawking souls, I pause and cast my hands heavenward.

"Erupt, you beastly magic," I say through gritted teeth. A massive fireball shoots into the sky, spiraling upward with the intensity of a miniature sun. My onlookers cry out and cover their eyes. Many of them drop to their knees or prostrate themselves fully before me. For a solid thirty seconds, the fireball illuminates the camp as though it's noonday instead of the middle of the night.

"Worship me, peasants!" I yell. As the fireball winks out, I sweep into the tent, leaving a dumbfounded crowd transfixed in my wake.

This power might be going to my head. I should probably reflect on my behavior.

CHAPTER NINE

THE DRESS THAT ETRICOS BROUGHT ME to wear is Tora's wedding dress. Or, more specifically, it was supposed to be Tora's wedding dress. The old woman—her name is Huna, but everyone else calls her Baba—told me as much, a glimmer of disapproval in her eyes.

I thought it was disapproval for me, but I was wrong. She does not approve of Etricos.

Five days have passed since I came through the Gate, and I am as sick as a dog. After my spectacular display of power, Etricos arranged for me to occupy a tent removed from the rest of the cluster: a goddess cannot live among commoners, after all. They mounted the structure atop the same hill from which they watched my near demise. He acted none too soon.

Fever, chills, vomiting, diarrhea. I have dysentery, as best I can guess. It hit on my second day here, the natural outcome of whatever parasites colonize this place. Huna stays with me. She is my constant attendant.

Even wracked with deathly illness, I am yet a goddess. Or so the people beyond these tent walls believe.

She scrutinizes me as she ladles a cup of the brew she keeps over the fire at the center of the tent. I am listless, my short hair sweat-plastered to my neck and forehead. Behind her, on the opposite wall, Tora's dress hangs, butter-yellow against the rough brown of the tent.

That first night, after my tantrum, Huna alone followed me. In the midst of her scolding, she made clear the dress's significance, though I did not fully understand her words. I took it off, replaced with a simpler garb that she offered in its stead. Her insistence unwittingly spared it from the effects of my impending illness.

I left it behind, too, when Etricos transferred me to this tent. Tora herself brought it, eyes downcast, sorrow on her face. She would not meet Huna's gaze as she presented it. Huna said not a word, but she received the gown and hung it where it still remains.

It is an offering. If I reject it, I reject Tora. What a ridiculous culture this is.

Huna sets the cup of brew beside my sickbed and helps me sit up to drink. I'm as weak as a newborn, completely dependent on her aid. The delirium has passed, though—thankfully—and I believe I am on the mend. She holds the cup to my lips. Its herbaceous contents scalds my tongue and slides down my throat.

One small sip at a time, I drink the whole of it.

"Tell me about Tora and Etricos," I say as she helps me recline again. I am acquiring the language bit by bit, like assuming a new dialect. Huna, in her ministrations, is happy to talk, and the more she does, the more I understand.

A dark cloud crosses her face. She glances towards the dress on the opposite wall.

"Why are they not yet married?" I press.

"The tribal elder died," Huna says, and her wrinkled

mouth presses into a thin line. "There is no one to perform the ceremony."

Of all things, this seems trivial. These people, to the best of my understanding, represent the last of their tribe. My studies of this time period maintained that Etricos was the only warlord to withstand the invading demon army. At this point, then, all the other tribes have been conquered and enslaved.

And some warlord Etricos is. There are, at most, three hundred people in this encampment, including women and children.

"Is there no rite they can perform?" If the officiating elder is dead, surely there must be some other means provided to recognize a couple as husband and wife.

"He is inconstant," Huna says.

The bitterness in her voice startles me. "Etricos? He loves Tora." It might seem stupid, but this is important to me. I have seen his letters in the National Archives. His adoration for his wife is legendary. I don't want that veneer stripped away with all the others I've already lost.

Huna shrugs, and she gestures back and forth from one hand to the other. "He loves her, he loves another, he loves her again, he cares nothing for her. So it has always been, since they were children. And now, he gives her dress to a goddess and visits that goddess daily."

I can't fully contain my scoff. Etricos visits, but not on any amorous errands—and Huna knows that better than anyone. I understand her bitterness, though. This tribe has fled from their homes. They are refugees. That Tora brought along her wedding dress, an extravagance amid the bare necessities required in their flight, speaks of its significance to her.

For Etricos to hand it to another, then, is a terrible crime.

And yet, it too makes sense.

"I am a goddess, after all," I say.

It's Huna's turn to suppress a laugh. The smile tugs at the corners of her mouth. Kindly she smooths a damp lock from my brow.

After five days, she is well aware that I am no goddess at all—if she ever believed it in the first place. No goddess would succumb to such an illness. We use the term between us more as a joke than anything else.

"Etricos loves Tora," I tell her. "Is there no way for them to marry?"

That clouded expression reappears. I understand her concern. Everyone else may call her "Baba," but Tora alone can lay claim to that name; she is Huna's granddaughter, and her only surviving family. "I cannot have him make excuses afterwards, should his desires change. Should he say it wasn't a true marriage, Tora would suffer. He serves his own needs first."

This is not the Etricos of legends, a self-serving, inconstant lover. I squelch my burgeoning dissatisfaction. Our legends, romanticized as they are, hold no meaning here. But I do have truth to anchor me.

"He will not leave her. He will become a great leader, with Tora beside him."

Huna regards me, skepticism and hope mingling upon her wizened face. "Is that so?"

"Yes."

She does not question how I know such things. She understands that, though I am no goddess, I am no mere commoner either. Whether she believes my words or not, she does not say.

Instead, she pats my shoulder. "Sleep now. You need more rest, Goddess Anjeni."

I don't argue. Not only is she right, but fools alone would challenge her commands. I like Huna. It's a shame that her legacy did not carry down through the centuries.

If I ever make it home again, I will correct the omission.

A week more has passed. I long to see the world beyond these tent walls, even if it is only the expanse of barren fields and sun-blasted grasses. At night, I can glimpse the stars through the chimney hole at the center. I reek of campfire smoke and body odor.

That's actually my cue that I'm better. In the throes of illness, I couldn't have cared less about my hygiene.

Huna still makes me drink her herbal brew every hour or so, but she no longer has to hold the cup. I can sit up on my own. For the first time in days, I can walk, even. Weak as I am, I pace the tent under her watchful eye. I linger in the shaft of morning sunlight from above. She sews a length of pretty crimson fabric, her stitches small and precise.

I can't imagine where she got the overly-fine material, but she's been working with it for the past two or three days. If the resulting garment is meant for my use, I'm in no condition to receive it.

"I need a bath," I say. She has done well enough to sponge my arms and face clean, yet the stink of illness still clings to me. Resources are limited, especially where water is concerned, but a possible alternative exists. "The ocean is only a mile or two away, is it not? Can I go?"

The Eternity Gate stands at the end of the world, as the legends say. Etricos and his tribe fled to the furthest extremities of the land, and the nation of Helenia sprang from there.

A day at the beach would do me well.

"You are too weak for the journey," says Huna, but her voice harbors a hint of uncertainty, as if she doesn't believe her own words.

I stare.

"Cosi would have to arrange it," she reluctantly says.

Etricos has not been to see me yet today. Huna is hardly one to advocate for his authority, though.

"Why?"

"Because you are a goddess." The customary twinkle in her eyes does not accompany this reference to my supposed divinity.

My scalp prickles with suspicion. "What has Etricos done?"

Huna tips her head, a sardonic expression on her face as she draws her needle through another stitch. "It is your doing as much as his, Anjeni. I told you he serves his own needs."

As I muddle over the possible meaning of this, the tent flap parts and Etricos himself enters, a welcome breath of wind around him.

He greets me with a deep-swept bow. "Goddess Anjeni."

"I want to go to the ocean," I tell him without preamble. "Can you arrange it?"

He shifts from one foot to the other, his gaze flitting toward where Huna sits beside the exit. He looks almost squeamish. "Why should you want to go to the ocean?"

"Because I need a bath."

The squeamish expression lifts into charm. "But we can bring you a bath here. A tub, and water heated by the fire and—"

"With water dragged from the nearest river?" I interrupt. "That's more than a mile away, and you need the water for drinking and cooking." I could have asked to bathe at the river instead of the ocean, but it would be crowded with people fetching their daily supply.

"We will bring you a bath, Goddess Anjeni," Etricos says, dismissive of my objections. He turns to leave, and I start after him.

From beside the door, Huna hisses a warning. Etricos whirls, hands raised in a placatory stance.

"Please, Goddess Anjeni. Please remain here for now. We will bring a bath to you."

He backs out of the tent door, bowing as he goes.

I should here clarify: Etricos also knows I'm not a goddess. His visits during my illness confirmed as much. However, while Huna addresses me in good-natured sarcasm, he addresses me in appeasement, as if by treating me as a deity I might actually fulfill the role.

Today's apparent collaboration between him and Huna has my hackles raised. She tolerates him, but she doesn't buy into his nonsense.

Although, she's been sitting by the door all morning. My suspicions redouble. For whatever reason, she guards me from leaving.

"What is going on?"

Frankness settles upon her wrinkled face. "We need a goddess right now, Anjeni."

"We?" I echo. "You and Etricos?"

"Everyone," she replies.

"You're not going to let me go outside, are you."

"I am sorry. Cosi and Dima are doing their best to keep order. If you leave, it may cause a frenzy."

What frenzy? Everyone's already seen me in my divine worst. "I'm not going to hurl any more fireballs into the sky, if that's what you mean," I say, embarrassment staining my cheeks.

She chuckles. "You might have to." Then, with a secretive expression, she beckons me forward. Furtively she grips the edge of the tent flap. "Have a look, little goddess, but be careful not to show yourself."

Misgivings rise as I ease toward the opening. Huna holds it taut, so that I can only pry free a small slit, to which I put my eye.

There is a yard around my tent, with a low wooden fence to mark its boundary. Two braziers stand on either side of the gap that allows passage. Flames lick upward from their confines, their heat blurring the air. A warrior stands guard on either side of them.

"What on earth...?" I start. Beyond the fence, cloth bundles litter the ground in clusters and piles. Further down the hill, the mushroom-like tents extend across the valley.

I move my head for a different angle in the slit. More tents. It's the same in the other direction. The mushrooms are multiplying.

"Where did they all come from?" I ask, bewildered.

"Word of the goddess has spread. It was a few people at first, but more join us every day. They flee their homes and overlords to come here. Last night, over three hundred arrived—men, women, and children seeking refuge. They leave offerings at the fence, hoping to win the goddess's favor. Cosi has told them they cannot worship in person until the Hour of Fire, but they will come."

I back away from the flap, terror welling in my throat. The Hour of Fire refers to noon, when the sun is directly overhead.

"Huna," I say, "I am not a goddess."

She peers at me with knowing eyes, but a faint smile touches her lips. "You killed the demon champion and half the host behind him. The enemy scattered and fled. We came to the God's Arch not for a goddess, but for a miracle. And we received it."

"The God's Arch?" I repeat. "You mean the Eternity Gate?"

She frowns at this name.

I cast one hand behind me. "The stone arch out on the hill—you call that the 'God's Arch'?"

"It was put there by God long ago, Anjeni," she says. "It connects to the realm of the gods. You are not the first to come."

I swallow. "I'm not?"

"The Goddess Aitana came centuries ago," says Huna.

My stomach drops. Perhaps my sister followed me through the Gate after all. Perhaps she simply ended up somewhere else. "And what did she do?"

"She brought the sacred lore to our ancestors."

"What sacred lore?"

"The power of the gods, passed to humans."

"You mean magic? You're telling me that Tana's the one I get to blame for that ridiculous first fundamental?"

Huna tilts her head to one side in confusion. She doesn't understand my sarcastic question, so she mostly ignores it. "The lore is lost, Anjeni. Our enemies hunted and killed its bearers decades ago and burned all the records. Only a few still have the spark, but they have no teacher to help them harness it."

Why is my mouth so dry? I know the legends of this time like I know the back of my hand. "And what if I can teach them?" I ask, wetting my lips. That sentient magic within me thrums.

Her wrinkled mouth turns upward ever so slightly. "Then perhaps you are more of a goddess than you believe."

I let her words sink in. They sound nice. They flatter me.

They are, in short, ridiculous.

I change the subject. "You came to the God's Arch for a miracle? Is that why you did nothing when I first appeared?"

Huna regards me with narrowed eyes. "What do you mean?"

"When I passed through the arch and tumbled down the hill, when the demon champion attacked me, your people only watched from afar. You did nothing."

She leans forward, elbows resting on her knees and a stern expression on her face. "We prayed for your victory."

A scoff erupts from my throat. "That does *nothing*."

"The demon horde demanded for a champion to meet theirs. We answered that we would send one. Dima was to go, but you appeared before he could mount his horse. What could we do then but pray? For another to step on the battlefield when two champions meet signals an attack. The demon hordes outnumbered us seven to one."

My mouth hangs open. I shut it with an audible click. From the way she talks, I'm the one who inconvenienced them in that moment I appeared.

Not that I could help it.

She leans in even closer, a grin lighting her face. "And our prayers were heard, Goddess Anjeni. You won the battle, did you not? Though you gave us quite the scare."

Doubtless I did. "What would have happened had I lost?"

She sits back. "Death for the warriors. Enslavement for the elderly, the women, and the children, as with other tribes. It may yet come. Those gathering to us will bring more demons in pursuit."

Again the magic within me thrums. It's brash of me, but I already know the outcome. "It won't happen, Huna. You have a goddess to protect you now."

The old woman smiles. I have earned her approval.

CHAPTER TEN

Of all the modern conveniences I miss, I might miss running water the most. The bath, in a beaten metal tub that looks suspiciously like a repurposed enemy shield, spikes and all, is glorious, if rudimentary. Huna kindly leaves me to it. I barely fit, but I can wash away my acquired grime.

The lye soap is harsh. I take care not to get any in my eyes as I scrub my short hair clean. I'm thankful once again for Renado's superb skills, and for my own boldness in hacking off my hair to start. Washing it long under these circumstances would be a nightmare.

I rinse with the extra pitcher of water that was left for this purpose. Etricos called the whole lot a water offering and assured me that the people are only too glad to give it. And really, with as many people as there are in the valley below, they need only have donated a thimbleful each.

I dry my skin with a cloth and wrap my hair atop my head. Huna has left me a clean set of clothes. I slip into them and feel, for the first time in ages, something like myself again.

The sun, directly overhead, shines through the hole in the top of the tent. The Hour of Fire is upon us. Noise beyond the tent walls has steadily escalated, fervent murmurs like the drone of a hive of bees. I rub the excess water from my hair and comb it with a narrow-toothed comb that Huna has left me. In the heat of the day, my hair dries quickly.

Someone outside wails, their ululation more ceremonial than frantic. Even so, it draws my nerves taut. These people, wrapped in their worship, expect favor in return. They are placing all their hope in an unseen, unknown goddess.

If I'm to fulfill that role, I must learn control over my beastly magic. Should they discover I'm a fraud, Etricos is not the only one who will suffer.

On impulse, I point my index finger toward the hole in the top of the tent, as though aiming a gun. I focus on the sky beyond, one eye shut, three fingers curled back toward me as I sight my target among the wispy clouds.

Calmness. Control. Hundreds of lives depend upon me.

"Bang," I whisper, and I flick my thumb.

A fireball whips through the opening and explodes in the sky above. It's not the miniature sun I produced on my first night here, but it's also not the tiny spark I intended.

On the bright side, I now know how to stop that ceremonial wailing.

The shocked, deathly silence outside breaks with a renewed murmur of voices. From beyond my tent's entrance someone speaks.

"I, Etricos of the Helenai, request an audience with the goddess Anjeni."

Insofar as I'm aware, Huna is sitting just outside the door. She was kind enough to give me privacy, but I can't imagine that she would stray far.

Sure enough, her voice carries inward. "Does this request please the Goddess?"

There must be quite a crowd out there if they're putting on such a show.

I play along. "Etricos of the Helenai may enter."

The tent flap opens. Huna comes in alongside Etricos, her crimson sewing bundled in her hands. Stricken masses cluster beyond the wooden fence, their hands clasped as though in prayer, their eyes seeking even a glimpse of divinity. The interior of the tent is dark, and the flap falls back into place as quickly as it moved aside. I am hidden well enough from prying eyes.

I kneel upon a rug next to the banked coals of a smoldering fire. From this position I lift challenging eyes to Etricos, waiting to hear if he will rebuke me for my small show of power.

If he's using me as a stage prop, he should be grateful for the spectacle.

"Goddess Anjeni," he begins, and he tips his chin in a perfunctory sign of respect, "we have received many refugees who desire your protection. They seek your good favor, not your wrath."

"Does a fireball in the sky signal wrath to your people?" I ask.

Amusement flashes across his face. He checks it, pursing his lips together until he can answer me seriously. "It alarms the faithful."

"If I leave this tent, will it also alarm them? I need to get out, to have fresh air and open space. And I need a place I can practice my magic."

He blinks. Instinctively he looks to Huna.

"You cannot keep a goddess like a prisoner," the old woman says, a hint of satisfaction hovering around the wrinkled corners of her mouth.

"For a goddess to appear among mortals…" says Etricos, hesitation thick on his voice. He does not finish the sentence, but I can guess the direction of his thoughts. I've grown up around politicians, and Etricos practically bleeds politics. If I'm out among the people, he cannot control the narrative.

"There will be more demons," I tell him. "How can I protect your people if they fear the very sight of me? And how can I teach those who bear the spark, if you keep me here?"

"We will appoint a high priestess to precede you," says Etricos.

Confusion draws my brows together. "Is not Huna my high priestess?"

"She is your attendant. If it be to your liking, Aitana shall fill the role of priestess."

Instinctively I scowl. My expression is fierce enough that he steps back, surprised. I can't help it, even if they're not talking about Aitana my sister. They're talking about the Aitana who loves Demetrios, the Aitana whose superior feminine wiles render me a tragic, jilted figure for centuries to come. I'm supposed to accept her as an acolyte?

"Goddess Anjeni," says Huna with delicate tact, "Aitana bears the spark. As a child she was consecrated to the Goddess Aitana, her namesake."

My annoyance surges. "The Goddess Aitana is my sister. I should not take those who have consecrated themselves to her."

I don't know for a fact that Tana is the goddess they're talking about, but it's a logical enough guess. Part of me wants desperately to strip her of every last follower she has, but I don't want her namesake for a priestess.

"The Goddess Aitana is not here," says Etricos. "Unless Goddess Anjeni would like to summon her, we will worship the goddess we have, not the goddess of our ancestors."

Oh, he's good. Like an eely politician, backing me into a rhetorical corner. If I could summon Aitana, would I?

If it meant she'd end up with the same dysentery I've just survived, I might.

"Why not Tora?" I ask. "Can she not be my high priestess?"

Huna arches her brows. Etricos frowns, but he schools it away with an apologetic expression. "Tora has no spark. She cannot be a priestess."

I look to Huna for confirmation. She nods briefly, almost imperceptibly. Tora is no magician.

"Aitana will make a fine priestess," Etricos continues. "She is willing, obedient, loyal—"

"She is someone you can control, in other words," I interject.

"She is someone *you* can control," he retorts. "Tora is mine. I don't want to share her."

Huna glares, but his childish candor pleases me. I press the point. "She is your plaything?"

His jaw tightens. A telltale glance toward Huna conveys that he knows from whence I've received this impression. "Tora is *mine*." Almost as an afterthought, he tips his attention toward the old woman at his side. "Baba, I have told you I will be faithful," he says in an under-voice.

"I've seen many miracles in my day," says Huna dryly. "That one would eclipse them all." He bristles, but she continues to speak. "Goddess Anjeni believes that you love Tora, Cosi. She was concerned throughout her illness. She does not wish to separate you."

An unspoken addendum hangs in the air: "As I do." Though Huna does not say these words, Etricos and I both understand her meaning.

His back stiffens, pride hardening his face. "I will send you Aitana, Goddess Anjeni, and all others who bear the spark. You may choose your priestess from among them." He pivots to leave, but I speak up quickly.

"Send them to the God's Arch. I will choose from them there."

Etricos studies me, his critical glance scanning me from top to toe. His eyes flit toward where the butter-yellow dress hangs against the brown of the tent. "If you are to appear outside, you should wear clothing more befitting your station, Goddess."

"A goddess doesn't wear another woman's wedding dress, Etricos."

"I would happily marry her in rags," he says.

Although it's a lovely sentiment, he has failed to take Tora's feelings into account. "But would she happily marry you?"

Etricos scowls. He assesses both Huna and me. In the end, he sweeps wordlessly from the tent.

I give him points for knowing when not to argue. That trait will serve him well in his coming years of leadership.

"Why could she not love Dima?" Huna murmurs. "Even if he is the younger son, he is better suited."

Her preference for a younger sibling to an elder one raises my hackles. "It's Tora's choice," I say in a clipped voice as I rise to my feet. "But Huna, bear in mind: Etricos is the better brother."

Huna disregards my remark. Instead she unfolds the crimson fabric in her hands and holds it aloft. "Try this on."

It is a shirt—a tunic that looks like it serves some religious ceremonial purpose. The square shoulders and banded collar give it that formal atmosphere. Its deep red color reflects the sunlight as I receive it from her. "Where did you get this?"

"It was an offering, Anjeni. I have adjusted the size for you."

Whenever I consider my room full of junk back home, I cringe. These people have next to nothing, and they treasure every small item. An article of clothing such as this, like Tora's wedding dress, represents a personal sacrifice, an extravagance spared in a time of hardship and now proffered to deity in hopes of salvation.

I examine the sleeves, troubled. They are capped—similar to the sleeves of the shirt I was wearing when I came through the Eternity Gate. In my limited experience, such a style does not exist among the Helenai. I suspect Huna has altered more than the size, but it makes sense that she would use my own shirt as a template in her alterations.

"Who left it?"

"I do not know. It is a man's style, but the material is good, better than the shirt you wear. Cosi is right. A goddess cannot emerge before the masses in common clothing."

I turn my back to her and strip away my simpler shirt. She has seen my bare skin often enough, having attended my battle wounds over the course of my illness. The fresh pink scars, still sensitive to the touch, create a raw pattern from my waist to my shoulder blades. I have felt the tattered ridges with my fingers but cannot twist far enough to glimpse more than their very edge. I shrug the crimson tunic over my head to cover the scars from sight again.

Thanks to Huna's alterations, the garment fits, neither too tight nor too loose. The hem falls to my mid-thigh, with side-slits up to my hip bones. I fasten the series of hooks up the front but leave the two at the top undone, so that the decorative banded collar remains open at the base of my throat.

I turn to Huna for her assessment. She frowns, her discontented gaze lingering on the stiff red material.

"It is so mannish," she says.

I don't mind the mannishness as much as how the skirt beneath, with its gathered waistline and broad hem, does not match at all. "I like it, but I'd rather wear pants with it," I say.

Huna is silent. I fiddle with the tunic's hemline, tucking it into the skirt to see if that might look any better. It doesn't. I glance up again, only to discover Huna frowning at me—not an angry frown, but a perplexed one.

"Women should not wear pants," she says.

"I'm a goddess. I can wear what I want." I return my attention to the shirt.

"I think you are right."

This admission startles me. I jerk and stare at her, dumbfounded, but she only regards me with a pensive set to her mouth.

I jettisoned into this era clad in pajama pants, a casual shirt, and a light sweater. The shirt and sweater are fit for rags now, too damaged from my battle with the monster. Huna washed the blood from them both, but the gashes made them unsalvageable—at least as a shirt and sweater. She grudgingly returned my pants to me during my illness, but every time I wear them, she tuts in disapproval.

"You think I should wear my pajama pants?" I ask dubiously. They don't have pajamas in this time period, but she knows the term by now.

"No," she says in scorn. "Those are baggy and spotted—"

"They're called polka dots," I interject. "Spotted pants" denotes something else entirely.

"An unsightly, childish pattern." Huna never minces words.

"Then what pants would I wear?"

"Cosi can get you a pair of his, or Dima's. A goddess in men's clothing will give the people an image of strength. You are a warrior-goddess; perhaps you should dress like one."

There's more than one politician in this tribe of cast-offs. "Huna," I say, "you're just as bad as Etricos."

She sloughs off the comparison with a shrug. "I will speak with Cosi. You remain here, unseen, until I return."

I sigh but agree. From beyond the tent walls, the murmured worshipping has renewed. I haven't the first clue how these people expect me to behave as a goddess, so the safest choice is to remain hidden, even though I'm eaten with impatience to get beyond the prison of this confined space.

As Huna passes through the tent flap, I glimpse the gathered crowd. Many figures kneel beyond the wooden fence, their pleading eyes fixed upon the sky above my tent.

Are they looking for another sign? It's not going to happen. I might miss the opening next time and set the tent on fire. I pace, restless as I wait, my fingers fiddling with the slit edges of the stiff tunic. The murmurings beyond the walls come in waves, as though people are taking turns with their worship.

A ripple of excitement passes through their ranks, a signal of some change in their dynamic. It draws my nerves taut like a bowstring, so that when the tent flap parts, I jump.

It is only Huna.

Sorry. It is *not* only Huna.

Behind her, ducking to enter, Demetrios follows. I have not seen him since the night he waylaid me from getting to the Eternity Gate. I haven't wanted to see him, either, the philandering scoundrel. Once safely inside, he straightens to his full height, an aloof expression on his tanned face. I favor Huna with a stink-eye.

"Cosi elected to send Dima with the clothing," she says delicately.

Etricos is still in a snit from our earlier conversation, in other words. Why could Huna not have brought the clothing herself, though?

Demetrios does not make eye contact. Instead, his calculating gaze darts around the interior of the tent before he fixes it directly over my head. He extends the folded bundles he carries. "Goddess Anjeni, we the Helenai present these offerings to you."

He sounds almost as annoyed as I am. I glance again at Huna, perturbed. She knows I'm no goddess, and Etricos knows, but whether Demetrios is in on the secret I cannot tell. She tips her head, a minute gesture for me to take the clothes.

I obey. My hand brushes against his by accident, and I pull back too soon. Half the pile topples to the ground as I scramble to keep my grip on the rest of it.

Demetrios makes no effort whatsoever to catch anything. Nor does he demean himself by stooping to pick it up. Shoulders back and spine erect, he flits his attention downward to the tumbled pile. I stare at it as well, my breath caught in my throat. Hidden among the fabric were a collection of knives. They glint against the hard-packed floor.

I drag my eyes up to his face, mutely demanding an explanation.

Does he have to be so tall? My glare isn't nearly as effective when I'm staring up at someone's chin instead of looking down my nose at them.

He in turn studies me, ever assessing. "Cosi says a warrior-goddess should have weapons. We did not know what weapons you desire. We give these in offering, but if they are not to your liking—"

"Demetrios," I interrupt.

He jerks on instinct and averts his attention to the walls of the tent. A flush of self-consciousness crawls up his neck even as the muscles tighten along his clean-shaven jaw. "What does the goddess wish of me?"

The words alone sound subservient, but insolence infuses them. He doesn't like me using his proper name, that much I gather. Everyone else calls him by his nickname, but I'm not about to enter into such informality. An adversarial relationship suits me fine.

Huna interjects on his behalf. "Goddess Anjeni, Dima intends no offense. He is only Cosi's messenger in this matter."

"He hasn't offended me," I say, annoyed. Even I can admit I sound offended, though. I stoop to retrieve the clothing and blades, since Etricos's chosen messenger obviously won't ingratiate himself to perform such a menial task. The knives, sheathed in decorative covers, are mismatched. Given the huge influx of refugees, Etricos probably has to control what comes in and out of this tent. I suppose, small as they are, these were the easiest weapons to smuggle in here.

I straighten again, blades and fabric alike bundled in my arms. As I cross to dump the load on my cot, I ask, "Why did Etricos send so many pairs of pants?"

"He did not know what would fit you," says Huna.

Suspicion laces through me. I can't imagine this tribe has a lot of extra clothing lying around. "Where did they come from?"

"They are offerings," says Demetrios, his voice bland.

"Offerings from where?" I press. If half a dozen tribesmen are going pants-less right now, I need to know.

"They are offerings, Goddess," he repeats, as if to emphasize that I should be grateful rather than questioning. The tenseness of his shoulders finally registers in my brain. He was not this belligerent the first time we met.

What right has he to be angry with me? "Are they your pants?" I ask.

"No," he says, scorn dripping from that single word. It makes sense: any pants of his would puddle around my ankles.

I change my line of questioning. "Am I just supposed to strap the knives somewhere on me for show? Etricos doesn't expect me to use them, does he?"

The scorn on his face magnifies as his eyes meet mine. "You don't know how to use a knife?"

The attitude on this one—he thinks he's the only one who can act all high and mighty? I tip my nose in the air. "Where I come from, knives are used to prepare food, and for little else. Only the basest of thugs choose them as weapons."

His expression flattens. He stares at me, assessing my statement.

"We have weapons you've never even dreamed of," I say. This tribe has yet to discover black powder, the substance that will revolutionize warfare forever. In some ways, that's a good thing. In others, it's bad. The primitive nature of their weapons is part of what allows magic such a firm cultural hold on the infant nation they are about to form. If they had guns and cannons, magic with its many rules and restrictions would fall by the wayside.

"Why did you not bring these weapons with you, Goddess?" he asks, his voice arch.

I raise one hand. *Just a spark on the fingertip will do.*

As if I have any such control. Flames engulf my hand to the wrist. I force my expression to remain neutral; the beast within always overreacts, so I'm learning to anticipate as much. "Is my magic not weapon enough?"

Demetrios looks unnerved at last, though the emotion is fleeting. He inclines at the waist—five degrees at most, a purely symbolic bow. "The goddess bestows her favor upon the Helenai, for which we are grateful."

And I suddenly feel like a child showing off to a grown adult. The fire on my hand snuffs out. "You're dismissed. Tell Etricos that I thank him for the offering, and that I will return the pants that I cannot use."

"They are an offering, Goddess," says Demetrios yet again, as though I have failed to understand the import of this detail.

"And I shall offer them back to you. Do the Helenai refuse the gifts of a goddess?"

He meets my gaze. Grudgingly he tips his head in acknowledgment. Then, he leaves.

"Offerings are sacred," says Huna from her corner.

"Then a goddess's offerings should be doubly so. What am I supposed to do with half a dozen pairs of pants? Hang them up next to Tora's wedding dress, to decorate the tent walls?"

She grunts, but a sad smile pulls at her mouth. "I can alter them to fit you. If you return them, you will cause injury to those who offered them—to the mothers and sisters of our honored fallen."

I jerk my attention first to her kindly, wrinkled face and then to the pile of pants. Apprehension crawls up my spine. "Those come from the dead?"

"Clothing is sometimes kept as memorial," says Huna. "Please, Anjeni, the offerings are sacred."

I swallow my distaste. Unlike Tora's wedding dress, these pants cannot return to their original bearers. As long as no pants-less warriors lie shamefully hidden in the cluster of mushroom tents down the hill, what quarrel have I?

CHAPTER ELEVEN

OF THE HALF-DOZEN PAIRS OF PANTS, only one really fits. The others are too loose or too snug. I fold the rejects nicely and place them in a pile for Huna to mend when she has opportunity.

She observes in disapproval as I roll tidy cuffs on the dun-colored pair that fits, exposing my ankles to view. I have no shoes, but I'm used to going barefoot. The crimson shirt sits much better atop a fitted waistline than it did over my discarded skirt.

Huna's final inspection tells me she still has misgivings. She deigns to smooth my hair with her fine-toothed comb.

"Can we go now?" I ask, antsy to get out of the tent.

She glances to the exit, uncertain. The worshipful murmurs still buzz in the air beyond.

My patience stretches thin. I have to appear before the teeming masses at some point, and the longer I stay inside, the closer the tent walls get. As I open my mouth to say as much, though, a voice speaks from outside.

"Goddess Anjeni, Tora of the Helenai requests an audience."

Huna darts across the space. I didn't know the old woman could move so fast. She opens the flap and hisses for Tora to enter.

Her granddaughter comes, apprehension upon her face. I have vague recollections of Tora helping Huna tend me during my illness, but she has kept her distance for the past few days. If I were in her position, I would be suspicious of my fiancé and the goddess he so often visits. Tora has been leery of me from the beginning, though.

She fears magic. Naturally she would fear its bearer as well.

She bows low the moment she steps into the tent. Huna asks her why she has come.

"Cosi sent me," Tora replies. She holds out her hands.

Or rather, she holds out the thin packet she has been twisting between her hands. Huna unrolls it as I crane my neck to view its contents.

There's a narrow paint brush and a tiny pot. What on earth?

Huna understands its purpose. "Goddess, it is tradition among our people to make ceremonial markings upon the body for important occasions."

"What kind of markings?" I ask, suspicious.

"Around the eyes." She motions above and below.

Enlightenment dawns. "You want to put makeup on me? That's fine. If I had a mirror I could do it myself."

Huna and Tora exchange a glance. Tora looks ready to retreat, but Huna drags her further in.

"Goddess, kneel there." She points to the puddle of sunlight that streams from the opening overhead, after which she fetches a footstool for Tora to sit upon. When her granddaughter protests, she says simply, "Your hands are steadier than mine."

Tora reluctantly obeys.

I've had someone else do my makeup before, for public events with my parents when everything has to look perfect. I tilt my head upward. The sun blazes through the hole in the ceiling. I fix my gaze off to one side.

Tora uncaps the tiny pot and works quickly. I can only imagine what's in the black concoction she paints around the rim of my right eye. She traces her brush almost all the way to the top of my ear and embellishes the mark, the tip of her tongue caught between her teeth as she works.

There's lead in this paint, I just know it. I'm going to get lead poisoning and die.

She transfers to the opposite side and continues, her brushwork light and quick. Her hand is steady, though her anxiety bubbles beneath that surface of concentration.

When she sits back to assess the overall effect, I blink, the dazzling light of the sun burned on the backs of my eyelids. Huna hums in approval.

Yeah, this death-paint better look good. I glance around for something reflective to inspect it myself. My bathwater in the tiny battered tub, opaque with grime, doesn't quite serve the purpose. I try one of Demetrios's smuggled blades. The polished metal isn't as clear as a mirror, but if I angle it against the light, I can see a dim reflection of my black-rimmed eyes.

And what a sight they are. Lines flare from the outer corners, curling and flicking like fire, punctuated with specks of coal in their midst. Flame and ash mingle together in the motif.

If I were in my own time, I'd document the sheer awesomeness of this artwork with half a dozen pictures. "Ahh, I love it," I say, the words ushering from my lips on instinct. Tora blushes in her corner, one hand grasped around her other elbow in a semi-protective stance.

"Am I ready? Can I go out now?" I ask.

Tora looks to Huna, who looks back at her with an unspoken question in the quirk of her brows.

"Cosi told me to accompany you both," Tora admits.

I clap my hands, startling her. "Yes! Let's go!" I'm on my feet in an instant. Huna grips my arm before I can bolt for the exit, though.

"We will precede you, Goddess," she says wryly.

The fanfare is going to kill me. Tora and Huna step in front of me. In a whisper, the granddaughter inquires of her grandmother, "Do we announce her? Do we have the sentries announce her?"

I answer before Huna gets the chance. "Don't say anything. Part the tent flaps for me to pass through, and we'll be on our way."

My freedom is so close I can almost taste it. If I'm stuck in this tent for a second longer than necessary, I might turn feral and cause some real destruction among these people.

Perhaps Huna can sense my unrest, because she accepts my suggestion with a nod. She and Tora step through to the exterior. As they draw the curtained tent flaps back, the murmurs from beyond the wooden fence die to a hush.

I tuck my short hair neatly behind my ears, ignoring the twist in my gut as I glimpse hundreds of bodies beyond that gap in the tent.

Relax, Anjeni. You're a goddess. You're their *goddess.*

I square my shoulders, take a deep breath, and step into the full light of day for the first time in weeks.

Jaws drop. Eyes bulge. I meet a few of the stares in turn, my face impassive. I'm as arrogant as I possibly can be, looking down upon the worshippers for three, four, five breaths. Then, I pivot and cross around to the back of the tent.

Huna and Tora follow, clumsily, Huna hissing under her breath. "Goddess, what are you doing?"

There's no way I can wade through that crowd. The butterflies in my stomach will erupt out of my mouth before I get more than five yards into their midst. Even as I sidle out of view, my knees half-buckle and I catch myself in a jarring step.

Anyway, the hill with the Eternity Gate is behind us. It's much more efficient to hop the wooden fence in the back and go straight there.

The remnants of my battle with the demon monster cut black across the valley before me. The Eternity Gate overlooks it, a familiar edifice in the unfamiliar terrain.

The land around the Gate is littered with spots of pale brown and objects that glint in the light. I'm already over the fence, but I pause to squint at these strange ornaments.

"Goddess," says Huna from behind me. I turn. She's too old to hop a fence, low though it may be, and too dignified to climb astride over it. Worshippers are crowding around the edges of the enclosure, mostly children trying to get a better glimpse of the goddess.

"You may stay," I tell her with a tip of my head. I look to Tora.

She glances at her grandmother apologetically and swings her legs over the fence—quite dainty in her long skirt.

I proceed, uncaring whether Tora gets nerve enough to stick close to me. I'm out. The wind rustles through the tall grasses as I stride barefoot down the stony hill. I don't even care about the rocks. There's no one to stop me from getting to the Gate this time, no one to keep me shut inside.

Tora does follow, but at a distance of ten or more feet. She can't walk as fast in her skirt as I can in my pants.

The ornaments on the hillside come into focus the closer I get. They are small packets similar to those left outside my tent, more offerings, but at the God's Arch. I pick one up to examine its contents. A gold bracelet slips from the scrap of cloth into my palm. I dangle its glittering links aloft in the sunlight, guilt and wonder warring within me.

"This has to stop," I say to Tora as she joins me. "Your people can't keep giving away their most precious belongings."

"Our lives and our freedom are most precious, Goddess," she replies, her brown eyes searching mine for understanding. "You have spared us. How else can we repay you?"

Shame floods through me. I wrap the bracelet in its packet again, but I hesitate to replace it on the ground. The crowd watches from a distance. I cannot reject an offering.

In discontent, I continue my climb toward the Eternity Gate. The rugged earth bites into my callused feet. I nearly trip over a jutting stone. "If it's an offering the people want to give, they can remove the rocks from this hill," I say, half-joking and half-serious.

"I will tell Cosi," says Tora demurely.

I spare her a glance over my shoulder. Impulsively I ask, "Do you love him?"

She blushes but does not answer.

"Huna says he is inconstant. Is that true?"

"Please, Goddess," says Tora. "Please, I do not wish to speak of it. Baba and Cosi do not get along."

Her loyalty is split between the two, in other words, and it pains her to discuss the situation. But I'm pretty sure that goddesses are supposed to meddle in mortal affairs. "I think you should marry him," I say.

The rosy color of her cheeks betrays her feelings, though she refuses to answer aloud. I pick my way over the last few yards to the Gate, my breath short from the exertion up the incline.

Nostalgia strikes a chord within me. The weathered stones, warm from the sun's rays, retain no remnants of that pulsing energy that possessed them on the morning of my birthday. They are not as worn as in my time, either: the writing patterned over their surface cuts deeper.

"Do you know what this says?" I ask Tora.

She shakes her head.

Suspicion lances through me. "You can read, can't you?"

She bites her lower lip and looks to my tent perched on the other hill. "Not that language, Goddess. What does it say?"

"I don't know." She jerks in surprise, meeting my gaze. "No one knows. I suppose, if it's been here for thousands of years, the language of its first users must be long dead. Too bad." I trace the pattern of a character with one finger. If I could activate the Gate and step back through this instant, would I?

Tricked out in my awesome death-paint and my manly red shirt? Absolutely I would.

But where would that leave all these refugees and the offerings they have made in good faith? Etricos still has a long way to go to establish his sovereign nation.

"Cosi is coming," says Tora, "with Dima and Aitana and those others who bear the spark."

"Dima bears the spark?" I ask sharply.

She frowns. "No. He guards Aitana and the others. Our enemies hunt the spark-bearers first and foremost."

A grunt twists up from my throat. Mr. High-and-Mighty can sit on his laurels back in camp, for all I care. "Have there been any more demons since I came?"

"No. Only scouts near the river," says Tora. "Dima took care of them before they could return to their master to report."

"I see." I shouldn't be annoyed, but I am. I was sick, so of course it's good that someone else could watch out for the safety of the encampment, but why Demetrios?

I mean, aside from the whole "capable warrior" swagger he has going on.

"Who is their master?" I ask. She regards me with open astonishment. "We only ever called them the demon hordes where I come from, Tora. Who is their master?"

"The Bulokai—the tribesmen that summoned them from the netherworld, and Agoros the Fifth, the present leader of the Bulokai."

In my native time, Helenia dominates the international discourse in our corner of the world. I don't recall any of our neighboring countries tracing their roots to a people known as the Bulokai. "I guess Etricos wipes them out," I remark offhand. Tora starts, a troubled furrow between her brows as she fixes her attention on the approaching group. Some of the worshipping crowd has followed as far as the valley basin, but only Etricos's chosen candidates mount the steep incline toward the Eternity Gate. The spark-bearers straggle out in a broken line as they come, the younger, slower members toward the back. Etricos and Demetrios lead the way.

Aitana, to her credit, pauses in her ascent to wait for the smallest of the group to catch up.

I plant myself directly between the two pillars of the arch as they approach, my hands outstretched to each column. Etricos has brought me seven souls from out of his hundreds. Seven meager souls, ranging in age from five to twenty, their faces and hands washed but their clothing tattered at the edges.

Tora descends eight steps to meet her betrothed. He draws her to him with a possessive arm, his eyes flitting upward to where I observe him, as though to say, "I have loaned her briefly to you, and now I claim her as my own again."

He doesn't need to play the macho games here. I'd officiate their wedding myself if I thought it would stick in their culture.

"Goddess Anjeni," he says with a formal bow of his head, "I, Etricos of the Helenai, have brought you those of the Helenai who bear the sacred spark, according to your request."

"The Helenai," I repeat, fixed upon his wording. "Do all the people in your encampment belong to the Helenai?"

He blinks. I recognize that reaction as a politician caught in a scheme.

I pin him with a stern gaze. "Etricos, I need you to bring me *all* who bear the spark, not just those among the Helenai."

"We are here that you may choose a priestess, Goddess," he replies. Meaning he wants my priestess to come from among his own tribesmen and not from the other tribes that join his encampment daily.

And it finally registers that the seven he has brought me are all female. "Are there no men among the Helenai who bear the spark?" I ask in confusion. Magic is a trait shared among the sexes in my time.

"No," he says, his voice hushed. Hardness infuses it as he continues. "Does the goddess prefer a priest to a priestess?"

I'm embarrassing him in front of his tribesmen. "No. I prefer a priestess. I only wondered whether the men of the Helenai could bear the spark."

"It is possible," he says. His tight-lipped answer leaves me to draw my own conclusions: the Helenai men who bore the spark have already died. As warriors they would be singled out first by the enemy. The spark is easier to hide among women, who do not serve on the front lines in battle.

Tragedy has plagued this people, and now they pin their hopes on the magic borne by a false and foolish goddess in their midst. But for their sake, I must play my part.

I settle cross-legged on the ground beneath the arch, training my attention upon the girls Etricos has brought me. "All right, spark-bearers. Show me your power."

Aitana carries the youngest in her arms, but she lowers the child to the ground and urges her forward. Shyly the girl approaches, her hands aloft. Uncertainty clouds her dark eyes, but she manages to produce a crackling spray of magic between her fingers. She lacks the control to pass the candle test except by chance, but she will grow into her power as she ages.

And I hate that I'm mentally deferring to the evaluation methods of my despised magic tutors. There's not even a candle in sight, yet that's my first instinct upon seeing the erratic sparks.

"Very good," I tell the girl. She retreats, hiding behind Aitana's legs.

The rest of the candidates come from youngest to oldest. They have hardly more control than the first. Without the fundamentals to focus their minds, they can only muddle with their sparks of magic. Aitana is the last and the strongest. She can center her power on the tip of her finger in a single flame, but not for more than a few breaths.

As it winks out, she looks not to me for approval, but to Etricos and Demetrios. There's no question where she seeks favor.

I, with my elbow propped on one knee and my chin cradled in my hand, contemplate the small group before me. Having only come into my power a mere two weeks ago, I shouldn't be so critical. I expected more, though. I expected at least someone to shoot a burst of power into the air or something. Not a soul in this group has progressed past the first awakening stage.

Etricos clears his throat. "Goddess Anjeni, which of these shall you take as your priestess?"

His attention flits towards Aitana, the strongest of the group. She is the obvious choice.

Call me petty, but I don't want to give her the honor. "They are all my priestesses," I reply, rising to my feet.

The fourth fundamental of magic is that it divides upon the user's will and understanding. Command and it shall be done.

I raise both hands, four fingers aloft on my left and three on my right. "Seven bearers of the sacred spark," I say. "Seven priestesses."

Sparks rocket upward from each of my raised fingers, like firecrackers shot into the sky: seven balls of flame burst in succession high above. My power divided is smaller and more controlled than when I try to produce a single manifestation, but the crowd in the valley below gasps and ducks nonetheless. The spark-bearers, too, fall away in apprehension. I keep my gaze fixed on Etricos, who stares back at me.

Faint amusement tugs at the corners of his mouth. "Be it as you wish, Goddess Anjeni. Will you return to your tent?"

"No," I say, much to his chagrin. "I remain here for today. You may return to your people, if that is your desire."

He tips his head in acknowledgement and, Tora's hand tightly clasped in his, pauses only to whisper a command to his brother before he descends the hill with his betrothed. Demetrios remains behind, the guard I did not request.

"Goddess, what do you wish of us?" Aitana asks. The youngest still clings to her uncertainly.

"Collect the offerings on the hillside," I say. "They are sacred and should not be left to the elements." My stance between the pillars and the memory of candle tests has pulled another issue to the forefront of my thoughts. "If you find a small silver item, flat and polished and about this big"—I gesture roughly three inches long by an inch-and-a-half wide with my fingers—"bring it directly to me. It is mine."

Unless I'm vastly mistaken, I came through the Eternity Gate with my lighter in my pocket. It was not among the clothing returned to me during my illness. Most likely it fell free as I tumbled down the hillside, or in my ensuing battle with the demon champion.

I may not need it anymore, but if it's here I want it back.

CHAPTER TWELVE

"**M**AGIC IS LIKE A VOLCANO. It builds up in pressure and then bursts. You are the volcano."

My collection of priestesses looks up at me with mirror-image blank expressions. They huddle together just below the Eternity Gate, with Demetrios off to one side, his arms folded and his attention divided between us and the crowds in the valley's basin.

I demonstrate what I'm talking about, the buildup of pressure, the release in a fiery ball that shoots into the air.

What a liberating discovery, this connection between the theoretical and the practical sides of magic. I'm itching to experiment with all the fundamentals, all the intermediates, all the superlatives I thought I had memorized in vain. My pupils need to start at the beginning, though. They need to start with that very first fundamental.

Magic is like a volcano. None of this river rubbish.

"Try it," I urge.

They do. And, one by one, they fail. Repeatedly. Even Aitana's flame sputters and dies in the same breath that she creates it. I single her out, leaning in for more pointed instruction.

"Force it out. Shove it through the gap. It's a beast in a cage, so let it free."

Mere embers spit from her fingertip. Her breath quickens as panic sets into her eyes.

I fling out my arms. "What is wrong?"

"I don't understand, Goddess," she says in trembling voice. "The volcano, the beast—they're not here within me." She dissolves into tears upon this admission, burying her face into her hands. From the side, Demetrios takes a concerned step forward.

"Back off," I snap, holding up my palm to arrest his movement. The last thing I need is the diligent lover comforting and coddling his favorite in her failure.

"Aitana," I say, and I kneel in front of her so that we're at the same eye level. I pry her hands away from her eyes. "Look at me, Aitana."

She ventures to meet my steely gaze, but she averts her attention just as quickly.

"Look at me," I say again. The hopelessness that dances across her face triggers a harrowing guilt within me.

I know that despair—not from my apathetic teenage years, but from when I was a child struggling against an unresponsive spark, desperate to please my parents, to please my teachers, desperate to measure up to my phenomenal younger sister. It never worked. I urged and pled, prayed and sobbed, and all for nothing. The memory ricochets through my mind, still painful after a decade of smothering indifference.

I'm doing to Aitana exactly what my tutors did to me, demanding the impossible and getting frustrated when it does not occur.

But in her case, this is a matter of life and death. Her people are on the verge of extinction, and only magic will save them, for they have no stronger weapon against the demon hordes.

And she's not my sister. Same name, but completely different person. She's *not* my sister.

I release her wrists and back away. She chances to look at me again, uncertainty warring upon her face, tears tumbling down her cheeks and a sob in her throat.

We're not the same. There's a reason I couldn't manifest magic for all the years I studied it. I'm not the same as other magic users. Either I don't interpret my power in the same way, or it doesn't respond to me as it does to others. Telling her she's like a volcano is as effective as telling me I'm like a riverbed. It will never work.

Well, crap.

There's got to be a way around this. That first fundamental has been the bane of my existence, a dam that kept me from progressing through all the practical applications. I don't want to teach it.

But my little class is in shambles. The younger girls huddle together, breathless as they wait upon my judgement. Aitana trembles in fear and misery. Demetrios looks ready to snatch the whole group away from my charge and lead them back down the hillside to safety.

"Close your eyes, all of you," I say, training my voice to a calmer timbre. "Interlace your fingers, with your forefingers pointed to the sky. Breathe in and out. Empty your mind."

I wait for them to comply, strolling along their line as their tension slowly ebbs. Only my youngest pupil fidgets. The others gradually relax, their breaths becoming smooth.

I hate myself right now, but what else am I supposed to do? "Everyone, repeat after me: *The first fundamental of magic*—"

"The first fundamental of magic—"

"—*is that it flows like a river.*"

"—is that it flows like a river."

Their voices ring out in unison as I proceed through the rest of the recitation. Seven fledgling riverbeds before me align their minds with the fundamental. Four of them have steady flames flickering atop their fingertips before we finish the second sentence.

Why has fate sent a volcano to teach these rivers how to flow? I am probably the worst possible person for this job.

"You are the riverbed," I finish on a mumble. "Say it: I am the riverbed."

"I am the riverbed," seven voices intone together, the youngest piping an octave above the eldest. Seven flames burn bright. One by one, they open their eyes to the sight.

The youngest yelps and breaks her grip, snuffing her power. The flames of the pair just older than her sputter out because of their surprise.

The others maintain the flow, their eyes wide and fixed upon the dancing tongue of fire. Aitana is crying again, but with joy and wonder now.

And I? In bitterness I pivot on the ball of my foot and walk away, past the Gate, up the hill to its apex.

The hilltop spreads out before me, its other side gently sloping downward, the land undulating toward the horizon where a ribbon of ocean glitters in the afternoon sunlight.

Why could I not be like them? Why should it come so innately to others when I struggled and muddled and shoved against a channel I did not fit?

The dry wind rustles through my short hair, bringing the scent of late summer. The sun beats down upon my head, merciless. I stand alone, separate from the rest of the world.

Stubborn. Defiant. Refusing to cooperate. My father's accusations on my birthday eve rake across my mind. He might as well have been describing my brand of magic. It's ingrained into me, this non-conformity. So it was from the beginning. I didn't *want* to be different. It wasn't a choice. It's part of my nature, something I'm powerless to change. I am made of different stuff than my sister, than my magic tutors and the ragtag cluster of pupils down the hill.

They are riverbeds. I am a volcano. They are tranquil. I am a beast.

Afar off, a feral screech cuts through the air. I whirl, my hand ablaze, that beast within me responding before I'm really even aware. Afar off, a cluster of demon riders pursue a line of refugees, their weapons raised as they close the distance between them and their quarry.

"Afar off" is nothing to magic. In an instant, my inner beast rockets across the gap, across the black-scarred valley to the plains beyond, piercing through the demon ranks with a precision that only hyper-heightened awareness makes possible. The magic connects, spiderwebs across the enemy raiders, and destroys them in a twisting executioner's blow.

The seventh intermediate of magic is that it governs temporal space. It connects every infinite point at once. Distance is but an illusion on the magical plane.

The valley below echoes with cries of alarm. Demetrios bounds up the hill to join me as Aitana gathers my other pupils in a protective embrace. None of them can see past the rise of the land, but I, at the highest point of what will someday be Monument Hill, have a far-flung view. The cluster of refugees, two or three miles away yet, straggles out in a ragged line.

The enemies I eradicated were only the first wave of pursuers.

I focus on the distance, on the second wave, a larger cluster of demons perhaps a mile behind the first. They have slowed their pace. A few have turned back.

In theory, the seventh intermediate should allow me to destroy them, because all space converges into one single point. In practice, the distance intervenes. My second attack flashes into their midst, but fails to connect with more than two or three of its targets. It's like trying to catch a chain link with a hook on the end of a pole—an extremely long pole.

"C'mon," I mutter under my breath. I focus my concentration, my throat tight as I shove my captive beast among them yet again. The deadly blow cuts through the second wave, but those who turned back already gallop beyond its effect.

I gulp air, a lance of pain shooting through my head. I shake it off. My arms tremble from the strain.

"Goddess, it is enough," says Demetrios with urgency in his voice. He is at my side, one hand hovering near my elbow as though ready to catch hold of me. Wary of his touch, I jerk away and focus again on the retreating demons.

They can't escape. I can't let them.

Even as I raise my hand for a final attempt, Demetrios catches my wrist and yanks it downward. "Goddess, they are too far."

I wrench free, shock racing through me.

He doesn't acknowledge the rebuff. "They're not attacking anymore, Goddess. They're running away."

"They'll attack others fleeing to safety," I retort with a flinging gesture that direction. "We have to destroy them while we have the chance!"

He grabs my other arm, his large hand gripping just below my armpit, reining me in. "It is *too far*."

Again I twist free. My attention snaps to the cluster of fleeing demons, but they're already at the horizon, barely visible in their retreat. My magic won't focus anymore. I swallow, trying to force it.

Distance is but an illusion.

It's a powerful illusion, though. My vision sparks and shudders. The enemies on the horizon, mere specks, are too far now and the distance increases with every passing second.

"You should not overexert yourself when a battle is already won," says Demetrios. He does not attempt to touch me again. I glare a mute accusation up at him.

He's not sorry. If anything, he's fully resolute in his interference.

I gather every last ounce of strength and pride within me and turn my back on him. Spine erect, I stride down the hillside toward my gaping pupils.

"G-Goddess," Aitana stammers, cringing in fear. From this angle on the hill, even the approaching line of asylum-seekers is beyond her sight.

I ignore her terror and speak directly. "There are refugees on the plains, that direction. They have been chased by demons. Tell Etricos to prepare for their arrival: food, water, shelter, and healers ready to treat their injuries."

I continue down the hill before she can respond, my steps controlled so that I don't slip and tumble like a fool into the gawking crowd below. Behind me, Aitana calls for my priestesses to gather up the offerings and return to camp. Before me, the spectating worshippers scramble to create a path. Demetrios treads close on my heels, though he has sense enough to hang back two steps as we progress to and through the basin. My worshippers fawn and prostrate themselves, awe in the few sets of eyes that dare to flit up toward me. I fix my gaze forward and focus all of my attention on the hillside yet for me to climb, and upon my tent perched atop it.

The intermediate magic, its distance and intensity, has sapped my strength and meager stamina. The outer edge of my vision blurs as I mount the second hill. Static fizzles in my ears. I push stubbornly forward, my breath forced, my legs trembling. The blurred vision spreads. Darkness eats away at the nebulous colors.

I crest the hill, and there my knees give out.

Strong, solid arms catch me, sweep me up, and carry me the remaining several yards into my tent.

CHAPTER THIRTEEN

Darkness suffuses the area around me when I open my eyes. The fire at the center of my tent has burned to mere embers. Above, through the vent, a gauzy pattern of stars shines against the black sky.

My head throbs like I've been run over by a truck. Gingerly I push away from my cot. The throbbing intensifies and my dim surroundings swim. "Huna," I croak, but there is no response.

She's not here.

A chill courses down my spine. I gather my blanket around my shoulders and stand on wobbling legs. "Huna," I say again, my eyes adjusting to the darkness. I stumble toward the tent's exit.

The flap parts, and a shadowed figure steps through. "Goddess, you should not be up."

Why is Demetrios here? I ignore his rebuke. "Where's Huna?"

"Tending to the sick among the newly arrived." Without ceremony he scoops me up, blanket and all.

I buck in his arms. "Put me down, you cretin!"

He obliges by depositing me back on my cot. "You are to rest," he commands, his voice as hard as stone.

My face burns with indignation. He hovers too close, ready to catch me again if I should try to stand a second time. Not that I can. He's effectively caged me in.

Oh, he wants to be imposing? I tip my head in defiance. "How long was I asleep? How late is it?"

"Second watch," he replies, his guard never faltering.

It's close to midnight, then. I have already slept for eight or nine hours. "I'm rested."

"A goddess must not overexert herself."

My expression turns cynical. If he doesn't already know the truth, he's being awfully sarcastic in his address. "But I'm not really a goddess, Demetrios. I'm just an ordinary girl."

He scoffs, actually scoffs, derision upon his shadowed face. "Ordinary? You don't come within two leagues of 'ordinary.' Lie down and rest, Anjeni."

I start to argue, but my name on his lips dismantles my senses. "Wh-what's that supposed to mean?"

His fingers close around my wrist. In the dimness he lifts my palm to eye level. "This is not the hand of anyone ordinary, Goddess. Ordinary hands are rough and callused. Your hands have never seen a day's work. Who but a goddess can afford such luxury?"

My heart sits in my throat, its erratic rhythm like a knot that binds my voice. Demetrios stares, waiting for my defiant rebuttal.

But I have no words. My treacherous thoughts fixate on the intimacy of this exchange, the darkness around us, the warmth that emanates from his nearness.

This man is supposed to be my inconstant lover.

I have nowhere to retreat. Do I want to retreat? I can't bring myself to push him away, lest I fail in the attempt and look completely pathetic. I can only meet his shadowed gaze, apprehension raising gooseflesh along my arms.

Abruptly he releases his grip on my wrist and steps back. "Sleep, Goddess Anjeni. The Helenai need your strength, not your stubborn will."

Stubborn. Defiant. Are my faults really that obvious?

I settle on my cot, lying on my side so that my back is to him. "Go away, Demetrios," I say. "This goddess does not require your presence now or ever."

"Even goddesses have their limits. You would be wise to honor yours."

A rustle of fabric follows this remark. I wait three breaths and chance a look over my shoulder. He has left me to the dim interior. The blanket upon me is stifling, my earlier chill banished by the warmth of embarrassment and internal dismay.

Butting heads with Demetrios is more fun than I expected, and much too dangerous a game for me to play.

Huna returns near dawn, as the glimpse of sky through the top of the tent lightens to a grayish blue. I pretend to be asleep, my breathing steady and rhythmic. She settles on her cot with a groan. Two minutes later she is snoring softly.

I'm going to have words with Etricos about keeping old women out until all hours of the night. Her lateness worries me, though. The refugees must have been in a dire state if they required such prolonged treatment.

I roll over onto my back and stare up at the patch of fading night sky. The web of stars vanishes against the growing light. As Huna's sleep deepens, I throw back my covers and rise. Someone—Huna, I sincerely hope—changed my clothing during my unconscious state. A quick check of my face reveals that the death-paint has been washed away as well.

The encampment beyond my tent walls is silent. I venture to part the flap. Guards still stand beside the braziers that mark the entrance to my hilltop domain and more offerings litter the ground, but there is not a worshipper in sight.

Boldly, I slip from the tent into the cold predawn air. One of the guards glances over his shoulder, stiffens, and immediately returns his attention forward again. He mutters something to his fellow under his breath. I straighten my spine and cross around to the back of the tent. I don't need their permission to leave.

I hop the fence but settle on the hillside just beyond, with a perfect view of the Eternity Gate. A breeze wisps around me, salt-laden from the ocean a mile away. The silent repose beneath a gradually lightening sky does wonders for my soul. I lean back on my elbows and drink in the tranquility.

I am alone for maybe a quarter of an hour. Footsteps tread upon the grass. I look up as Etricos joins me. He sits cross-legged, much more formal than my languid position. "You should not be out here alone, Goddess Anjeni."

"I'm not alone anymore, am I?" I fix my gaze forward as I absently pluck at the scrubby grass.

Etricos says nothing. A glance up at him reveals consternation upon his face.

"The newest refugees, were they in such poor condition?"

"It was mostly women and children. The men that escaped with them turned back to face the demons, to stop the tide of attacks. A good number were badly wounded. Even more were killed."

This disclosure sobers me. "There will be others, other groups coming to the safety of this place, with demons pursuing them, slaughtering them."

"Yes," he says, the single word heavy in the chill around us. I give him my full attention. "What will you do?"

He glances askance at me. "I need the spark-bearers fully trained, Goddess. How long will it take?"

My brows shoot up. "That all depends on them. It can take years for full training. What will you do in the meantime?"

"I cannot march our warriors beyond the protection of this place. We are too few, and the enemy too strong in their own domain. How far does your influence extend? If they learn of your weakness—"

"My weakness?" I interrupt. "Excuse me?"

His expression darkens. "Goddess, your power is great, but it comes at a high cost. If Agoros learns that you must sleep for half a day after an attack, all he need do is send two waves of soldiers upon us. You will sleep as the second wave slaughters us all. I need our spark-bearers fully trained."

"I will get stronger," I say. "I will train the spark-bearers as well, but I do need all of them, Etricos, not only the seven from among the Helenai. *All* of them, do you understand?"

His jaw tightens, but he curtly nods.

"And you need to establish your city here." He jerks, twisting around to stare at me in full. I continue. "This will be your stronghold. You cannot live forever in tents. You need to organize the people. They can work. One day, this city will cover this land as far as the eye can see."

"We wish to return to our homeland," he says.

I focus on him, my brows drawing together. Their homeland? The idea of the Helenai having a homeland beyond this place is foreign to me. They are refugees as well, though. They fled to the God's Arch from afar.

I temper my voice. "This is your homeland now, Etricos." Denial flashes across his face. I emphasize my statement:

"*This* is your homeland. You cannot gather other tribes under your protection and expect them to return with you to a place unknown to them. This is the meeting place, the rally point, the beginning. This is your homeland."

He blinks, shifting his gaze as he processes my words. "Our ancestors are buried elsewhere."

His thoughts are with his parents, grandparents, and loved ones. My memory flits to my family in another time, and that sense of separation floods through me. I wall it off, suppressing the instinctive tears that sting the corners of my eyes. "You must look forward, not back."

Silence stretches between us. He stares at his hands, contemplative and stubborn. I wait. If he is to become the great uniter, this decision must be his. But he doesn't have to make it today.

A gust of wind streams around us, carrying crisp ocean air upon it. Etricos sighs and meets my steady gaze. "You know things, Anjeni—things that mortals should not know. Are you a soothsayer? Is that a power you bear?"

For once he does not call me "Goddess"; for once he acknowledges my humanity.

"My knowledge has its limits, Etricos, but this I can promise you: your name will be held in reverence and honor for generations to come *if* you let go of the past and work to establish the future instead."

He bucks his head and stares the opposite direction. I shift my attention to the Eternity Gate, its surface pale and golden in the first rays of the rising sun. In a way, his dilemma is my own. Since coming here, I have shoved aside my regrets, my grief and anxiety of separation from my family and everything I know, but it lurks within me. No one knows where the goddess Anjeni goes from here. I might never see my home or my family again.

I cannot allow that grief to control me. In this moment, I have a purpose. So too does Etricos. I change the subject.

"What will you do for food? You don't have enough resources to feed all those who will flee here for safety, and they bring next to nothing with them."

"We have fish from the ocean," he says. "All else is quickly depleting. We have only a small number of livestock. Milk and eggs were a luxury even before the others began to arrive."

"Is there no means to grow crops? You must establish a colony here, where people can live in safety." It will do them no good to survive the attack of a demon army only to starve for lack of food.

"There is another option, if our needs should outstretch our resources," he says. To my questioning gaze he continues. "We can raid—send expeditions out to the nearest regions not to fight but to steal their livestock and their grain."

This guy, this wily, amoral opportunist. What am I supposed to do with him? "The word is 'liberate,' Etricos. You must liberate those regions, including the people in bondage, and gather them here. I can go with you—"

"You must remain, Goddess," he interrupts, his voice hard. "If we lose you, we lose everything. And if the demons were to attack this place while you were away, while the warriors were away, they would destroy everything."

He is correct. I must protect the fledgling colony above all else. Any military campaign will fail without magic behind it, though.

A bitter taste enters my mouth. I shuffle it away with the rest of my suppressed grief and anxiety. "Send Aitana to me. She is the strongest; I will train her personally. Find me any other spark-bearers among the refugees as well. If I must remain here, other magicians must be ready to go with you, when that time comes."

He tries not to look pleased as he rises from the ground, but he largely fails in the effort. "Do you have any other instructions before I go, Goddess Anjeni?"

"Yes," I say, much to his dismay. "Organize the people into groups: some to build, some to gather, some to grow. You need farmers and fishermen and masons."

An irritated look dances across his face. "There are not enough men in the camp to divide them, or to focus their efforts on any but the most pressing of needs."

"There are plenty of women," I say. "Food, shelter, and fuel are the most pressing of needs, and all must work together to establish them."

CHAPTER FOURTEEN

B Y NOON, THE HILLSIDE beneath the Eternity Gate crawls with bodies, women and children bearing every rude implement imaginable to pry up the many rocks and stones. They roll them down to the basin, where others wait with carts to haul them away. They have few tools in the encampment, and every last one is put to work somewhere.

Etricos has either a genius for organization or else he knows how to delegate responsibility. I suspect the latter.

I watch them work in spurts, my attention divided between their industry and the small cluster of spark-bearers who have joined me at the apex of the hill. Etricos gleaned fifteen newcomers from among the other tribes, bringing my class to an unmanageable twenty-two. Demetrios stands removed from the group, on his guard as he scans the surrounding terrain for any approaching danger. I mostly ignore him.

Aitana has had her personal instruction. She advances at a pace that would make me sick if I didn't absolutely need her to excel. Already she has mastered the first three fundamentals. She helps with the newcomers now; not all of them speak the same dialect as the Helenai.

I have broken them into groups by age and tend to the elder ones. Two among them, Ria and Ineri, have abilities similar to Aitana.

Below, the workers continue to toil beneath the blazing yellow sun.

Movement from the encampment hill draws my attention. A line of people processes like a twisting snake toward the basin. Etricos runs alongside them, catching up to the leader, arguing as he keeps pace.

I squint. The leader of the snake-like processional is an older man. He appears to be dressed in ceremonial clothing, his arms folded into trailing sleeves as he carefully picks his way down the slope. He never looks at Etricos, but maintains a stony façade.

Demetrios is at my side almost before I realize it. I glance up at him, but he pins his attention upon the approaching group. The workers on the hillside pause and step out of the way as the line ascends toward the Eternity Gate. The leader takes a twisting path again, skirting around the torn earth. He and his entourage zigzag slowly toward me.

Etricos has given up his argument and keeps pace beside the man. Both of them look up, and I meet their gazes.

"Aitana," I say over my shoulder. She straightens in my periphery. "Take all of the spark-bearers to the ocean side of the hill and continue to practice there."

She glances downward to the approaching visitors and, without question, herds the younger students away.

"Go with them," I tell Demetrios.

"No," he says.

"If they are attacked, all is lost for the Helenai."

"They're in no danger from that direction."

"Am I in danger from this direction?" I ask him, an edge to my voice.

He looks down, meeting my arch expression with one of his own. "That is Moru, the elder of the Terasanai, the plains people who arrived yesterday."

"The people I rescued? Why would he pose a danger to me?"

Demetrios scoffs. "A tribal elder who has survived Bulokai enslavement? He could only have done so through treaty. He sacrificed the lives of others to ensure his own safety."

I fix my attention again upon the approaching line, assessing. "There is value in survival. He has led his people out of enslavement, has he not?"

Demetrios does not answer, which is probably for the best. The group is within earshot now. As they come to the Eternity Gate, Moru pauses to touch its weathered stones. The reverence of this action, the elegance of his long fingers pressing against the warmth of the arch, thrums through me as though he had pressed those fingers to my heart instead. Etricos sidesteps around the edifice, but each of Moru's entourage in turn touches their hand to the sacred relic as they pass.

I think I might like the Terasanai.

Moru climbs the last several yards to the top of the hill, but he stops six feet from me and stoops into a low bow. "Goddess Anjeni, Moru of the Terasanai desires an audience."

His accent differs from the Helenai, but I can understand him well enough. I look to Etricos, who is silently, almost imperceptibly, communicating that I should send this upstart visitor on his way. I tip my head in rebuke, and his expression plummets into a glower.

"Speak, Moru of the Terasanai."

The man freezes midway in his bow, his attention fixed upon my bare feet. He raises inquiring eyes, but rather than question my lack of footwear, he says, "Forgive me, Goddess. I wish a private audience, such as you often grant Etricos of the Helenai."

He has counseled with other refugees in the encampment and learned the way the wind blows here. Beside me Demetrios tenses, ever on his guard. I slide my attention to his older brother who, for the moment, holds his tongue. He cannot dictate my actions before others, lest he undermine my divinity and thus his perceived influence with the divine.

"Etricos of the Helenai holds my favor," I say. "What claim have you upon a private audience, Moru of the Terasanai?"

He meets my steady gaze, scrutinizing me, calculating. "The Terasanai, too, hold your favor, Goddess Anjeni. You would not have spared us yesterday were it otherwise."

The corners of my mouth curve upward. I incline my head. "Come."

"Goddess," Etricos protests as I turn away. I spare him a questioning glance. He pauses long enough to collect his wits. After a deep inhale he says, "Please do not forget your promises to the Helenai."

As if any promises have been made. But I know where my loyalty must lie first and foremost. The Helenai are my people. The Terasanai can only receive my blessing if they acknowledge Etricos as their leader. I nod my reassurance to him—though it does not allay his fears in the least—and lead Moru away from the cluster.

Demetrios, thankfully, has sense enough to remain with his brother, though he watches me like a hawk as I separate from the group. I walk thirty yards from them on the hilltop, far enough that our voices won't carry on the wind.

"Speak," I command Moru, examining his weathered face.

He bows again. "The Terasanai thank you for your favor, Goddess Anjeni, that you have spared our lives and offer us protection from our enemies."

Politicians are the same in any age: none of them gives thanks except as an opportunity to request further support.

"What additional favor do you seek?" I ask.

He straightens. The flash of surprise on his face quickly gives way to grudging respect. "Lands designated for my people. The Terasanai wish to live under your protection, but as the Terasanai, with our own customs and our own space."

My instinctive frown troubles him.

"Goddess, if we must lose our identity, we may as well have stayed in captivity to the Bulokai."

"Is that so?" The question leaves my tongue much sharper than I intended, but the nerve on this guy has my hackles raised. Playing nice with the Helenai is tantamount to demon enslavement? Who is he kidding?

But I can't excoriate him. If there's one thing I've learned from my father, it's that the necessity of making political allies trumps any personal offense one feels. I have to set boundaries without driving up a wall between us, if possible.

"Moru of the Terasanai," I say, picking my words carefully, "I grant my protection to my people, the Helenai. You may live among them here, you may even carve out lands upon these hills for your people, but if you cannot unite under one banner with all others who seek refuge in this place, I cannot support you. Only through unity will the people of this land overcome the demons who seek their destruction."

He ruminates upon my words, resentment lingering at the edge of his expression. "You would have us abandon our traditions, then?"

"Far from it. I would have you contribute them to the united culture that will emerge. What skills have the Terasanai brought with them?"

He cocks his head to one side, studying me as he considers his response. "We are farmers and builders. Our women are weavers and gatherers. But we have escaped with little more than our lives, Goddess."

I glance down upon the stone-gatherers at the base of the hill, the women and children who toil with minimal skill or knowledge of their work. "Why, when you have so little, do you seek to separate yourselves from those who would be your allies? You do not wish to contribute your strength to the efforts of those who offer you protection?"

Moru stiffens, drawing himself up to his full height. "The Terasanai are a proud and ancient people. We wish to subjugate ourselves to no one."

It's a pretty speech, but one glaring contradiction remains. "Moru, how did you survive the Bulokai?"

His bravado falters. Hesitantly he glances up at me. "Goddess?"

"How did you survive?" I ask again. "The Bulokai demons kill the tribal elders of those they conquer, do they not? How did you, Moru of the Terasanai, survive their slaughter?"

His expression turns brittle. I scrutinize him, waiting for his answer, observing every minute movement he makes: the squints at the outer corners of his eyes, the right side of his mouth tugging slightly downward. He battles an inner demon, unable to meet my gaze for more than a fleeting instant. At last he steels himself to reply.

"I treated with them, Goddess, for the sake of my people. It was a grave mistake."

The firmness of his voice speaks volumes above his words. If the Bulokai exploited their treaty, of course the Terasanai would not wish to enter a similar agreement with anyone else.

And yet, he is a politician. I know better than to take a politician's word as absolute truth.

"How can the Helenai trust one who has treated with the Bulokai? How do we know you are not a viper in our midst, come to infiltrate and destroy?"

His expression hardens, his gaze fixed upon an unseen vista in the recesses of his mind. "They required our labor, heavy burdens upon our backs from sun up till sun down. They took our children as tribute to Agoros, the firstborn of each family slaughtered in ceremonial sacrifice. They defiled our daughters and tortured our youths. It would have been better to die."

A chill crawls up my spine as he pins me with an iron gaze.

"We will *not* bend in fealty again."

This is the true purpose of his errand, the true reason he stuck out his neck to encounter a volatile, fickle goddess. "Does Etricos of the Helenai require fealty from you?" I ask.

He presses his lips together in a firm line, his silence my answer.

And my blood boils. "I will speak to him."

"Goddess Anjeni," he says as I start back toward the waiting group. I glance over my shoulder, expectant. "The Terasanai thank you for your favor and protection."

"My favor and protection yet remain to be seen, Moru," I reply. "The Helenai need your strength and skill. You must remember: your enemy is the Bulokai."

He bows his head. I resume my course, reining my temper even as the beast within prowls its cage. Etricos sulks as I approach, but he says not a word. His attention flits to Moru, who follows ten paces behind me. Demetrios steps between me and the leader of the Terasanai, as though I need his protection. I fix my attention upon the ocean side of the hill, where Aitana instructs the younger students in the first and second fundamentals. For the moment I control my fury.

Behind me, no words pass between Etricos and Moru. The emissaries of the Terasanai withdraw. The laborers cease their stone-gathering, their tools silent as the foreign tribe crosses through their midst. Only when the noise of their work resumes does Etricos speak.

"Anjeni, you will not interfere with my leadership over this people."

His voice trembles with rage, with the echoes of his wounded pride. I do not face him. Instead, I look down at my hand, at the magic that flares upon it. With concentration, I reduce the flare to a controlled ball and dance it across the tops of my fingers, a seemingly careless effort that partially vents the wrath of my inner beast. It requires more focus than I'd ever admit to the likes of Etricos.

The display serves as a quiet, potent reminder. I am not a goddess, but neither am I a pawn for Etricos to manipulate as he pleases.

"If your positions were reversed, would you subject yourself to Moru of the Terasanai?" I lift my eyes at last to meet his gaze, the ball of magic a bright burning ornament upon my hand.

He jerks irritably, refusing to answer my question.

"I do not interfere in your leadership, Etricos," I say, "but you will *not* use my power to subjugate others beneath your rule. A true leader earns loyalty; he does not take it by force."

With those words, I abandon him on the hilltop to join my students below. Demetrios follows, a silent shadow in my wake.

CHAPTER FIFTEEN

J`UTTING WATCHTOWERS BECOME` the first sign of a permanent settlement on these hills, beacons of protection and vigilance. Other hallmarks of civilization follow. The people dig wells and lay foundations for homes. They haul trees from the forest beyond the river and stones from the hillsides. A handful of masons and one blacksmith survive among the hundreds here; they have banded together to establish a brickyard and foundry.

Fires are ever burning, smoke ever curling into the air as a signal of industry and fearlessness.

The Terasanai have their own enclave in the camp. They refuse assistance with their needs, poor though they are in earthly goods. Etricos blames me for the separation. He blames me, too, that other refugee groups send their leaders directly to me to request freedom from his rule. As more and more refugees arrive, the Helenai become a greater minority, and Etricos's influence diminishes.

"It is good for him," says Huna with a satisfied grunt.

"He is supposed to be a leader," I argue, wracked with guilt. Have I ruined the founding of my country?

She snorts. "He should act like one, then. Everything has been handed to him since he was a child because he was his father's eldest son. The firstborn always has advantages."

Her words chafe this firstborn. "Not always. Sometimes the second child is too spectacular."

She cocks her head, her eyes narrowed. "What is 'spectacular,' Anjeni?"

I still inject modern vocabulary into my speech, partly out of habit and partly because I cannot fully express myself in their tongue. Most of the time, Huna and the others brush off the unfamiliar terms—as I do with their use of archaic words I have not yet acquired—but every so often she questions me.

"'Spectacular' is something that catches the eyes because it is so wonderful."

Huna nods. She focuses on the sewing in her hands, muttering the word under her breath as though trying it on for size. She has fitted me with enough pants to last the year and more shirts than that. The material she works with now is a flimsy, silky offering from one of the encampment's more recent arrivals. I think I must own every piece of jewelry and scrap of fine cloth within a fifty mile radius, and yet the people insist upon giving me more.

I spend my days on Monument Hill—what will one day become Monument Hill—training my students and practicing control over my magic. I have run through every trick I used to watch Tana produce. I have not her agile, liquid manipulation of power, but I make up for it in sheer intensity.

And I am getting better at the fluid aspect of magic, even if I'm still nothing like a riverbed.

Aitana progresses in her studies as well. She reminds me of my sister in how quickly she learns. How apt it is that they share a name. We do not have the luxury to spend weeks upon weeks in mastery of one fundamental or one intermediate, though. Whereas Tana could build up her strength in each principle at a time, her namesake learns the basic concept and moves on.

I reason that it is better to have a magician weakly versed in all the fundamentals and intermediates than to have one who knows the first few fundamentals thoroughly. But that's not the whole truth. Deep down, I struggle against feelings of resentment as I watch her swift progress. She is not my sister, but she is my rival—at least insofar as the legends will report. What if the student surpasses the teacher? What will become of the goddess Anjeni if the mere mortal Aitana displays greater magical acumen?

The intermediates deal with space and distance, useful for attacks. I start teaching them to her to assuage my guilt, but I also don't give her deep enough instruction to master anything.

The superlatives I do not discuss with her at all. I have scant opportunity to practice them myself, but I run through the memorized principles in my head each day while Aitana and my other intermediate students tutor the younger spark-bearers.

The rainy season is almost upon us. Clouds build in the afternoon afar off to sea, but they have not rolled to shore yet. Soon they will come. I have warned Etricos, and he encourages the builders to make haste, as tents will prove miserable when the torrents begin in earnest.

A salty wind flutters through the grass. Below, on the ocean side of the hill, one of the younger students yelps at sparks of magic that flare much larger than she expected. Aitana jumps to her aid. I refocus my attention elsewhere, self-conscious that the fledgling magicians might expect me to help.

I shouldn't practice the superlatives against a crowd of novices. My magic is too volatile.

Quiet footsteps tread toward me, my only warning of Demetrios's approach. I glance up, my confusion mounting as he settles upon the ground next to me.

Did *he* notice what I was doing? A self-conscious blush starts up the back of my neck. He doesn't have a spark. He shouldn't be able to sense my toying experimentation, but I can't read him at all. He usually keeps his distance when he stands guard over us, ever alert for demon attackers on the far-off plains. Up close, I can observe the afternoon stubble on his jaw. The breeze waffles through his hair as his dark eyes scan the surrounding hills. My mind registers the straight line of his nose and the disciplined manner in which he carries himself.

"Why do you not teach the younger students?" he asks.

I jerk my attention from his profile with the embarrassing realization that I was staring. "Teaching brings better understanding," I say. I draw my knees to my chest and rest my arms on them, trying to quell my instinctive nerves.

He tips a questioning glance towards me.

I fidget. "When you teach others, you absorb the principles more fully. Teaching becomes a form of learning. Thus, as the more advanced teach the less, all progress together."

My magic tutors once attempted this method with me, but it backfired. When I was twelve, I taught fundamentals to children half my age, and those children immediately surpassed me. It was a magnificent means of destroying my last shreds of hope.

Demetrios leans back on his elbows and regards me fully now. I train my gaze upon the ocean and mentally recite the first superlative. What is he trying to do?

"Cosi told me to get close to you, to gain your favor and influence you back into submission to him," he says.

I turn, wide-eyed, every defensive nerve on alert. One corner of his mouth pulls upward in the merest hint of a smile. He enjoys my discomfiture, that wry expression says.

My treacherous heart flip-flops, but I douse it with a measure of cold, forced wrath. "And you think telling me this will help your cause?"

He shrugs, his attention sliding again toward the students on the hillside. "It is Cosi's cause, not mine."

"And yet, here you are."

The smile grows somber. "My brother is persistent. If I refuse, he'll give the charge to someone else. Perhaps he might undertake it himself. Don't you prefer that I pretend the part and warn you of his intentions, Goddess Anjeni?"

Abruptly I stand. He looks up in mild inquiry and I glare down upon him, my heart thudding in my chest as a thousand scattered thoughts flurry through my head like a flock of butterflies.

"What do you gain by disclosing your brother's plans to me? He is your brother. Do you turn traitor to him?"

Demetrios maintains his calm. "You and he are not enemies. How can I turn traitor?"

"We are at odds. What do you gain by pretending a greater allegiance to me?"

I can well believe that Etricos has instructed his brother to flatter and flirt with me—it's exactly the sort of scheming a politician undertakes to bring a contrary underling back into line—but for Demetrios to tell me as much strikes me as even more manipulative. What does he expect me to do? Does he seek to undermine Etricos? Is this a play for greater power on his part?

He remains maddeningly unmoved. "What greater allegiance do I pretend? If I wish to gain your favor, is not honesty the best method?"

The scheming cad. My fingers itch to hit him, but I clench them into fists to control the urge. He obeys his brother's command by divulging his instructions? He's playing both sides, and the worst part is that it works: I do prefer his honesty to any false flattery.

"What do you seek to gain?" I ask.

The corner of his mouth tips upward again as he observes my flustered state. "Your favor, of course. That is what Cosi told me to do."

I glance toward the encampment on the opposite hill, toward the watchtowers and the stretches of wall that are going up between them. Discontent writhes within me. "You should let Etricos do his own dirty work."

"I don't want him to," says Demetrios, drawing my startled attention back to him. He has caught hold of the hem on my right pant leg, pinching it between thumb and forefinger as though it is a curiosity he has just discovered. I could jerk it from his grasp, but for the moment I remain fixed in place. A studious frown pulls at his brows as he toys with the hem. His hand brushes against the top of my bare foot. "If Cosi seeks your favor, he will get it, eventually. And what will become of Tora in the meantime?"

A half-dozen implications bounce through my head. "You seek to protect Tora, then?"

He flips my hem away and looks up. "She is like a sister to me. Should I not protect her?"

"And what of Aitana?"

His gaze flits downhill, to the magic students and their main instructor. "What of her?"

"Do you not protect her as well?"

To my heart's delight and my mind's utter horror, he favors me with an intoxicating smile. "I protect all among the Helenai. That includes you, Goddess Anjeni."

"I don't need your help," I reply, my spine stiff.

He scoffs. "Those who do not know their own limits always need help."

My face burns with chagrin. I crouch beside him, my arms resting on my knees as I meet his stare. "Shall we test my limits, then?" I ask, a dangerous note in my voice.

His broad smile returns. "Certainly. It's good exercise for me to carry you around after you faint."

Does he have a retort for everything? "That's happened once."

"Twice. It was tricky the first time. The injuries on your back were so dire that I had to carry you like a child tucked against my chest. We marveled that so much power could come from one so small and slight of frame."

My embarrassment magnifies tenfold, though I contain it as best I can. Like a child, small and slight of frame—the description throws my heart into turmoil. If he truly views me as a child, I should be safe from any amorous advances.

And yet, I'm pretty sure he's flirting with me. Even worse, I half revel in it.

He catches my hem again, a casual movement. I cannot jerk away in my crouched position. "Why do we not spar, Goddess? We can test your limits, as you say."

My thundering emotions need bridling. Much as I might enjoy our verbal encounters, I can't let them get out of hand. I rise from my squat to look down upon him. "We do not spar because I do not use your weapons and you do not use mine. One of us would die."

My words fail to impress him. He tugs on my hem as though inviting me to sit again. I pull it from his grasp in a backward step.

The move offends him: his expression shifts from charming to distant. "Is your control over your power so poor?"

I'm done playing games for today. "Yes, it is."

"Then you should practice more."

If only it were that easy. My brand of magic is too volatile. I can practice the fundamentals, certainly, but the intermediates involve attacks and the superlatives combine offense and defense. Safe practice would require a partner of equal strength to keep me in check, or else a battle where no one worries about casualties.

As a warrior, he should know as much.

"You have a strange way of currying favor," I say.

"The Helenai need you, Goddess," he replies. "You alone stand between us and complete destruction. Cosi is correct in that regard: we cannot survive without you."

How am I supposed to answer that? The safety of an entire nation rests upon my shoulders alone?

I don't think so.

"You will have to learn to survive without me. One day I will leave the same way I came, through the God's Arch."

He sits up, genuine displeasure on his face. "When?"

"When the Gate opens again. I will pass through it to another realm. I was not meant to remain here forever."

The muscles along his jaw tighten as he looks to the cluster of spark-bearers further down the hill.

"I will see Helenia established as a nation, and Etricos as its first ruler," I say, my gaze following his. "He must be elected by the people, though. Winning their favor is his task, not mine, to accomplish."

"And what will you see me become, Goddess?" he inquires, his face in profile to me.

A philanderer. A faithless lover. The man who will render me a tragic figure for centuries to come. But I cannot tell him any of that. I hope to avoid the full brunt of it, even if the stories remain.

"Your destiny is of your own choosing. It is none of my concern."

From below, Aitana looks to us. She has finished her instruction, and the spark-bearers spread out across the hillside for free practice.

"My own choosing?" Demetrios echoes. He rises from the ground to stand beside me.

"Yes," I say. "Choose wisely." I leave to walk among my students. He remains at the top of the hill, his gaze following my every step.

Demetrios maintains his higher ground for the rest of the day. He doesn't dog my footsteps when I make my daily commute to the ocean and back, but stands guard near the cluster of spark-bearers on the hillside. I focus anywhere but him, and yet I'm aware of the constant sentinel.

The sun hangs low in the western sky, almost kissing the spot on the distant horizon where sea meets land. My younger students have returned to their families. Aitana, Ria, and Ineri remain, practicing their fundamentals and intermediates with one another. I might abandon them for the comfort and quiet of my tent, but they're at that stage where practice can become dangerous. As the only one present who knows any superlatives, I have to keep their powers in check should something get out of balance.

Up on the hilltop, Etricos has joined his younger brother and they are deep in conversation. I turn my back on them.

Aitana separates from her fellow learners and approaches me with caution, her attention flitting nervously past me to the top of the hill.

"Do you have a question about your studies?" I ask her.

She ducks her head. "Forgive me, Goddess. It is my studies, but it is not. I am grateful for your teaching, but I am worried. I do not progress quickly."

Is she crazy? She bounced through the first fundamentals within a few days. She's well into the intermediates after only a month. Granted, she practices for ten hours a day instead of the one or two that my sister and I had growing up, but her pace is still accelerated.

However, she also has no one to measure her practice against. She is the most advanced of the spark-bearers.

"What makes you think you don't progress?"

Again she ducks her head. "The difference in our powers, Goddess. I am nowhere near your ability. I worry that I will never approach it."

I hold back a scoff. Part of me wants to squash her presumption that she could ever approach the power of a goddess, but I'm not actually a goddess and she may well surpass me one day. Her greed to rival me drives this thorn of resentment even deeper into my heart.

"If you pass too quickly through the intermediates and beyond, your power will be out of balance."

Her mouth pulls to one side and her attention darts up the hill again. I deign to glance that direction. Etricos has a hand on his brother's shoulder, drawing him closer as he speaks. The orange sunset creeps across the sky beyond, casting deep shadows around them.

"I must become strong for the Helenai, Goddess," says Aitana, still looking upward to the pair.

I itch to tell her that *everyone* has to become strong for the Helenai. She's not a one-man army. I get the impression that she wants me to fish for more information, though, so I keep my mouth shut and wait.

(Because I'm insolent like that.)

Sure enough, she blurts what plagues her mind. "They have protected me since I was a child. When my spark emerged, my people sent me away, fearful that the Bulokai would attack them to eliminate me. The Helenai took me in. They kept me hidden and safe. I must become strong for them."

She doesn't resemble the other members of the Helenai with her ash blond hair and pale eyes, but I had never thought to question why. So she's a transplant into their community. I take the liberty of my divine status to study her. A deep blush rises on her cheeks and she looks again to the top of the hill.

"Dima has always guarded me," she murmurs.

Against my better senses, I perk in interest. She twists her fingers together as she continues.

"I was nine when I came to the Helenai. He was only thirteen but already well into his warrior training. He became my guard, my shadow, always there to keep me safe, always near my side, until—" Her voice falters as she favors me with a telltale glance. She swallows the rest of her sentence.

Not that I need her to speak it aloud: Demetrios guarded her until a goddess appeared in their midst. He stayed at her side until there was someone more powerful to protect.

I have supplanted her, in other words.

And she's trying to send me on a guilt trip for it. My resentment wells.

"Demetrios guards you still," I say, my voice tighter than I would like. "He guards all the spark-bearers in this settlement."

"He was my constant companion in times past, Goddess, the one person I could rely upon."

She maintains an innocent tone, but I recognize her motives. She's laying subtle claim to him, appealing to my sense of pity to warn me away.

Unbeknownst to her, I have no sense of pity. I also have no desire to get tangled between her and Demetrios, but I'm willing to push a few buttons.

"You think he has become unreliable?"

Her eyes widen. "No. I only meant—"

"You want him to guard you alone? I can give him such an order."

He probably won't obey it, but that's beside the point. I am on a different plane than Aitana and Demetrios both, and the sooner she recognizes that, the better.

She fidgets, discontent flashing across her face as she glances again to the brothers on the hilltop. "I need to become strong enough that I don't require a guard."

I suppress a derisive laugh. "Among the Helenai, it seems the stronger you are, the more they insist upon guarding you."

She considers this with a frown. "I must become stronger," she says at last.

It has been a long day. I'm tired and frustrated and restless, and I don't have the patience to extract her true intent through subtlety. "What would you have me do, Aitana?"

Whether the tip of her head is from appreciation for my bluntness or from self-important conceit I cannot discern. "I have been practicing," she says. "I practice on my own—late into the night sometimes. I think I have mastered the attack you used to save the Terasanai—the attack itself, not to your degree of strength, of course."

"You think you've mastered the seventh intermediate?" I have not taught her this principle yet. She lingers between the third and fourth.

"May I show you?" she asks.

"It requires a target," I reply, still skeptical. Even if she's some kind of magical genius, manifesting the seventh intermediate without knowing the principle itself is a risky endeavor.

Her expression turns innocent—a ploy that, I am quickly learning, masks when she is being sly. "I thought, perhaps, that you and I might—"

"Spar?" I interject. Disbelief snakes through me. "You want to spar with me?"

"We use the same weapon," she replies, childlike simplicity in her voice.

My earlier conversation with Demetrios floods through my mind. She has spoken to him, perhaps while I trekked to and from the beach. Do they conspire against me?

"You are not strong enough," I tell her flatly.

"I cannot become stronger if you refuse to teach me, Goddess."

The beast within me has begun to pace its cage. "I am teaching you. You are not yet strong enough for the upper intermediates. Certainly not the seventh."

The warning in my voice should cue her to drop the subject, but she presses it instead. "How can you know unless you test me?"

"I have seen you work the earlier intermediates. I know."

Her restraint breaks. "You wander on your own and pay scant heed to our progress. We do not learn as swiftly as we might, were you more attentive."

The beast snarls in my ear. I rub away the phantom noise. "You have no idea how swiftly you learn because it comes too easily for you. If anything, I should be forcing you to slow down, to build up each principle to perfection before you move on to the next."

Her eyes flash. "I have mastered all you have taught me."

A scoff cuts from my throat. I studied the principles of magic for a dozen years and more, memorized them from beginning to end, pored over theses and academic essays in the hopes that it would somehow trigger my supposed spark. Yet even now, with ready magic at my fingertips to answer the theories crammed into my brain, I would not claim to have mastered it.

"Your ignorance has bred false confidence, Aitana. Until you can manifest each principle across the full spectrum of its application, you have mastered nothing."

Our argument has drawn attention from Ria and Ineri further down the hill, and from Etricos and Demetrios at its top. A restive silence curls upon the breeze around us in the falling dusk. Aitana tips her chin at a haughty angle and I simply wait, a volcano biding its time.

"I am stronger than you think," she says, backing away step by step.

She's going to force me into a confrontation. I can see it in her eyes, the calculation for how best to display her hard-earned skill against her adversarial teacher.

"You claimed only moments ago that you were not strong enough," I say.

"You can judge for yourself how strong I am." She raises her hands.

"Aitana," Etricos calls from the hilltop, worry in his voice. He starts towards us, but he is too late.

If she could truly use the seventh intermediate, I might be in trouble. The magic that gathers within her falls within the fourth, however, similar to the attack I used against the demon army when I first arrived, but with less power behind it.

And, unfortunately for her, I'm in no mood to allow it to erupt my direction.

The first superlative of magic is that it governs all energy. Twist it upon itself, but beware the stronger will.

She doesn't even know I can control her spark. She unleashes the attack, but it reflects back upon her in a clap of light and flame. The force ejects her from her practiced stance. Her body slams into the earth, and she tumbles across the slope of the hill to lie facedown in the grass.

"Aitana!" Etricos dashes for her prone form. Ria and Ineri gape from below, frozen in place.

She's not dead. She's only had the wind knocked out of her. I remain rigid as she pushes up to her elbows and gasps for air. Etricos is on his knees beside her, speaking to her, offering her assistance, coddling her in what he perceives as her accident rather than my attack.

Because that's what it looks like, that she attempted a feat of magic and failed. I didn't do anything more than clench my fist.

"You didn't kill her," says Demetrios at my side, his attention upon Etricos and Aitana. "Perhaps your control is better than you believe."

I adopt my most carefully bewildered look. "What has my control to do with anything?"

"I have seen Aitana practice. This has never happened before, even in her early attempts. You interfered."

No hint of rebuke colors his words. He merely states a logical conclusion.

And I state my own. "You goaded her into attacking me."

He glances sidelong at me, amusement tugging at his mouth. "I encouraged her to spar with you, if you were willing."

"Why?" I ask.

"Because it's good for people to know their limits."

I'm starting to question whether the legends from this time appeared out of thin air. Demetrios exhibits no signs of affection whatsoever for his supposed paramour. His actions speak more towards animosity.

Aitana, meanwhile, sobs her woes into Etricos's chest. One arm around her shoulders, he helps her stand. It makes for a poignant scene.

"What will Tora think of that?" I ask.

A muscle moves along Demetrios's jawline. He leaves my side, striding across the distance to take his brother's place. Aitana transfers from one set of arms to the other, sniffling the whole time as Demetrios leads her up the hill. She clings to him like an injured child, though I'm sure the initial shock has worn off by now.

Etricos watches them until they disappear over the hilltop, at which point he stalks toward me, fury upon his face. "Why did you not stop her? She might have killed herself!"

Sometimes, the best way to infuriate someone is to remain unmoved. "She's not strong enough to kill herself," I say. "At worst she might singe her eyebrows, but they'll grow back."

"Goddess!"

"I told her she was not ready, Etricos. I told her repeatedly. Poor choices have consequences."

He vents his anger in a snort, raking one hand through his hair as he glances up the hill. "She only wants to protect the Helenai. She loves our people. She feels the burden of her gift and wishes to turn it to good use."

"She wants attention," I say. "Were she only concerned with the Helenai, she would obey her teacher." I let him stew over that as I call to my two remaining students farther downhill. "Ineri, Ria, it's time to return. If you wish to practice more tonight, focus only on the principles you have learned completely."

They each nod, still wide-eyed over the spectacle they have witnessed. Some good may have come of Aitana's rashness after all.

"Anjeni," says Etricos in a low voice, pulling my attention back to him, "the Helenai need you, but we need Aitana as well. Please do not allow her to injure herself like this again."

I'm in no mood for him to lecture me. My annoyance, built up over the course of the day, spills over into sarcasm now. "Perhaps you should encourage your brother to coax *her* back into submission instead of me."

Surprise flashes across his face. On impulse, I shield Demetrios from blame for divulging this plot.

"I know things that no mortal can know, Etricos," I remind him. "You would do better to focus your schemes elsewhere."

CHAPTER SIXTEEN

A ITANA'S INJURIES AMOUNT TO nothing more severe than a burn on one forearm and a severely wounded sense of pride. Resentment simmers within her from that day forward, and I develop a sudden, acute empathy for the Dean of Magic and all of my former instructors. My empathy for her is non-existent, though. It's not like someone is forcing her to study magic with no results to show for her efforts. She continues to improve daily.

And I take a more active role in training her and the younger spark-bearers both. I can't trust her anymore with sole responsibility for their education. Granted, I probably shouldn't have foisted it onto her shoulders as much as I had, but I still maintain that it was good for her, and for them all.

My passive observation gave me opportunity to experiment with my magic. Active instruction helps me hone it, to exercise better control over that raging beast within.

The number of refugees in our settlement has leveled to roughly a thousand people. There are forty spark-bearers now. We divide into groups of ten, with Ria, Ineri, and Aitana each assisting me.

As the days pass, Etricos sends scouts onto the plains and into the forest beyond the river. The Bulokai have isolated us within a five-mile radius. Their demon patrols will not come closer, and they cut off any asylum-seeking outsiders from reaching the safety of this place. The warriors among the Helenai and its allied tribes train daily. Soon they will ride out against those patrols, to pick them off one by one.

These people, poorly equipped as they are, have found their anchor in this land and will root it firmly in the ground. They till the earth in preparation for the coming rains, and they continue to lay the groundwork of their city-fortress.

Among the many buildings under construction, Etricos has ordered a pavilion. At present it is nothing more than a canopy upon Monument Hill, above the Eternity Gate. He plans a stone floor with a permanent structure above it, but it's still too dangerous to quarry granite from the cliffs further up the coast.

I refrain from telling him that he's building on the site of what will become the presidential residence. There's no telling what extravagances he might work into the design if he knew he would one day occupy its vicinity. There's no pavilion in my native time, so I see no reason to aggrandize a structure that will not last.

The canopy at the top of the hill provides me and my students with shade from the sun during our long days of training. My skin has become a lovely, glowing brown from daily exposure, but I value the canopy's shade more as the humidity increases. The heat of each afternoon turns sticky and sweltering, a portent of the approaching rainy season.

I wish it would come, anything to break the suffocating summer.

"Goddess, you have visitors," says Demetrios from his sentry point beyond the pavilion.

I stand from among the cluster of students I am teaching and peer toward the settlement. "Who is it?" From my position, I cannot glimpse anything.

He beckons me to his side. "See for yourself."

Aitana watches from among her assigned class, a sulk on her face. I ignore her. Ordinarily I would ignore Demetrios as well, but he doesn't usually alert me when people from the settlement approach. This atypical behavior prompts me to join him.

Below, a group of seven people journeys up to us. At their head, Etricos walks alongside Moru of the Terasanai. A deep scowl cuts into Moru's weathered face, his hands tucked into his sleeves as he mounts the hill. Etricos, in contrast, looks relaxed, even triumphant.

"What's he done now?" I ask.

Demetrios slides a glance in my direction. "You think the worst of Cosi without knowing their cause for coming?"

"He's always scheming something."

He suppresses a laugh. It manifests only in a slight curve of his mouth that he quickly schools away. "You said he must become a leader to this people. He takes your instruction to heart."

I sigh and return to my class to give them practice time and send them further downhill. The other three groups can stay beneath the canopy, but there's no point in my students remaining idle without an instructor.

I join Demetrios again as Moru pauses to touch reverent fingers to the Eternity Gate. Etricos continues past him. Three of the followers, one young woman and two old, pause to pay the same respects. The other two, a woman and a man, pass the monument without more than a glance. I recognize the man as one of the warriors of the Helenai.

"Goddess Anjeni," Etricos says, dipping into a theatrical bow as he stops in front of me.

Moru bends with more control. "Goddess, we desire an audience with you."

I cannot keep the suspicion from my face. "The audience is granted. What brings you to me, Moru of the Terasanai?"

"Not I, Goddess." He bows and moves aside. Etricos does the same. The warrior behind him joins hands with the young woman and together they step into the newly created gap. He bows and she curtsies.

"We wish your blessing to marry, Goddess Anjeni," says the warrior.

My suspicions redouble. The girl—large eyes, softly curling hair, feminine in every aspect—looks no older than sixteen. I might withhold consent on that count alone except that her lover doesn't look much older, roughly my age. She smiles shyly, her gaze downcast as she sneaks a glance at him. He squeezes her hand and waits upon my word.

Within this fledgling community where monsters lurk along the borders, waiting to marry seems like a fool's decision. The objection to this union can have nothing to do with their ages. It lies in other quarters.

"You are of the Helenai?" I say to the boy.

"Yes."

"And you are of the Terasanai?"

The girl nods, a blush climbing her neck.

I turn my attention upon Moru, who still scowls. "Do you object to the match?"

"How can I?" he asks, bitterness in his voice. Behind him, the two older women—the bride-to-be's mother and an aunt, I would guess—exchange a sorrowful glance.

"Why come to me, then? Should not the consent of the tribal leaders suffice?"

"I believe so," Etricos pipes up from beside his warrior. The woman behind them—the warrior's sister, I can only surmise—maintains a neutral expression. Whether she is for or against the match I cannot discern.

I favor Etricos with a less-than-enthused examination. Anyone can see that he's over the moon about this proposed union. He likely orchestrated it. There have been other marriages within the settlement, and none of them requested my blessing. The very fact that Moru brought this situation to me—and I have no doubt he required it rather than Etricos—tells me he wishes for divine intervention.

As if that's in my power to give.

"Moru, walk with me, please."

Momentary relief flashes across the tribal leader's face. He spares a glance over his shoulder to the pair of older women. The bride-to-be looks crestfallen, her hand still firmly clasped in her lover's grip. Etricos's triumph of a moment ago has tempered into something more guarded, though he does not appear upset at my request.

I lead Moru away from the group, much as I did the first time we met. "Tell me the truth," I say when we are beyond earshot. "What are your objections to this marriage?"

"She is my granddaughter."

And there goes any chance of this attachment having been spontaneous. Etricos probably ordered his underling to make love to this specific girl.

Moru continues. "Goddess, women outnumber men in this settlement three to one. Among the Terasanai, that disparity is even higher. We have not the luxury to decline a marriage, but she is my only surviving granddaughter."

"Do you suspect her lover's sincerity?"

Frustration dances across his face. "I don't know."

"Do you wish me to forbid the marriage?"

He does not immediately answer, but casts his gaze back toward the group. His granddaughter and her would-be groom clasp both hands together as though standing at their marriage altar already, their hopeful eyes upon us. If Etricos did put his warrior up to this, he chose a magnificent actor.

"I worry that we will lose our culture and traditions if we intermarry with the other tribes," says Moru.

"And if you do not intermarry, you risk extinction," I reply. The men among the Terasanai are few enough to make this a viable threat. "Do you value your culture and traditions more than you value the continued existence of your people?"

My question troubles him. "My people and my culture are one and the same."

"They're not," I say. I crouch low to pluck at the dry grass around me as I speak, choosing my words carefully. "A people can outlive a culture, but not the other ways around. Right now your culture is changing rapidly, and it will continue to change in the coming years."

I look up at him, a seasoned tribal elder who has come to an eighteen-year-old girl for help. In my own time, no one would consider me a reasonable source of advice and support. I have no business telling others how to live their lives or what decisions they should make. They worship me here—falsely—because of my magic, because I appeared through their God's Arch by no efforts of my own, because I offer them the promise of deliverance from a foe they cannot defeat by their own power.

But because I come from another time, I interpret their world through different eyes.

"Shall I tell you the truth?"

My question jars him. He peers down at me, suspicion and reluctance upon his face. I straighten, twirling a stalk of grass between my fingers, my posture firm and formal as I meet his gaze.

"What truth?" Moru asks, his voice guarded.

I'm torn. I have studied history and legends alike. How much to disclose of either one presents me with a dilemma, but my heart whispers that Moru has a right to know a piece of the future that lies before him.

I break the news gently.

"The Helenai will absorb the Terasanai and all other tribes who seek safety within this settlement. Centuries from now, the nation of Helenia will hardly recall that any other tribes existed."

I watch him closely, gauging his reaction. Despair and disbelief both seep through the cracks of his schooled façade.

Should I have kept my big mouth shut? "I do not tell you this to force you into subjection, Moru. Change is inevitable. Centuries from now, the Helenai in their present form will no longer exist, and few will believe that I ever existed at all. I will be nothing more than a story told to children."

I can't help the wistful smile that curves along my mouth. How I once despised those scholars and intellectuals who declared that the goddess Anjeni was only a romantic fabrication. Will I correct them if I ever make it back to my own time?

I wouldn't know where to begin. After playing deity to a thousand people here, the mere thought of taking my stories to millions of modern faces nauseates me. If I ever do get home, I might hole up in my bedroom and never come out again. Regardless of what I do, in the modern world, people will think I'm crazy.

"Why do you tell me this, Goddess?" he asks.

"Because you must decide which is more important: the legacy of your past, which will disappear, or the prosperity of your people going forward." On impulse I ask, "Would the marriage be more to your liking if it were someone else's granddaughter?"

He grunts. "I would be less suspicious."

I concede that point and make my own. "The woman brings as much tradition to the union as the man, Moru. She will teach her children the ways of your people. A blended culture will emerge—neither Terasanai nor Helenai, but something in between."

"If her husband allows it."

"He cannot suppress the innate influence of a mother." My mother's influence on Tana and me comes to mind. Not every woman will be as assertive, but especially in a warrior culture, Moru's granddaughter will hold more sway with her children because she will assume primary care of them. It's "women's work" among these people.

Moru still nurses his doubts. He shifts his weight from one foot to the other, his hands folded in his sleeves as he considers the awful truth before him.

"What would you have me do?" I ask. "Forbidding their love will likely strengthen it. Requiring them to wait could have the same effect."

"They have known each other only three weeks," he says.

"You gotta be kidding me," I mutter under my breath. I don't know exactly how the cultures here treat courtship, but if I tried to convince my dad to let me marry someone I'd only known for three weeks, he would have the boy arrested.

But, again, time is a luxury that belongs to a nation at peace.

"I would prefer to arrange a marriage for her," says Moru.

I blink, hard-pressed not to clench my jaw at the massive displeasure that sweeps through me. I forcefully remind myself that this is not my culture; it does not follow my beliefs and traditions.

That being said, I'd sooner die than agree to an arranged marriage for any woman. "In an arranged marriage, she will not have known her groom for any time at all—unless you have a suitable candidate among the Terasanai already."

He doesn't. I can tell by the irritation that dances across his face. "We would come to know the groom and his family during the arrangement, to ensure that he will take care of her and treat her well."

"Why do you not do that now, with the groom she has chosen for herself?"

He looks away, avoiding eye contact and my question both. But the answer is obvious enough.

I rub my temples to ward off a growing headache. "Can you not work out an agreement with Etricos? I know he has faults—believe me, I know—but can you not come to an arrangement with him? Your continued quarrel breeds unrest within the settlement. Is there no compromise?"

"She is my only granddaughter," Moru snaps.

Etricos struck him where it hurts, in other words.

"Do you believe he is tricking you?"

"I do not know what to believe, Goddess Anjeni. If, as you say, we must submit to the Helenai—"

"I did not say you must submit," I interrupt. "I only said that the tribes will merge under the banner of the Helenai. The influence your people have upon the culture that results will depend largely upon your attitude. If you resist, your traditions will vanish."

I don't know that for sure, but it makes sense. I wouldn't observe any rituals of a people who openly scorned me.

Moru's scowl deepens. He breathes through his nose to calm his turbulent emotions. At last he comes to a decision. "I will support this marriage *if* I may officiate at the ceremony, and *if* it may follow the traditions of the Terasanai."

"Done," I say. He jerks, fixing wide eyes upon me. "You needn't look so surprised. The Helenai have no tribal elders to perform such a rite. It's the reason Etricos himself is not yet married to his betrothed."

Suspicion crosses his face. "And you do not preside over such unions?"

I scoff and avert my gaze. "I am *not* a goddess of marriage." Before he can make further inquiry on this subject, I end our conversation. "If we are at an agreement now, will you please send Etricos to me? I will inform him of your conditions."

He studies me from head to toe but ultimately bows and retreats. I watch from the corner of my eyes as he delivers my summons to Etricos. To my annoyance, Demetrios trails behind his brother.

"Did you orchestrate this marriage?" I ask when Etricos comes within five paces of me.

He stops short. "Orchestrate?" he asks, in much the same tone that Huna uses when she does not recognize one of my words.

"Did you arrange it? Is it a trick to force the Terasanai into a closer alliance?"

Etricos cocks his head in an unspoken rebuke.

"Did you arrange it?" I press.

"I encouraged the courtship, but they met without my help. The betrothal itself comes much sooner than I hoped, but I recognize its advantages."

"Doubtless," I say. "Moru will officiate at the wedding, and it will follow the traditional ceremony of the Terasanai."

He scowls.

"Perhaps, if you are friendly enough, he will one day perform the same service for you."

That suggestion makes him scowl all the more. He turns on his heels and starts back, but I call after him.

"Etricos!"

He favors me with a sour, questioning glance.

"Does your warrior truly love her?"

I can't prevent concern from creeping into my voice. The youth of Moru's granddaughter and the vulnerability of her people infest my mind in a discordant tangle. If I am committing a girl younger than myself to a lifetime of deception, contempt, and abuse, I need to know it.

To Etricos's credit, his expression softens. "I believe he does."

For once, there is no guile in his words. The situation is to his advantage, but he has not played the unscrupulous part that I feared. I accept his statement with a nod. He continues on to the small group.

Demetrios hangs back alongside me. "Is it important that a man loves the woman he marries?"

My hackles rise. "Of course it's important. If he expects her to support him, to bear and rear his children to honor him, of course he must love her."

"But should she not love him as well?"

My brows pull together as confusion twists through me. "What are you going on about? Yes, she should love him. They are meant to be partners to one another."

I stalk past him, following Etricos's path, silently formulating how to give the blessing I must now bestow upon the waiting couple.

Behind me, Demetrios's footsteps rustle through the grass. He does not speak a word.

CHAPTER SEVENTEEN

THE WEDDING IS SIMPLE and beautiful, with decorations no more elaborate than some wildflowers from the forest and gifts no more extravagant than the most rudimentary household items, each a sacrifice from the family that gives it.

Moru conducts the ceremony before my canopy, the afternoon sunshine spilling around his dignified shoulders and upon the happy couple. Etricos defers to him with a show of respect. This union represents more than the joining of two young people in marriage. Half the settlement stretches down the hill and into the valley to witness the alliance.

If Moru of the Terasanai can entrust his own granddaughter to the Helenai, the other tribes must reevaluate their positions.

I observe from beneath the canopy, with Huna and Tora at my side and my crew of spark-bearers fanned out around me. I have the unfortunate blessing of a beautiful dress—Huna's flimsy, filmy creation in a rich, indigo shade—and a death-paint motif around my eyes, courtesy of Tora. I have, too, a headdress of beaten gold, worked by the one smith in the settlement, who wrought it by melting down many of the precious offerings given to me.

It has a pattern reminiscent of flames rising to a point, and it rests heavy on my skull. An armlet and necklace echo its golden brilliance, as does a delicate anklet I keep hidden beneath the flowing fabric of my skirt.

You can bet I fought against wearing any of my opulent trappings. I succeeded only in remaining barefoot. I make more of a spectacle than the bride.

When I utter as much to Huna, she dismisses my concerns with a wave of her hand. "A goddess should look like a goddess. You would insult the bride and groom if you were to appear in less than your finest clothes."

My one consolation—and it is significant—is that Tora wears her own wedding dress. As the betrothed of Etricos of the Helenai, she too must look her best out of respect to the couple. The butter-yellow gown compliments its rightful owner well.

I do not know the traditions among the Terasanai, but the wedding ceremony appears normal to me. Moru gives a lecture to the bride and groom, they join hands and exchange vows, and the groom kisses her before the company of onlookers.

"Such things should happen only in private," Huna mutters.

"I think it's lovely, Baba," Tora says, her eyes shimmering with unshed tears.

"Is this very different from a Helenai ceremony?" I ask, training my voice with an innocent note.

Huna grunts. "Yes."

And my heart floods with relief. I see my modern world reflected in the scene before me. The Terasanai may be forgotten by name, but their traditions—some of them, at least—will survive.

In the aftermath of the wedding rite, as the couple greets their well-wishers, someone strikes up a tune on a pipe. A drum, fiddle, and lute join in merry harmony. Etricos bounds beneath the canopy.

"Goddess, do you dance?" he asks.

I answer with a very flat, "No."

The grin on his face reveals that he suspected as much. He extends his hand to Tora, who takes it with a blush, and together they join the gathering revelers. Many of my spark-bearers cluster to the dance as well, forming sets with their friends rather than seeking partners from the scant number of boys. Amid the growing assembly, Demetrios and Aitana flash into view. She laughs and he smiles as they circle one another in rhythmic steps.

"Can I go back to my tent now?" I ask Huna, dire and dismal feelings crowding within me.

She sways and claps along with the beat of the drum, her gaze fixed on the dancers. "If you want the party to end, you may. Unless you can slip away unseen, everyone will stop to pay you deference as you go."

I should have withheld my blessing on the marriage. Look at all of the trouble I might have avoided if I had.

"Can you not enjoy the celebration, Anjeni?" she asks, sliding a concerned glance toward me. "For all the time I have spent at your side, I do not believe I have seen you smile more than twice."

I can't prevent the scowl that answers her comment. I'm not a smiling sort of person. I'm more brooding and intense, and when I am happy I tend to keep it knotted up inside myself. I have tried to be cheerful and bouncing before, but that persona doesn't sit well on me. In its aftermath I always feel contrived and hypocritical.

Huna reads all of this and more in my expression. With a sardonic quirk of her mouth she pats my hand. "Suffer through this as best you can, my little goddess. It will not be forever." She returns her attention to the dancing grounds. Offhandedly she says, "It is nice to see Dima and Aitana on good terms again."

I fight to keep my scowl from deepening. If they want to be on good terms, it's none of my business. Her words, though, prompt a question. "Were they at odds before?"

"He was her guard from the time she came among us," says Huna, watching the pair flash in and out of view. "He grew to love her, but she—"

Her abrupt stop draws my attention. She looks like she's trying to swallow a bitter pill. Forcing a smile to her face, she turns fully to me. "She set her sights higher. For a time, we thought that she would become the tribal leader's wife."

She's speaking in circles around the true subject. It takes a split-second for my brain to connect her words with her meaning. "Etricos? You mean those other women you spoke of? Aitana was one of them?" I search the pair of couples out among the crowd, Tora and Etricos on one side of the dance and Aitana and Demetrios on the other.

Huna's gaze follows mine. She banishes her bitterness from her face but she cannot withhold it from her voice. "Dima loved Aitana, and Aitana loved Cosi. And Cosi was fickle, but always with an eye for greater power."

"Aitana is a spark-bearer," I conclude. My mood plummets even further. "What happened? Etricos doesn't favor her anymore."

"The Bulokai attacked us in earnest," says Huna. "Amid the calamity that followed, Cosi declared his love for Tora and swore he would end his days with her or no woman. In the face of certain death, mere scraps of power become meaningless."

"They should be meaningless anyway." I speak the words, but having witnessed politics my whole life, I know a leader must consider more than his personal feelings. He must act in the best interest of his people. In a tribal culture such as this, marriage alliances must factor in strength and power before love even enters the equation. I can almost forgive Etricos his inconstancy.

Almost.

"So after Etricos returned to Tora, Aitana turned her affections to Demetrios?"

Huna frowns, her attention upon that second couple. "I wonder."

"What do you mean?"

"For a time it seemed so, but she often looks to Cosi with longing. Perhaps she hopes he will yet change his mind. Dima has grown cynical because of it. But today they dance and smile at one another, so perhaps their quarrel is resolved. Perhaps she realizes that, should Cosi decide to marry for power instead of love, he would focus his efforts upon someone other than her."

She favors me with a tight smile. My brows pull together in a deeper scowl. "He would fail, and he knows it."

Huna laughs, her bitterness dissipating. "This is why I like you, little goddess. You know your mind and you stick to it."

I don't know my mind. That's largely my problem. It's what sent me seven hundred years into the past: I wouldn't have been anywhere near the active Eternity Gate if I had known my mind.

Right now, though, I'm more concerned with others who know their own minds. If Demetrios has been in love with Aitana from the beginning, his flirtation with me has been a weapon against her, a mechanism to trigger envy or regret. He egged her into a confrontation with me to demonstrate my greater power, then? To put her in her place and center her attentions back upon him instead of Etricos?

The thorn of resentment within me branches out in wicked spikes. He uses me like a prop to needle her with jealousy and remind her that she's not the salvation of this people, that she's not important enough to draw Etricos's attention.

The rotten lout.

But why am I so angry? I said from the beginning I would not play the role of my legendary namesake where Demetrios and Aitana were concerned. All things considered, I'm lucky that legend does not paint me as the "other woman," because right now that's exactly how I appear. He has loved Aitana from his youth. I am a stranger he guards for the safety of his tribe.

And I have guarded myself against his attentions for no reason at all. From the beginning I was only a tool to him.

I wallow in cynicism and self-pity, the music and laughter around me an insult to my injured soul.

As the afternoon wears on, Moru joins us. He bows before me with his customary dignity.

"You are not a goddess of marriage, and you are not a goddess of dance," he says, a gentle twinkle in his eyes. "What are you a goddess of, then?"

"Chaos and destruction," I reply, sounding every bit the part.

His brows arch. Self-consciously he checks over his shoulder to where his granddaughter and her new husband hop to a lively jig. "If that is true, perhaps it was unwise to invite you to a wedding."

Before I can respond, Huna speaks up. "Anjeni is a goddess of prosperous future and good fortune. Her presence ensures many blessings to your granddaughter on this day. You have my congratulations as well. I only wish I could see my own granddaughter so happily married."

He studies her, silently assessing what this speech might mean.

"Huna is the grandmother of Tora, Etricos's betrothed," I say. "She does not approve of him."

"Then we have much in common," says Moru with a smile, and Huna actually chuckles before she schools her mirth. He returns his attention to me. "Goddess, do you stay for the wedding feast?"

I look first to Huna, and then to the dancing throngs beyond my shaded position. There are hundreds here. "Do you hold a wedding feast for all these people?" Established as the settlement now is, resources are still scarce.

He shakes his head. "Only the wedding party: the bride's family, the groom's family, our tribal leaders, and you, Goddess, if you will remain. All others are welcome to dance and make merry, but they know to attend to their own suppers. And it will not be a feast, exactly."

The worry that crosses his face prompts me to say, "I would be honored to stay, Moru."

He bows again, murmurs his gratitude, and moves on to speak with another cluster of guests.

"I thought you wished to leave, Anjeni," says Huna beside me. Her guarded eyes shift from me to Moru and back again. "You show much favor to the Terasanai."

She is worried. Much as she might butt heads with Etricos, her loyalty lies with the Helenai above any other tribe. I suppose it troubles her for me to show kindness elsewhere.

But it's not kindness on my part, exactly. Perhaps it's a sense of kinship for a people whose identity will soon be cast aside.

"Huna, within two hundred years, the Terasanai will vanish from memory." I can give this date because that is roughly when the library of records will burn. No account of them emerges thereafter. "The Helenai will absorb their people, their traditions, their culture. Should I not show favor to a tribe in the twilight of its existence?"

She shifts uncomfortably upon the ground. "You claim you are not a goddess, Anjeni, but sometimes you speak things that no mortal can know."

I smile faintly, my heart burdened with the weight of seven hundred years upon it. I sincerely doubt that Huna adds this smile to her meager list of two.

The wedding feast is to occur beneath the canopy, which necessitates that she and I vacate to another place so they can prepare. I rise from the ground, grateful to move about, grateful that so many are too absorbed in their dancing to notice my movements now. Huna drifts toward the merriment, her attention fixed upon Etricos and Tora in its midst. I tread the opposite direction, down the ocean side of the hill, my indigo skirts trailing behind me on the humid breeze.

If I were not arrayed in such finery, I would trek to the ocean itself, and straight into the water's embrace. I could do with a swim, with a struggle against something larger and more powerful than I am.

I don't belong here. I don't belong anywhere. Whatever greater force delivered me here did not do it for my benefit, but so that I could benefit others. And that's all right, as long as I keep myself separate from them. Swathed in the wind and the lowering sun, I construct a metaphorical fortress around myself. There is nothing for me here. I will receive nothing but misery.

I must fulfill my purpose regardless.

And Huna complains that I do not smile.

The grass behind me rustles. I glance up to see Tora approach. The brilliant orange of the setting sun bathes her in golden light.

"Goddess, the wedding feast begins."

How can she yet love Etricos when he would have put her aside for greater prestige? How could she remain faithful when she looked to receive nothing in return?

But Tora is goodness personified. I am a selfish, resentful wreck.

"Thank you," I say. I gather my skirts and climb the hill, the wind at my back as I go. The music continues, and revelers still dance across the hilltop, but a small group clusters beneath the canopy, where low planks serve as tables. The wind shifts directions, carrying the aroma of spices and savory foods. Nostalgia strikes me like a hammer to the chest.

Moru hurries from beneath the canopy to usher me inward. "Goddess, we have saved the place of honor for you. Please, if you will be seated, we will begin."

He guides me to the centermost seat, the only place at the low tables that has a cushion. The guests of the feast are divided, the Terasanai at a perpendicular table to my left and the Helenai at one to my right, with the bride and groom directly to one side of me and Moru and the bride's mother opposite. All stand, awaiting my arrival. Tora joins Etricos, Huna, and the groom's sister. Demetrios, Aitana, Ineri, and Ria fill out the table designated for the Helenai.

I sink to my cushion without a word, my heart in turmoil. The rest of the company sits. A serving woman carries a covered dish from the fire pits they have built further downhill and presents it to me.

"This is a traditional dish of the Terasanai," says Moru from beside me. My mind registers a nervous tremor in his voice, but I am fixed upon the earthenware bowl. The servant removes its lid, and that nostalgic aroma billows into the air on a steam cloud.

"This is curry." I shift my attention to him, tears stinging the corners of my eyes. "You have brought me curry."

"If it is not to your liking—"

But I have already picked up my spoon, have already dipped it into the dish. The flavors are not the same, but the spices flood my senses. So, too, does a homesickness stronger than any force I've yet encountered. It engulfs me, transports me momentarily to the world I left behind and then drops me back in place with a crushing ache for what I have lost.

I can't cry here. I'll have death-paint rivulets running down my face.

"Is there more spice to add?" I ask Moru as the company gapes at me. The food of the Helenai, even at its very best, has been bland. I have missed this burning heat, just as I have missed the father who indulged me with it, the mother who shunned it, and even the sister who despised it. Moru passes a small jar from further down the table. To my great joy, its spices tingle my nostrils when I sniff the contents. His jaw drops as I ladle a heaping measure into my bowl, and when I take a generous bite of the result.

I have nothing precious in this world except a bowl of curry. Some things never change.

A laugh bubbles in my chest at that thought. I'm ridiculous to be so emotional over a humble dish, but I can't help it. My mouth burns as I eat. The warmth spreads through me, both a comfort and a harrow to my soul.

The Helenai cannot stomach spicy food. Etricos gulps his drink after the first bite, fanning his mouth against the heat. The others laugh but take this as a cue to proceed with caution. They raise their spoons cautiously, taste the fragrant sauce, and reach for their cups. Some recoil, force themselves to remain calm, and try again, wary of offending their hosts.

On the other side of the feast, the Terasanai heap more spice into their bowls, as I did. They exchange amused glances at the antics of their rival tribe.

"It is different from our traditional style," says Moru to my left. "We have not the same vegetables or meats, but substituted with what this land provides."

"It is wonderful," I tell him. I am still closer to tears than I would like. I shore up my emotions behind a temporary wall. They are an injury I must not touch or nurse until I am alone. For now, I focus on the heat of my food and the mannerisms of my dinner companions. I watch them through new eyes.

Etricos and Tora attend to one another. He squeezes her elbow in encouragement as she drowns her curry in more of the bland, boiled root the Terasanai have provided as its base. His eyes water and his nose runs because he is too proud to dilute the spice of his meal.

Aitana often glances in his direction. Why had I not seen it before? She has sought his approval, has sought to impress him many times in my company. Demetrios was always beside him, though. I assumed her affections went toward the younger brother instead of the elder. Perhaps they are split. She favors Demetrios with her attention throughout the meal as well.

He sees her glances towards his brother. His face remains unreadable. He alone among the Helenai consumes his food without any external signs of discomfort. He does not add to the spice, but he does not dilute it, either.

He also notices my observation. It does not matter. I am nothing but a path to salvation for these people. I may observe them as I please, for I will never be one of them.

Night is thick around us as the feast comes to its close. Only the piper remains in the darkness, twiddling a quick tune to the stars overhead. The dancers have returned to their homes beyond the opposite hill. The bride and groom rise to depart.

"Goddess, will you bestow a blessing upon them before they go?" Moru asks.

"A blessing?" I repeat. "What blessing would you have?"

"A sign, perhaps," he says. "Something to send them forward into their lives with hope for the coming days and years."

Under the collective gaze of the wedding party I rise and pass from beneath the canopy. Straggling wisps of clouds spread low against their stellar backdrop. I gaze upward, my mind racing for what I might say.

The second superlative of magic is that it answers from afar. Bid, and it will obey.

The superlatives instruct the manipulation of magic not at one's fingertips. They allow for control of a spell even after you release it, and of sparks that were never yours to start. That makes them the most difficult to learn and the most frustrating to master.

The feast-goers have followed me out into the night. I turn to the bride and groom at their center, she with her lovely smile and he attempting to look stolid and mature. They are both babies, embarking on a life together.

"May the stars in heaven smile upon you all your days," I tell them, and I cast a ball of magic upward. It grows as it arcs higher and higher into the air, mesmerizing in its brilliance. As its reaches the apex of its path, I twist my hand. The magic explodes into a thousand pieces trailing across the sky.

Like fireworks in a world where they do not yet exist.

The astonished cries of my audience delight me. From the corner of my eyes I can see some of them cringe. I focus, though, on the sky above and the thousand shooting stars that fade across its expanse.

My smile fades with them. I want to go home.

The bride and groom must leave together first. They bow in thanks and wander arm in arm into the darkness below. She touches her fingers in reverence against the Eternity Gate as she passes it, then rests her head upon her husband's shoulder. Moru and his daughters follow with Etricos and Tora in their wake.

Huna sidles up to me as others pass beyond the canopy's firelight. "Twice tonight you looked supremely happy, little goddess. And twice you looked as though your world had ended. Why did one always follow the other so quickly?"

I cannot answer her. My emotions are too near the surface to speak of them. They will overtake me if I try. Instead, I remove my magnificent golden headpiece and proffer it to her. My scalp aches where the ornament sat for so many hours. "Can you take this back to my tent, please? I think I will walk to the ocean tonight."

I entrust my necklace and my armlet into her care as well. The anklet can remain.

"Will you be very upset if I get the hem of this dress wet?" I ask.

She favors me with a reproving glance. "You are like a child, Anjeni. Take this."

To my confusion, she hands me the satchel she has carried with her throughout the day. It's the same one she keeps her sewing and mending in, her habitual companion wherever she goes. I look inside to discover a pair of pants and a shirt—one of my plainer shirts, even.

"I thought you might want a change of clothes," she says. "You have lasted far longer than I expected."

I soundly kiss her forehead. "Huna, you're a doll."

She shoos me away with an exasperated breath. "Do not stay out too late. I will worry."

I smile but make no promises. Shouldering the bag, I start toward the distant shore.

Huna's voice calls behind me, but she is not speaking to me. "Dima! Help an old woman down the hill in the dark." I check back over my shoulder in time to see Demetrios cross beneath the canopy to the other side. He is my self-appointed guard. It's likely he had started after me.

Silently I thank Huna yet again.

The moon is rising beyond a haze of clouds along the eastern horizon. The ocean before me reflects its light in glimmering waves. I pause beneath a shadowed outcropping of rocks to pull the pair of pants on beneath my dress, then I strip the filmy creation off over my head and replace it with the more comfortable shirt. I stow the dress in the bag and the bag in the rocks at the edge of the beach. I walk along the shore far enough to know I was not followed.

Then I plop into the sand, look up at the vast and starry sky above, and cry until my tears run dry.

I am alone, as I always have been. Most of the time the burden is easy to bear. Tonight it is a torturous weight upon my chest.

CHAPTER EIGHTEEN

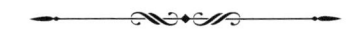

NIGHT-SWIMMING DOES WONDERS for my mood. Within the cold water, I scrub the remnants of Tora's painted motif from my face. I spend my pent-up homesickness in battling the ocean waves as they crash to the shore one after another. Centuries from now, tourists and vacationers will clog this beach in the daylight hours. Statutes will require them to leave when the sun goes down. Tonight, the whole ocean is mine, with no one to order me otherwise.

The moon has risen forty degrees in the sky when I finally gather Huna's bag from the rocks and start my sodden journey back to my tent. I have exorcised my internal demons for the present. My cot beckons me from my hill a mile away.

Halfway down the dark trail, a shadow detaches from the jutting rocks. I shriek and jump back.

Demetrios falls in step beside me with no acknowledgment of my start. And why should he acknowledge it? I'm not a real person to him. In some ways, that's better than if I were. I don't have to analyze everything he says and does.

I breathe in to calm the adrenaline that races through my veins. "How long have you been there?"

"Cosi was worried," he says, dodging the question.

Etricos sent him?

"Why?"

"Because the goddess Anjeni gave him reason to worry tonight."

I stop in my tracks. He proceeds two or three paces but pauses to look back at me.

"What reason did I give?"

His gaze shifts skyward, downward, over his shoulder, before it finally settles on me. "You have not forgotten the Helenai, have you?"

Uncertainty tinges his voice. It is so uncharacteristic of him that I question whether I only imagined it. "How could I? Everything I do is for the Helenai."

"Tonight the Terasanai held your favor."

Etricos and Huna are more alike than they care to admit, especially where their fears are concerned. I resume my path. "Your brother worries too much. The Terasanai were our hosts. Should I have met their hospitality with disrespect?"

He keeps pace beside me. "It was more than that, Anjeni. You were happy—happier than you have been."

I stop again and glare at him. "So because I was happy Etricos worries? I was also miserable, more so than I have been. Does he worry about that as well?"

"Yes," says Demetrios. "The Helenai still need you."

"I know." The phrase falls from my lips in a whisper more bitter than I had intended. I square my shoulders and start again toward the settlement. "I know the Helenai need me. I have a future to ensure. But I am not one of you. I do not belong here."

"You do not belong among the Terasanai."

As if I need the reminder. "I do not belong among any tribes in this place. I come from another world, but I don't belong there either. There is *nowhere* I belong."

On that declaration, we walk in silence. I don't care if he broods. For all I know, he's reminiscing on his wonderful evening with Aitana—and well he may, as long as he doesn't intend to use me again to secure her affections. I climb up the back of Monument Hill. The cook fires and canopy torches have long since extinguished. The grass of the dancing ground lies trampled flat. I pass through it and start down the other side, past the Eternity Gate that keeps its solemn watch over the valley below.

"Goddess," says Demetrios out of the blue, "what do you do if you want something you cannot have?"

Is he seriously asking me for advice in the middle of the night? Aitana's wistful glances towards his brother must really be preying on his mind. It's not my responsibility to encourage him in that matter, though.

"Despite what Huna says, I'm not actually a goddess of fortune, Demetrios."

"What do you do if you want something you cannot have?" he presses, undeterred.

My memories chase through a dozen years of magic lessons: the anguish, the yearning, the fruitless study and the crushing despair. I heave a sigh. "You convince yourself not to want it."

"Does that work?"

I scoff into the night air. "Not in my experience."

For all my resentment, all my denial, deep down I wanted magic more than anything. The façade that I didn't care only made my failures that much more painful.

"So what do you do?" he asks again.

My patience wears thin. "I don't know. You keep working for it until heaven and earth move and the fates align to give you what you want. And then you muddle through the million responsibilities that come attached to getting it."

He is silent for a breath. "Is that so? Do the fates align, then?"

No worries about the resulting responsibilities, I see.

We have reached the bottom of the basin. The gibbous moon overhead casts silver light across the landscape. Tired as I am, I pause to face Demetrios. My epiphanies this night have liberated me, enabling me to view him and the world around me from my objective metaphorical fortress.

"The fates might align, and they might not. But if they do, you might sometimes regret it as much as if they never had."

He studies me, his gaze intent. "What did you want, Goddess Anjeni? What did you want so much that the fates aligned to give it to you?"

I half chuckle. The last thing the Helenai need to know is that my entrance into their world also marked my magical awakening. "None of your business. But I pursued it for years, almost from my infancy. I learned everything I possibly could about it, tried everything I could think of to obtain it, and still it eluded me. And then, I gave up. Completely and utterly gave up."

A puzzled frown descends between his brows. "But you received it in the end?"

I lift one shoulder in a wry shrug. "The fates aligned."

He looks like he can't quite wrap his mind around my words. "But you regret it."

Do I? I'm certainly cynical tonight, but do I actually regret my magic and this journey that finally triggered it?

"No," I say. "It's not what I expected, and it has brought much difficulty, but my whole world depends upon it. I cannot regret it."

"Was your wish to pass through the God's Arch?" he asks, casting a suspicious glance toward the stone silhouette on the hill behind us.

I'm not about to encourage a guessing game. "No. I am tired now, Demetrios. You don't have to follow me all the way to my tent. You can return to your brother and tell him not to worry any longer."

He stubbornly keeps step beside me as I climb my last hill. "Everyone worried, Goddess. Tonight you looked at a bowl of over-spiced stew with more adoration than the bride looked at her groom."

The visual is too much. I laugh in spite of myself. "That's not true."

Demetrios, pleased with my mirthful response, pushes the issue. "It is true. If we had known your affection could be so easily won, we would have crammed peppers into our supper pots for you long ago."

He's treading too close to my guarded emotions. Removed as I now am, I don't need to hold a grudge against him, but neither will I subject myself to being used. I'm not a weapon he can call upon to keep Aitana in line. We are not friends.

"The Helenai have my loyalty. They have no need of my affection."

"What if we want it?" he asks.

I frown, too exhausted to muddle over his meaning. "You can't always get what you want. You'll have to learn to live with disappointment."

"Unless the fates align," says Demetrios knowingly.

The conversation has come full circle. I spare him a tight smile to acknowledge it, but this feels too much like he's flirting again. I am detached, a goddess in a fortress.

An *annoyed* goddess in a fortress. Who does he think he is, to moon over Aitana all afternoon and then sidle up to me in the dark of the night? I'm not playing this game.

"Good night, Demetrios," I say, and I swing my legs over the fence that lies around my tent.

"Good night, Anjeni," he replies, his voice resolute.

I seriously might hit him. I knew from the start that he was a philanderer, and today only proved it. This flip-flopping of my heart is ridiculous.

He follows the circumference of the fence as I circle around to the tent flap, as though I might steal away somewhere else if he doesn't watch my every move. I duck into the quiet interior, discard the satchel from my shoulder and collapse upon my cot, the lingering dampness of my clothes notwithstanding.

"You have returned at last, little goddess," says Huna from her corner.

"Thank you for letting me go," I mumble. Already my mind drifts. She answers me, but I cannot discern the words as I slip into a welcome, dreamless slumber.

CHAPTER NINETEEN

THE MERRY SPIRIT BROUGHT BY the wedding lingers across the settlement. The various tribes have made friendships through dance and celebration. Even my magic students seem happier as they practice. Aitana in particular holds her head much higher than before.

And why should she not? She has won back her beloved Demetrios.

I focus on training, renewed in my resolve to see Helenia established on this land. And I face a new dilemma. The offerings from the people had tapered off in recent weeks. They resume, but now they are food offerings.

I must have looked at that bowl of curry like it was my newly birthed firstborn.

My spark-bearers have fun sampling the many dishes with me. Some are better than others. Some are more familiar to me than others, too. It's strange to taste the culinary ancestors of my native time's "traditional cuisine."

And it's a wonder that the goddess Anjeni won't become renowned for gluttony. Some of the offerings are too good to share.

The people are transitioning from tents to houses. The builders complete more structures each day, so the valley of mushrooms is quickly becoming a grid of homes instead, with wagon roads and yards cleanly marked. From the top of my training hill, though, I can see only the jutting watchtowers and the wall that slowly grows along the ridge that separates us from the settlement. The basin is too much to include in this first line of fortification. The completed wall will not encompass the Eternity Gate.

The early morning sun and the humidity combine to raise perspiration on my forehead. Clouds build and dissipate over the ocean, but they refuse to come inland. I fan myself beneath the canopy, watching over my class of spark-bearers in their practice.

A horn cracks through the air. My head snaps up, orienting toward the sound. Demetrios is on his feet, one hand shielding the sun from his eyes as he peers into the distance.

"What is it?" Aitana asks, bounding to his side.

He looks over his shoulder and addresses his answer to me. "That's a signal from the watchtowers. A party approaches."

"Friend or foe?" I ask.

He shakes his head. From where we are, we can see nothing but specks near the horizon.

"Return to your homes for now," I instruct all of my students. I stride from beneath the canopy.

Demetrios catches my arm as I pass him. "Where are you going?"

I shake free. "To the watchtower. They might need me."

"I'll come too," Aitana says when Demetrios falls in step beside me. I consider denying her, but I bite my tongue. I have begun her training in the upper intermediates. She has memorized all the principles. As the goal is for her to use her magic in combat, I can't keep her sequestered forever.

I stride into the basin with the pair trailing in my wake. Demetrios tries to catch my eye but I fix my gaze straight ahead.

"Goddess," he says as we mount the hill where my tent sits, "you will need shoes."

I stop short and stare, a question on my face.

"You never go down into the village. There are nails in the road there, from the builders. You need shoes. Unless you would like me to carry you," he adds, an innocent lilt to his voice. Aitana looks like she just swallowed a bug. Are they on the outs again, that he needs to flirt with me?

"I have shoes," I say shortly. I've received sandals as offerings, but I've lost the habit of wearing anything on my feet. The risk of contracting medieval tetanus holds no appeal, however. We mount the hill and I duck into my tent to retrieve the footwear. Another blast from the horn echoes across the landscape.

The shoes feel funny on my feet. The sandal straps rub against my ankles as I quickly descend from my hill. People have retreated into their homes and tents for safety. They peek out as I pass with Demetrios and Aitana behind me.

"Goddess, what is it?" Tora calls from an open door, half a dozen children crowding around her.

"Stay inside," Demetrios says to her. "We will tell you when it is safe to come out."

Obediently she shuts the door.

"Who are all those children?" I ask.

"Orphans," he replies, his voice curt.

"She helps care for those in the encampment who have no parents," Aitana says.

Tora is a saint. I have never asked where she spends her days—or where she sleeps at night, for that matter. That she cares for orphaned children does not surprise me in the least.

Further up the road, the gates loom, set into the wall that marks the boundary of our encampment. Etricos stands beneath it, amid a cluster of tribal elders. Though in theory they all bear equal authority, any observer can see that he is the de facto leader.

Moru is speaking as we approach: "I warn you, do not under any circumstances open the gates to them."

"What is happening?" I ask as I join the group. Several of the leaders bow and fall back, allowing me space to speak directly to Etricos.

"A party of riders approaches beneath a white flag, Goddess," he replies. "They bear the standard of the Bulokai."

"They are scouts," Moru interjects. "This is how it begins: they come to treat with you, and to take back as much information as they can to Agoros."

"What do we do?" I ask.

"If we harm someone under the white flag, it is an act of war," Etricos says with a sidelong glance to several of the tribal leaders.

"If we let them leave here alive, they will report our fortifications and weak points to Agoros," one of the men replies.

I tip my head in uncertainty. "Are we not already at war with the Bulokai?"

"They bear the white flag," Etricos insists. "They may be defectors."

"They are scouts," Moru says again.

From above, the horn trumpets another warning call.

"Let's have a look at these scouts." I head to the ladder that leads upward into the nearest watchtower. Three or four of the gathered warriors peel off to climb the second tower. Etricos, Moru, and a couple other tribal leaders follow me. Aitana in her dress must remain below, but Demetrios mounts the ladder behind us.

I surface on a platform twenty feet above ground with a bird's-eye view of the surrounding countryside. The warriors stationed here bow out of my way, allowing me to examine the party of riders that approaches: a dozen men astride horses not of the mutant variety, with a white flag raised aloft. Beneath this flag flies a black and red banner, a symbol of the Bulokai tribe. The party is well protected in their spiked armor. The hilts of their sheathed weapons gleam in the morning sunlight.

"They look like they come for battle," I say to Etricos on my right.

At my left, Moru grunts. "They are spies. The Bulokai send them first under the guise of requesting a treaty. Even now they observe and assess our fortifications."

"The Bulokai never offered to treat with us in our homeland," Etricos says, his voice low as he watches the group of riders. "They attacked us outright."

Moru says, "A treaty only determines whether or not their armies will brandish their weapons when they enter the city. They will come as conquerors regardless"

I shift my attention to Etricos. "What will you do?"

To my astonishment, he looks to Moru and the other two tribal leaders for counsel.

"There will be a spark-bearer embedded among them," says one of the men. "If we attack, we must kill all of them swiftly, or he will cause great destruction."

The four leaders shift their attention to me, expectant. My brows arch. "You want me to execute a dozen men?" It's risky. Without knowing how accomplished the magician among them is, I cannot guarantee that my attack will be successful. At worst, it might ricochet back upon us.

Add to that one minor technicality: even from this distance I can discern that these riders are all men, with not a demon among them. They have not that hulking shape or the profusion of black, bristling fur emerging from every exposed area beneath their armor. Demons I could gladly obliterate. Playing executioner to fellow humans—especially prior to any overt provocation—makes my insides squirm.

But their approach, in Moru's estimation, appears to be provocation enough.

"We cannot execute them when they come beneath the white flag," Etricos says.

"If we do not, we are ensuring our own executions," Moru replies. "If they are here to treat, their armies are not far behind. Agoros has suffered us to exist for too long already. That they come now means they believe they can defeat us."

"Or that they acknowledge we will only grow stronger, and that they must attempt to crush us before that happens," says another of the tribal leaders.

As they discuss, I turn my attention to the enemy delegation. Their approach slows. "They're stopping," I say. Four tribal leaders turn to verify my words. "Why are they stopping?"

The group is perhaps a hundred yards from our gates. The rider who carries their banners holds his staff aloft.

Moru grunts. "They want us to send a delegation out to meet them, or to open the gates and invite them inside."

My heart thuds against my chest. Is this part of my responsibility as the goddess Anjeni, to meet an enemy party in negotiations? I part my lips to ask the question, but the words don't make it off my tongue.

"I'll go," says Demetrios.

I frown. "Alone?"

"Yes. They can give me their message. I will bring it here. They can wait outside the walls until it suits us to answer them."

Etricos looks to the three tribal leaders with him for approval. Each nods their reluctant agreement to this plan. The four descend the ladder to confer with those leaders in the opposite tower. The platforms on the watchtower are mostly shielded from view, except for the eye-level openings that allow for observation of the horizon in every direction. Our unwelcome visitors cannot see more than the slightest of movements within. Beyond the wall, they study our fortifications through the slits in their visors.

"Will you watch over me from above, Goddess Anjeni?" Demetrios asks.

I spare him a glance, wary of the two tower guards who still occupy this platform with us. I'm sure a number of rumors about me circulate the settlement already, but a familiar exchange here will only augment them. "Do you need someone to watch over you? If Aitana can climb the ladder, she can serve that purpose. This might be an apt opportunity for her to practice the seventh intermediate."

His expression shutters as I speak. At my conclusion, he tips his head in acknowledgment. "I will send her up to you. If you believe this circumstance harmless enough to entrust my life to a novice, so be it."

The guards behind him exchange a telling glance at his familiar manner of address.

Perhaps Demetrios means to establish a narrative of friendship between us to lend to his brother's right to rule. In that case, I cannot fully object, but I will not engage with him as though we are comrades. My metaphorical fortress protects my image as much as it protects my heart. "I trust you to gauge the danger and act accordingly. She and I will be here together."

"If she can climb up to meet you," he says.

Rather than dignify his taunt, I turn my back upon him, facing the enemy. The ladder creaks behind me as he descends.

I should have dictated from the start that all spark-bearers must wear trousers. Skirts are too cumbersome and can get in the way at critical moments like this.

The tribal leaders converse in the yard between the watchtowers. Demetrios, meanwhile, retrieves and saddles his horse. Half an hour passes. Warriors assemble on the ground and along the wall, ready to respond should something go wrong. The tribal leaders, even the most elderly among them, have their weapons in preparation for a coming fight.

And Aitana has found a pair of pants. She climbs into the watchtower, self-conscious of her unfeminine attire.

Yes, I definitely need to make this an official uniform.

A cry from below alerts us that they are opening the gates. The massive bar-lock lifts on a pulley, and one door swings inward far enough to allow Demetrios astride his horse to exit, but provides no more than a sliver's glimpse of the interior to our settlement before it shuts again.

Aitana stands rigid as the horse and rider canter away from us. Beside her, I forcibly remind myself to breathe, more unnerved than I care to show. The enemy party a hundred yards off makes no movement whatsoever as Demetrios approaches.

The encounter proceeds with nerve-shredding tension. Demetrios's voice carries back to us on the wind as he hails the group. They deliver a rolled message to him. He returns to the gates at a leisurely pace, because he's such a maddening piece of work.

At his approach, he glances upward, and our eyes connect through the observation panel.

He winks and focuses ahead again.

An unfamiliar relief sweeps through me. I orient my attention to the enemy messengers. In the aftermath of Demetrios's errand, they remain astride their horses.

"Should we not see what the message says?" Aitana asks beside me.

"Diplomacy is for Etricos and the other tribal leaders. Our duty is to keep our people safe from the enemies on our doorstep."

It sounds like a noble response, but at its heart it's only an excuse. I don't want to face Demetrios right now. As he rode out alone toward a dozen men armed to the hilt, I was more afraid for him than I've ever feared for anyone in my life. The intensity of my attachment has tipped my senses off balance.

Betrayer. Philanderer. I know where this path ends from the beginning. I can choose not to walk its length.

But is there anything wrong with recognizing someone as likable and valuable? Affection doesn't have to be romantic, does it?

Crap. I might be further along than I realized.

The guards below have barred the gates again. The tribal leaders' voices carry up to me in a murmur of cadences only. The ladder to the platform creaks, and a warm presence joins me in my observation of the enemy delegation.

Demetrios leans his head close to mine. "The spark-bearer is there on the far side," he says in a low voice, pointing to a rider at one edge of their staggered formation.

A goddess in a fortress. Don't do anything stupid, Anjeni.

"How do you know?"

"He has no sword and no gloves."

I look up at him on instinct. He is too near. Our eyes lock as though we are having an intimate interlude. Perhaps we are. Conscious of our audience and my jittering heartbeat, I resume my inspection of the enemy.

Demetrios is correct. The rider he has pinpointed wears no gloves.

A shuffle jostles my arm. "Where is the spark-bearer?" Aitana asks as she sidles between Demetrios and me. She peers at the enemy beyond as though her movement comes from natural curiosity rather than a desire to separate us.

Demetrios withdraws a pace. "There, on the end."

I'm torn between gratitude and annoyance for her interference. I squelch the latter emotion. She is here—on my command—to receive instruction, not animosity. "Can you concentrate on him? Do you think you could use the seventh intermediate against him?"

She bites her lower lip. "Shall I try, Goddess?"

"No," Demetrios and I say at the same time. I glance up at him and avert my gaze back to Aitana.

"Never attack an unknown magician unless you absolutely must," I say.

Demetrios adds, "The Bulokai sent this man to the gates of our refuge knowing that we have a goddess who protects us. He will be strong."

"But if we attack him first, before he has a chance—" Aitana starts.

"He may turn the attack back upon us," I interject. "If he is strong enough, he will."

Her expression turns faintly mocking. "You worry that he is stronger than you, Goddess?"

I meet her stare. "Perhaps the Bulokai have a god of their own, Aitana. We do not know."

She shifts under the intensity of my gaze, fixing her attention forward again. "But how can he control an attack he does not own?"

"The superlatives of magic allow it."

"You have not taught me those yet."

Her flat accusation chafes me, but I can strike at her nerves just as well. "You have not been ready to learn them."

Aitana's eyes flash. "I am ready now."

Behind her, Demetrios grunts. The two tower guards observe with interest from the corner where they have taken refuge.

Before such an audience, I deign to indulge her. "Listen closely, then: 'The first superlative of magic is that it governs all energy. Twist it upon itself, but beware the stronger will.'"

A contemplative frown descends across Aitana's face. "What does it mean?"

"It is a warning. For all the manipulation you learn in the fundamentals, for all the movements and attacks you discover through the intermediates, if your control wavers even slightly—if your strength lags in any small measure—another magician may steal your spark, your spells, everything. Never attack an unknown spark-bearer, Aitana. It could mean your death."

"Then why did you ask if I could use the seventh intermediate against this enemy?"

"For instruction only. Should I not train you how to sight a target?"

She grumbles under her breath as she focuses again on the enemy delegates, like I can't hear her. From below, a voice calls to me.

"Goddess Anjeni!"

I stoop to peer through the ladder's hatch. Etricos stands at the base, the message in his hands and the other tribal leaders clustered around him. "Will you come down?"

As if I'm here to do his bidding. "No. You come up."

He scowls at my disobedience.

"We must guard against an attack from their spark-bearer, Etricos. I can't see him if I come down to you."

Etricos concedes my reason and mounts the ladder. The tribal elders behind him bargain over who else will go up and who will remain below. One man volunteers to stay on the ladder as a vocal relay between the two parties.

This tower is sturdy, but the space is limited. Six people it can accommodate. Eight is pushing it. Moru and two of the other tribal leaders bring the numbers to nine. Aitana and I are crammed against one corner as we maintain our lookout. Demetrios, for a purpose known only to him, has positioned himself on my other side, so that I divide him and Aitana.

She is annoyed, as am I, but amid so many bodies there is little room to breathe, let alone rearrange our stances.

Etricos thrusts the enemy's correspondence toward me. "The message, Goddess."

A mere glance shows me the meticulously narrow script of ancient times. I can barely read that chicken-scratch when I have a side-by-side transliteration of it to reference. I'm certainly not attempting to decipher it in this crush, where the temperature rises with every breath.

"Read it to me."

Surprise flashes across his face, but he obeys. His voice rings out in clear tones:

> Hail, Etricos of the Helenai and all those who cower under his protection.
>
> I am Agoros, of the mighty Bulokai. I seek the dominion that rightfully belongs to me, granted by divine ordination to govern all lands. The Bulokai offer you generous peace and freedom if you will accept my rule, but if you refuse, we come upon you by the sword.
>
> As a show of your submission and goodwill, we demand that you deliver to us your fire god who has so unrighteously misled you against us. Your god keeps you in suppression. Join us and be free.

We descend upon you with sword and fire unless you submit to our offer of peace.

Should you choose to fight, be forewarned: my divinely granted right to rule will carry the Bulokai to victory. I am Agoros, a mighty warrior and commander of the hallowed Bulokai. Etricos and the Helenai must submit or perish.

Silence blankets the crowded space through this reading. All eyes fix upon me, awaiting my reaction.

"He thinks quite a lot of himself, doesn't he," says Demetrios at my side.

He would certainly know arrogance when he sees it. He's snaked one of his arms behind me on the pretense of bracing himself against the corner joint, but with the slightest twist of his wrist he could have a hand around my waist. I suspect that Aitana has discerned this arrangement, because she's staring hard at the minuscule gap behind me.

I hazard a glance toward the enemy party beyond the walls. They remain on their horses, battle-ready as they wait for a response.

"You may send me to the Bulokai, if you so choose," I say lightly.

A chorus of voices cries out in protest. Amid the uproar, the hand behind me twists and yanks me into a protective hold. My eyes bulge. I push a flattened palm against Demetrios to get away.

He doesn't budge, and I am left with the mortifyingly pleasant awareness of his muscled chest.

The tribal leaders here and below cry out their objections.

"Goddess, we will not submit!"

"We will fight to the last man!"

"Goddess, we trust in your power!"

Etricos calls for silence.

"Let go of me," I hiss to Demetrios as the clamor dies. He obliges, but with a reproving frown. I'm grateful for my corner position beside the observation openings. It allows me a thread of air in this ridiculous crush of bodies. Another glance over my shoulder shows that some among the enemy party have angled their heads toward our watchtower.

"Goddess Anjeni," says Etricos, "we will not submit to this intimidation." The leaders above and below utter their assent.

"Craft your response as you see fit, then," I say, maintaining my watch beyond the walls.

"We will fight them to the death, if you will support us, Goddess," says Moru.

I meet his gaze with a short nod. Thus reassured, he descends the ladder, with the other tribal leaders following.

Etricos hangs back. He whispers to me, "The Helenai would never abandon you. Do not think so poorly of us."

I keep my voice low as well. "I exist to protect your path to freedom, Etricos, but you must choose that path. If, for the good of the Helenai, you offered me to the Bulokai, I would go."

"The Bulokai would kill you."

"If I didn't kill them first. I never said I would go peacefully." I favor him with a faint smile. "But it was an easy bluff to make: I know you would never send me." He meets my gaze, acknowledges my words with a grateful nod, and climbs down the ladder to the waiting group below.

"You should not speak of submitting to the Bulokai, even as a bluff," says Demetrios beside me, an edge of anger in his voice.

I step away from him, to the opposite side of the tower as though searching for a different angle of the hills and plains that spread before my view.

"Anjeni," he says sharply.

"We all do things we should not. *You* should not face a delegation of enemy riders on your own."

The flash of surprise on his face morphs into interest. "You were worried?"

I'm well aware of our audience. The two guards shamelessly observe, and Aitana seethes in her corner, a resentful frown pulling at one side of her mouth. Demetrios is using me to needle her again.

I refuse to acknowledge his question directly. "It was dangerous. Returning the Helenai's response will be even more so. They will have no incentive to keep the messenger alive."

"I am not so easy to kill."

I slide a dry glance at him. "I suppose that depends on who is trying to kill you. Aitana, come here. We will practice the first superlative."

She sweeps past Demetrios with her head high. I keep my attention focused upon the riders outside as I recite the superlative principle to her and she recites it back in turn. After several rounds of this exchange, she has it memorized word for word.

The enemy riders, for all their attempts not to move a muscle, have begun to sag beneath the rays of the bright sun amid the building clouds. I continue my instruction of Aitana.

Half an hour later, Etricos climbs the ladder to the platform. "We have agreed on our response. Goddess, do you wish to read it?"

"No. I trust you."

He nods and turns to his brother, who sulks in one corner, neglected. "Dima, are you willing to take it back to them? We discussed sending it out on an arrow, but they might regard that as an act of aggression."

"The response *should* be an act of aggression or it's not worth giving to them," Demetrios replies. "I will carry it to them if that is your desire, however."

"Not yet," I say.

The pair of brothers looks to me. I drag my attention from the armored riders to meet Etricos's gaze. "Make them wait. From the formation they keep, they must have orders to appear as frightening as possible. The longer they're out in the sun in that full armor, the more uncomfortable they will become. The longer it will delay Agoros from receiving your response, too."

Etricos smiles at his brother. "You should have some lunch. The message will hold until this afternoon. Goddess, are you hungry?"

"No, but I could do with some water."

"I'll get it for you," says Demetrios before Etricos can offer.

Aitana bolts from beside me. "I'll go with you."

I have returned to my exterior observation. From the corner of my eyes I see Demetrios glance my direction. When I make no objection, he nods. Aitana precedes him down the ladder.

In their retreat, Etricos joins me at the platform's edge. "Is there a quarrel between you and Dima?" he asks, his voice pitched low enough that the tower guards would have to strain their ears to eavesdrop.

"No. Why?"

"You are on edge."

"Bulokai scouts stand without your city walls, with a spark-bearer of unknown prowess among them. Should I not be on edge?"

He dips his head in quiet acknowledgement.

I could let the subject drop, but my self-consciousness presses me to continue. "Why would you expect my being on edge to have anything to do with your brother?"

"Dima was brooding when I came up," Etricos says, with no indication of guile about him. "With you both off your usual humor, I assumed it was connected. It seems I was wrong."

I study his shuttered expression, searching for any gaps that might betray his motives for this discussion. "What about Aitana?"

"What about her?" he says negligently.

"Was *she* on edge or brooding?"

He meets my gaze with a grim smile. "I never observe Aitana, if I can help it." Before I can recover from my surprise, he switches to a different topic. "The tribal leaders are in disagreement for how to treat this Bulokai delegation. Moru suggests that it only requires one man to return the message that we send."

Smooth transition. He doesn't want me asking anything else about Aitana—not that I can blame him. He already knows my favoritism for Tora. "You wish to execute the other riders? Surely you don't mean to take them as captives."

"No. We could use their horses, though, and their armor and weapons."

"I thought you would not attack those who bear the white flag."

He scans the horizon beyond the delegation. "There is reason to suspect they will attack us. It seems these delegations deliver an act of destruction upon the tribes they treat with, as a symbol of their greater power."

Among the tribal remnants that found refuge with us are many who treated with the Bulokai. Their insight now is a boon. "What kind of destruction?"

"It has been different for different tribes: executions, buildings burned, kidnappings. From the message the Bulokai sent, from our stands against them before this, they cannot expect us to agree. It is likely they sent their strongest warriors to strike a preemptive blow when we refuse this demand for surrender."

I survey him through half-lidded eyes. "And yet you send your own brother out to meet them."

He tips his head in acknowledgment. "I trust you to keep him alive."

"Ah. You wish for *me* to kill all but one of the messengers."

Etricos doesn't bat an eyelash. "The majority of the tribal council agrees that only one should be permitted to leave this place alive. Who kills them doesn't concern us, as long as they die. I will tell Dima as well."

The danger of our situation strikes me anew, churning my nerves into a snarled mess. But this is why I am here, to help the Helenai meet and overcome the threats that seek to wipe them from the face of the earth.

If Etricos senses my misgivings, he makes no indication of it. He claps me on the shoulder and moves to the ladder, leaving me on the platform.

CHAPTER TWENTY

Soon after Etricos goes, a change of guard occurs. The pair who has observed me through the morning descends and another set comes up. I step to the back of the platform during the transition. My vantage point here overlooks the city and a most unsettling scene.

Demetrios and Aitana stand together in the street below. She clutches his sleeve with one hand, pleading on her face as she speaks. His back is to me. When he glances at a passerby, I withdraw a pace, still watching but less visible should he check this direction.

He gestures toward the tower, a water-skin gripped within the hand that points. Aitana shakes her head. Is she crying? She crumples against him, resting her forehead on his chest. Again he looks around, and then he wraps one arm around her shoulder, tucking her close to him.

In that cozy position, he guides her out of view.

Where they go together is none of my business. This leaden knot in my chest means nothing.

The guards' transition has finished. I resume my observation of the enemy messengers, my thoughts far from attentive to the task. What excuse will Demetrios and Aitana give for how long it takes them to retrieve water? There are probably half a dozen wells within three minutes of here.

When at last the ladder creaks behind me, I move not a muscle. The sun beats high overhead, and our unwelcome visitors are wilting. They have begun muttering to one another as their restless horses paw their hoofs against the ground.

The newcomer is neither Demetrios nor Aitana. It is Moru, and he bears a cloth-wrapped bowl.

"Goddess, for you," he says, proffering the food without asking whether I want it.

I can't stop a smile, faint though it is, from lighting my face. A savory scent rises from within the bundle.

But offerings such as this always come with strings attached. "What do you wish of me, Moru?"

He dips his head, apologetic. "I wish to have a word about the Bulokai riders, Goddess."

"Etricos has told me that you feel their numbers are unnecessary."

"They will attack us, a taste of the army yet to come."

"You wish for me to attack them first?"

Sometimes I forget that Moru is just as much a politician as Etricos. The practiced innocence on his face right now serves as a sharp reminder. "I would not presume to make such a request, Goddess. You are our divine protector and can fulfill your office without my guidance."

He knows I recognize his bald attempts at manipulation. It's his open manner that draws me in. I smile despite myself.

And Demetrios surfaces upon the ladder at this exact moment, my requested water slung over his shoulder. A scowl deepens on his face as I assume a more neutral mien.

"Thank you," I say to Moru, cradling the food he has brought me. He bows and retreats with no further requests.

Demetrios holds his peace until the elder of the Terasanai has fully descended to the ground. Only then does he shift an accusing gaze upon me. "I thought you weren't hungry."

I ignore the remark. I don't owe him an explanation for my caprice. "Where's Aitana?"

"She went to check on the other spark-bearers," he says. I mentally record the flicker of his eyes, the only visual cue that he is lying to me.

"I see." I attend instead to the covered bowl in my hands. Beneath the cloth I discover round, savory dumplings: vegetables and bits of seafood tossed with spices and fried in a batter. I pop the first one in my mouth as I resume my watch of the Bulokai delegation.

But I pause to revel in the explosion of flavor on my tongue. It's akin to the dumplings I sometimes bought from a street vendor on my way home from school. Silently I thank the Terasanai for their untold influence upon the traditional cuisine of Helenia. Under the stress of my current circumstances, I could probably eat a truckload of these.

The bowl in my hands dips, jerking me back to the present. Demetrios helps himself to its contents. I glower up at him as he thoughtfully chews, but he never even looks at me. Instead he stares outward in careful surveillance of our visitors.

"Too many spices," he says.

I shove another dumpling into my mouth.

He glances askance at me. "Do you have this kind of food in your world, Goddess?"

I can't answer without exposing a full mouth, so I only nod.

"Strange food for a realm of gods," he says, and he reaches for another.

I pull the bowl out of his range. Hastily I swallow. "Don't waste them if you don't like them."

He stretches nimble fingers past me. "Don't be stingy. I never said I didn't like them."

"Moru brought them for me, not for you."

"You don't have to be such a glutton, Anjeni. There's enough to share."

Our squabble results in me hunched against a corner, shielding the offering from his grasp. Meanwhile, the two guards gape at the familiarity between us.

"Don't be so stingy," Demetrios says again, trying to pry my arm back.

I hunch even closer around the bowl. "Go away. I don't share with liars."

He stiffens like a board, angry and offended. "When have I ever lied to you?"

How rich. I could probably give half a dozen instances if I took the time to catalog them, but I only need one to drive home my point. "Where did you say Aitana went?"

Rigid, he steps back, his mouth a hard line. I throw a challenging glance up at him, waiting for a response that does not come, that will not come.

Because she didn't go to check on any other spark-bearers.

Chagrin reddens his face. "I didn't lie."

"But you didn't tell the whole truth, either. It's the same as lying."

"I *didn't* lie," he insists. "She *will* check on the other spark-bearers. It's not my place to tell you Aitana's business beyond that." I scoff, and he bristles all the more. "Why do you always get this way after you have dealings with the Terasanai?"

The accusation spears me. "Stop it."

But he presses on instead. "Moru is not the only one who seeks your favor, Anjeni. Why do you show him and his offerings such preference? Every time—"

"*Stop* it. This has nothing to do with Moru or the Terasanai."

"Does it not? You care more for a bowl of dumplings than you do for the people who would die for you!"

My temper snaps; I fling the bowl. Demetrios ducks to one side, wide-eyed. The pottery cracks against the wall behind him, scattering the half-dozen remaining dumplings across the floor amid the clatter of the falling bowl. Silence floods the platform.

And I break it.

"You don't understand *anything*," I utter. In one swift movement, I swing onto the ladder and descend, trembling with fury, my mind a wreck. He accuses me of colluding with the Terasanai? He, who wraps a protective arm around my waist and that same arm around Aitana's shoulders all within the space of an hour? It doesn't matter how strong I build my fortress. He keeps knocking down its walls and then injuring me in the aftermath.

My feet hit the dirt. My shoes are up on the platform still, discarded early in my surveillance, but I don't care. I'll risk tetanus before I climb that ladder to retrieve them.

Besides, the ladder is occupied. Demetrios is following me.

"Anjeni," he calls. "Anjeni, come back."

I ignore him, stalking through the fledgling city with every intention of taking refuge in my tent and staying there for the remainder of the day, the murderous Bulokai delegation notwithstanding.

Demetrios catches up to me within ten steps, though. He blocks my way, his hands on my shoulders. "Please, Anjeni, I can't deal with two crying women in one afternoon."

"I am *not* crying."

I want to—oh, how I want to! The tears sting my eyes but I keep my emotions at bay behind a stony façade.

Demetrios glances around us. The area is mostly deserted—the people have orders to keep away from the gates while a

Bulokai presence is so near—but the few souls in the vicinity goggle at the altercation between their tempestuous goddess and her sworn protector.

Decisively he grabs me by the wrist and yanks me into the passageway between the nearest pair of houses.

"What are you—?" I bite my tongue mid-question, glowering as I trip along behind him. We emerge on a smaller road. Demetrios leads me past several homes and into a large tent.

If I'm not mistaken, it's the same large tent that I awoke in when I first arrived. The fire burns at the center of this main room. A low couch surrounds it, with two branching rooms hidden behind curtains. He checks them for unseen occupants as I stand stiff-backed near the exit.

"Aitana is my friend," he says as he pushes aside the flap that hides the second room from view. "It's not my place to expose her faults. She was upset, yes. But it has nothing to do with you."

"Nothing?" I challenge.

He meets my gaze. "It's not your doing."

I have no mental filter at this point. I'm too angry to consider the prudence of my words. "No, it's yours. You flirt with me to make her jealous."

"To make her *jealous*?" he echoes, disbelief upon his face. He jabs an accusing finger toward the exit. "She wishes I were my brother. She would trade me for Cosi in a heartbeat."

My indignation swells. "And I'm not a toy you can use to punish her for that."

"I'm not *punishing* her."

"Then why was she crying?"

He rakes one hand through his hair as he paces the length of the room. His path runs too near me. I step closer to the fire pit, stubborn in my silence as I wait for the explanation he's cooking up.

"Aitana is a good person, but she is spoiled," he says at last. "From the time she first came to the Helenai, she has received everything she has ever wanted—everything except Cosi."

The statement hangs in the air. I expound upon it. "And now she wants you instead."

Demetrios explodes with frustration. "I don't care what she wants! I care what *I* want."

"What *you* want?" I say, hardly believing my ears.

"What I want," he confirms. "I want you to look at me, Anjeni. Not at Cosi, not at Moru of the Terasanai, not at your dozens of spark-bearers, and certainly not at a bowl of dumplings! Only at me!"

The intensity of his words roots me in place. He meets my stare, holding my gaze, never wavering in the wake of this impassioned declaration.

Why is the air so close in here? The charged silence between us smothers me, so that I blurt the first thing that comes to mind just to break it.

"Why would you want that?"

He throws his hands up and paces the opposite direction. "Because you fascinate and confound me. Because in the same breath you're both fragile and formidable. Because whether you admit it or not, you need someone to want you. Why should I not?"

Half a dozen reasons bounce through my head, but none of them stick. I panic. "You don't know what you're saying."

"I'm asking for the fates to align," he replies without missing a beat.

My ears buzz, my thoughts clouded. I shake my head to clear it, but the muddle remains.

Demetrios, meanwhile, approaches, his gaze intent as he takes my hands in his. "If you are an ordinary woman, as you've claimed, you have no duty to play the role of goddess forever. I want you to look at me, to hold me dearer than anyone or anything in this world as long as you remain here. And that is the whole truth, Anjeni."

I stare, speechless. I have heard his words, but my brain can't wrap around them. What manipulation is this? What political game? Nothing makes sense to my mind, though my leaping, jittering heart telegraphs a ready response.

Demetrios reads my silence as skepticism, it seems, because he fidgets under my prolonged gaze.

"It's not the whole truth," he admits.

To my heart's dismay, he releases my hands and steps back a pace. My confusion mounts as he fishes into his pocket. He extends a fist to me and turns it upward to reveal its contents.

Upon his palm sits a small, silver case.

My lighter—my lighter that's been missing since I tumbled into this world.

Memories clobber me, bitter and sweet jumbled together with a pang of homesickness. A sob squeaks in my throat, but when I reach for my treasure, Demetrios jerks his hand away.

"No. It's an *object*. Don't look at it like it's your long-lost child."

I glare. "That is mine. Where did you get it? How long have you had it?"

He tucks his hand behind his back. "It's an object, Anjeni. Objects can be destroyed. They can disappear. They're meaningless."

I lunge for his arm. "It means a lot to me. Give it back."

He twists around, evading my grasp. "Everything you love can be gone in the blink of an eye. Why do you fixate on objects instead of flesh-and-blood human beings?"

I freeze, hanging upon him, my hands wrapped around his fingers as my brain processes his question. My voice creaks, barely above a whisper. "Everything I love *was* gone in the blink of an eye. When I passed through the Eternity Gate, I lost everything and everyone I love."

But I had lost them long before that. Bitterness had infused my soul for years. I had wallowed in misery, compelled by my self-hatred to hate everyone around me, too consumed by what I *didn't* possess to appreciate my own family and the many other blessings of my life.

What had I loved?

Nothing. I had loved nothing at all.

My emotional barrier cracks. Tears tumble down my cheeks on this stark revelation.

Demetrios reaches for me, but I recoil, retreating halfway across the room, my eyes unfocused as I wipe my face with the back of one hand.

"Anjeni—" he starts.

"Don't. Don't offer me false comfort. I don't deserve it."

He stands still, tense as I rein in my despair with a shuddering gulp.

In the wake of my returned composure, he extends his hand, offering my lighter to me again. I'm not sure I want to receive it, not with the venom it represents.

Decisively he crosses the distance between us and presses it upon me, the metal warm against my palm. Demetrios closes my fingers around it and cups my hand between his.

"I should not have kept it from you. In the beginning, it was a curiosity. I only wanted to study it as something from another world, something that a goddess brought with her from her native realm."

My eyes remain unfocused, my voice dull. "When did you find it?"

"It fell from your pocket when I carried you from the battlefield."

I jerk my gaze up to meet his. "You had it from the first? And you kept it, knowing it was mine?"

He opens his mouth, a defense on his tongue, but he shuts it again without a word. A simple nod answers my query. He withdraws his hands. My fingers feel suddenly cold.

I move to the low couch and sit. Deftly, mechanically, I flick the lighter open and strike a flame upon its wick.

Demetrios starts but catches himself. "How did you do that?"

"What?" I say, bewildered.

"How did you create the flame so quickly? It took me weeks to discover it even made a spark."

I flip the cap back in place and open it again, my thumb snapping against the flint wheel. "Really? Weeks?"

"Yes, weeks," he shamelessly says, still riveted on the lighter. "Do it again."

I flip it open and shut in quick succession, summoning a flame every time. Demetrios stares. I can practically see the gears in his brain turning: he itches to try it himself.

Suddenly he is the one fixated on an object, and I am fixated on him—exactly as he wants, and exactly as I never should.

"The Bulokai," I say.

He looks up from the lighter in my hands, accepting my change of topic without protest. "We should go back."

"Yes." I rise from the low couch, turning the silver case over and over again. As I pass him, Demetrios puts out a hand to stop me.

"It is a curious treasure," he says to my inquiring gaze, "but affection is wasted on objects, Anjeni."

Self-consciousness crawls up my spine to my face. I nod and avert my eyes. Demetrios falls in step beside me as he always has, as if the whole world didn't just rearrange into something new and terrifying.

CHAPTER TWENTY-ONE

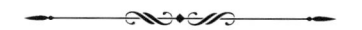

E TRICOS MEETS US ON THE WAY back to the watchtower, concern on his face. "Where did you go?"
"To get some fresh air," Demetrios answers before I can speak. He sounds nonchalant, as though our contentious scene had never occurred. I half marvel up at him before I catch myself.
"Has something happened with the Bulokai delegation?" I ask, hiding my still-reeling emotions behind an indifferent façade.
Etricos falls in step beside me. "No. Some of our warriors are getting restless, though—especially those who come from tribes once conquered. The longer the delegation remains, the more likely it is that someone from our side will make a preemptive attack."
"I will deliver the return message immediately, then," says Demetrios.
"I will go with him," I add. Both brothers wrench around to stare at me. I'm not about to explain that my nerves can't handle watching from the tower a second time as Demetrios ventures out on his own. I have a viable reason to participate

in the errand. "If their magician attacks, I need him in full view. The watchtower is too constricting for an effective counter-attack."

They exchange a glance. I hold my breath as I wait for their assessment.

"You cannot come with me," says Demetrios.

"But—"

"Goddess, we cannot put you so directly in harm's way," says Etricos. "You may not approach the Bulokai, but perhaps we may send a small group of warriors to wait outside the wall, and you among them to guard against an attack, as you propose."

It is a better option than remaining in the tower.

"What of Aitana?" Etricos asks his brother.

Demetrios maintains his unreadable expression. "Has she returned?"

"Yes, and with two of the other spark-bearers. They wait in the tower."

The two others must be Ria and Ineri. "What is she doing with them there?" I ask suspiciously.

"I believe she was instructing them. They were repeating phrases back and forth."

If that little minx has taken it upon herself to instruct in the first superlative, I'm going to wring her neck. Even from a hundred yards away an enemy magician might seize control of their magic should they choose to practice the principle among themselves. I increase my pace.

Demetrios drags me to one side by my elbow. "Watch your step."

He has nicely skirted me around a handful of dusty nails lying in the road. Grateful as I am to avoid such an obstacle, I glare at him.

"Shall I carry you, Goddess?" he asks blandly.

With utmost dignity, I train my attention upon the ground and continue on my own strength.

Warriors line the interior wall, with archers ready to climb to the defensive positions. Etricos parts from us to join a cluster of tribal leaders. I proceed to the watchtower, Demetrios at my side.

"I'll only be a minute," I tell him. "You don't need to follow me up."

He arches a brow but does not protest the command. As I mount the ladder, he stands attentively below.

I surface on the platform to find Aitana with Ria and Ineri crouched in one corner, deep in discussion. They start upon seeing me. Aitana looks first guilty and then defiant.

"You haven't done anything foolish, have you?" I ask.

Conveying the principle itself isn't a problem. I had the full set memorized ages ago. I couldn't manifest a spark, though, so there was never any danger of hurting myself in unsupervised practice.

"We await your demonstration, Goddess," says Ineri, her nervous gaze flitting toward Aitana and back. She at least realizes that they should not be here.

But, as long as they're receiving instruction, I might as well make it worth their while. "I will demonstrate below with the Bulokai, should the occasion arise. You three may remain here and observe from the tower."

Rebellion streaks across Aitana's face. The other two look relieved. I cross to the observation point and check the delegation. They yet wait astride their horses, the sun beating down upon their full body armor.

The gloveless warrior at the far end flexes and clenches his hands—a common exercise among magicians to keep their joints limber.

I descend from the tower again.

Etricos and the other tribal leaders have chosen a group of warriors—archers and pikemen—to accompany me beyond the city walls. Demetrios leaves me in their midst to retrieve his horse.

"Goddess, do you wish for some armor?" Moru asks.

I doubt they could find anything small enough for me, but it doesn't matter. "Metal conducts magic too easily," I reply. When performed in armor, it can readily get out of hand. The Bulokai magician in his spiked battle-wear must have incredible control over his skills. Perhaps he uses the armor to amplify his attacks outward. I tamp down the flutter of nerves within me as my mind races through the possibilities.

Agoros would not send a faulty magician to face a fire-god. I cannot underestimate this one. I must remain vigilant.

Demetrios is ready too soon. He climbs astride his horse and waits at the gate. Tension mounts in the midst of my small contingent of guards. Archers scale the ladders to defensive points along the walls while the remaining warriors fall into lines to await orders should an attack occur.

The gate opens on its pulley, and Demetrios rides through the gap.

I swallow hard, my hands trembling as my group passes to the other side.

Breathe, Anjeni.

A hundred yards away, the Bulokai messengers straighten in their saddles. As Demetrios canters toward them, I recite the superlative principles in my mind. He is only halfway across the divide when I sense it: the build of magic that precedes an attack.

And Demetrios draws steadily closer to its source. My breath hitches.

The second superlative of magic is that it answers from afar.

With a twist of my wrist I seize the gathering spark and flare it back upon its bearer. The explosion of power, amplified within his shell of armor, throws him from his saddle to the ground in a steaming, hulking mess.

Demetrios stops short and whips his sword from his belt. For a split-second, deathly silence reigns upon the scene.

As one body, the remaining Bulokai warriors tear their gloves from their hands, power flaring on their fingertips.

Horror seizes me. They are magicians to the last man.

"Demetrios, get back!" I scream, shoving past my contingent.

The sixth superlative—or the seventh—?

I snatch at several sparks at once as I barrel across the ground, but there are too many for my mental grasp. I've never actually practiced the sixth, seventh, and eighth superlatives, the principles that govern catching magic from multiple users at the same time. Shouts sound behind me, and arrows fly across the void toward the Bulokai cluster, but the shafts incinerate before they reach their targets. A flare of power—the fourth intermediate—jets toward Demetrios on his horse, but I shove it back into the Bulokai ranks, my feet pounding across the scrubby earth.

Chaos, fire, and smoke. Voices shout warnings and battle cries. Magic is so thick upon the air that I can hardly breathe.

A crack of energy shoots from behind me into the midst of the Bulokai. Aitana in the watchtower has unleashed her attempt at the seventh intermediate. As it strikes one of the rogue magicians, another snags its spark and twists it back to its origin point. A flare of magic rips through the tower, splitting my attention before and behind me.

The Bulokai magicians know at least the first two superlatives. Her attack was weak. The rebound couldn't have been fatal. I swallow my terror and refocus on the battlefield. Half a dozen intermediates course through my brain, but if I invoke one, I risk their master-magician snatching it from me. It is safer to deal with the superlatives, manipulating from afar. I catch another set of sparks and flare them out upon the enemy.

The Bulokai abandon their horses as the animals turn skittish in the cloud of magic. I can't see all of them anymore, my eyes dazed by their movement and my mind overwhelmed with the divided threads of power. Another fourth intermediate rockets from their midst, headed straight for me. I divert it into the ground. Rock and dust explodes into the air, and a circle of dry grass succumbs to flames.

"Anjeni!" Demetrios shouts. He has dismounted his horse and runs with the animal as cover. Three more intermediates arc from the Bulokai, honing in upon him.

And I panic.

"Get down!" I scream, sweeping my arm to deflect the attack. Three intermediates I can catch. Three is a reasonable number.

A seventh intermediate blindsides me, like being hit by a train I never saw coming. The force launches my body sideways. I slam into the hard-packed ground, my head smacking against a low-lying rock.

"Anjeni!"

Demetrios calls as though from a distance. For the barest moment, my body refuses to respond. Shock suffuses me, my mortality never so palpable before as it is now.

But the beast within its cage howls. I jolt free of my stupor and sit up, adrenaline pulsing through me. Blood streaks from my forehead down my face, running into my left eye. I swipe at it with a tremulous wrist. A smear of crimson decorates my arm.

"You're hurt." Demetrios skids to his knees beside me, grabbing at me to pull me back toward the presumed safety of the gates.

I shake off his grip, my attention fixed upon the enemy. "Go back. I will finish them."

And I will, even if I must die in the effort.

The Bulokai have banded together, rallying their magic. Three of them incinerate the barrage of arrows from the city wall, while all the others cluster amid a thickening miasma of energy. It's a prelude to the eighth superlative: their strongest magician will pool and augment the multiple sparks in a destructive attack.

If he gets the chance.

Amid a hail of streaming arrows and smoldering grassland, I climb to my feet. The beast within prowls its cage, fixed upon the exact moment it can break free and ravage all in its sight.

Only vaguely do I register Demetrios's continued presence. He withdraws a pace, his sword drawn and his stance protective, ready to shield me from any attack that might rocket my direction.

A streak of lightning flashes in the cloudy skies above, followed by a roll of thunder. It distracts a handful of Bulokai, who look skyward. One of their fellows barks a command.

Their master-magician has revealed himself in their ranks.

They might outnumber me, and their practical experience with the superlative principles gives them an advantage. I am untried, a novice who knows how magic works but has never actually worked these higher laws. My body aches, my joints sore and blood still coursing freely down my face.

A mere girl in their eyes, a minor obstacle to overcome.

One element stands in my favor, though: they are only riverbeds. I am a volcano.

The eighth superlative of magic is that it amplifies all discernible sparks. In unity may one conquer many.

Their master-magician lifts his hands. A scream tears from my throat as I hijack the colossal surge of power and wrench it down into their cluster. The explosion hurtles them away from one another, slamming them into the ground, snapping necks and spines.

The mass of energy diminishes with each magician's defeat, and still I clutch it tight, blasting it against their heads, feeding it with my fury. Thunder resounds across the sky again. The clouds crack and rain lets loose upon us.

Magic, with its kinship to fire, quickly fades in the torrent. Nevertheless, I swipe a final blow against the master-magician. He lies prone upon the ground, his men scattered, their horses running for cover from the downpour. The murmur of rain engulfs the battlefield as all other noises fade into silence.

My inner beast snarls, eager for more destruction. I stalk forward to inspect its prey.

Demetrios sweeps past me, his stride longer. He reaches the first fallen figure and thrusts his sword through the man's neck with a twist to sever sinew and bone.

I halt in my tracks, shock coursing through me. The scene before me shifts into focus: these are men, humans, lying broken and defeated upon the ground.

Demetrios repeats his ruthless sword-work with two more of the Bulokai before I gather my wits. I dart to his side, carefully averting my eyes from the gore I pass. The rain washes his blade clean as he readies it to strike his next victim.

"What are you doing?" I cry, snatching at his arm.

My strength is nothing to his. He decapitates this warrior, dragging me forward in the act. I nearly stumble into the body, but he catches me and rights me on my feet.

"They will carry no reports back to Agoros," he says, his voice as hard as stone. He strides onward to complete his task, leaving me beside this fallen corpse. My contingent of warriors crosses the gap from the city walls, some to haul the bodies away for disposal and others to retrieve the scattered Bulokai horses.

And for the first time since my arrival in this backward era, the reality of my circumstances hits me like a brick to the head.

Whether any of the enemy magicians survived my frenzied attack is immaterial. Demetrios beheads them all, a swift and deadly executioner. I watch his every move, a punishment for my bloodthirsty instincts of moments ago. Sickness swells within my windpipe.

In my rage, I intended to slaughter them all. Is a cold and calculated blade through the neck so very different?

By the time he returns, we are both soaked to the bone. Demetrios stands before me, broad-shouldered, muscled, water streaming from his head to his toes. I look up at him, wordless and—I'll admit—awestruck. Is this the same man who only an hour ago declared his feelings for me? This man has no feelings. He is terrifying, a conqueror, a merciless tyrant.

If he had died, I would want to die as well.

He breaks the silence between us. "I will carry you back to your tent, Goddess."

The statement jars me from my maudlin self-reflection. My spine stiffens as a sense of dignity floods through me. "You will do no such thing."

He reaches for me, but we're both drenched and I slip easily from his grasp. My toes squish through the mud as I start back toward the city gates. Demetrios keeps pace beside me.

"Anjeni, you are barefoot and injured, and with as much magic as you expended, you might faint at any moment. You must honor your limits."

"You only want an excuse to pick me up," I retort, my attention fixed stubbornly forward.

"I do."

The bald admission startles me. I stop short and stare.

His gaze is deadly serious. With the rain falling in sheets around us, he reaches one strong hand to my face, grazing my cheek with his knuckles. That simple touch, calculated and controlled, is all he ventures, but his intensity consumes me. Despite the frigid rain, heat blossoms in my chest.

Terror follows quickly on its heels.

I could have died. *He* could have died. I am in this mess so far over my head now that my only hope of success lies in what the legends of my native time report, but while the legends boast of Helenia's triumph over evil, they are not kind to the goddess and her lover.

It is yet another reality check. Woodenly I back away and resume my path to the gates. Demetrios, silent, follows on my heels. We pass through the opening, only to be met with rows of solemn-faced warriors and leaders. They stand beneath the shelter of the watchtowers, their eyes almost accusing upon me.

Their goddess fell before magicians of the Bulokai. They are more vulnerable than they believed.

Etricos approaches his brother. From his pocket Demetrios produces the message he was to deliver. "Agoros can draw his own conclusions about his delegation," he says.

Etricos nods.

"What of Aitana and the others in the tower?" I ask.

"All are injured, but not fatally, Goddess."

"See to their treatment. I will be in my tent."

The street is a river of mud. Thankfully, the homes are on higher ground than the roads and alleys that run between them. My tent, at the very top of the hill, will provide shelter from storms and floods alike. As I near that safe haven, though, on impulse I bypass it. Demetrios, ever my shadow, does not question my chosen path.

From the back of the tent, my vantage point overlooks the Eternity Gate on the adjacent hill. Already the basin between here and there fills with water. The Gate, barely visible through the mist, might as well be a hundred miles away.

Demetrios brushes gentle fingers against my arm, sending a wave of goosebumps up my spine. "Come inside, Anjeni. Come in where it is warm and dry."

I look at him—really look at him, at his steady eyes and strong jaw, at the face and physique I was determined to dismiss from the moment I realized where the Gate had brought me—and I break.

This isn't a story. It isn't a legend. It is deadly. The weight of my task presses down upon my shoulders, but it is nothing to the weight of emotion that crushes my heart.

The rain masks my tears, but it cannot hide the agony upon my face. Demetrios enfolds me in his arms and tucks my sodden head beneath his chin. I sob against his chest, the trauma of this day too much to contain.

CHAPTER TWENTY-TWO

"You should not be here. It is indecent." Huna prods at Demetrios with a stick meant for the fire.

"Baba, would you truly send me out into the cold and wet?" He lounges beside my fire pit as though he owns the place, a far cry from his usual regimented stance.

I, meanwhile, peek from behind the curtain where I'm supposed to be changing clothes, but a hiss from Huna sends me back into my sheltered corner. I pull a dry shirt on over my head and fasten its collar in place.

Huna resumes her scolding. "You know better than to linger in an unmarried woman's home."

"Cosi lingers here all the time."

"He has tribal business. You have none. People will talk."

"Maybe I want them to talk, Baba."

A hearty thwack echoes through the tent. I emerge from behind my curtain, freshly clad, to discover Demetrios in a mock cower while Huna fumes over him. The grin on his face testifies how much he fears her temper.

She straightens when she sees me. Tossing her stick on the fire, she snatches up a blanket, which she flings around my shoulders. "You'll catch your death of cold, little goddess. What were you thinking, standing out in the rain until your very bones trembled?"

She rubs my arms through the fabric, watching my face as she works. I meet her inquiring gaze, but I give no answer. I don't know how long we were out there, Demetrios and I. By the time he coaxed me indoors, my teeth chattered and my shoulders shook from the chill brought by the rain. Huna received me with disapproval and instantly shooed him away.

Only he didn't go.

He observes me from the ground, his expression guarded. I suspect he can read my every jumbled thought, but I can read none of his.

"Anjeni, sit by the fire." He pats the spot next to him.

He's as drenched as I was, but if I send him home to change, there's a chance he won't come back. After my terror of this afternoon, I don't want to let him out of my sight. Neither he nor Huna seems at all concerned about his health, only mine.

"She'll sit here," says Huna, and she drags me into a chair she has placed on the other side of the fire, opposite Demetrios. I settle on it, bewildered, only for her to drape a towel over my head and vigorously rub my wet hair. "Where would we be if you got sick again?" she mutters under her breath. "The Bulokai march boldly to our gates. What would we do?"

"We would fight to the death," says Demetrios.

Dread plunges through me. "I won't get sick," I say from beneath the towel.

Huna tuts and continues her ministrations. She retrieves a comb and drags it through my hair. It's a good thing I'm not tender-headed.

As she works, my gaze meets Demetrios's, and I look away again, ceiling-ward. The rain beats against the tent roof. A hood blocks the cloudy sky from view while leaving space for the smoke from the fire to vent. I pretend to study this arrangement as Demetrios continues to study me.

The curtain from the outside parts. Etricos enters, with Moru right behind. He hones in on his brother. "Aitana is asking for you," he says unceremoniously.

Demetrios tenses but remains silent—defiantly so, to my eyes. The knots in my stomach twist tighter.

"Dima, you know how she can be," says Etricos. "Tora can do nothing with her right now. Go help."

A mutinous crease appears between Demetrios's brows, but it disappears almost as quickly. He hefts himself from the ground and inclines his head toward me. "Goddess, I will return." After a brief glance at his brother, he sweeps out of the tent into the steady rainfall beyond. I clench my fists in my lap and swallow my irrational fears.

From behind Etricos, Moru watches this entire interchange with scrutinizing attention.

Huna abandons my side to fuss with things in her corner of the tent, pretending she is otherwise occupied lest Etricos order her away as well. He ignores her presence.

"What happened, Anjeni?" he asks me. Moru steps wordless to his elbow.

My tattered emotions have no place here. Despite my wet hair and informal clothing, I straighten in my chair like a queen. "Agoros of the Bulokai sent a dozen magicians to your gates."

"Why did you not defend us from them?"

The accusation in his voice triggers a scowl upon my face. "Excuse me?"

"You did not attack them, Goddess. We are lucky their powers misfired."

I open my mouth and then snap it shut again. I used no intermediates during the battle. From afar it would have looked as though no magic originated from me.

Mostly because it *didn't* originate from me. But the assumption that I did nothing except uselessly run around on that battlefield infuses me with cold wrath.

"Their power didn't misfire, Etricos. The superlatives of magic allow for it to be controlled from a distance. I did not directly attack. I used their sparks against them instead."

He digests this information. Moru does the same. Before they can question further, I twist my wrist. The flames in my firepit spark a ball of light into the air. The two men jump, surprised. The bright-burning spell bobs before their eyes.

I squash it with another flick of my wrist. "It's a higher skill. There are nine superlatives. And the Bulokai magicians knew them. They tried to use the eighth at the end of the battle."

Etricos pulls at his collar, gathering his wits. "But why did you allow them an opportunity to attack? Why did you allow yourself and your students to be injured?"

"Allow?" I repeat, my hackles rising. "Why did I *allow* it? Do you have any idea how difficult it is to control a dozen foreign sparks?"

"You are a goddess, are you not?" Moru softly inquires.

A hush settles upon the tent. Etricos, rigid, watches with bated breath. Moru studies me, disquiet dancing upon his face as he awaits my answer. Even Huna in her corner has halted her token tasks.

I lean forward, resting my elbows on my knees. Locking gazes with Moru, I clasp my hands together so they will not shake too much. "In my world," I say, considering each word before I speak it, "magic is a skill, not a weapon. We know it can attack, but we have no cause to use it for that purpose. I am sorry. In this, my power falls short of your needs."

"In your world?" Moru repeats. I can see it on his face: he wants to believe I am the goddess I have pretended to be, but doubt has crept into his heart. "Is that the world of the gods?"

"It is a completely different realm." My eyes lose their focus as I ponder just how different the two worlds are. "Battles are fought with fire-laden artillery and more destruction than you can imagine; machines carry us across the land and through the air. We can travel halfway around the world in a day. And magic is a luxury, not a necessity."

Absently I pull my lighter from my pocket, its solid weight familiar in my hand. I glance up to gauge Moru's expression. He fixates on the silver trinket as I turn it over and over again. When I flip it open and spark a flame on its wick, he recoils, his eyes huge.

"I am not one of you," I say, my voice low. Moru jerks his attention from my lighter to meet my gaze. "I do not belong in this world, and I bear power to a degree that none among your people yet manifests. Whether that makes me a goddess is your decision, not mine."

He blinks, contemplating my words. Briefly he glances towards Etricos, who eyes him warily, then shifts his attention back to me. With great reverence, he angles his body in a formal bow. "Goddess Anjeni, forgive my boldness. I questioned you out of turn."

Moru has chosen faith, unaware of how close I came to defeat on the battlefield this afternoon. The burden of my responsibility weighs even heavier upon me.

"There is nothing to forgive," I say. "You have the right to question."

Etricos has bided his time throughout this exchange. With my divinity for the moment settled, he steers the conversation elsewhere. "Goddess, how long will it take to train your priestesses in these higher principles you speak of?"

"I can teach them the superlatives, but true proficiency requires time and practice. How badly were Aitana and the others injured?"

"Scrapes and burns among them. Mostly they were in shock."

Not surprising. The seventh intermediate has an effect akin to electrocution. The weakness of Aitana's attack likely spared her life when the enemy twisted it back upon her.

"I will give them tonight to rest and resume their instruction tomorrow." I say this as though it's a well-measured response, but really I'm too shattered myself to focus.

Etricos makes no sign that he suspects as much. He simply inclines his head. "We need them trained quickly. When Agoros learns of what happened today, he may well descend upon us with his entire army."

My stomach twists again. "How will he discover what happened? All of the Bulokai magicians are dead."

Etricos and Moru both straighten their spines, dignity descending upon them like a mantle—the same stance my father always took to defend a decision for political reasons rather than rational ones.

My hackles rise. "How will he know, Etricos?"

"We have sent him his magicians' heads bundled on one of their horses."

"He will think twice before threatening us again," Moru adds.

This is why I hate politics. A show of strength can quell or incite the enemy. From what little I know of Agoros of the Bulokai, he will likely react with vicious force.

I run my fingers through my wet hair, as though I might smooth away the indignation that flashes through me. "You could not send your response in a less aggressive manner?"

"Agoros communicates through aggression," Moru says. "We must answer him in kind."

"The tribal leaders agreed upon our response," says Etricos, as though this justifies everything.

I bury my face in my hands, burdened with new anxiety at the growing danger of the situation. Etricos and Moru make no apologies before they depart into the rainy evening. In their wake, Huna presses food upon me, chattering at me to eat as she finishes drying my hair. For the next hour, my eyes intermittently stray toward the tent flap, but it remains in place.

Demetrios does not return.

I might as well be breathing water for how humid the air is. Every inhale sits heavy in my lungs, and my instinct is to sleep it off.

The rainy season always has this effect on me, though.

Huna mops at her brow with a handkerchief as she stirs the breakfast pot over the fire. She ladles me a bowl of broth, which I accept with listless gratitude. I slept poorly, too consumed by my anxiety in the wake of yesterday's battle and its revelations.

"Where will you train with your priestesses today, little goddess?" she asks, and with good reason. The basin between here and the Eternity Gate is awash with rainwater. In my day there are culverts and drainage systems to divert the runoff toward the ocean; in this era it can only take its natural course to that ultimate destination. A mile away, the river will have swollen in its banks.

"Here, perhaps. We need someplace dry. The rains will start again this afternoon."

The expression that crosses her face speaks of discomfort. However accustomed I am to the wet and dry seasons of this area, the Helenai are not. Their homeland must be somewhere to the north, in the more temperate regions.

I swallow the last dregs of my broth and wipe the corners of my mouth. "I should start. Practicing magic in the rain becomes difficult, even when you're sheltered." Or so I've heard. Tana used to complain about it all the time, how even the sight of a downpour disrupted her concentration. Fall and winter magic classes always focused more on theory than application.

One would think that riverbeds would receive strength from rain, but apparently the first fundamental's metaphor doesn't carry that far.

"Don't overdo it," Huna admonishes me. She holds aloft my sandals, returned by who-knows-whom. I receive them from her but sling them over my shoulder by their laces. Her disapproving grunt follows me from the tent into the muggy morning air.

Thick clouds obscure the sun. Its luminous disk hangs near the eastern horizon, its light diffused into gray stillness across the fledgling city before me. Mist veils the grid of houses and tents, with smoke from home fires rising into its ranks. Even this early, the city is rife with activity.

The guards outside my fence nod in deference as I pass. I spare them a grateful glance. These men stand sentinel outside my tent regardless of weather or time of day. Unlike my father's security detail, they receive no pay for their work. Payment is a luxury. Here, only survival matters.

But why does my mind keep drifting toward home? I did not expect the rains to trigger such nostalgia.

Dew plasters broken strands of grass against my feet as I descend to the village. My heart jitters in my chest with every step. Ignorance of the Helenai might be my undoing: for all the time I have been here, I do not know where anyone else lives. Today's practice makes me nervous enough, but I have to track down my students from among the residents of our half-walled city.

If Demetrios were here, he could guide me. There are plenty of other people to ask, though. Not all of them are terrified of me.

I cross into their midst. Those attending to morning tasks—chopping wood, washing clothes—stop to eye me with uncertainty through the morning haze. I might speak to any one of them, but instead I walk onward, head high and shoulders back.

And I recall that I do know where someone lives: Tora's house lies just up the road.

(At least, I hope it's hers. These huts are remarkably similar.)

The door stands ajar as I step into the yard. Tora herself slips through the opening, a bucket in one hand and worry upon her face. She stops short upon seeing me, her hand falling from the door pull so that it does not shut. Within, a woman's voice takes on a keening note.

Tora glances self-consciously over her shoulder and hurries to intercept me. "Goddess, what brings you here?" she asks, her voice hushed.

Whatever altercation is happening within, she would rather I not be party to it. I'd rather not myself, actually.

"I came to gather my students, but I don't know where they might be. Can you point me to their houses?"

She raises a hand as though to lead me away but catches herself before she touches me, ever wary of causing offense. "I know where some of them live. If you'll come—"

"Dima, don't leave me! Please!"

This cry from the open door cuts through whatever Tora meant to say. She freezes, a blush flooding her face. My stomach drops into my feet. As I look instinctively to the house, Tora clears her throat.

"Aitana is here, Goddess. I don't know if she is well enough yet for training."

Demetrios's voice answers the plaintive request within. "Aitana, let go of me. I've stayed too long already. It is my duty—"

"Goddess Anjeni doesn't need you, Dima. *I* do."

So Demetrios spent the night here. My anxiety deadens in my chest. What did Huna say yesterday? Something about it being improper for a man to linger in an unmarried woman's home because of the rumors that would result?

"Aitana was too upset to go to her own home last night," Tora says. "I kept her here with me and the children."

Tora's orphans. I had completely forgotten about them. This house has two or three rooms at best, and none of them large. There's no privacy to be had under its roof. "Where are the children now?"

"Gone to the fields to help with planting. Yesterday's rain will have softened the earth enough to plow more land." She is desperately trying to divert my attention, and I am trying to be courteous enough to listen, but my mind remains keyed upon the argument that has continued within the house. Aitana has launched into the screed of an injured female.

"You promised, Dima! You promised you would always watch over me! You promised by the moon and the stars and the sun in the sky!"

"We were children, Aitana."

She barks a laugh. "Is that the extent of your word? You can abandon it if you gave it as a child? Not even a year ago you told me you loved me."

"And you said you loved my brother."

Beside me, Tora flinches. Her fingers tighten around the handle of her bucket.

"Does your love mean nothing? Or are you only concerned with power?"

"You're being ridiculous, Aitana."

"Cosi at least is true to his declarations of love. Even if his heart has changed, he remains true to his promise—a promise made when *he* was only a child."

Tora's face turns ashen, guilt chasing through her haunted eyes.

"Did you need to fetch some water?" I ask her, my voice low. "There's a well nearby, isn't there? Don't let me waylay you."

Despite her relief that I would give her the opportunity to escape, she holds her ground. "You should come too."

"I should," I say, "but I will remain here."

Tora, the lovely soul, does not press her goddess further. Instead she passes into the street with only a worried backward glance. She does not have to listen to this quarrel and its damning implications, but it's good for me, good for my runaway emotions.

So Demetrios has confessed his love to Aitana. He only confessed his fascination to me.

Within the house, Aitana has resorted to a blubbering moan that masks her words in gibberish. Perhaps I should have gone with Tora after all. I ease closer to the door, peering inward through the narrow gap. She crouches upon the ground, her head buried in her bandaged hands as she sobs.

"You're going to make yourself sick again if you keep crying like that." Demetrios, beyond my sliver of sight, sounds less compassionate and more put upon. "Tora will be back soon. You should rest."

And the door swings open. I start like a child caught in mischief, but quell my instinct to hide. Demetrios, halfway across the threshold, halts in surprise to see me standing in his path. A frown pulls his brows together. He shuts the door behind him, muffling the high-pitched wailing that escalates within.

"You should be wearing your shoes, Anjeni."

My sandals dangle from one hand at my side. Of course he would hone in on that detail.

"I probably should," I say, numbness infusing my spirit. I cast my mind about for how to act natural in front of this man, especially after the conversation I just overheard. "Is Aitana too injured to resume training today?"

His frown deepens into a scowl. I have no chance to collect my wits before he wordlessly sweeps me off my feet and carries me from the yard to the road.

"What're you doing? Put me down!"

"If you won't wear your shoes in the village, Goddess, you will be carried. We cannot afford your injury, even if it's only to your feet."

My heartbeat pounds like a drum in my ears. "I have them. I'll wear them. Put me down."

The morning haze is nowhere near thick enough to obscure us from onlookers. Luckily for my dignity, Demetrios deposits me on a low stone fence some twenty yards down the road from Tora's house. He looms over me, waiting for me to comply.

I glare up at him as I slip my right foot into its leather sandal.

"How long were you there?" he asks.

I'm in no mood to play along. "How long was I where? I've come to collect my students and crossed paths with Tora. She said Aitana stayed with her last night."

His lips press together in a thin line. Has he kissed Aitana with that mouth? He declared his love to her with it. What other ties lie between them?

And since when did I become such a jealous shrew? I divert the conversation elsewhere.

"Etricos has asked me to redouble my students' training. Now that the rains are here, morning practice will be even more important."

"I'm sorry I didn't return."

His blunt statement catches me off-guard. "What?"

Demetrios looks me straight in the eyes. "I promised you I would return last night. I meant to, but I didn't. I'm sorry."

I ignore the fluttering rhythm in my chest. "I'm sure you had duties to attend. I have mine to attend now. Do you know where my other students are?"

I plant my newly shod feet on the earth and stand. Demetrios holds his ground, which puts us at an uncomfortably close proximity. I skirt to one side, but he catches my arm.

And I jerk away from him as though burned.

What is wrong with me? So he once told Aitana he loved her. So he spent last night watching over her. Tora was there. Half a dozen or more children would have been there too. It doesn't mean anything.

Except that I wanted him to come back, and he didn't, and no candid apology now will change that. It was a selfish wish on my part, the peace of mind that came from having him in my sight. I survived on my own last night, and I'll continue to do so from now on.

"Anjeni—" he says.

"I need to start training again before the weather breaks," I interrupt. "Magic is more difficult to handle when it rains."

He snaps his mouth shut and nods. With his spine stiff, he leads me through the grid of homes to collect my magic students.

Not a word passes between us for the remainder of the morning. Demetrios keeps watch over the group as I instruct, but he never looks directly at me. The set of his jaw tells me he is angry.

Good. He can't always get what he wants. I certainly don't.

CHAPTER TWENTY-THREE

THE AFTERNOON RAINS DRIVE US to theory lessons—my specialty, except that I can't always find the correct words in this ancient dialect. I instruct in my own tent, with my students seated around the fire pit as the storm patters above and the winds press against the fabric walls.

The air here is close. Huna has taken refuge with Tora down the hill. Only ten of my forty students can fit comfortably into the tent's confines, so I have to train in shifts. The others practice in the nearest houses, which Etricos has transferred to us for the cause. They sleep there as well, a cluster of dormitories for students of magic.

Two days have passed since the skirmish with the Bulokai magicians. Aitana, her hands bound in salve and cloth strips, has recovered well enough to join us. Tora tells me that her burns are severe, but I have seen no evidence of them beyond the bandages. I suspect Aitana's presence has more to do with the guard who watches over our training sessions. She sticks to Demetrios like glue, her gaze defiant whenever I glance in her direction.

Demetrios doesn't look happy either. In two days, he and I have exchanged only a handful of words. He makes no attempt when my students are present, and when lessons conclude, he has the task of escorting everyone back to their new dormitories in safety. He has yet to return afterward.

Maybe he remains with Aitana. I'm too proud to ask.

The rain does interfere with magic, but not to the degree that Tana always complained. I manipulate a spell around my fingers as I instruct on the intermediate theories. The bright-burning ball twists a golden path from my knuckles to my palm. The longer I manipulate it, the easier it is to maintain.

Which makes me wonder if Tana simply didn't practice enough.

"The intermediates govern the relationship between magic and the space around it," I say, my hand outstretched and the ball perched on the tip of my middle finger. "Some believe that the magic itself never moves, but that space moves around it, or that space itself is an illusion."

From beyond my tent walls, a horn trumpets through the storm. I palm the ball of magic, squashing it from existence as Demetrios pulls open the tent flap to peer into the rain.

"What is it?" Aitana asks, her voice strained.

"A warning from the watchtower," he replies.

I already have one sandal on. "Goddess," Demetrios begins.

I yank the other shoe in place. "You may escort everyone home," I say, snatching up my cloak. I flip it around my shoulders as I bolt for the door, but Demetrios blocks my way.

"It is only a warning signal," he says. "They will signal again if there is a true threat."

"I'm going to the watchtower."

He gives in to my resolve. "Aitana, take the others back to their homes."

She starts to protest the order. Their quarrel has nothing to do with me, so I sweep past the pair into the downpour, pulling my hood up over my head as I go.

Demetrios falls in step beside me. Faces peer at us from open doors, the sodden streets devoid of any other activity. Closer to the walls, soldiers dart from eave to eave. A second blast sounds from the nearest watchtower.

"That's the warning signal again," Demetrios says.

I have to take his word for it; I can't tell one call from another.

From between two houses Etricos dashes to our side, a messenger boy in his wake. "They've spotted people beyond the walls. They cannot tell whether they are friend or foe."

He mounts the tower ladder ahead of me, with Demetrios and the messenger boy behind. Moru has preceded us.

"Goddess, come look." He gestures me to his observation point. Wind sweeps the rain in sheets, obscuring the horizon in gray. Visibility is less than half a mile. Across the landscape, water runs in rivulets headed for the basin to the south or the river to the north. Amid the rocks and tall grass, a handful of figures struggle out in an uneven line.

A more pathetic sight I have never seen. "Who are they?"

Moru shakes his head. They have sent no one to intercept these newcomers.

I pivot toward the ladder. Demetrios catches me by the elbow.

"Someone has to go out there," I say. "We can't leave them on the plain in this weather."

He looks to his brother, who nods his curt agreement.

"I'll come with you," says Demetrios. "Let me call for horses."

"We will send others with you," says Moru. "If these are enemies, we should have strength in numbers. If they are friends, they may be injured and need help."

Anxiety thrums through me. "Be quick about it."

Within five minutes they assemble a dozen men to accompany me beyond the walls. Thankfully they opt against horses. The newcomers are within a quarter mile. It would take longer to fetch and saddle our mounts than it will to walk the distance.

(Which is lucky for me because—confession—I've never actually ridden a horse, and I don't particularly want to admit it to anyone here.)

As the gate swings open, the second watchtower sounds another warning signal. I look to Demetrios beside me.

"They must have sighted more people," he says, his eyes sharp beneath the hood of his cloak. He steps past the city walls, leading the way into the full brunt of the storm.

The spongy ground squishes beneath the soles of my shoes. Water splashes against my bare ankles, my sandals sodden as we trek through the frigid downpour. The newcomers loom like spectral shadows, obscured by sheets of rain that flutter on the wind. Demetrios draws his sword as we approach. The other warriors do the same. The storm around us muffles the sounds.

The nearest figure is not one person. It is two women huddled together as they stagger forward step by step. One leans heavily upon the other, head downcast and limbs all but limp. The second woman looks up. Shock flashes through her hollow eyes. The pair stumbles and falls to their knees, and the first woman sinks to the ground, her face ashen.

The second woman speaks through blue-tinged lips. "Please. Please, have mercy."

She gathers up her companion to shield her from the rain. A streak of red seeps from their dark clothes into the puddling water around them.

Alarm claws up my throat. I shove past Demetrios. "They're injured. Fetch a cart to carry them back."

The ashen-faced woman's eyes flutter. She has only a sluggish pulse. Her companion clutches a tightly bound arm to one side—an arm not long enough to have a hand at the end of it. Blood stains the pale, soaked bandages almost black.

A chill sweeps through me as the warriors around me move into action. My gaze travels further up the straggling line. The next nearest figure presses a hand into his gut as he trudges through the elements. Behind him, another person crawls across the water-logged earth. Through the mist, someone stumbles and pitches forward.

They are all injured—horrifically, terribly injured.

"Please," the woman at my side says, drawing my attention back to her and her unconscious friend. "Please, we beg of you to spare us from your fire god."

"Our fire god?" I echo sharply. "To spare you from our fire god?"

She whimpers, curling in on herself in agony. "Please. We want to live. Have we not suffered enough?"

Demetrios touches my shoulder. "Anjeni, move aside. We will treat them."

I'm in the way. I rise from my crouched position, and two warriors take my place to triage the injured women. Demetrios draws me further back, even as a protest erupts on my lips.

"They are terrified. What if one of them lashes out at you?" he asks, his voice low in my ear.

It's a possibility, if these refugees are desperate enough and believe that we only mean to slaughter them. But surely I should help regardless.

"Let us tend to them," he says. "Return to the city. Help prepare our arrival there."

"What if one of them lashes out at you?" I ask. I can't be the only one in danger of an irrational attack.

Demetrios touches a thumb to my cheek, as though flipping away a piece of debris. "I'm expendable. You are not."

And then he actually smiles at the full-fledged scowl that darkens my expression.

The lout. He delights in my worry for him, and even so I worry all the more.

Before I can turn away, he cups my face with his rain-chilled hand. Goosebumps chase down my neck. "Shall I return with you?" he asks, studying me as though at leisure.

I gather up what shreds of my dignity I can find. "If you won't let me help here, you should stay to help in my stead."

His thumb flicks across my cheek again. Is this how he shows affection? It's more effective than I would have guessed. My lungs tighten and my heartbeat races.

Has he touched Aitana's face like this?

On that thought I buck my head and turn away. "We will receive the injured in the city," I call over my shoulder. "Be quick to bring them."

Either he does not answer me, or the wind carries away his response.

Fifteen souls arrive within the city walls. Four die within the hour. Their injuries are extensive: missing limbs and eyes, puncture wounds, burns and brands. The Bulokai tortured these people to within an inch of their lives and then set them loose within our tiny pocket of land.

"An offering to the fire god of the Helenai." Etricos studies me closely as he delivers this information. "The Bulokai told them each the same thing."

"Agoros taunts us," Moru says quietly.

We sit in counsel, I and the tribal leaders, in Etricos's tent, with Demetrios to guard the door.

"To what end?" I ask. "What good does it do him to maim these people and deliver them to us?"

"He shows us his level of depravity and tests our own," says Etricos. "We did not have to shelter these people, Goddess. We might have left them beyond our walls. They would not have survived the night. Most of them may not anyway."

A sick anguish twists through my heart. "You would have left them out in the rain, to freeze as they slowly bled to death?"

"Agoros would have done so," says Moru. "We sent him back the heads of his magicians. Perhaps he tests whether we respond with such force to any who come to our gates."

I snap my mouth shut. If we had sent nothing back to Agoros, would these people still have suffered? Will he send others?

"We should be careful about who we take in," Etricos says. "We have few enough resources to care for our own people. We cannot deplete them further on those who are dying already."

I stare at him, disbelief flaring within me.

"Etricos is correct, Goddess." Moru tips his head in apology, but several of the leaders around him nod their agreement. "If we spend our strength tending the deathly ill, we will be vulnerable when Agoros attacks."

I understand what he's saying. With a scarcity of resources, we cannot sacrifice for futile causes. That doesn't override the moral necessity of assisting others—even if that assistance only amounts to giving them shelter where they can breathe their last with dignity.

"If we leave people to die without offering help, are we all that different from Agoros?" My voice catches on this question.

"We must honor our limits," says Demetrios by the door. He watches me closely, his dark eyes always assessing. "Those who do not honor their limits will fall by the sword when the Bulokai come."

He rarely speaks in settings such as this, usually deferring to his brother's authority. This warning is more for me than for the rest of those assembled. Nevertheless, the tribal leaders nod.

Moru sees the misgivings upon my face. "We will do what we can, Goddess. Our first responsibility lies with the people already here."

Reluctantly I agree. According to the legends, Etricos will liberate and unite the other tribes of this region. I must trust that he will exercise compassion when the circumstances do allow it.

After the meeting, Demetrios escorts me to my tent on the hill. Warmth envelops me as I pass into the interior. Huna attends the injured with Tora and will remain with them tonight, but she banked the coals of my fire before she left.

Demetrios ducks in behind me. "Will you be all right here by yourself?"

Is he offering to stay? Huna would have a fit, to say nothing of Aitana, should she hear such a tale. I'm half tempted to invite him for that spectacle alone.

"Is there another choice?" I ask, curious about how he might respond. I crouch beside the low flames of the fire and feed it from the store of fuel Huna keeps nearby.

Demetrios bends to assist me. "You might sleep among your priestesses."

I meet his steady gaze. He's serious. I cast aside the disappointment that flits through me. "I'll take my chances by myself."

"You always do." He drops a length of wood on the flames and straightens as a shower of sparks crackles in the fire pit.

"Remember to change into dry clothes before you go to bed, Anjeni. If you venture outside, don't forget your shoes. But don't venture outside."

He's treating me like a child. I rest my elbows on my knees and glare up at him. "I know how to take care of myself."

"But you don't always apply the knowledge." He sounds tired, like I exhaust him. I straighten to my full height, still so much shorter than him.

He brushes a strand of hair out of my eyes. "If Baba were here I would stay longer."

My patience for his mixed signals has long since vanished. "I'm sure you can find her easily enough if you want to see her so badly."

One corner of his mouth quirks in a rueful smile. He shakes his head as he moves to the exit. "Good night, Anjeni. Sleep well."

I murmur a reciprocal sentiment, though probably not as sincere. Demetrios passes into the rainy night, leaving me alone in the orange glow of my meager fire.

He never lingers when only he and I are here. I would have liked his company for longer tonight, but I know better than to ask such a favor. Listless and morose, I change my clothes and huddle beneath the blankets on my cot.

Sleep flitters in and out. Tired though I am, my body and mind cannot sync their rhythms tonight. The fire dims to a faint glow as my thoughts drift toward elusive dreamscapes.

But instinct draws me back. I open my eyes to darkness, to the sound of rain on the fabric ceiling overhead and the unmistakable sense that I am not alone.

Whoever—whatever—has come moves with incredible stealth. My every muscle clenches in terror as gradually I slide my gaze toward the low-burning coals in the fire pit. Beyond them, beside the tent's opening, a shadow shifts.

My breath hitches in my throat. Keen, piercing eyes stare at me through the darkness—eyes that burn like embers, that stand out in an otherwise nebulous phantom.

"How interesting." The words spoken aloud crack my stupor. I sit up, flinging aside my blankets, half-coiled and ready to attack this intruder.

My voice comes out in a rasp. "Who are you? What are you doing here?"

"I have come to pay my respects to the fire god of the Helenai," the phantom replies. His keen gaze flits into the shadowed corner of the tent. "Does he sleep elsewhere? I expected to find more than his concubine here." He looks me over from head to toe. "Fire gods have strange tastes in women, it seems."

Throughout this speech, an icy grip clutches my heart and squeezes it tight. The Bulokai refer to me as a fire god. But how—?

"Agoros." The name falls from my lips. The specter's attention had strayed elsewhere in the tent's interior, but it snaps back to my face. He glides toward me in the darkness. Lightning-quick I unleash a fistful of magic.

The projectile passes straight through him, splattering against the far wall in a luminous cascade. I cancel the spell before it can cause any lasting damage.

"Oh," the specter says, looking down where the magic should have hit him. "*This* is even more interesting. The fire god is a fire *goddess*, but one that does not recognize astral projections. Where did Etricos of the Helenai discover such a novelty?"

I clamp down on my rising terror. He is here, but he is not here. Through the shadows I discern facial features that drift in and out of focus, as though a pattern of rippling water overlays them: a square chin, a scar that runs from jawbone to temple, a crooked nose. In all of my years of magic lessons and supplementary studies, never have I encountered even rumors of such a technique. If I can't harm him, he likely can't harm me either.

Except that the seventh intermediate converges all space into one point. Distance is an illusion, just like this spectral Agoros.

"Did you like my offering, Goddess?" he asks, a crazed smile twisting up one side of his face. "If I had known you were a woman, I would have sent you more. I have plenty more to send."

My blood runs cold at the threat. "Is that what you do with those you conquer? Are they playthings to torture and dispose of?"

He reaches a hand toward my cheek, but I jerk away. A chuckle erupts from his throat. "I shall make *you* a plaything when I come in the flesh." His sharp eyes almost devour me whole.

"I will kill you if you come in the flesh." The ferocity of these words as they cross my lips surprises even me.

Agoros, far from being intimidated, only laughs again. "You can't touch me, child—not now or ever."

My mind races. If he could perform this astral projection all along, why has he not come sooner? Why did he not show up at the city gates himself instead of sending his dozen magicians? An untouchable Agoros would have struck more terror into the hearts of the Helenai than any band of warriors. Why would he not scout our city, walk among our people, observe our fortifications or lack thereof from every possible angle?

Only one answer satisfies these questions: this brand of magic must come at a high cost.

"You make yourself vulnerable by coming here," I say. His mouth curls in a sneer, but apprehension flashes through his eyes. I press on, gesturing toward his shadowed figure. "This requires more focus and more energy than you would have your enemies know. How long will you sleep when you return to your body? That's it, isn't it? You have to overextend your limits to accomplish this feat. Otherwise you would have come here many times before now."

I can feel it: from a great distance, the power of the seventh intermediate builds. It's more firm in my mind than in the physical world, as though a thread extends between this phantom and his physical location. He can strike at me, but as long as I trace that thread, I can strike at him as well.

I build my own seventh intermediate, focusing on that pinpoint of energy a hundred miles away, forcing myself to remain calm, to become the aggressor instead of the victim. "Will you really attack? You use a technique that drains your strength, yet you want to test your control against mine?"

Agoros gnashes his teeth. "You will die, Goddess, and the Helenai will die with you. I will destroy every last soul and burn this pathetic refuge to the ground."

Before I can respond, a breath of wind courses over him. The phantom Agoros disintegrates into ash and shadow, his tattered remnants swirling into the glowing coals of my dying fire. The pinpointed energy from afar winks into nothingness.

Thank the fates.

My knees buckle. I crumple but catch myself on my palms as my pulse thuds in my ears and stars dance in my vision. Sweat breaks across my skin. For several moments I gulp deep breaths, seeking to calm my frayed nerves.

Footsteps and voices sound outside. The tent flap parts.

"Goddess, is everything all right?"

I look up at the silhouette of Etricos framed against the lowering rainclouds in the nighttime sky. How did he know to come?

"Were you practicing your magic this late at night? The guards said a spell erupted inside your tent."

My failed attack—of course someone outside would see it.

"Agoros was here," I say, my voice hoarse in my throat. "He was here, but he wasn't. He projected his image into my tent and spoke with me."

Etricos regards me through the dim light, unsure of how to respond. "It was a dream, perhaps...?"

"It was no dream. He was here, and he will attack us. I need to know that technique."

Was it a variation on the seventh intermediate? If magic converges all space into one point, why should a person not be in two places at the same time? Technically, one could be everywhere at once.

But it *can't* be the seventh intermediate.

The ninth superlative of magic is that it is everything and nothing converged into one universal whole. The true master governs all.

The scholars of my day consider the ninth superlative to be an unattainable ideal, the epilogue to the more practical series of principles. Agoros, it seems, lies closer to that ideal than I do. If that projection technique is an indication of his power, he lies closer than any person I've ever heard of.

If I can't rise to his level and quickly, the Helenai will perish.

CHAPTER TWENTY-FOUR

THE FIRST RAYS OF DAWN CUT through the edges of a low cloud cover. I sit outside my tent, swathed in the gray morning mist with only a blanket around my shoulders to ward off the chill. Sleep tugs at me, but my thoughts are too active to give in.

Through the night, I have rifled through all the theories I know to find one that might match Agoros's astral projection. Nothing aligns. The principles of magic overlap and intertwine, but this pattern of projecting one's consciousness out into the world defies the boundaries I have always understood.

But then, my inner beast defies the boundaries as well. I should know better than anyone that the principles cannot specifically account for all variables.

Two figures approach through the low mist: Huna and Demetrios. He supports her elbow as they trudge up the hill together. She looks like death warmed over. I gather my blanket close and rise to my feet as they pass between my guards.

Demetrios regards my bare feet with silent disapproval.

"Have you slept?" I ask Huna.

"It has been a long night, little goddess," she replies, her voice hagged.

"How many still survive?"

For a breath she does not answer. She looks askance at Demetrios as though seeking his approval. When he gives no gesture either to speak or withhold information, she says simply, "Three."

Shock suffuses me. Huna brushes past, into the warmth of the tent and the comfort of her own bed. Demetrios watches her go, concern knotted in his shoulders.

The savagery these refugees faced at the hands of Agoros looms before us all. He will repeat his torturous acts upon us if he triumphs. I box my emotions, wary of succumbing to instinctive despair. "Is Tora getting some rest?"

Demetrios looks me over from top to toe. "Yes. Moru sent some of his tribe to tend the survivors. Did *you* rest?"

I guess he hasn't spoken with his brother yet this morning. If he spent the night in Aitana's company, I might scream.

"No," I say, holding his gaze.

"Why not?"

"Don't you share a tent with Etricos?"

Demetrios blinks. "Cosi was with Baba and Tora last night, helping with the injured. What does that have to do with you resting?"

I had not considered Etricos to be the nursing type. More likely he was stealing time with his betrothed while her grandmother played chaperone. "It's nothing," I say, feeling suddenly foolish. In the light of day, my phantom visitor seems ridiculous.

Except that I know Agoros was here.

I step away, intending to cross around to the back of the hill where I can observe the Eternity Gate through the morning haze, but Demetrios catches my arm.

"Why did you not rest, Anjeni?"

"If you wanted me to rest, you should have stayed with me." I speak the words lightly, but they fall flat. Truly, if Demetrios or any other man had been in the tent last night, Agoros would have assumed him to be the fire god of the Helenai. It's better that he was elsewhere, for a multitude of reasons.

"It would not be proper for me to stay with someone to whom I am not married," says Demetrios.

My lack of sleep and the stress of my nighttime encounter together loosen my self-restraint. "Are you married to Aitana, then?"

He bucks his head, rolling his eyes skyward. "That was not what you think."

I almost laugh. Death and destruction lurk, and I'm needling a man for whom I have ambivalent feelings. It's surreal, but I desperately want to hear his defense. "What do I think, then?"

"Tora was there, along with the children she cares for. I made the mistake of sitting in a corner while she coaxed Aitana into cooperation, and I fell asleep there. And they left me like that."

I can picture the scene: Tora allowing her betrothed's little brother the rest he had more than earned after a horrific day. If his presence made Aitana more cooperative, that was all the more reason not to disturb him.

And I have been nothing but petty to him over it. "I'm sorry."

"Why would you believe the worst of me?" Demetrios asks.

I can't explain to him that I came here expecting the worst of him. I know how the story goes, so it will be my own fault if I get hurt. *When* I get hurt. That seems like more of a certainty every day. After facing my mortality so many times already, though, a broken heart seems trivial.

"Agoros of the Bulokai has a power that I do not," I say abruptly. "I need to learn it."

Surprise flashes across Demetrios's face. "How?"

"I have to experiment, to push myself beyond my limits."

He shakes his head. "You must honor your limits, Anjeni."

"If I fail, it could mean the death of the Helenai and all those they protect."

"If you overexert yourself, it could mean our deaths as well."

His concern, endearing and unfounded, brings a smile to the corners of my mouth. "Will you watch over me when I lose consciousness, or must Huna take that responsibility?"

Demetrios scowls. "What about your students? Did not Cosi tell you to focus on their training?"

"This is more important."

"What is this new power?" he asks. I summarize the ability and how I learned of it. A growl rumbles in his throat.

"I have to acquire it, Demetrios. Agoros cannot have abilities beyond mine if I am to defeat him."

"Agoros summons demons from the netherworld. Will you strive to acquire that ability as well?"

I had not considered this. If his demon warriors—the burly, hairy hordes that follow his bidding—are not native to this world, perhaps Agoros truly opened a portal, something akin to the Eternity Gate.

That would represent yet another area in which he surpasses me.

"Anjeni," says Demetrios, his voice a low warning.

"Let me work on one skill at a time," I say.

He cups the back of my head with a strong hand, forcing me to meet his gaze. The world almost stops as we consider one another. He could kiss me right now if he really wanted to.

But of course he doesn't. "You will be careful." It's a command, not a request. "You will not push your limits unless I'm there to watch over you."

I nod, warm anticipation spreading through me. "Does that mean I can begin now?"

He doesn't understand my eagerness because he doesn't know the life I once lived. Only three months ago, in my native time, I routinely failed in all my attempts to learn magic. Now that I can control my spark, the possibilities seem endless—as endless as the promise that the ninth superlative makes. *One universal whole.* Agoros, contrary to his intentions, gave me a glimpse of what I might achieve.

I would be ungrateful if I let such a gift go to waste.

The mystery technique eludes me. It's like trying to levitate by lifting both feet off the ground at the same time: impossible, unless one can somehow defy the laws of gravity.

But the ninth superlative says that magic is everything and nothing at all. If the true master governs all things and space is only an illusion, this should be an attainable skill.

Whether I can attain it is the true question.

"It is enough for today, Anjeni."

Demetrios stands over me, resolve upon his face. The gray daylight casts him in somber light. For propriety's sake, the entrance to my tent gapes open so that anyone from the outside can see in. Huna insisted as much when she left us an hour ago, but with the rain, not even the guards at my fence peek at us.

A scowl draws my brows together. "It's not enough. I'm nowhere near figuring this out."

I shouldn't be so testy with him, but my frustration keeps mounting in layers the longer I sit, the longer I try to force a technique that refuses to manifest.

It's the first fundamental all over again. It's twelve years of fruitless magic lessons, vain attempts, abject failure. Despair swells in my throat, constricting my breath. The bitterness of my former self, on hiatus since I arrived in this realm, has quietly returned.

I roll my neck, as though I can simply release this onslaught of negativity.

"It is enough," Demetrios says again.

My temper flares. "If you're tired, go somewhere else."

His mouth presses in a thin line.

I shake my head to clear it. "I'm sorry. You don't understand. I have to do this, but it frustrates me."

"How will it help us defeat Agoros?"

The question gives me pause. If I acquire this skill, what does it merit? In answer, the seventh intermediate skates through my thoughts. "It connects places and allows for direct, precise attack from a great distance. It will help us defeat Agoros because we will be able to bring the battle to him instead of waiting for him to come to us."

He crouches to eye level with me, his face solemn as he holds my gaze. "There is no 'we' in this. You alone will be able to take the battle to him."

"All the better. No one else will be in danger."

Lightning-quick, Demetrios grabs me by the shoulders, as though to shake me. "It is *not* all the better. Stop thinking you have to do everything alone!"

I can only stare, too off-kilter from his outburst. My brain stutters as blood rushes to my face. I say the only response that comes to mind: "But I'm the only one who can do it."

He releases me with a discontented growl, flinging himself away to sit hard upon the ground. The two guards at the fence sneak a glance in our direction. Our voices have carried out to them through the downpour. Demetrios cradles his forehead in his hands, displeasure radiating from him.

I, meanwhile, flounder in bewilderment. "I don't understand why you—"

"Always alone, Anjeni," he interrupts. He fixes dark eyes upon me, a muscle tightening at his jaw. "From the moment you arrived, you have insisted on doing everything alone."

Stubborn. Defiant. Forcing my own way. My father's stinging accusations, almost forgotten in the tumult of living in this barren time, flash across my memory.

It's not fair. I didn't arrive in a place replete with strong magicians—not friendly ones, at least. I carry the burden of a legacy far greater than anything Demetrios can imagine. My whole world depends upon my success here. His life and future depend upon my success.

I lean forward and repeat the only salient point in this argument. "I am the only one who can do this."

"You can share the responsibility rather than shouldering it on your own," he says.

A scoff cuts from my throat. "How? With who? Aitana still fumbles to control the greater intermediates. The others straggle out behind her in their training—"

"I'm not talking about the spark-bearers. You can rely on Cosi to plan attacks. You can rely on me to fight by your side. You don't have to… to dash a hundred leagues away on your own and leave us all behind. You don't have to hold yourself apart from everyone else. This is *not* your fight, Anjeni. It belongs to the Helenai, and to the tribes who have sought refuge here with us."

Is he telling me to stay out of it? "It is my fight."

"Not your fight alone," he says.

Something in me snaps. "But I've always *been* alone, Demetrios. I never even fit in with my own family. Where sparks are concerned, I'm a volcano among riverbeds. If the fates wanted me to work well with others, they would have fashioned me differently, but they *didn't*. And if I have to abandon even my own body to defeat the Bulokai, *I will do it!*"

I slam a fist against the ground, and my inner beast roars. For the barest instant, power flings me outward, across the fire pit—except that I'm still seated solidly upon the ground. I can see both of my selves as though through a blurry mirror.

My split consciousness snaps back together like a pair of magnets. The force sends my head reeling, and I pitch to one side, my stomach in my throat and a sheen of sweat across my skin.

Demetrios scuttles to me. He holds my head and rubs one sure hand against my back as I retch. Thankfully nothing comes up. Water leaks from my eyes and my esophagus burns. I gasp for breath, my senses in shambles.

A fraction of a second. For a fraction of a second, my consciousness tore in two and my senses occupied separate spaces.

It was agonizing, like my head was cleaved and all of my bones were on fire.

But I did it.

I latch onto this meager triumph, desperately suppressing the after-effects of shock that resonate through me.

I did it once, and I have to do it again. And again, and again, and again, until I can calmly stride into a house a hundred miles away and converse with the occupants at my leisure while I focus a seventh intermediate on them from afar.

The extent of Agoros's power strikes me anew. If a split-second at a couple yards of separation does this to me, what agony did he endure to visit me in the night?

From the depths of my soul I force my consciousness out again. The rift and reunion follow in quick succession, faster than a heartbeat.

"Anjeni, stop!" Demetrios scolds as my insides lurch again.

I gasp, half pain and half jubilation. "I have to do it. I have to."

He crushes me to him, presses my head into his shoulder, tightens his arms around me as though he can keep me contained through physical restraint.

But I shove my consciousness outward again anyway. What an interesting spectacle we make, joined together like that. No wonder all the legends call us lovers.

With my head tucked tight against Demetrios, only my other-body eyes work. The split lasts half a second longer this time. Having one source of vision blocked allows me to focus more on the other. The magnetic pull snaps me back with a jolt.

"Anjeni, please," Demetrios whispers in my ear, his warm breath sending a wave of chills down my spine. My senses churn and reorient themselves, my every nerve prickling as though under attack from a million tiny, fiery pins.

This is my limit. Three attempts, hardly more than the blink of an eye, and my stamina is spent. Feebly I push against the muscled chest of my faithful guard. He allows me to withdraw a degree. My tattered breath rattles in my lungs as I look up at him with a welling sense of victory.

His expression, in stark contrast, speaks only of defeat. To my astonishment, he plants a fervent kiss upon my cheek and then rests his brow against mine. I gape, terrified and enraptured at the same time. His eyes are shut, his breathing steady as he calms his nerves.

"You will rest," he says, drawing back to pin me with a stare. I nod. Even were I not exhausted, I would not dare argue with him.

His determination renewed, he scoops me from the ground. I can't contain an instinctive yelp of protest. He deposits me on my cot only a few feet away and drags a blanket over me.

"I'll stay by the door until Baba returns," he says brusquely. His gaze doesn't quite meet mine anymore. "You will honor your limits for today, Anjeni, please."

Already I melt against my bed, my strength sapped from the duel shock of over-extended magic and such affectionate scolding. I try to speak, but my words are incoherent, my thoughts are incoherent, everything is incoherent.

As Demetrios moves away, sleep swoops down, a bird of prey capturing its quarry. I welcome it, gratification thrumming through me.

CHAPTER TWENTY-FIVE

I AWAKE TO DARKNESS. The coals of my fire have burned so low that only the reddest of light emits from their depths. The flap between my tent and the outside world lies closed, and I can just discern a figure huddled on the cot across from me.

Huna has returned and Demetrios left me to her care.

I stare up at the ceiling of my tent and contemplate. It's the middle of the night. If I were to practice this fledgling magic skill, Demetrios would scold me. But then, he's down the hill in his own tent and won't come back until morning. If I exhaust myself into another sleep, who would be the wiser?

On this thought, I sit up. My blanket rustles softly as it falls away. The figure on the other side of the tent stirs and rolls over.

It is not Huna after all. It is Aitana. She peers at me through the darkness. In surprise, she rises on one elbow. "Goddess, you are awake?"

Sleep infuses her voice. I fight the surge of annoyance that wars within me.

"Where is Huna?" I ask.

Aitana's mouth presses into a thin line. "She is with Tora… and Cosi," she mutters. "Dima instructed me to remain here with you through the night."

I flop back onto my cot. "You should rest. I'm sorry I woke you."

Across from me, Aitana yawns, but she does not curl up against her bed. "You are displeased to have me, Goddess," she says. "Is it true you have abandoned your students, then?"

"Abandoned?" I frown at her. "Who says I've abandoned my students?"

Aitana doesn't answer the question but meanders down a tangential path. "Perhaps we do not progress as quickly as you would like. Perhaps my failure in battle displeased you. It is difficult to live to the high standards of a goddess."

So she's the one telling the others I've abandoned them. That's just what I need, a mutiny among my spark-bearers. I drape one forearm over my eyes. "I've told you before that you progress faster than most. Do you need constant coddling to progress further?"

She rolls over, her back to me. A sullen silence settles between us. Aitana has always resented me, and I have always resented her. What could have possessed Demetrios to assign her here?

Maybe I should go ask him.

Safe in my own bed, I force my consciousness outward. That splitting sensation crackles through me, and I stand by the fire, looking down upon my supine self.

This projection feels more stable. I raise one shadowed hand. Wisps of darkness flicker around it like black flames.

Does the nighttime help?

My split consciousness snaps back together with a rippling wave of pins and needles. I gulp a deep breath, my heart racing.

On Huna's cot, Aitana turns. "Are you crying?" she asks across the gap between us.

"No. Go back to sleep."

Contrary woman that she is, she sits up instead.

"Go back to sleep, Aitana."

"Dima said you might practice a dangerous skill when you woke up. You would not put the Helenai at risk with such reckless behavior, would you, Goddess?"

I grind my teeth together. So Demetrios warned her, did he? "I came here to liberate the Helenai. Agoros is the one who puts you at risk. Go back to sleep."

She scowls and sullenly lies down again. I steady my breath and listen to the breeze that wafts through the vent overhead, biding my time.

A seeming eternity passes before sleep claims Aitana. I should probably sleep myself, but her words and Demetrios's warning have sparked rebellion within me. If I want to practice magic in the midnight hours, who are they to say otherwise?

I cannot trigger the projection with any degree of finesse, but I can hold it for longer on each attempt. By the seventh time, I can sustain a full fifteen seconds outside myself. Lying flat on my back helps. I'm not fighting against gravity in my physical body, for one thing. The shock that comes when my two sides collide is easier to bear as well.

Exhaustion eats at me. I don't know at what point in my practice I fall asleep, but I am content.

My eyelids flutter against the brightness beyond my open tent. A silhouette crouches before me, haloed by the brilliance.

"You practiced during the night," Demetrios says.

I blink and rub the grit from my eyes. My voice emerges with a sandpapery cadence. "What time is it?" If I look half as bad as I sound, I must be a wreck.

He combs my mussed hair away from my face with strong fingers, a surprisingly gentle action. "Morning is half gone. Will you eat?"

My self-consciousness multiplies. I sit up and run a hand over my face, eliminating any evidence of drool from the corners of my mouth. "Yes. Am I needed somewhere?"

"You are always needed." He speaks casually, his attention upon the low pot on the fire as he ladles some broth into a wooden bowl. He proffers the vessel to me along with a wedge of flatbread. The presence of such food tells me that Huna has come and gone while I slept like the dead.

The broth scalds the roof of my mouth, but it's the best thing I've ever tasted. Or I might be so deliriously exhausted that anything would taste good.

"Anjeni," says Demetrios, "you promised you would not practice when I was not here to watch over you."

The flatbread sticks in my throat. I did promise, and I promptly broke that promise on the first opportunity that presented itself. The legends paint Demetrios as inconstant and unreliable, but perhaps those descriptors would better apply to the goddess he abandons.

I swallow, trying to catch his eye, but he will not look directly at me.

So I make excuses for my conduct. "You left Aitana to watch over me in your stead."

His gaze snaps to my face before he averts it again. A muscle ripples along his jaw. "Aitana was best suited to pass the night here. I did not expect you to break your promise and train without me."

Better that she pass the night with me than with him. That eventuality will come soon enough.

He's lying, though. "If you didn't expect it, why did you warn her I might?"

Demetrios scowls, caught in a snare of his own making. He doesn't favor my question with a response.

I rally my dignity enough to say, "I was careful."

"You *promised*."

A sigh whispers through my lips. "I'm sorry, then. Now that you're here, I should practice again."

He regards me with a scrutinizing eye, but in the end he nods. I swallow the last of my breakfast and set the bowl aside, but I hesitate to proceed.

I hadn't considered how awkward it might be to stretch flat upon my cot with an intense and attractive man watching over me. He doesn't need to know his presence affects me. I can't give him that advantage. Reluctantly I lie back, my embarrassment boiling faster than Huna's broth on the fire. "It works better when I don't have to worry about my physical body," I say as I cover my eyes with one forearm.

"I'm here. You don't have to worry."

I glance sidelong at him from beneath my arm, a blush traveling up my neck to my face. Why does he have to be so endearing even when he's furious? In the broad light of day I can recognize that I wronged him. Is this the type of behavior that will drive him from me? My stomach flutters with pent up nerves—silly emotions I don't have time for. If I'm only allowed to practice in his presence, I shouldn't waste the opportunity on a bout of overactive hormones.

This was so much easier when Aitana was here and I didn't care.

I force my consciousness outward and land beyond the tent wall, in the yard. Puffs of clouds billow against a backdrop of azure sky. The sea glitters afar on the horizon. The world is full of color, of green grasses sprouting up from the ground, of the white and umber mushroom-tents and huts that spread down the hill, with dabs of orange, brown, and red moving between them—people attending to their morning chores on this glorious day.

I absorb as much as I can, enjoying the vibrance around me.

For all the pain this technique causes, it brings immense pleasure as well. *Everything and nothing in one universal whole.* Is that what the ninth superlative means? Does the great enigma of this principle amount merely to finding balance in opposition?

But that concept is easier said than done. I jolt back into my body, my nerves aflame from the energy I've expended.

"You have gotten stronger, Goddess," says Demetrios beside me.

"I have to get stronger still," I reply.

He nods, his attention still trained upon the exit. "Soon you will leave us all behind."

I roll my head to study his profile, that straight nose and strong jawline. Doubt twists through me. "I was always meant to leave the Helenai. You know that."

"And yet I would petition the fates to make it otherwise."

In this moment, I would almost petition them as well.

He turns at last to look at me, his dark eyes searching for answers I cannot give. My self-consciousness multiplies. I'm at a disadvantage, lying flat while he sits by my cot. I rise and swing my legs around so that I perch on the edge of the thin mattress, higher than him now, the balance between us restored.

"Was Etricos with Huna and Tora again last night?" I ask.

"I don't want to talk about Cosi," says Demetrios.

That effectively shuts me down. What does he want to talk about? Or are we just to stare at one another until I conquer my sudden shyness for practicing this projection magic in his presence?

My attention drops to my hands that grip the edge of the cot. "Are you *very* angry with me?"

"Yes."

Don't ask a question unless you want an honest answer, I guess. I lift only my eyes to lock gazes with him. He dips his head, the better to meet my stare.

"Anjeni, you know what I feel for you. Why do you disregard my feelings? When you act so recklessly—"

"I only fascinate you." I blurt these words as my heart attempts a desperate escape from my ribcage.

"What?" says Demetrios.

My nerves escalate. "I only fascinate you. That's what you told me, that I fascinate you. What would my recklessness have to do—"

Frustration leaves his throat in a grunt. He rises to his knees and drags me forward into a solid, ardent kiss.

Like, a full-on-the-mouth, whistles-and-bells-ringing kiss. I can feel it all the way to my toes.

My senses ignite and my self-imposed restraints crack. I wrap my arms around his neck and kiss him back. His hand presses against my spine, fingers spread, drawing me close as his mouth effectively—and I mean *effectively*—conveys that "fascination" doesn't begin to describe what he feels for me.

It is too much and not enough at the same time. The kiss ends, but he rests his forehead against mine as if to savor how close we still are. His ragged breath matches my own. My heart must be racing a thousand beats a second.

"You should marry me," he says.

I recoil, as though he dashed cold water in my face. Did we really go from a first kiss to a marriage proposal in the space of five seconds?

"What?" I croak.

He pins me with a determined gaze, deigning not to repeat himself.

"I—I can't marry you! I'm not— You don't— This doesn't turn out like—"

Demetrios silences me with another kiss, but this one is quick and to the point. "You should marry me," he says again, and then he withdraws.

I am a reeling, boneless wreck, more so than when I overextend myself. I sit hard upon the ground, dazed, my brain tracing his words over and over while my senses scrabble for equanimity. Demetrios, meanwhile, retreats to the door, scanning the world beyond, performing his ordinary duties as though nothing is amiss.

What is he trying to do? Ruin my focus? Throw my heart into turmoil?

Mission accomplished.

"Anjeni, if you love me, you should marry me," he says over his shoulder.

Is it that simple? Maybe it is. I mean, if I'm destined for a broken heart, why not go whole hog?

Except that I don't *want* to go back alone through the Eternity Gate as a married woman. Do they have divorces in this time period? Can I get a cross-dimensional divorce after everything is over, or would I just pretend that a marriage never took place? Should I commit to a lifetime of solitude?

Technically, in my time Demetrios is long dead. I would be widowed, free to date other men.

But I don't want to date other men. I don't want him to be dead. I want him to be alive and living, with his arms around me and his mouth against mine and—

If he runs away with Aitana, though, I might want him dead. Maybe that's why the goddess Anjeni steps back through the Eternity Gate. Maybe that's her method of legally killing her wayward husband.

Should I be plotting like this when all we've done is kissed each other?

At the wide-open tent exit, Demetrios ruefully shakes his head and steps into the full light of the morning sun. Did anyone outside see us? Do rumors of the goddess and her lover already ripple through the city?

Do I care? The closest I've ever come to making out with someone before was the time I dated a guy for three weeks and when I *thought* he was going to kiss me, he dumped me instead.

"Sorry, Jen. I expected you to be more like your sister."

Demetrios has never even met my sister, and honestly, if he perfected his kissing with the Aitana of this era, it was time well spent.

"Are you going to practice more today?" he asks.

I sit in a disheveled heap upon the ground. It takes me a split-second to realize he's talking about my magic. "I should," I mumble. But I'll need an hour just to regain my focus. Maybe I should go back to bed and sleep away this irresponsible interlude.

Not that I can sleep with Demetrios nearby. My nerves are practically singing.

Ridiculous, twitter-pated teenaged girl!

"I should," I say again, and I pull my wits together.

So what? A man just kissed me and told me to marry him. Miracles happen every day, if one knows where to look for them.

CHAPTER TWENTY-SIX

THE CLOUDS DON'T QUITE MANAGE an afternoon storm. I wander beyond the confines of my tent for little spurts at a time, shadow-flames flickering from my projection. I can see evidence of the spitting rains, but I can't feel anything aside from the cot against my back within the tent. Every time I notice that sensation, I get sucked inside again.

This whole process is like dreaming while I'm still awake. My energy and awareness come in waves.

Demetrios remains beyond the door, and I take my wanderings down the back of the hill because I can't look at him right now. He sits, unaffected, and I get thrown into turmoil if I catch even a glimpse of his profile. So I avoid him.

A muddy sludge coats the valley between here and the Eternity Gate, with sprinkling droplets that pepper the low puddles. Soon I'll be strong enough to reach the Gate. I'll have free rein of this area and become a regular terror to its inhabitants, the goddess who walks among them in a nest of black flames.

I can hardly wait.

From the city, a warning call blasts through the air. I spin, but my surprise and the quickness of my movement wrenches me into the dimness of my tent. Demetrios ducks through the opening.

As I sit up, a wave of nausea plows into me.

"You're not to go, Anjeni." He wraps his hands around my shoulders, moving me to lie down again.

I fight against his efforts. "I have to. What if it's Agoros with his army?"

"It's messengers or more refugees. You've outspent your strength. You won't make it ten steps without collapsing."

The truth of his words thrums through me. This is the double-edged sword of practicing heavy magic: I am not able to respond when I might be needed.

Whatever emotion Demetrios reads upon my face softens the hardness of his expression. "I'll go. Promise me you'll stay here and rest, and I'll go and return with word of what's happening."

If I were stronger, I could go with him, a creature of shadow and flame.

"Promise," he urges.

I nod, disappointment twisting through me.

"Keep your promise this time, Anjeni." He squeezes my shoulder and leaves as another signal trumpets through the air.

My inward streak of rebellion prompts me to follow him, but I quash it. Lying back upon my cot, I close my eyes and listen to the noise beyond my tent. The trump blares intermittently. My restlessness grows the longer I wait, until I can't take the suspense anymore.

Fifteen minutes after Demetrios has left, I sit up.

Deep breaths, Anjeni. Don't pass out.

I stand, about as steady on my feet as a newborn calf. My head hangs low while a wave of dizziness rolls over me, fizzling my vision into nothingness and back again. I inhale deeply and step toward the tent door.

Demetrios is coming up the hill with Tora beside him. He sees me and scowls.

In my defense, I did rest.

He passes between my guards. I straighten my spine, waiting in dignified silence within the canopy of my tent.

Before he says anything, he tugs on the restraints that hold the doorway open. "The tribal leaders are coming to you. Tora will help you get ready."

Tora slips inside. The flaps fall into place, cutting both Demetrios and the outside light from view.

"What's happened?" I ask.

She rummages through the trunk that holds my clothes. "More injured are making their way across the plains to us."

"Why are the tribal leaders coming to me?"

"Because they are divided about what to do." She extracts a flowy dress from amid the pile of clothing and offers it to me, a question in her eyes.

I retreat behind my dressing screen and strip the shirt I'm wearing. I quickly wash with water from the pitcher and basin. As I slip into the dress, Tora appears with my jewelry ready.

I balk. "They've all seen me without my ornaments."

"The more official you look, the better," she says.

Reluctantly, I slip a bracelet over my hand to dangle at my wrist.

"Goddess, they intend to leave the injured outside our walls to die." Sickness darts through me. Tora continues in a whisper. "Please. Please, intervene."

My gut twists. I partition my emotions behind a fortress of logic. "If it's like last time, most of these people will die. All of them may die."

"But some may survive," Tora says. She positions my golden headpiece in its proper place. It digs into my skull. "Please, we cannot be monsters and refuse aid to those who suffer."

"Which leaders are in favor of helping them?"

She rattles off three names, men with whom I am only vaguely familiar.

"Not Etricos? Not Moru?"

Tora shakes her head. Bitterness taints her voice. "They claim we cannot waste our meager resources."

The excuse sits no better with me than it does with her. What resources we expend will be minimal if, like last time, most of the refugees die within hours of their arrival. "If there are more tribal leaders against helping than for, why do they come to me?"

"Because a goddess should have final say in matters of life and death."

I quell my instinct to scream. I'm not a goddess. I'm an eighteen-year-old, barely an adult, barely able to take care of myself, let alone determine what to do with other people.

But the thought of leaving the injured to die exposed to the elements violates every sensibility I have.

From outside the tent, Demetrios hisses a warning. The tribal leaders are ascending the hill.

Tora motions me to sit and quickly applies the death-paint around my eyes, a simple outline. Demetrios pokes his head inside to check our progress.

"Put a cushion for her by the door," he says.

She obeys and motions for me to sit. The skirt of my dress is ample enough that I settle cross-legged. She steps back, regards me speculatively, and adjusts my crown a degree to the left. Then she exits the tent.

The curtains draw back. The afternoon light, diffused by clouds though it is, pierces my eyes. I flinch and refocus my gaze as Demetrios and Tora secure the opening. Before me, within the fenced yard of my hill, the tribal leaders stand in a line. They bow in a sign of obeisance.

Etricos steps from their midst to address me. "Goddess, the Bulokai have sent more injured into our territory. We seek your counsel."

His expression, hidden from the others, holds a warning that I should not overstep my bounds to contradict him.

He should know better by now than to attempt intimidation.

I tip my head at an angle. "How many injured are there?"

"Between fifty and eighty. Many have already died on the plains."

Agoros has been busy, the sadistic ghoul. "What will you do with the dead?"

Etricos frowns. Behind him, the tribal leaders exchange uncertain glances. Their concern has been with those yet living, those who bear down upon our safe haven in search of sanctuary.

I lean forward, pinning him with a hard stare. "What will you do with the dead, Etricos? Will you bury them in a mass grave? Throw them in the river to be carried out to sea? Burn them to ashes? You cannot leave them to rot on the plains. They will draw scavengers, and disease will follow."

"We have buried those who came the first time," says Moru.

"Burial is not the issue," says one of the other leaders. "These people have suffered. They are yet alive. We must do what we can to keep them that way. For all we know, some of our kinsmen may be among them."

"It would require too many of our resources," Etricos argues. "If we bring them into our walls, use our supplies to treat them, watch as they die one by one, what good does it do us? The brutality they have endured will weaken our people's morale should they have to witness it."

At the opening of my tent, Tora trembles with tightly bound emotion. Her hands clasp one another in a death grip, as though that alone restrains her from crying out. Etricos avoids meeting her gaze, and little can I blame him.

"Isn't your morale weakened already?" I ask. The leaders start, their expressions troubled. "Do you exult in leaving people to die beyond your city walls? Will that inspire confidence among the Helenai and her sister tribes? Does it send a message of strength to Agoros, and to those who yet labor under his captivity? And what if there *are* tribal kinsmen in the midst of these injured? Will you alienate your own people when they discover their kindred were left to die in the elements rather than being treated with dignity in the final hours of their life?"

Etricos presses his lips into a thin line. "Goddess, I fear that—"

"Fear has no place among the Helenai, Etricos. You did not come to the ends of the earth to cower, but to stand in defiance to your last breath."

Several of the men shift in their stances. I have successfully shamed them. Etricos looks to one side, his jaw clenched as he contemplates my words—and possibly how he can weasel out of their implications.

"You are correct," he says at last, the statement tight in his throat. "We cannot lose our humanity."

Moru opens his mouth as though he would speak, but he catches himself. He glances my direction, a plea in his eyes.

"Do we agree to treat those injured who travel here, then?" asks one of the three who stood in favor all along. A cluster of voices answers in the reluctant affirmative. Moru remains silent, observing me as I observe him.

"Does this please you, Goddess?" someone asks, jarring me from my study of the Terasanai elder.

"If it pleases you," I say, a self-conscious blush rising to my face.

They bow in homage and start back down the hill, discussing the arrangements required to meet the needs of so many. Etricos walks mute and stiff-backed in their midst. Moru lingers.

"Speak," I command him when his peers are out of earshot.

He approaches the entrance to my tent, his gaze flitting from Tora to Demetrios. "Goddess," he says in a low voice, "it is possible that Agoros would hide his agents among these refugees."

Agoros doesn't need to hide agents. He can walk through the city on his own power, if he so desires. Moru is better acquainted with his tactics than I am, however, so I cannot dismiss this counsel. "How can you determine one way or another? Would he injure his own people? Would they remain loyal to him afterward?"

Moru only shakes his head. He doesn't know the answer.

"Treat them as though they are allies. Guard them as though they are enemies," I say. "What more can we do?"

"What more, indeed?" His echo whispers across my ears as he bows before me. The resignation of his tone—more than anything else from this afternoon's encounter—sends a chill of misgivings up my spine.

Have I acted foolishly? Did I choose wrong?

As Moru retreats in the wake of his fellow leaders, Demetrios sweeps the opening of my tent back into place—but not before Tora darts inside. Shadows fall with the curtains. Tora drops to her knees and engulfs me in an embrace, nearly bowling me off my cushion.

Her tears flow freely, her whole body shuddering as she murmurs her overwrought gratitude. "Thank you, Goddess Anjeni. Thank you."

Fatigue weighs heavy upon me. "Don't thank me, Tora. This may well bring calamity within our gates."

She pulls back, her watery eyes searching mine in the dimness that surrounds us. "It is better to die as humans than to live as monsters," she says. She hugs me again and withdraws, slipping through the exit to leave me alone.

Absently I pull the golden crown from atop my head, rubbing at the tender spot where it sat. "It is better to live as humans, most of all," I mutter to the empty space around me.

I sincerely hope that belief is not yet another luxury I carry from my own time.

Demetrios insists I rest for the remainder of the afternoon. Admittedly, the counsel is good. I nap within my tent and awake to dim and faded light at my door. In my first waking disorientation I cannot discern whether it is dusk or daybreak.

I stumble from my cot, the flowy skirt of my dress nearly tripping me. I can only imagine what my face looks like, whether the black paint around my eyes has smeared or half rubbed off.

Demetrios ducks into the tent from his post outside. "Anjeni, you should not be up."

Even as he guides me to the nearest chair, I wave aside his concerns. "What has happened while I slept?"

He pours me water from a flask and proffers it to me. "Our people have collected refugees from the plains. They already dig the graves."

I contemplate the cup in my hands. "It's the same as last time?"

"To a greater degree. There are more women and children this time."

Dread floods through me. "Children?" I start from my chair, my throat closing over with sick disbelief. "He injured children?"

Demetrios catches me by the shoulders before I can dart to the opening of my tent. "We are treating them as best we can. Agoros is a monster in the flesh."

I swallow, half-wanting to seclude myself from the brutal reality that takes place down the hill. I can't do it. "I wish to go down there."

His eyes darken and his mouth thins. He's going to refuse my request.

I pin a stern look upon him. "I will go one way or another. You cannot stop me."

He knows he can't. His jaw tightens as he considers his options. "I will go with you," he says at last. "Put your shoes on first."

I obey the command and, for good measure, wash my face to rid any remnants of death-paint. The dress will suffice for now; changing clothes is too much of a hassle.

Demetrios offers me his arm, as though we are a gentleman and lady about to take a civilized evening stroll. I eye him, masking my rising self-consciousness with suspicion. He told me to marry him. He watches over me like a lover might. Am I tacitly accepting when I don't even know my own mind yet?

I mean, yes, he's attractive, but I barely know him as a person despite all the time we've spent with one another.

Reluctantly I take his arm. Halfway down the hill I am grateful for the support. My stamina drains from me with every step.

Perhaps it would have been easier to project myself down the hill instead.

"It will be difficult," Demetrios says. "Many are dying; many are already dead."

I steel my nerves. Darkness encompasses us as we pass into a city seeming at rest. Lights twinkle among the houses and tents, but the residents are quiet. The quarantine lies on the far side of the settlement, near the river and the crop fields, almost a mile from my tent on its hill. Demetrios supports me the whole way. I wilt against him when we finally arrive.

The wounded occupy a series of tents connected to one another like the chambers of a honeycomb. Light sets the area aglow, and shadows move within.

"Are you ready?" Demetrios whispers. I nod. Together we duck inside the nearest entrance. The twin smells of death and sickness assault me. I breathe through my mouth as we progress from room to room, from victim to victim. There are no beds, only blankets upon the earth. The women who nurse the injured pause in their ministrations to dip their heads to the goddess in their midst, and then they return to their work. I observe bloodstained bandages, ashen faces, glazed eyes—again and again and again. My chest constricts and I huddle closer to Demetrios as I walk.

"We should leave," he says to my growing distress.

"No." I need to see this. I need to understand the monster I am up against. This is not a romantic legend woven from brave and noble deeds. This is pain, suffering, trauma, the true and dark reality that history will gloss over when it paints its account of this storied era.

The children are the most difficult to see. They don't whimper or cry out. They lie in shock as women tend to them, washing away dirt and blood, sewing together gaping injuries with needles made of bone. Infection will follow in the patients that survive. Nothing here is sterile. Flies and fleas already abound.

"Anjeni," says Demetrios. He pauses to wipe away tears I did not realize I was crying. His thumb is warm against my cheek. "We should go."

I swallow and nod. I have seen enough.

We cross through the honeycomb of tents and emerge to warriors arriving with more injured. Tora directs them. Etricos stands nearby, his expression closed.

Tora sees me but continues her work. She separates the conscious from the unconscious patients, assesses injuries, and reassures fears with a gentle touch.

"They take the dead directly to the graves."

I jump at this unexpected voice beside me. Moru meets my gaze with a sad smile.

"Are there many?" I ask.

"Roughly half."

Demetrios tightens his hold on my arm, tucking me marginally closer to him. If Moru notices this protective act, he makes no indication. He gestures to Tora.

"She is admirable in her resolve. Etricos has chosen his future wisely."

"He has," I agree. A cluster of women separates from the shadows of the nighttime city, Huna and Aitana among them. They approach Tora for instruction on where they might help. Huna notices me off to the side and tilts her head in wordless rebuke—whether because I have left my tent on the hill or because I'm hanging upon Demetrios's arm is anyone's guess. Aitana spies us as well, and resentment flashes across her face. She lags behind the group and then parts from it to join us.

She greets me with forced civility. "Goddess, you have descended from your solitude."

I fix my gaze forward. "How goes your training, Aitana?"

"Self-study is difficult. I have no direction." She crosses her arms, her eyes flitting to my hand wrapped around Demetrios's elbow.

Yes, dear, for the moment, I've stolen your boyfriend. Time will bring him back to you.

"It's good of you to help with the injured," I say, an unsubtle hint for her to move along.

She deigns not to take it, parking herself on the other side of Demetrios instead. Amid the cluster of women, Huna receives her instructions and passes into the honeycombed infirmary. Tora sighs and rubs her forehead in the momentary lull. When she turns to enter the tents as well, Etricos forestalls her.

"You need to rest," he says.

"I can rest later." She tries to skirt around him, but he blocks her path again. "Cosi, step aside."

"You are exhausted. Please."

"I can rest *later*," she says again, bobbing to one side to get past him.

He grabs her by the shoulders. "Tora, I'm worried about you."

She wrenches away from him. "You have no right to worry about me! You're not my husband, Cosi, and you never will be!"

Dead silence blankets the scene. Etricos, stricken, stares at his betrothed. Tora covers her mouth, aghast at her outburst. She glances toward her onlookers—Moru, me, Demetrios, and Aitana. A sob escapes her throat, and she bolts into the night.

Etricos remains behind as though in a trance.

"Cosi," Demetrios murmurs. On his other side, Aitana watches with ill-contained satisfaction.

Something in me snaps. "Etricos, if you don't go after her, you're a bigger fool than I thought."

He jolts from his stupor. He glances at us as though noticing our presence for the first time. With a distracted buck of his head, he darts off in the same direction as Tora.

I start after them, but Demetrios yanks me back. "Let Cosi take care of it."

"Like he was taking care of it when he just stood there?" I fling my hand toward the shadows. "He's going to bungle everything!"

"Let him take care of it," Demetrios says again. Behind him, Moru and Aitana observe, ever alert.

"You can't stop me from following," I utter, my voice low.

Demetrios rolls his head skyward. "*Anjeni,*" he says in exasperation.

"You can't," I insist.

"It's late. We must return you to your tent, Goddess," he says, and he hooks my arm in a strong grip. "If you'll excuse us, please," he says to Moru and Aitana, and he leads me away.

"What do you think you're doing?" I hiss.

"Quiet. Do you want Aitana to follow us?"

I glance back over my shoulder. Aitana and Moru stand apart from one another, each of them watching our retreat into the shadows. When we pass the first line of huts, Demetrios veers me off in another direction.

"This is a terrible idea," he says. "Whatever happens between Cosi and Tora is private."

But we're headed on roughly the same course they went now. "Admit it. You're as curious as I am."

He doesn't deny the charge. "Cosi has been worried sick about her since the first wave of injured arrived. She will work herself to death if she's not careful. That's why he would have left these people beyond the walls rather than bringing them into our protection."

"Then he should have told her as much."

"You think he hasn't, in a hundred ways? He even applied to Baba to intervene, but she and Tora are too similar. Where there is work to be done, they're in the thick of it."

I contemplate this in silence.

From further down the road, a voice rings out. "Tora, wait!"

Demetrios drags me behind the nearest hut as a silhouette darts into the road, followed quickly by another.

"Cosi, please. Let me go." Misery infuses Tora's words. She is crying.

We peek around the corner to see Etricos tightly holding her wrist as she angles away from him.

"Why would you say such a thing?" he demands. "Why would you cast me aside like this? What have I done?"

"You have done nothing," she says, pulling against his grasp.

"Then why, Tora? You know my heart is yours."

But Tora shakes her head. "Don't lie."

"Do you doubt my words?"

"I doubt your actions. You have done *nothing*, Cosi." She tugs her wrist from his grasp and retreats a step. Etricos stares, his mouth agape. Tora continues. "How long have we been in this land? Weeks. *Months*. You might have married me a thousand times. There are half a dozen tribal elders now, but when one excuse disappears, you find another. I understand. This isn't what you want. I release you from your promise."

"No," he says, even as she turns away. "No, Tora. You are my soul." Before she gets two steps, he tugs her back, his mouth seeking hers in the darkness, his arms crushing her to him in a passionate embrace.

My fascinated observation ends as Demetrios yanks me back around the corner and places himself as a barrier to prevent me from looking again. "Give them their privacy, Anjeni."

I suspect, were we not puddled in shadows, I would see a lovely blush rising on his cheeks. It would mirror the heat on my own. We listen in awkward silence, but no sounds travel to us. Demetrios checks around the corner, only to withdraw again.

"Baba will have his head if word of this gets back to her," he mutters.

Meaning that Etricos and Tora are still locked in their fervent kiss. "Is it really that bad?" I ask.

"Such intimacy should happen only between a husband and wife."

I stare, my expression flat and one eyebrow raised. Demetrios has the decency to meet my gaze. "I told you you should marry me," he says, unapologetic for his earlier conduct.

From the street, Tora protests. "Cosi, please. This isn't—"

"I wanted everything in perfect order," Etricos says. "You deserve so much more than I can offer. I was trying to get—but I was wrong. I will marry you tonight, Tora, this very hour."

She hisses in rebuke. "Cosi, people are dying."

"Who makes excuses now? People will always be dying. Or are you the one who wishes to be rid of me?"

I poke my head around the corner in time to see Tora take Etricos's face in both hands and plant a solid kiss upon him. Demetrios draws me back again.

"You see?" he says. "Cosi took care of it." He sounds worried, though.

A frown pulls at my brows. "Does Huna still object to their union?"

"Baba can have no complaint as long as they do marry."

"You think they'll go through with it tonight?"

"I don't know. That is their decision. We should go."

I want to protest, but at this point I'm nothing more than a would-be spectator to the intimate encounter. Demetrios is correct: they deserve their privacy. In resignation I allow him to lead me away, between the huts to another street and another road back to my hill.

"Where will you go tonight if they do marry?" I ask as we approach my fence with its ever-present flames and guards. Demetrios frowns at the question. "You share a tent with Etricos. You wouldn't go back there on his wedding night, would you?"

He grimaces and looks away. "I can pass the night at one of the guard houses."

A knot of misgivings within me releases. I suppress the sigh of relief that results.

"Do you worry about where I sleep, Anjeni?" Demetrios asks.

Heat floods my face anew. I open my mouth for a quick denial, but I meet his gaze and recognize the teasing glint in his eyes. I scrape together some dignity and speak with stiff words. "No more than you worry about where I sleep."

"That is worry indeed." He takes my hand and squeezes it. With a nod he motions me to complete my journey alone. I slip from him, inner turmoil raging as I cross between my too-interested guards. Demetrios's gaze follows my every step. I pause for one last look over my shoulder before I pass into the deep shadows of my tent.

He smiles, a muted curve of his mouth that, despite its subtlety, sets a flurry of butterflies loose within me. With a sigh I let fall the flap that separates me from the outside world.

"Does my gift distress you, Goddess Anjeni?"

I whirl, fury incinerating my twittering emotions. A specter moves against the dark backdrop, Agoros in his projected form, his burning eyes upon me.

Control, Anjeni. You might lose everything if you lose control.

I temper my voice. "You know my name."

He waves a ghostly hand. I can just discern the flickering black flames that emanate from him. "A triviality to discover."

"You didn't even know I was a woman before."

"I did not think it worth knowing."

I fixate on that ephemeral thread that connects him to his physical form. Surprise courses through me. "You are nearer to here than last time. Have you left the safety of your stronghold, then?"

His lips curl into a sneer. "You would do well to focus on the threat before you rather than seeking enemies afar."

My beast of magic prowls within me, its hackles raised, a snarl vibrating in its throat. "Why? *Distance is but an illusion.*" I twist my hand into a fist and jerk it down.

Something answers, something far away. It spikes out, jolting through bodies that go rigid and tumble to the earth. Agoros wrenches his attention over my shoulder. The shock on his face contorts into hatred.

"You filthy minx!"

The specter vanishes, taking with it my connection to that distant locale.

I stagger to one side, my breath short and a cold sweat on the back of my neck. What have I done? I attacked at a distance beyond physical sight, more on instinct than any sure knowledge of success. My skin crawls with apprehension, but the beast within practically purrs with delight.

I need Demetrios. I didn't hit Agoros. There were others around him—magicians protecting him? Did I kill them, or simply injure? Regardless, I have attacked our enemy. I need someone to know, and Demetrios is the only person in whom I can confide.

As I pass again through the curtain that separates my tent from the outside world, faces of the wounded in Tora's honeycombed infirmary flash through my mind. This is life and death. I will not apologize for my boldness.

And perhaps Agoros will think twice before seeking me out again.

My strength is failing. I muster every last ounce and stride between my guards with my head high, as though nothing is amiss. Demetrios has already disappeared down the hill.

Where is he? I need him.

He might have returned to his own tent. I orient my steps that direction.

"Goddess Anjeni!"

I whirl. Tora and Etricos emerge from an alley I've already passed, hand in hand. I halt, my nerves humming with alarm.

"We thought you had returned to your tent," says Etricos.

"I... did." If he's really about to get married, I can't ruin this moment with talk of warmongers and attacks. "I needed to get some air."

Confusion registers on Etricos's face, but he dismisses it. "Tora and I are getting married tonight. We would be honored if you will attend."

"Oh," I say. *Stupid Anjeni, act surprised or something!* "Yes. Congratulations. Where will you have the ceremony?"

"In the tribal council's common hall." Etricos gestures to an adjacent street. "Moru has agreed to officiate. He's bringing Huna from the infirmary with him. Will you help Tora prepare, Goddess?"

Tora peers wistfully at me, biting her lower lip.

"Yes, of course." Why shouldn't I help with an impromptu wedding? It's not like I might fall over if I stand much longer, or that I may have just triggered an enemy attack against us.

(Please, let me not have triggered an attack against us.)

"I leave her in your care, then," says Etricos. "Tora, I will see you soon." He kisses her goodbye, so passionately that I have to look away in embarrassment.

As Etricos brushes past me to depart, I blurt, "Will you bring Demetrios to the wedding?" He pauses, giving me a look that makes me blush to the roots of my hair. Thank heavens for the cover of darkness. I temper my voice to minimize its trembling. "I need to speak with him."

"How could I marry without my own brother present?" Etricos says with a grin. He favors Tora with another loving glance and continues up the road.

"Goddess, you may think it strange—" Tora begins.

"It's not strange. You love him and he loves you, and you should have married ages ago." And the sooner they get it over with, the sooner I can counsel with Demetrios on my rash long-distance magic.

"It's not a traditional Helenai ceremony," she says as I hurry her toward her home.

"Helenai traditions must adapt," I reply. "The important thing is that you marry."

"Baba might not approve."

My fatigue robs me of any patience for this exchange. "Are you trying to talk yourself out of your decision? Your grandmother will be happy not to guard you against Etricos anymore. Moru will make the marriage known. There will be no dispute over whether it is valid."

Tora breathes a sigh, her shoulders sagging, but she nods.

"Are your orphans here?" I ask as we approach her house.

"No. I was supposed to be at the infirmary. Others care for them tonight."

"Perfect." I pull her through the door, determined to exit again as quickly as possible.

Tora's butter-yellow wedding dress fulfills its purpose at last. The bride, elegant in her simplicity stands with serenity beside her groom as Moru recites the marriage covenant before them. Two tribal elders act as witnesses, allowing Demetrios to sit with Huna and me. We are the only guests to this sacred rite.

If I weren't so tired and worried, I might cry for joy. Instead, my ears buzz with low white noise and I struggle not to let my eyelids droop.

Moru instructs the couple to kiss one another. Tora sends a self-conscious glance toward her grandmother and shyly pecks Etricos on the lips. Huna grunts but makes no other sound of disapproval. The tribal leaders congratulate the couple, their well-wishes sincere despite the restive atmosphere that surrounds this event.

Demetrios leans over to whisper in my ear. "Anjeni, what is wrong?"

I look askance at him. "I need to talk to you alone."

He tips his head to the door of the hall and helps me rise. "Baba, I am taking Goddess Anjeni back to her tent," he says.

Huna favors him with a reproving glance. "See that you don't go inside with her. People might talk. And don't say you want them to talk," she adds when Demetrios opens his mouth to reply. "You should not eagerly defile a woman's reputation."

Apparently my reputation is still intact. That must count for something.

"We're not going to my tent," I say. "I will sleep in one of the dormitories with my students. You will be at the infirmary until dawn?"

She studies me, suspicion lingering on her face as she nods. "The Helenai are to watch the injured through the night. The other tribes will relieve us in the morning."

I would lay odds that Tora devised this arrangement to ensure that proper treatment occurs. She would trust her own tribesmen to offer care that others might consider futile.

Whether they live up to her expectations is anyone's guess. She will spend the night elsewhere, if Etricos has any say.

I leave the council hall on Demetrios's arm, relying on his strength more than might be proper under Helenai standards. As we step into the night, he asks, "You will sleep among your students?"

"Agoros came again." The muscles in his arm flex beneath my touch. Briefly I relate the encounter.

"You should have come for me immediately," he says, which is beyond unreasonable.

"I did, but I came across Etricos and Tora first."

"You're not hurt? He didn't attack you?" He lifts one hand to caress my face, his fingers tangling in my hair.

My heart thuds in my chest. This was not supposed to be a romantic interlude. "No."

He brushes his thumb against my cheekbone and withdraws the warmth of his touch. "I'm glad. I'll warn the city guards to watch for attacks through the night. You're not to return to your tent. Do you wish me to stay with you and your students?"

Yes.

"I don't think that's necessary," I say, squashing my instincts to keep him by my side. This attachment to him grows at a pace much faster than I anticipated. "You need your sleep as well."

He looks around us, checking the shadows for potential threats. "I can sleep anywhere, Anjeni. I won't sleep if I'm worried for your safety, though."

"I don't think Agoros will confront me like that again."

"I hope you're right," he says.

I hope so too, though the magic within me itches for another chance to strike.

CHAPTER TWENTY-SEVEN

Fear taints the darkness. I sleep only fitfully amid my younger students, and when the first rays of dawn crest the horizon, I leave the small house and its silent occupants.

Figures trudge through the morning mist: Demetrios escorting Huna and Aitana from the infirmary. I trusted him to rest, but it doesn't surprise me that he's up so early. Sometimes it seems like he's the personal guard of everyone among the Helenai.

I gather my blanket tight around my shoulders and sit upon the low stone fence that borders the street. Will the little group notice me, or will they pass? Aitana droops against Demetrios's arm as though she belongs there, her golden hair cascading against his shoulder where she rests her head. If not for Huna on his opposite side, they might look like a pair of lovers returning after a long night's revelry.

Demetrios halts as our eyes connect through the morning haze. Huna arches her brows at me. Aitana lifts her head in confusion and, upon perceiving me, scowls. Her hold on Demetrios's arm tightens.

Payback for my similar conduct last night, I'm sure.

The possessive motion draws his attention. "Aitana, you need to rest. Hurry inside." He gestures to the house across from where I spent the night, the second of my students' dormitories.

She ignores him and calls to me instead. "Goddess, have you come down to train us today?"

Pettiness cannot occupy a place in my heart, especially after my impulsive attack last night. But I indulge it anyway. "Perhaps I should. We need stronger magicians."

Demetrios gives me a warning look. Aitana straightens on his arm.

"I am refining my superlatives," she says.

My harrowed night has drained my self-restraint. I steel my nerves and split, my shadow-self rising from the fence, darkness wisping from my edges as I close the distance between us.

The color drains from Aitana's face.

"Is that so?" I ask, mere inches from her. At the same time, upon the stone fence, I calmly watch the scene of my own specter menacing a terrified girl.

Truthfully, I'm no better than Agoros in using this technique.

The specter evaporates in the mist as my twin senses recombine. I rise on legs that quiver beneath my clothes. My blanket fails to ward off the chill that comes from magic exhaustion, but something within me has changed. I can't explain it exactly. The attack upon Agoros last night broadened my understanding to a degree I had not thought possible. My body lacks the stamina to follow through with all the new options open to my mind, but I can build that stamina with practice.

On my own two feet I approach the trio—Aitana, who cowers; Demetrios, who scowls; and Huna, who regards me with a troubled eye.

"Did you sleep at the guard house?" I ask Demetrios.

"Yes," he says.

Relief floods through me, that Aitana has not commanded his attention for long. I turn my focus elsewhere. "Huna, you should sleep."

She detaches herself from Demetrios and latches onto me instead. "If you will come with me, little goddess," she says. Before she can walk more than two steps, I tug her toward the nearby house.

"Sleep here. There will be no more sleeping in the tent on the hill."

Either Demetrios has already warned her or Huna is weary indeed; she does not argue. We enter the house and I settle her on the same bed I vacated only a short while earlier. My students stir in their slumber.

"What strange power have you discovered now, little Anjeni?" Huna asks as she lies back upon the mattress.

I tuck a blanket to her chin. "You don't have to worry. I have discovered everything and nothing at all."

She rolls to face the wall. "If that is true, watch that it does not consume you."

I think, perhaps, her caution comes too late.

This wave of injured refugees continues throughout the day. Our people commit the dead to an ever-growing mass grave beyond the city walls, with casualties in the hundreds already.

Etricos finds me among my students, overseeing a cluster who practice their intermediates. He tips his head away from the group. I give instructions and detach myself to join him. Demetrios accompanies me.

"Our scouts have returned," Etricos says in a low voice. "The Bulokai have set up small encampments beyond our borders. It looks like they are shipping their captives in, torturing them, and setting them loose upon our lands."

My stomach turns. "What will you do?"

"We will raid the camps. Goddess, will you help us?"

Demetrios tenses beside me. I look askance at him as I reply, "Of course I will."

Etricos nods. "We leave within the hour. I will send Tora to you to prepare."

"I can prepare myself. They need Tora at the infirmary."

He pauses as though he might protest, but in the end he accepts my decision. I return to my students and issue a few final words of instruction before proceeding to my tent.

"I can't ride a horse," I admit to Demetrios as we climb the hill. He looks sharply at me, so I elaborate. "Few people ride horses in my realm. We have machines to carry us from place to place."

"Machines?" Confusion wrinkles his brows.

"Cars, trains, airplanes," I say, even though he can't possibly understand. I pin him with a stare. "Is horse-riding difficult?"

"I'll be with you to keep you safe."

That doesn't answer my question, but I quell my nerves. If I can attack an enemy a hundred miles away, I think I can manage a few hours on horseback.

He waits outside my tent as I trade my sandals for boots. Etricos probably wants me to wear the black paint that Tora so nicely supplies, but I would rather not distinguish myself from the other soldiers on this raid. I have every intention of destroying the encamped Bulokai before any among the Helenai can engage with them.

I tuck a couple of knives into my belt and bundle up in a hooded coat. The low, sullen clouds threaten rain at any moment. It is late enough that we will not return until after nightfall.

As we trek back down the hill, Aitana emerges from her dormitory, swinging a cloak around her shoulders. "I'm coming with you," she says, her glare defiant.

She must have eavesdropped on my conversation with Etricos.

"Aitana, that's not—" Demetrios begins.

"Fine," I interrupt. "Bring Ria too. Tell Ineri to supervise the younger ones while we're gone."

I sweep past her as she gawks, robbing her of her triumph with such an easy victory.

"Anjeni," says Demetrios beside me, "this will be dangerous."

"Of course it will, but the Helenai need warriors, not hobby-magicians. They must start somewhere."

He concedes the point, as does Etricos when we inform him that two more will join us.

Half an hour later, I ride stiff-backed, my every thought on keeping my balance. Demetrios runs his horse alongside mine, but we are falling behind the group. My confidence drains like sand in a sieve the further we get from the city.

If I were strong enough to project directly into these encampments, I wouldn't have to travel there by horse. No one would.

We keep close to the river with its trees and greater vegetation rather than riding exposed out on the plains. The foliage overhead allows scant shelter from the intermittent rain. Etricos has scouts in the area to watch for any Bulokai encroachers. More than once I avert my eyes from a body in the underbrush—one of the many injured striving to reach our sanctuary. This is not a mission of mercy. We come to confront the enemy, and I must steel my senses to that purpose.

As night falls around us, Etricos halts the group in a small grove. "The nearest camp is a little over a mile away, on a hilltop. They will have sentries posted, watching for an attack. Speed and darkness will be our greatest ally."

Even if the encampment is small, the Bulokai have the advantage. We have thirty warriors, but getting them up a hill robs us of the element of surprise.

"I'll go alone," I say. "If I can destroy the Bulokai here, you can leave men stationed in their place to wait for the next shipment of captives, and we can move on to the next encampment."

Etricos looks uncertain. "Goddess—"

"I know what I'm doing, Etricos," I say. That's not entirely true, but I'm sure I can cast magic through my projection. I only have to follow the thread that runs between my two selves.

"I'll go with her," says Demetrios.

I glare at him. "I'm not going there in my physical form."

"I will get you as close as possible, Goddess. This is only the first encampment. We will take Aitana and Ria as well. They can watch from below and guard against any Bulokai magic."

To my surprise, Etricos agrees to this plan. In fact, he embellishes on it: his warriors will fan out across the terrain in watch of Bulokai scouts and guards.

We leave our horses in the grove and proceed on foot, spreading out as we go. The trees break and a hill rises before us, with torches flickering between the ghostly tent silhouettes.

"Do not overexert yourself," Demetrios whispers in my ear.

Images from Tora's infirmary play through my mind. If I fail, more people will suffer and die. My determination solidifies. I sit upon the ground and tuck my knees to my chest, resting my head atop them.

Distance is but an illusion.

In a flare of power, I launch up the hill to land in the midst of the encampment. Bristle-faced demons look up from their sloppy meals. A shout echoes through their ranks as weapons scrape from sheaths.

The fifth intermediate of magic is that it favors a radial plane. Fear no aggressor; you are never blind.

Magic blasts from me in a cutting ring. It slices through the converging Bulokai, tossing them backward. I unleash a seventh intermediate among them in its aftermath. Smoke rises from the hulking figures on the ground. Stubbornly forcing my projection, I stalk through the area in search of enemies I may have overlooked and finish any who yet show signs of life.

Low cages dot the encampment. Frightened captives cringe from my spectral image, whimpering as I pass—and little can I blame them.

Their tormentors lie dead, but a greater monster prowls among them.

My senses shudder. I release my projection and surface in my own body with a gasp. My head reels, overwrought in the wake of so much power expended. Demetrios kneels beside me, his hands clasping my shoulders as he examines me for evidence of trauma.

"The camp should be clear," I say, my tongue thick and clumsy, as though I am drunk. "They have people in cages."

On that final word, my eyes roll back in my head and I pitch into darkness.

CHAPTER TWENTY-EIGHT

THE RHYTHM OF THE GALLOPING HORSE beneath me rouses my senses. Gradually I focus. My head, weighted like a ball of lead, rests against Demetrios's shoulder. He holds me tucked close, his body hunched and one arm tight around my waist as he rides like a demon through the night.

My heart lurches. Sideways in the saddle as I am, one false move might send both of us pitching from the horse to our deaths. Instinctively I tighten feeble fingers around the leather strap that fastens his armor at his chest. He glances downward, meeting my gaze in the darkness. I can just make out the shadow of his stubbled beard.

He says nothing, but the hand at my waist draws me a fraction closer as he returns his attention to the path we follow.

A second horseman keeps pace behind us, one of the other warriors. My still-muted senses heighten by degrees as we travel, but my limbs have scant strength. I entrust myself to the care of my guard, certain that he will keep me from harm. Rain begins to fall, a light and quiet distillation. Demetrios hunches further inward to better shield me from the wet.

Exhausted, I close my eyes, indulging in his proximity and the sense of security it brings.

How did it come to this? Am I injured more than I realize, that we ride like this through the night?

I was supposed to help liberate the other border encampments, not become a liability to the cause.

We return to the city by a back pass, skirting along the river until dots of lamplight pepper the darkness. Demetrios calls a command to his underling. "Fetch Baba or Tora, quickly, and come to Cosi's tent." The second horseman separates, headed toward a cluster of lights to the left. Demetrios plunges ahead, through the dirt roads of the sleeping city.

Why are we headed to Etricos's tent? A feeble protest rumbles in my throat. My tongue won't cooperate enough to form words.

Demetrios reins in beside the familiar shelter. He clasps me protectively to him as he swings from the saddle and hits the ground with jarring force. My teeth click together in my mouth. We pass from the sheen of rain into the low, dry interior. He crosses straight to the adjoining room and deposits me on the cot—his cot, and the same cot to which he brought me when I first arrived in this world. He checks to make sure I am comfortable, and then he cups my cheek with one strong hand, intensity bleeding from him in the shadows.

I study his face and the worry etched upon it, as though I might engrave his image on my mind.

The moment ends. He turns away to remove the boots from my feet.

Again I attempt to speak. Only a garble of sounds emerges.

"Anjeni," he says, his voice as hushed as the rain that whispers against the tent walls, "I thought you were dead. What am I to do if you die?"

He does not say, "What are *the Helenai* to do?" I cannot answer him, and my heart might burst because of it.

The curtain parts and Tora enters, terror upon her. "What has happened?"

"She overextended her powers. Keep her resting. I will return to Cosi and the others. We should be back by daybreak."

"Dima—"

"Tora, she mustn't be left alone, do you understand? She's stopped breathing more than once already."

I did? I don't remember.

Demetrios kneels beside my bed. He cups my face again, but this time he stoops to kiss my cheek—so near to the corner of my mouth that he might as well have closed that distance. "Rest," he whispers. He holds my gaze in the dark as though to reinforce that single word. A chill supplants his warmth as he withdraws. He passes through the exit. Moments later, muted hoofbeats signal his departure.

Tora stands beside the curtain as though in a trance. Is she mortified by the intimate exchange she witnessed? I don't care. There was nothing improper about it.

She shakes off her stupor and, with her customary composure restored, bends to check my condition.

I would apologize for causing her trouble, but my tongue still refuses to cooperate. My heart has gone out the door with Demetrios. Truthfully, so has part of my awareness. It's as though I can pinpoint his presence even as he retreats from me.

Everything and nothing. I drift to sleep on those words, a splinter of myself galloping through the shadowed rains alongside the man who claims he loves me.

Huna attends me when I next awaken. Muted daylight illuminates the tent walls, but it cannot be long after dawn. I roll over and attempt to sit up, my strength renewed to a degree that allows me control of my own limbs at least.

My crabbed attendant thrusts a bowl of broth into my line of sight. "Drink."

I sit up to receive the food. My vision fizzles into darkness and back out again. I keep my head low, pretending that my full attention is only on sipping my savory breakfast.

After a few swallows, I test my voice. It crackles in my throat. "Did Demetrios return?"

Huna grunts. "Not even an hour ago, with Cosi and Aitana and the others. What did you do, my foolish little goddess?"

I pause, the bowl near enough to my lips that its heat wafts against my nose. "I stretched beyond my limit."

My head is much clearer this morning. This abject weakness resulted from expending magic through my projected form, I'm sure of it. I wasn't anywhere near this drained when I attacked along Agoros's thread to his physical sanctuary.

Projection magic must obliterate physical stamina. No wonder Agoros has yet to attack in that form.

I want to know the outcome of last night's raids, but I suspect that Etricos will retreat to his own bed rather than reporting to me. Demetrios should probably do the same, but will he come here first or head straight to one of the guardhouses?

I'm selfish. I want him to come to me.

Almost unbidden, my senses expand. He is in the city—like a familiar face in a crowd his presence beckons me. I glance toward Huna, who has turned her back on me to ring out a washrag in the basin. Surreptitiously I set my drained bowl on the ground and lie again upon the cot, as though resuming my rest.

My eyelids flutter shut. I focus on that beckoning presence further in the city.

He's going to scold me.

A ghost of a smile curves along my mouth. I don't care if he scolds. I only want to see him, to know that he and the others are safe.

So I *jump*.

"You know by now what she is, Cosi! You know her nature! When you ask her to do these things, she will throw herself into the task—the gods alone know why!"

I stand within the council hall amid empty chairs while voices carry through the partially open door of the one private room at the back.

"All of our lives are at stake, Dima. She is no different than the rest of us."

Who are they talking about? Aitana? Tora?

"She *is* different. She doesn't belong to this world."

Oh. They're talking about me. I shouldn't eavesdrop. I should return to myself, but something pins me here, keeps me fixated on the pair of brothers in the next room.

Demetrios presses on. "I don't know what drives her to act the way she does, but if she continues like this, she will die. Where will the Helenai be if she dies? Aitana and Ria exhibit mere shades of her power. She wiped out an entire encampment on her own, while they could barely handle a pair of Bulokai foot soldiers."

"That's exactly why I need her," Etricos replies. "Would you have me leave her in safety on her hilltop while the rest of us risk our lives to fight? We have given her everything she could possibly want. The full wealth and reverence of the Helenai rest upon her. She can sacrifice for us as well."

A scuffling ensues. Half-numb, I ease up to the door that separates this room from the next. The slit of an opening reveals

Demetrios with his hands fisted in his brother's shirt, his face only inches from Etricos's. "*Not* to her death."

Etricos remains unperturbed. "Death may claim any one of us. It is the nature of this fight." His brother shoves him back and stalks to the other side of the room. Etricos straightens his shirt. "Of course I don't want her to die. She might have cleared all of the Bulokai camps within an hour with her magic if she hadn't collapsed. It cost us all night and the lives of four good men without her. I need such a weapon to be strong, to be reliable."

"She's a human, not a weapon," says Demetrios over his shoulder, a snide twist to his voice.

"In war, we are all weapons. The more she fights, the better she will control her power."

"If she survives. If you ask the impossible of her, she will die trying to achieve it."

Etricos grunts, a satisfied sound that rankles his younger brother.

"You think that's something to gloat about?" Demetrios asks.

The elder brother shrugs. "I gave her to you, Dima. It's your job to inspire her towards restraint, not mine."

"I've tried—believe me, I've tried. She disregards my efforts."

"You'll have to try harder. Engage her sensibilities. Manipulate. She's not that different from Aitana."

Humiliation plunges through me. *Is his treatment of me nothing more than calculated manipulation?*

Demetrios rakes one frustrated hand through his hair. "You're wrong. She's completely different. Cosi, if she dies, any hope we have dies with her."

The sympathetic smile on Etricos's face lacks sincerity. "I know. That's why you need to do your job. But don't get in the way of me doing mine. A weapon at rest is no weapon at all."

Demetrios growls his dissatisfaction. He stalks toward the door that separates us, and I back away on instinct. He wrenches it open. As he passes through, our eyes meet. He stops short, the blood draining from his face.

Somehow, in the intensity of their conversation, I forgot that I'm not really here.

"Anjeni," he says, reaching one hand toward my spectral form. I wink out of the hall and back to his tent, landing in my body with a jolt. Huna still fusses at the water basin, oblivious to my small excursion.

I can't stop the tears that leak from my eyes. Quickly I roll to my side, my back to the old woman. What exactly did I overhear? Etricos *gave me* to Demetrios? I knew he told him to flirt with me, but this goes beyond that. Has everything been an act, two brothers orchestrating my emotions to accomplish their desired ends?

I know I'm a weapon. I didn't know it in such bald terms, but what else would I be? My purpose in this era is to establish Helenia, and certainly I must survive for that to happen.

But I have been willing. They didn't have to meddle with my heart to persuade me.

The curtain flies open. Demetrios stands wild and breathless upon the threshold. I hunch deeper into the cot, my face to the wall.

"Baba, I need to speak with Anjeni, alone."

"It is improper—"

"Baba, I *need* to speak with her. Alone."

His intensity spurs Huna, who silently vacates the room. The curtain falls behind her.

I remain motionless, my breath trapped in my lungs as I listen for his approach. What am I supposed to say to him? I should not have overheard his conversation. Does it change anything?

It doesn't have to—at least not externally.

"Anjeni—"

"I'm glad that you're safe," I interrupt, my voice more watery than I'd like. Carefully I wipe my cheeks with my sleeve. "The raids were successful, then? I'm sorry I wasn't more help."

"Anjeni, look at me."

My eyes slide shut as I burrow fractionally deeper into the thin mattress. "I'm still tired, Demetrios. I only meant to see that you and Etricos had returned." It's a paltry lie—Etricos had nothing to do with it—but I squelch any sense of guilt. The pair of brothers has worked me as they might work a mule, Etricos to spur me on and Demetrios to rein me in.

"Anjeni, please."

He's not going to leave until I talk to him. I exhale a sigh and reluctantly push myself up. I can be calm. My purpose here still aligns with their goals. We are allies in this fight. "I'll be more careful on future raids," I say, my back still to him. "I didn't know how far it would deplete me. I should have started with the lower intermediates instead of the higher ones."

"You should not have done any of it. This is not your fight."

I look up at him, wonder and sorrow and muted anger all at war within me. "It *is* my fight."

"Why? You are not of this world and you will not remain here."

I meet his gaze even though my heart feels like it's breaking into jagged shards. "But my world depends upon it." Demetrios recoils, and I elaborate. "My world cannot exist if the Helenai perish. It is as much my fight as yours. Perhaps it's more. You hope to spare a few hundred lives, but millions depend upon my success."

His brows furrow and his mouth tightens. "Is this the burden you carry?"

The question turns over in my mind. From the beginning I was a mistake, useless for anything but sarcasm and resentment. My advent here and the magic that it triggered give me purpose—something I wholly lacked in my own time. Resignation bleeds into my quiet response. "It's no burden. The fates aligned to grant my desire, but at a price. I must see the Helenai establish a sovereign nation in these lands. I won't die, if that's what worries you."

"Of course it worries me," he says. "How could it not?"

How sweet. If only I could trust his motives.

"I'm tired," I say, returning to the mattress, my back to him. "You must be tired too. You should sleep."

"I will sleep here."

My head snaps toward him. I half rise on my elbows, alarm lacing through me. "You can't—!"

But he already curls up on the stretch of ground beside what should be his cot, where I rest instead.

"Demetrios," I hiss, crouching on the bed as I look down upon him. He lies on his side, his back to me. "Huna will have your hide." I prod him in the shoulder to drive home this point, but he ignores me. "*Demetrios.*"

"Sleep, Anjeni," he says. "The Helenai need you to be strong."

The Helenai need me. Their hope dies if I die. He acts to benefit his people.

The wall between us solidifies, and something in me breaks.

"Don't tell me that!" I swat at him, tears spilling from my eyes. "I already know it! Don't tell me that!"

Demetrios twists and sits up, astonishment on his face. My vision blurs, but when he reaches for me, I recoil beyond his touch.

"I don't need your sympathy. I don't need you to offer false comfort to keep me in line."

"It's not false comfort," he says. He grabs my arm, but I wrench away. "Anjeni, please. Don't misunderstand."

"I'm not misunderstanding. I'm a weapon. I already knew it. And you have to take care of your weapons or they might fail you when you need them most."

"You're not a weapon! Cosi has no right to treat you like one!"

"He has every right! My whole world hinges on his success!"

He catches my flailing arm and yanks me from my perch on the cot, toppling me down on top of him. When I attempt to rise, he crushes me to him, tucking my head against his shoulder, wrapping me in strong, restraining arms.

"Don't, Anjeni," he murmurs. "Don't misunderstand."

More tears escape unbidden. In such a tight embrace, there's no point in my continued struggle. I lie stiff, fighting the urge to melt against him, to accept the comfort he offers.

He sighs, and my body follows the movement of his chest. "You already know I love you," he says.

Why must my treacherous heart flutter so much against a few paltry words?

"Is this where you engage my sensibilities to manipulate me?" I ask, miffed at both him and myself.

For the barest instant he doesn't respond. Then, "I'm trying, but you never cooperate."

And I laugh, a cynical response, because I'm too far physically and emotionally spent. Demetrios's hold loosens enough for me to roll to one side of him. We lie next to each other, each breathing deep, each staring at the tent ceiling.

He clasps my hand in his. I should pull it away, but I don't. Instead, I curl my fingers into a firm grip.

CHAPTER TWENTY-NINE

Etricos has no clue that I overheard any of his conversation. He sits in the main area of his tent, with the afternoon sunshine spilling through the wide-open doorway. A practiced smile leaps to his face when I exit from the side room. He asks my condition.

"I'm better," I say, which is true. I'm able to stand on my own two feet without blacking out.

Demetrios, beside me, glares at his brother.

"No doubt Dima has told you our raids last night were a success," Etricos says. "We have left men garrisoned at the camps to receive the next shipments of refugees."

"Will they be strong enough to overcome the Bulokai who bring the shipments?"

"They will have the element of surprise."

That doesn't answer my question, but I decline to press the issue. "And what of Aitana and Ria?"

Demetrios speaks before his brother can. "They exhausted their magic last night and required rest."

"Your students practice up the hill, Goddess." Etricos points through the open doorway. "Dima can escort you there."

"Where are you going?" Demetrios asks, suspicion on his voice.

His brother stands and straightens his shirt. "The other tribal elders wish for a report. Now that our goddess emerges unscathed, I go to speak with them."

"I'm sorry if I caused you trouble," I say.

Demetrios lays gentle fingers on my elbow, turning me toward the door even as he glowers at his brother. "Don't apologize to him. You caused no trouble."

A glimpse of Etricos shows amusement plain upon his face. Demetrios and I pass from the tent to the street beyond, where dozens of Helenai tend to afternoon errands and chores. They glance our direction but avert their eyes again when they realize who I am. Many heads bow in deference as I pass through their midst.

Puffs of white cloud dapple the sky above. My students have taken advantage of the fine weather to practice outside. Ineri oversees them, but she pauses their exercises when she recognizes me coming up the hill. Ria is with her. Aitana is nowhere to be seen.

My students greet me with reverence. Ineri exchanges an uncertain look with Ria as I approach. I take it that Ria has informed her of my condition the night before.

No matter. It's good for them to consider the consequences of their magic, should they ever reach that level of mastery.

"Are you rested?" I ask Ria.

She nods, wordless.

"And Aitana?"

"She is resting still."

My attention strays to the nearby dormitory. Is she actually resting, or is she being antisocial? Should I look in on her?

In answer to my question, as though summoned, Aitana exits the house. She holds her head aloft as she walks, her eyes looking past Demetrios and me as though she does not see us. She has been sulking, in other words.

She deigns to address me after she has joined the other two girls. "Goddess, I trust you are sufficiently recovered?"

I see. She and Ria reported my condition not only to Ineri, but to all of my students.

"I stand before you," I say. "Shall we continue training?"

"We can manage, if you would like to rest."

As if I would allow her to hijack my students. "I would not like to rest. My intermediates, follow me. Beginners, break into groups with Ineri, Ria, and Aitana."

I sweep past the trio. In my wake, several students peel away from the group and follow.

"Don't overdo it," Demetrios whispers under his breath.

"I won't. We're practicing the upper intermediates, not any forbidden principles."

I guide them to the back of my hill, with full view of the Eternity Gate across the basin from us. Without projection magic, the intermediates are child's play.

Which only makes me want to practice them in projection. Demetrios watches me like a hawk, though, so I refrain from following this impulse.

The cloud clusters tighten as the sun descends. Orange light glitters upon the distant ocean. The humidity, thick and heavy, is a portent of more night rains yet to come.

A trumpet signals from the city's watchtowers. I look to Demetrios for its meaning.

"People approach the gates," he says.

"Should we go to meet them?"

He considers the question, and ultimately nods. I disperse my small class to their evening activities.

Demetrios offers me his arm, and I take it as we climb the back of the hill together. I don't actually need to lean on him.

If anything, the afternoon's exercise has invigorated me, strange as that seems, but yet I allow this small indulgence.

We cross the other side of the hill and down through the streets. Etricos meets us near the watchtowers, with Moru beside him. "It is the first batch of our rescued captives," he says. "There are roughly thirty of them—men, women, and children—and all of them unharmed. This is an easy collection of allies to make."

"We should not bring them directly into the city," Moru says, his brows drawn together in a frown.

"Where would you put them?" I ask.

"We can give them tents beyond the city walls. We cannot assume these people are allies, Goddess. Many of them may blame us for their plight."

I look to Etricos, who grudgingly nods his agreement. Moru departs to give orders, but Tora joins us only moments later.

Her husband kisses her cheek. "What brings you here, love?"

She blushes under the open affection, her self-conscious eyes sliding toward Demetrios and me and then away again. "There may be relatives of the injured in this new group. Where will you bring them?" When he tells her that they are to remain outside the city, alarm flashes across her face. "Even the children? Cosi, you can't leave them beyond the walls. What if the Bulokai attack?"

"It is safer this way, Tora."

"But—"

"No arguments. It's not permanent, but only until we can assess their loyalties."

"Then let's go," she says, and she tugs him toward the gates.

He digs in his heels, confused. "Go where?"

"To assess them. Goddess, will you come?"

"No," Demetrios says before I can answer. "Goddess Anjeni must rest."

I glare at him, but he doesn't flinch. I play my one trump card. "You can't stop me from going with her, you know."

Etricos intervenes on his end. "Tora, there will be time to assess them tomorrow. Night is almost upon us. They are not injured and can stay beyond the city walls until morning. Please, don't argue."

She scowls but buttons her mouth, deferring to her husband for now.

"Do you tend to the infirmary tonight?" I ask.

"Yes," she says. "I've rested this afternoon."

The tightening of Etricos's jaw tells me that he'd rather his wife remain with him. He bids us farewell and accompanies her that direction. Demetrios angles me back toward the dormitories up the hill. "You must eat something and go to sleep," he says.

I bristle at being treated like an invalid. "I'm stronger than you think."

"Don't be stubborn, Anjeni."

"That's like telling a fire not to burn," I say in full glower.

Demetrios laughs. He catches my hand and squeezes. "It is exactly like that."

Overnight, the number of rescued captives grows from thirty to a hundred or more. "They crowd the tents that Cosi provided them," Demetrios says.

It has been drizzling since the dark hours before dawn. Guilt for our less-than-hospitable reception of them flits through me. "What a miserable night they must have passed."

He regards me with a wry glance. "Less miserable than being tortured and maimed by the Bulokai."

I concede the point. We pass from the shelter of my students' dormitory to the misting rain outside, our heads covered as we quickly walk the road toward the council hall. "What does Etricos intend to do with all of them? Does he make an assessment this morning?"

"Yes. Tora insists."

"Should I go with him?"

Demetrios hesitates. The concern that chases across his face, while heartwarming, is unfounded.

"I am rested," I say. And it's true. I haven't felt this refreshed in days. The weakness that plagued me after the encampment raid has vanished. My beast of magic within its cage purrs, eager to explore beyond its confines again.

"Moru fears there may be those hostile to our people among these captives. You are the goddess of the Helenai and would draw their ire if that is true."

"Who better to draw them out?" I ask.

"If someone were to attack you—"

"I don't have to go in my physical form."

He regards me, skepticism in the angle of his head. "You might project yourself into their midst, but will that not leave you weak again?"

"I cannot grow stronger if I don't practice."

He trains his attention forward, a discontented expression on his face. "We will put the question to Cosi."

We arrive at the council hall. Moru and a handful of tribal elders already assemble within. They greet me with nervous bows. Etricos has not yet arrived. I draw Moru aside to question the restive atmosphere.

"We did not expect so many captives," he says. "Our resources will not stretch much further."

He maintains a diplomatic calm. I have come to recognize this mannerism in him as indicative of unrest. "What is your true concern?" I ask.

Moru glances over my shoulder to where Demetrios eavesdrops on our conversation—on the pretense that he is my bodyguard and cannot leave my side, of course. I half-turn, trying to communicate with him to step away.

He arches his brows but receives my unspoken request. Silently he removes himself two feet. He can keep me within his sight while still allowing for a degree of privacy.

Moru observes this wordless interaction, but he refrains from commenting on it. His voice lowers to a whisper. "There is a higher ratio of men than expected. If we are not careful, we might offer the Bulokai free transport into our lands, and into our very city. Even if we keep them without the walls, there is nothing to prevent some in their ranks from slipping away and entering the city from the back. If they are allies, we need their strength as workers and warriors."

"How do you propose to discover their loyalties?" I asked.

He shakes his head. "We do not know, Goddess. We cannot continue to receive them into our care at this rate unless they are willing to work for their own fare, but it makes no sense for Agoros to send us those who would be a strength to us."

"Agoros will not send more captives when he realizes his encampments are compromised."

"Unless he wishes to use them as cover for his agents," Moru says darkly.

Across the hall, Etricos enters, his head high as he surveys the assembly of leaders. He hones in upon me almost immediately. If my private conversation with Moru bothers him, it does not show upon his face. He greets the other leaders as he passes. They follow in his wake. I can see a hierarchy of power before me: Etricos at the top, with Moru as a close second and the others tiered beneath.

"Goddess Anjeni, you honor us with your presence this morning," says Etricos, and he bows low before me.

Scratch my previous hierarchy. I'm at the top, with Etricos and Moru as my close seconds, at least as far as appearances are concerned. Etricos would not bow to me were it otherwise.

"Have you devised a means of assessing the rescued captives?" I ask, turning my full attention upon him.

He straightens with a guarded set to his shoulders. "We have already sent word to separate the women and children from the men, and to determine whether there are families among their ranks. They are less likely to be hostile to us if they are with their own people."

I nod. If Agoros did implant hostile agents in their midst, as Moru fears, they would be unconnected to the other refugees, strangers to their fellow captives unless he somehow recruited traitors from within the groups. Given his treatment of the people beneath his control, I feel this latter possibility to be improbable.

"We cannot continue to receive so many so quickly," one of the leaders behind Etricos says.

"The warriors we left behind to receive them have broken down the encampments," Etricos replies. "The last of them returned half an hour ago. We have taken the Bulokai tents they brought back with them directly to the refugee encampment, which should help with shelter."

A discussion of food and other resources follows this. I sidle up to Demetrios as I observe. His proximity calms my nerves—we are both outsiders to this meeting. Briefly he catches my hand in his, a momentary comfort to my inner turmoil, but he releases it again lest someone observe that minor intimacy between us.

I wish he had not let go. As a goddess, I should feel confident and composed. As a teenaged girl, I'm a fish out of water in a crowd of men. For the barest instant, my mind transports to the evening parties my family attended when I was growing up—those assemblies that masqueraded as recreational activities while providing yet another venue for politicians to bargain with one another. This era cannot afford such pretenses, but the bargaining is the same.

Tora enters the council hall, and Etricos breaks off conversation to meet her. Misting droplets of morning rain glisten against her dark hair.

"You've had a long night. You should be resting," her husband says.

She shakes her head. "You said we could assess the newcomers this morning." A hard look crosses his face—he doesn't want her involved—but she grasps his hand. "Cosi, let us see to the women and children, please. I'm not alone. A dozen of our kinswomen wait at the guardhouse to help. Do what you will with the men, but we cannot leave women and children outside the city walls, exposed to elements and attacks."

"It is a reasonable request," Etricos reluctantly says to Moru as he joins the pair.

"Send warriors with them," Moru replies, his hands folded in his sleeves.

I step forward to offer my presence as well, but Demetrios catches my arm and pulls me back. "Stay out of it," he whispers.

"Why?"

"Because you have other responsibilities, Goddess."

His use of my title instead of my given name raises my hackles. "Protecting the Helenai is my responsibility."

He tips his head in brief concession, but he still doesn't relent.

"What are you worried about?" I ask.

"If you venture beyond the city walls, you will be a target for anyone hostile to us."

"I don't have to go in my physical form."

"And that will drain you of your strength."

I purse my lips in a flat expression. "I'm getting better at it. The more I practice, the stronger I become."

"So you say. Your students expect more training this morning, Goddess."

"They can't practice in the rain. Most of them can't even manage a spark."

Our hushed back-and-forth has drawn attention from some of the tribal leaders, who regard us with suspicion. Demetrios flashes them a tight smile. Part of me wants to step away from him, to put some distance between us, but I hold my ground.

What do I care if rumors fly? Our relationship will become the ultimate in legendary gossip, so why should I try to prevent it?

"Goddess Anjeni," says Etricos from across the hall, "we go to inspect the newcomers. Will you come with us?"

A low growl sounds from Demetrios. I spare him a wry glance and say, "Yes, of course."

Moru and a handful of other leaders remain behind. The rest of us pass into the drizzling rain, headed for the city gates. Demetrios sidles up next to his brother to chastise him.

"If there are enemies among these newcomers, they will target the goddess in their midst."

Etricos slides a sideways glance at him, and that wordless acknowledgement speaks volumes. He knows I present a target. That's why he invited me: Tora will go beyond the city walls as well, and he wishes her safety above all else.

Demetrios glowers. It's nice that someone cares whether I live or die.

As we near the walls, several Helenai women join us, their heads shielded with scarves. A call to the guards signals for the gates to open. We pass through to the barren expanse beyond. To the left, a small encampment brims with activity. Warriors set up the stolen Bulokai tents amid the few mushroom-like Helenai ones already standing.

The assessment is a tedious endeavor, and one in which I play no part beyond onlooker. Tora and her band of helpers tend only to the separated women and children. In addition to physical needs, they determine languages and tribes, seeking to match these refugees with those tortured few who yet survive in Tora's infirmary, or with the larger tribes that earlier escaped the Bulokai.

These people have a strange tranquility to them, as though they are past feeling any pain or fear. What horrors have they already survived, to arrive at this dazed level of confidence?

"They did not need you here," Demetrios says. His grudging tone speaks of boredom.

"Perhaps not, but it is good for me to see." These liberated captives have no dire physical injuries, but they also have little in the way of worldly goods—only the clothes on their backs, and those clothes are in tatters. They receive meager rations of food with eager gratitude and divide the small portions between them as though they dine upon an enormous feast. I have never imagined such levels of abject poverty.

Etricos and most of his warriors remain among the separated men. Tora finishes her inspection of the women and children and joins him, but he quickly shoos her away. A short interchange ensues—she is pushing to help with the men as well. Her husband, short-tempered in his concern for her safety, denies the request and turns to escort her from the area himself.

One of the refugees moves in the midst of the men, his focus on the pair. Metal glints in his hand. A warning cry tears from my throat and an instinctive spell flashes from my outstretched fingers—

A split-second too late.

Tora crumples to the ground as my fourth intermediate strikes its mark. Her assailant jolts back into the crowd. Etricos shouts his beloved's name and Helenai warriors converge to protect him.

My feet pound across the sodden earth. Demetrios outstrips me, his sword in his hands, and plows into the clustered men. I stop short, my mind clouded as chaos sweeps through the encampment. A riot stands before me. Helenai warriors cut into the fray, forced to abandon their guard over Etricos. I pivot my attention to him instead.

"Tora, stay with me." He gathers his wife in his arms, her eyes wide with shock. A dark stain spreads against the rain-damped fabric of her dress, originating from the wound at her back, where a narrow blade protrudes.

"Get her into the city, quickly," I say.

He clutches her to him and lurches from the ground into a run.

Magic crackles from within the fray of rioting men. I whirl and turn it back upon its source. Power explodes and bodies fly. They crash upon the ground. I stalk into their midst, my mind aflame with seething fury.

I can discern the innocent from the enemy: one gibbers in fear while the other tenses to attack me off-guard. I strike any who dare to lift their eyes in defiance to the goddess of the Helenai and leave seventeen dead upon the ground.

In the aftermath, silence possesses the encampment. I scream—loud and long and hard.

CHAPTER THIRTY

K EENING PIERCES THE AIR, mourners in the crush of bodies that crowd the council hall. Tora lies at the head of the room in waxy stillness. Beside her, Etricos kneels, his gaze upon the ground, his body almost as motionless as his beloved wife's. He clasps one of her hands in his, her ashy skin a contrast to his bronze. Next to him, Huna grips his other hand and folds over herself in monumental grief.

This isn't how the story goes.

I know by now that the legends haven't gotten everything right, but this is too far outside the lyric narrative. Etricos rules Helenia with Tora by his side.

We have evidence of it in the National Archives.

Maybe the fog in my brain clouds my reasoning. I sit, dreamlike, at the head of the room but apart from the principal mourners. The goddess presides, but she does not participate. The other tribal leaders cluster near me, their faces drawn with somberness. The whole city cycles through to pay their respects, an endless line of grievers bearing condolences and offerings: flowers, trinkets, mementos of the deceased.

Divisive as Etricos has been among the tribes, Tora was universally loved. Aitana and Ineri escort her orphans through the line, and their sobbing faces might as well tear my heart from my chest. Everyone here has experienced death and destruction, but this is somehow worse.

A body settles beside me, and a hand thrusts a cloth into my line of sight. "Goddess Anjeni," Moru says, his voice hushed.

I stare at the cloth first and then up at him in confusion. He regards me with gentleness and pity. With a careful hand, he dabs my cheeks.

I blink and receive the cloth from his hand, completing the job myself. "Should a goddess not cry, Moru?"

His reply comes in a whisper, spoken in reverence. "Even the heavens weep tonight, Anjeni." He removes himself from my presence to join the other leaders.

Demetrios, on the far side of his brother, turns halfway to check on me. If I could banish the pain from his eyes, I would in a heartbeat. He sees my sorrow, matches it with his own, and returns to his vigil.

Tora was like a sister to him. She was a sister, mother, and daughter to everyone she encountered.

I can't break into the hysterics or moaning sobs that so many of the mourners indulge in. Moru has voiced his permission for my tears, but yet I must maintain some measure of dignity as a goddess amid humankind.

The wake lasts well into the night. Those closest to Tora linger the longest, finding solace in one another's company. The Helenai funeral tradition requires the family to remain with the body through the darkest hours, followed by a burial at dawn. There is no embalming, no preservation. They will wrap her in a shroud and commend her to the earth before a full day has passed.

I can't bear this. And, as I am not her family, I have no right to remain. When the crowds finally dissipate, I rise from my position and cross around to pay my last respects to a woman whose memory I have loved since I was a small child.

Etricos looks up with hollow eyes as I bow low before him.

"I am so sorry." The words feel cheap upon my tongue, but I don't know what else to say. He makes no reply. His fingers tighten around the cold hand in his grip.

"Goddess, you honor us," says Huna, her voice laden with emotions.

"No," I say, and tears brim anew in my eyes. "Huna, no. Tora honored everyone she encountered. Generations will sing of her goodness." She nods through her grief. We are crying together, and it will only get worse the longer I remain. I rub the back of my wrist across my eyes and straighten. "I will return to my tent."

Demetrios moves as though to accompany me, but I forestall him with one tense hand. Concern flashes across his face. I shake my head. In this moment, he belongs here with his brother, not trailing after the fickle, inept goddess who failed to prevent this tragedy.

He settles back upon the ground, and I withdraw.

Of one thing I am sure: this is my fault. Had I acted a split-second sooner, had I been more alert—

"Goddess, we will accompany you," says Moru. Four of them, tribal leaders, fall in step beside me. They carry a wide strip of heavy cloth upon four poles, shelter from the falling rain. "Do you sleep in your students' dormitory tonight?"

Word of my sleeping arrangements circulates through the tribal council, it seems. I wonder how much further the rumors travel.

But it doesn't matter, especially not tonight. "No. I go to my own tent."

My purpose in sleeping elsewhere, in having Huna sleep elsewhere, was to deprive Agoros of a ready, isolated target. If he shows up tonight, I will do everything in my power to shred him limb from limb.

Moru does not question the destination. We climb the hill in the dark and wet, a solemn procession headed for the two beacon braziers at the top. My ever-present guards bow their heads in deference as we pass. I speak quiet thanks to my escorts and slip inside the confines of my tent.

The place has a feel of abandonment to it. The fire pit at the center is cold, and only the patter of rain against the tent fabric meets my ears.

I deserve nothing better than this. A real goddess could have healed a knife wound on the spot instead of sending the victim to her hopeless and painful death. What use is magic, except to destroy?

In fury, I cast a third intermediate upon the coals. The fireball spatters and catches half-burned wood, splashing orange light through the tent.

"The goddess yet lives."

I whirl, my rage spiking dangerously. Agoros stands just within the entrance, shadows thick around him. The tension in his shoulders warns me against a rash attack: he is on his guard, ready to strike.

As am I.

"With the great mourning in the city, I assumed my agents had struck their proper target," he says. In our previous encounters he has been mocking, superior, arrogant. This time, he exercises caution. "Who did they strike instead? Etricos himself?"

"Etricos lives," I say.

Agoros shifts his gaze to my hand. I don't need to look to see what has drawn his attention. My beast of magic vents its frustration in a collection of flames that extend almost to my elbow.

"You can't attack me with that."

The thread of magic that projects him here extends to a place closer than ever before, though still afar. "Not yet. But I will."

He dismisses the threat. "If my men did not strike down Etricos or his lover, who did they kill? Or do I flatter myself that they succeeded in creating this great lamentation through the Helenai and her sister tribes?"

My eyes narrow as his words thrum through my head. Did he assume that Etricos and I were lovers? Is that why his agent honed in upon Tora? A case of mistaken identity? My guilt multiplies tenfold, but I will not give him the satisfaction of success.

"You flatter yourself," I say through gritted teeth. "Your agents are dead, to the last man. Come to me in person and I will provide you with the same service."

Something akin to admiration crosses his face. His gaze sweeps from my head to my toes and back again. "I think I have underestimated you too many times, goddess of the Helenai. Perhaps I should tame you instead of killing you after all."

My beast of magic snarls. I lunge, seeking that connecting thread to strike back along its path, but he vanishes before my eyes. The hint of a smile on his lips as he goes elicits a cry of wrath from my throat. I fling the magic from my arm into the fire pit. The flames erupt as high as my waist and spew embers into the air with a crackle.

In the aftermath, despair crashes down upon me. My knees buckle and hit the ground. I double over and pull at my hair, my carefully suppressed grief boiling over its confines.

Back in the council hall, with its crowds of onlookers, I could not give in to base emotions. Here, in the solitude of my own tent, I can wail and carry on until my heartbreak ebbs.

Though I'm not sure it ever will.

The dawning sun sees Tora consigned to her final resting place. She is not buried among the other dead on the far outskirts of the city. Instead, they give her a place of honor atop one of the solitary hills that roll softly toward the ocean. I can see the Eternity Gate in profile from her graveside, its solid arch swathed in gray mist. I search my mind for what stands upon this plot of ground in the modern world.

The National Cathedral, where heads of state are buried. My heart squeezes tight in my chest.

The salt-heavy wind ripples through the mourning party as the shrouded body lowers into the earth. Warriors cast dirt atop it. Huna leans upon Etricos's arm and sobs.

No one has slept. Remnants of grief—swollen eyelids and mouths pressed into thin lines—mark all of us. Aitana hangs upon Demetrios, her shoulders shuddering as she fights a wave of misery.

I'm so numb right now that I don't even care. At least she's not hanging on Etricos in his hour of bereavement.

As the dirt piles higher in the pit, I move away, my footsteps oriented toward my own tent. This signals others that they can leave, apparently, because the tribal leaders cluster around me like a protective guard. I glance back and make eye contact with Demetrios. He looks torn between accompanying me and remaining with his brother. I offer him a wan smile and continue on my path.

I can't face him right now anyway. Throughout the night, my remorse has blossomed like a rancorous weed in my heart. Agoros told his agents to kill the goddess of the Helenai, and he assumed that Etricos and the goddess were lovers. If Tora had been anywhere else, if I had approached Etricos to help with his cluster of refugees instead...

Hindsight has given me a thousand alternate ways to prevent her death. My insides gnaw upon themselves with guilt and worry. If the legend got Tora's death wrong, what else did it mistake? Or worse, have I triggered an alternate future? I have no certainty of success anymore. Everything I know is a lie.

The tribal leaders see me to my tent. I step inside and wait long enough for them to descend to the city before I slip back out again. I cross around to the back of my hill and settle in the dewy grass. Already the rising sun burns off the morning mist. The Eternity Gate stands across the basin from me, emblem of my journey here.

In times past, I drew comfort from its presence. No such comfort meets me now. It's too far removed from where I am.

I push off the hillside and trek down into the basin. The night's rainstorm flooded the area, but the water has mostly moved on. The season has created a thick layer of sludge. I remove my sandals and slog right through it, mud spattering my feet and ankles and squishing through my toes. Sick at heart, I climb the hill to the looming relic.

Its stones, cold to the touch, offer no consolation.

"What am I doing here?" I whisper the question, the words half-strangled. I'm little better than a child. Did the universe really entrust the founding of a nation into my hands?

A cry of frustration wrenches from my throat and I strike the arch. Pain lances from my fist up my arm.

It's nice to feel something. I strike again, and again, and finally bow my head against the stone monument.

There is no solace here. Even so, I settle between the two pillars as I did so often in my native time. I rest my head to one side, my eyes closed against the brightness of the morning sun.

Urgent footsteps draw them open again. Demetrios scales the hillside, his breath short in his lungs and panic on his face.

Dread strikes me like a lightning bolt. I sit up. "What's happened?"

He grasps my forearm and tugs me up from within the Gate, crushing me to him, burying his face against my neck. "You can't—you can't leave us, Anjeni."

I stand rigid with shock, unsure how to respond, taking comfort from his embrace and knowing all the while that I don't deserve it.

"I'm not leaving yet. The Gate is closed."

Had it been open, would I have passed through?

No. I owe this people my very life. I cannot go while they remain in peril.

Demetrios draws back and regards me. The raw concern in his eyes triggers my tears anew.

"I've ruined everything." My voice catches on a sob, but I'm going to burst if I don't confess to someone. "I'm sorry. I ruined everything. If someone else had come, someone wiser, someone who knew more than I did— It's all my fault. It should have been me, not Tora—"

He enfolds me in his arms again, pressing my head to his shoulder with a strong hand. "Hush, Anjeni."

But I don't deserve this comfort. I push away. "You don't understand. I can't do anything right. I've never done anything right in my life. Tora wasn't supposed to die!"

Stillness settles between us on that statement. Demetrios's hands close around mine, his face intent. "Death might come to any of us. It is the nature of this fight."

I rip away from him, up the hill through the Gate. Etricos said much the same thing in the conversation I overheard, and I don't like the remark any better when it's about Tora instead of me.

"You don't understand," I say.

He regards me with quiet patience. "Then explain it to me."

I toss my head, my gaze flitting across the scenery—the green, rain-soaked hills, the water-worn basins, the glittering ocean, and the tree line afar that marks the banks of the river. Tora's grave is a brown smudge atop a nearby hillside. The mourners have all returned to the city.

How will he react? If he knows the truth about me, how will he react?

But I can't have a lasting relationship with a man who believes I'm more than I really am.

A scoff cuts from my throat as this thought flits across my mind. Lasting relationship? I'm not supposed to have a lasting relationship with him. Why should I care if he knows the truth?

"I'm a fraud," I say. I chance a look at him. He takes one step up the hill toward me but catches himself. The intensity of his stare prods me to continue. "You already know I'm not a goddess, but it's much worse than that. Demetrios, I don't come from another world. I come from another *time*."

Confusion flashes across his face. He tilts his head to the right, his eyes in a contemplative squint.

"I will be born roughly seven hundred years from now, a citizen of the nation of Helenia. The Helenai are my ancestors."

The bald statement gives me pause. Oh, how I hope *he's* not my ancestor. I've kissed him. If we're directly related, that's just about the grossest thing I can think of. Why did that never occur to me before this moment?

He takes two more steps up the hill, though cautiously. I can practically see his brain turning over my statement, extracting its full import piece by piece. "And this is how you know things that only a goddess should know?"

I nod, backing up a pace to maintain a buffer between us.

"That doesn't make you a fraud. That makes you a miracle."

"I'm not—"

"The gods chose to send us living proof that we would triumph, that our people would survive. And we have survived because of you."

I shake my head. "No, Demetrios. You have survived in spite of me. That day I tumbled through the Eternity Gate, when I faced the demon champion on my own…" Uncertainty lances through me. I have acted brash and confident since my arrival here, and it was completely unfounded.

He takes that last step between us and closes his hand around mine, his fingers rough against my palm. "What is it?"

Tora lies cold in her grave. I meet his gaze, ready to receive punishment for my overconfidence. "That day was the first time in my life that I had ever used magic."

He guards his expression, but not enough to hide the surprise that flickers there. The hand that grasps mine is still, like a predator that watches its potential prey, taut with coiled energy that might spring at any moment.

"I was never a magician," I say, making the confession in full. "My parents forced me to learn the theories, but I had no spark—or not one that would respond. My sister was the magical genius; I couldn't even light a flame on a candlewick. The only reason my magic woke up that day is because I was that desperate not to die. You, Etricos, everyone—you have entrusted your future to a girl who knows nothing."

He blinks, and his grip on my hand tightens. "But you do know things, Anjeni."

I try to pull away, but he won't release his hold. "Don't you see? I'm barely eighteen. I have no experience. I've been figuring this out as I go."

"Then you're no different than we are," he says.

Shock squeezes my voice into a croak. "What?"

The corners of his eyes crinkle with a sardonic look. "You think Cosi knows what he's doing? The Bulokai slaughtered our tribal elders—our father included. We fled to this place as a last resort with only remnants of a once great people. You think he knows what he's doing, or that any of us do? You think I know?"

My chest tightens. "Yes," I manage to say, but my voice holds no certainty.

Demetrios leans in close, pinning me with his stare. "Survival was our only goal, Anjeni. We never thought we could conquer the Bulokai. We only wanted to survive, and we have done everything in our power—we were *that desperate not to die*."

He throws my own words back at me. I can't handle the tumult of emotions that they bring: fear, relief, gratitude, remorse, despair.

"But Tora—" I start, my tears welling anew.

Demetrios tugs me into another tight embrace, my head against his chest. He whispers comfort in my ear. "We all grieve for Tora. But if we give up hope, we dishonor her."

I relax in his arms, for the moment allowing the solace his presence brings. If we could remain like this forever, if there were no Bulokai, no Agoros, no impending death and destruction...

He withdraws far enough to cradle my face with one hand, running his callused thumb across my cheekbone. His gaze flits down to my mouth and back up again.

A blush floods over me, but when I try to push away, the hand on my back doesn't budge. "Demetrios," I say self-consciously, "you might be my great-great-something grandfather."

"I'm not," he says, with all the surety of someone who speaks only the absolute truth.

And he's probably correct. Nevertheless, I squirm. "You can't possibly know that, and neither do I."

He remains unmoved. "It's easy enough to know. I won't have children with anyone but you, and you can't be your own ancestor. Or, if you are, that's not my fault, is it?"

He's serious. What's more, he's going to kiss me on that magnificent pretzel of logic. My blush redoubles. "But what if—"

"Anjeni," he says, so close that our breaths mingle, "I don't want to repeat Cosi's mistakes."

The delays, the excuses, the need for everything to be perfect—Etricos had a scant few days with Tora when they might have married months or even years ago.

My heart is stronger than my head right now. I don't want to repeat Etricos's mistakes either. I wrap both arms around Demetrios and meet his mouth with mine.

CHAPTER THIRTY-ONE

"I WILL RAID THE BULOKAI HOLDINGS."

Etricos announces this to the tribal elders assembled in the council hall, his face a mask of solid indifference. A chill races down my spine. He only buried Tora this morning, and he makes this declaration before the sun has set. I look to his audience for their reaction and discover them equally unnerved.

"You must give yourself time to grieve," Moru says.

Etricos barely acknowledges the remark. "I will grieve in my own way. But I am done waiting here while the enemy encroaches upon our doorstep. I will take a party of warriors and raid the nearest Bulokai holdings. We will liberate the captive tribes and destroy the demons in their midst."

Moru only shakes his head. "The Helenai need their leader."

"This tribal council can fulfill that role," says Etricos without even a breath of hesitation. "The Helenai need not live separate from our allies. And more than a leader right now, they need a general who can protect them from tragedy and death. I will depart at daybreak with any warriors willing to take up the fight alongside me."

Someone further down the line of councilmen starts to protest. "But—"

"I'm not asking permission. I am informing you of my intent. I leave now to prepare." He sweeps from the council hall then, into the dying sunlight.

Several sets of eyes shift to me. I force a calm expression in spite of my thundering heart. Historically, Etricos liberates the captive tribes and unites them into a sovereign nation. It has to start somewhere.

"Goddess, what say you?" asks one of the leaders.

"Let him go."

Were Tora still alive, I could speak with more confidence. Instead, the phrase leaves my throat in a harrowed whisper. The outcome of Etricos's raids might be very different from the legends of my youth. I glance self-consciously toward Demetrios standing guard. He shows no sign of disagreement to my decree.

The tribal leaders murmur among themselves, some in support and some skeptical. One excuses himself from the group to convey this new development to his people. Others soon follow. As the council room empties, Demetrios leaves his post by the wall to stand beside me.

Moru hangs back from his fellow councilmen, looking as though he intends to leave but lagging further behind with every step. When the last man before him exits, he pauses, his hands in his sleeves as he studies the floor.

Demetrios helps me rise from my designated place at the head of the room. We approach the leader of the Terasanai, and I fully expect him to speak to me, but when he finally turns, his gaze instead hones in upon the warrior at my side.

"Will you go with your brother, or do you remain behind to take his position of leadership?"

Surprise laces through me. Demetrios stiffens his spine, and his hand upon my elbow goes still.

"I do not aspire to Cosi's position," he says.

Moru's gaze slides down to that slight contact between us and then back upward again. "Do you not?" Beside me, Demetrios bristles, but the leader of the Terasanai continues. "The people will follow the leader that our goddess chooses. They look to her for guidance. Naturally they will look to those around her for authority."

"I am a guard to the goddess," says Demetrios.

"And nothing more?" asks Moru.

Our intimate exchange at the Eternity Gate flits through my mind. Demetrios again pressed for marriage, but the only person I know to perform such a ceremony stands before us now as more of an adversary than a friend. I observe my guard—my lover, of a sorts—wondering how he will answer such a pointed query.

He does not answer at all.

Why does he not answer? He has been careless of rumors in the past. Why can he not state the truth?

Moru studies him with the eyes of a calculating politician. "I would not oppose you in your brother's place. I believe you would lead your people well, Demetrios."

"Dima." The tone of his voice makes me jump. His correction comes with a scowl etched deep upon his face.

His open hostility has no visible effect upon Moru, who only inclines his head. "My apologies. I sometimes forget that Helenai warriors are so particular about the use of their proper names."

I frown and look from one man to the other in confusion.

Demetrios keeps his gaze fixed upon the leader of the Terasanai, his every muscle taut. "I do not seek my brother's position."

"And yet it may come to you more readily than you expect." Moru adjusts his hands in his sleeves and turns to leave the hall, but he pauses for one final glance upon us. "If you do not seek power, Dima, you should not be so familiar with those who possess it, particularly at such a critical time as this. As I said, I would not oppose you, but a goddess's lover will always outrank a mere mortal, be that mortal his elder brother or anyone else."

He exits to the dusky streets, leaving us alone. Demetrios stands a monument of injured pride and close-kept anger. And I—

I don't know what to feel. A chasm yawns within me where my heart was only moments ago. I see the logic of Moru's words, the inherent warning. The people of this city look to me for protection, and they will look to any lover I have as one who holds inherent authority.

I'm not a private citizen. With Tora's death, Etricos is at his most vulnerable, and a transition of power could easily occur.

"I will speak with Cosi," Demetrios says. He starts for the door, but I snatch his wrist in both hands. He looks down at my grip and back up again.

That movement was on instinct. I fumble for an explanation to justify it, but ultimately abandon the attempt. "What will you say to him?"

He looks me straight in the eyes. "I will go with him."

"And so will I."

Demetrios opens his mouth to deny me, but the words stick in his throat. With a curt nod, he twists his wrist to catch one of my hands and pull me after him to the exit.

As we step onto the public street, he drops that contact.

Because he does not seek his brother's position. He will maintain his distance from the goddess whose favor would grant it to him.

Stupid, prideful man. Stupid, goddess-fawning society.

A rift grows between us as we progress up the street to the guardhouse. I do understand the logic, but my emotions are in shambles. An hour ago we stood in perfect harmony with one another, and now we cannot even make eye contact for fear of what others might think.

I maintain the silence until I can bear it no more, and then I only speak to distract my thoughts away from hurt feelings. "What did Moru mean, about Helenai warriors and their proper names?"

Demetrios, who searches the darkening street for signs of his brother, spares me a sidelong glance. "Warriors of the Helenai use their proper name only on formal occasions: birth, marriage, death. Our leader uses his when dealing with leaders from other tribes."

Meaning that Moru, in calling Demetrios by his proper name, acknowledged him as a leader in his brother's stead. No wonder the correction, then.

"Why did no one tell me? I've always called you Demetrios."

"You are a goddess. We do not dictate how the gods address us as mortals."

His careful indifference cuts me like a knife. "Dima," I say on impulse, a rebuke in my voice.

He turns like a whip, as though he might shield my use of that nickname from any onlookers. "Anjeni, please. The Helenai need my brother. I need him. Please, do not undermine him. I did not think—"

"You didn't think that intimacy with a goddess would have political consequences?" Disappointment, like a dead weight, presses upon me.

If he must choose between me and the Helenai, he will choose the Helenai. It's the choice I would have him make, too, but that doesn't stop the pain of rejection. It squeezes my heart like an overripe tomato.

"It should have no political consequences," says Demetrios. "Once Cosi returns to his right mind, no one will question his authority. Until then, I must support him as our leader. And so must you. Please."

"I understand." I speak the words with fatalistic resignation and slip around him to continue up the street. I do understand. The timing between us is off. But it was always off and—assuming that the legends get our story correct—it always will be.

I retreat behind my mental fortress, crushing my emotions back into the box I should have kept them in all along. I'm not sorry I let them out. Love unfulfilled is still love and I am a better person for it.

Which is scant consolation as the somber night descends around us.

"The goddess must remain here." Etricos doesn't even look up from the weapons inventory he pores over. Behind him, warriors assemble gear and tack in preparation for their early morning departure.

"I can help you, Etricos," I say. "It won't be like last time."

"It won't, because you're not coming. Dima, I will be glad to have you."

"But—"

"Goddess Anjeni," he says, and at long last he meets my gaze with his solemn eyes, "the tribal leaders have pledged the bulk of their warriors to me with the understanding that you will remain behind to protect the city. If the Bulokai send more agents into our midst, you alone are strong enough to fend them off."

We have discussed raids before, and we have discussed me staying behind for this very reason. Why, then, do I feel like I'm being pushed aside when I could be of better use?

"Give me your more advanced students instead," Etricos says, and the statement jars me from my introspection.

"What?"

"Aitana, Ria, Ineri, and any others you feel would be skilled enough. We do not have the luxury of hiding our spark-bearers anymore. We will strike the enemy as hard as we can."

I lean close to argue. "If that is the case, I should come with you."

"No. You protect the people here. We must defend as well as attack."

Again, he pushes me aside.

"Anjeni, he's right," says Demetrios.

A hint of betrayal winds through me. "You would take untried spark-bearers into battle, then?"

Etricos has returned to his weapons inventory. "We must try them at some point. Please don't argue. If you wish to support me, give me your best students and keep the people here safe."

He does not meet my gaze again. I swallow the bitterness that wells in my throat. A glance toward Demetrios reveals mingled regret and apology upon his face, but his eyes silently plead for me to avoid conflict.

"You will use wisdom in your attacks." I intentionally phrase the statement as a command.

"Of course," says Etricos, still engrossed in his task.

My voice hardens. "I mean it. If you sacrifice my spark-bearers unnecessarily, if you run headlong into a fight to soothe your broken heart—"

His head snaps up, jaw clenched and anger flashing through his eyes, a dangerous warning for me not to approach that sensitive subject.

It is enough. The deadly determination within him eases my fears. "I will send you my intermediates, Etricos. May you have good fortune in your battles."

His expression does not soften. "Thank you," he says as he returns to his preparation.

I spin on my heel and leave the guardhouse. Demetrios follows, but I tell him, "You should stay here."

"I will see you to your students."

"I plan to instruct them before I give them to you."

"All the more time I can spend with you before I leave," he says. After a glance up and down the dark street, he squeezes my hand.

I'm under too much stress to control my instinct for sarcasm. "Oh, did you want to spend time with me?"

Demetrios suppresses a smile and guides me up the street. He keeps close enough that he could saddle an arm around my shoulder as we walk. He doesn't, of course, but his nearness alone is almost good enough.

The streets lie deserted in the early evening shadows, but lamplight shines in the windows we pass and illuminates the handful of tents that yet remain. Tora's home, further up the road, has no light, no warmth.

I draw a fraction closer to Demetrios and clasp his hand tight in mine. "What happened to all of the children she cared for?"

He peers down at me. "The other tribes have stepped forward to help."

"And where is Huna?" I have not seen Tora's grandmother since the burial at dawn.

"At the infirmary, tending to the injured in Tora's place."

Of course. Tora and Huna were cut from the same cloth.

We pass the darkened house and continue to the first of my students' dormitories. Light blazes bright through their window covering. Demetrios knocks, and voices within hush a split-second before Aitana opens the door.

Her instinctive smile dies when she notices me behind him. With a formal bow she says, "The goddess truly honors us with her presence."

I'm not in the mood for her sullen sarcasm. I sweep past her into the room and survey its occupants. Ria is here, along with several of the other intermediates. Most of the younger ones occupy the second dormitory. I assume that Ineri is with them.

I lock my gaze upon Ria, who has trouble maintaining eye contact. "Etricos leaves at dawn with a company of warriors to strike against the Bulokai. He has requested spark-bearers to accompany him. Are you willing?"

Ria stiffens with resolve. "Yes, Goddess."

At the door, Aitana says, "Of course we are."

I spare her a sidelong glance and pass my attention to the rest of the girls. "Anyone who has reached proficiency in the fourth intermediate is eligible. Aitana, Ria, and Ineri will continue your training in the fifth, sixth, and seventh as you travel."

Aitana starts in surprise. "Goddess, you don't come?"

Again I glance at her, my spine straight and my chin up.

Demetrios answers for me. "The goddess Anjeni must protect the city. The other tribes have pledged their warriors on condition that she remain."

An eager gleam lights Aitana's eyes. Away from my presence she can shine—for Etricos and Demetrios both—but this is war, not a petty competition. I shift my attention to my other students.

"Who among you is willing to go?"

Nine raise their hands, in addition to Aitana and Ria. Two of them I know for a fact are stuck on the third intermediate. I cull them from the group with a promise that I will prepare them to join the next excursion. To the others, I say, "Etricos and his warriors leave at dawn. Report to the guardhouse nearest the city gates for your further instructions."

I exit as quickly as I came, with Demetrios beside me. Aitana, unbidden, dogs our steps to the next dormitory, where I repeat the call to Ineri and those within her charge. The students here are less skilled. Aside from Ineri, only two others qualify.

"Will a dozen spark-bearers be enough?" she asks, nervousness bleeding from her.

"You will have to take care of one another," I say. "You, Ria, and Aitana are the only ones who have started into the superlatives. Practice as often as you can. Don't overexert yourselves. Help the others grow stronger, and keep them safe in battle."

She nods, protective arms looped around the pair that has volunteered to come with her. As I depart, Aitana says, "I am the most skilled of your magicians, Goddess. Does that not make me the leader?"

I stop and pin her with a steady gaze. "You share that responsibility with Ria and Ineri."

"But—"

"I don't trust you, Aitana." My jaw tightens as I strive to keep my temper in check. "If you can learn to put the welfare of those beneath you above your own conceit, you may one day make an excellent leader. Right now you are too eager to showcase your abilities—"

"How dare you," she utters, her fists clenched to her sides. "How dare you accuse me of such a thing."

I refuse to rise to her provocation. "You are gifted with magic, but you allow jealousy to cloud your decisions." Demetrios lays a hand on my elbow as though to draw me away from the confrontation, but I shake him off. "If calamity befalls, if the Bulokai kill those in your charge, will you also take full responsibility for their deaths?"

She lifts her chin in the air. "I won't allow anyone to die."

A scoff cuts from my throat. Tora's fatal end flashes through my mind, and tears sting my eyes. "You think you have that level of control? On the battlefield, death can occur in a split-second, right beneath your very gaze, before you even have a chance to blink. You are over-confident."

Aitana presses her mouth in a firm line.

And people accuse me of stubbornness. "There is no dishonor in sharing leadership with Ria and Ineri. If you cannot do that much, you are unfit to lead at all."

I turn from her and head up my hill. Behind me, Demetrios quietly advises her to report to his brother. I have no doubt that Etricos will override my decision and put her in charge of the other spark-bearers. I only hope we have no cause to mourn that override afterward.

Sunlight pierces the horizon. Etricos with his band of warriors already thunders across the plain. I observe from one of the watchtowers with Moru and several other tribal leaders. A hundred warriors and a dozen spark-bearers plunge into the vast Bulokai territory, there to strike against our enemy by whatever means they can.

I should be with them, but I remain behind, a weapon of defense instead of offense.

As the dark line crosses beyond sight, I descend the ladder to the street below. The handful of warriors who remain in the city will share Demetrios's post while he is gone. One of them follows me up my hill. I dismiss him when my own tent looms before me. The guards outside my fence have received other assignments, on my request. A goddess who defends an entire city does not need token sentinels outside her home.

With their more advanced members gone, my students require all my attention. We practice fundamentals on the hillside until the afternoon clouds gather in darkening knots. I move our lessons indoors, to the closest dormitory. The sky rumbles and lightning spiderwebs out as the first fat drops of rain hit the ground.

My heart is leagues away, with the company that rides out in the elements.

Three days pass with no word. "The Bulokai have camps in this region, but the nearest settlements are at least half a week away," Moru says when I ask him what we should expect. "If Etricos means to liberate them, we must give him more time than this."

I worry that Agoros will trample the small army. The anxiety eats at me, and every spare moment I have I spend wandering the hills beyond our city—in spirit form.

I can project myself as far as the river to the north, and out upon the plains to the south. Each day I push those boundaries further, creating a quick surveillance of our territory as I jump from one point to the next. Within the city, rumors abound of the goddess who appears and disappears in the blink of an eye. Huna tells me the stories over our evening meals, and then she scolds me for my instinctive grin.

"You should not terrorize your own people, little goddess."

"I'm not terrorizing them."

"You look like an emissary of death with the black flames of the netherworld licking the air around you. And you *like* it." She pokes me in the ribs to drive home this point.

I drape an arm around her shoulder and pull her into a lopsided embrace. "I do it for the Helenai, Huna."

She snorts, ever the skeptic.

By week's end, I can walk among the scorched, abandoned enemy camps that used to mark the borders of our safe haven. Each sits atop a hillside that allows me far-spreading views of alien scenery beyond. My daily surveillance changes accordingly.

Ten days after the company departs, a single rider streaks across the rain-soaked plains. I see him from one of these hills, and the terror that strikes my heart wrenches me back to the confines of my tent. I sit up amid shadows, trying to calm my racing pulse.

Logically, this is a messenger. He bore no marks of the Bulokai, and it makes sense that Etricos would communicate with us, especially after so long an absence. But fear for the group—for Demetrios, more than anything else—shatters my concentration. I tear from my cot and throw on a hooded cloak and shoes. My students practice fundamentals and intermediates in their dormitories during the afternoon rains. Light flashes against their cloth-covered windows as I pass.

Below, in the city, I sludge through muddy streets to the council hall. Moru and a handful of others sit within, discussing the growing city. They pause as I enter.

"A rider comes," I say. "He should be here in another two or three hours."

They exchange nervous glances. "Is he friend or foe?" Moru asks.

"It looks like one of Etricos's men—a messenger, I presume. We cannot be sure until he arrives."

They set aside their local business and prepare instead for this rider's advent, sending word to the other tribal leaders and to the city guards upon their watchtowers.

In my modern era, communications take place at the click of a button and one may travel miles in only a few minutes. Here, where nothing travels faster than the speed of a horse, my impatience builds and my mind flits through a dozen or more terrible possibilities.

Failures, deaths, destructions.

Perhaps he is the last survivor, come with warning that Agoros leads an army of thousands to destroy us. And that would mean that Demetrios—

I box my emotions from following this train of thought. I cannot invest in anticipatory grief.

When the watchtowers finally trumpet their signal, I'm almost ready to die from the dread. The tribal leaders file into the council hall one by one to take their places. I sit in my designated spot, a token guard nearby.

And we wait.

Except that I'm so tired of waiting. I lean back against the wall and shut my eyes. In an instant, I am at the city walls, watching as the rider pulls up before the gate. Dusk and shadow obscure me from his view. From above, a soldier calls down for identification.

He gives his name and says, "I bear a message from Etricos of the Helenai."

The gates shudder and part wide enough for the rider to pass. He gallops through, and I recede to my body in the council hall. I open my eyes to a ring of councilmen. Moru alone glances at me, concerned.

I arch my brows and he turns his attention forward, the lines of his face smoothing. He alone in the room realizes that I was not entirely there.

Outside, horse hooves clatter to a stop and a parlay of voices ensues. The rider enters, wind-swept and bedraggled, with a pair of soldiers behind him. From the depths of his layered clothing, he produces a sealed and folded letter, which he presents to the council with deep reverence.

Etricos sends word of victory.

The tension in the room breaks as relief smothers us all. The rider precedes a supply of provisions and cattle, tributes offered from two of the conquered Bulokai holdings. The liberated people have pledged their loyalty to the Helenai.

I fight the sudden urge to cry. The legends were correct in this measure, at least.

The council piles questions upon Etricos's messenger, demanding details of the raiding band of warriors.

He bows low. "We owe our victories to the goddess Anjeni." Shock jolts through me at the sound of my own name. The warrior continues. "Word of her power spreads across the land. The demon soldiers of the Bulokai cannot abide the spark. They flee and perish before us at the first sign of magic in our midst."

"What of the Bulokai magicians?" I ask.

"We have encountered none."

The absence of magicians strikes me as suspicious. Even as my worry mounts, Moru speaks.

"Agoros keeps his spark-bearers close to him, goddess. They are not as plentiful as it may seem."

The dozen that approached our very doorstep were an anomaly, in other words.

The meeting disperses. The rider leaves to rest, and the tribal leaders carry news of Etricos's success to their respective quarters of the city.

The next day brings a caravan of wagons brimming with supplies—sacks of grain, crocks of oil, dozens of chickens in cages—along with herds of cattle that extend in a straggling line toward the horizon: sheep, cows, oxen, pigs.

The city rejoices at its sudden fortune. The council frets over where to store such wealth. They divide the goods among the households, so that hardly a yard exists that does not harbor an animal or two.

Agoros will not take this blow well. I resume my vigil upon the surrounding hills.

CHAPTER THIRTY-TWO

—⸘⸙⸘—

WIND SWEEPS THE FAR-FLUNG PLAINS, and the tall grass rolls like ocean waves. In my projected form, I feel nothing but the cot against my back in my tent miles away. Another ten days has passed, and I have expanded my range. I walk amidst foreign scenery, ever alert for intruders.

Twice I have discovered clusters of Bulokai agents sneaking onto our lands. Twice I have eliminated them. I cannot dwell on the blood I shed but keep my emotions tightly compartmentalized. Even so, their faces haunt me, the killer who fells them with deadly precision.

Use of magic in this form, even the lower intermediates, still saps my strength in the blink of an eye. Huna scolded me the first time she found me in a near-comatose state. Now she does not leave my side.

I crest a hilltop, black flames bleeding from me. A rumble of galloping horses carries on the wind. Alarm mounts within me. Is this Agoros come to take his revenge?

But the host that crosses the gentle valley below has too few in its numbers to be the great army of the Bulokai. I recognize, too, the proud leader at its head.

Etricos returns triumphant.

Someone in their midst spies me. A cry cuts through their ranks and dozens of heads peer toward my hilltop. I gather my strength and push my projection closer to them.

Etricos pulls his horse to an abrupt stop. He schools his shock when he recognizes me and inclines his head in greeting.

"Goddess Anjeni."

"Etricos, well met," I say. Briefly I allow myself to survey the men behind him. Demetrios is not among the front lines. Neither are my spark-bearers. I hope they are further within the crowd. "Do you return to the city, or do you only cross through to another destination?"

He smiles. "We return, Goddess, but briefly."

A rider urges his horse through the company, Demetrios forcing his way to the front. I fight the instinctive relief that bubbles within me as he reins in beside his brother.

A scowl marks his face. "Anjeni, who is with you?"

I arch my brows. Huna is there, but I suddenly don't want to tell him that. Before I can formulate a cheeky response, Aitana emerges from the crowd and directs her horse alongside Demetrios's. She lifts her nose proudly, but the reins in her hands betray a tremor of nerves.

"I trust all my spark-bearers are safe," I say to her.

She spares a self-conscious glance toward Etricos and Demetrios, but she wordlessly nods.

"Injuries are part of battle, goddess," says Etricos. "Not a man among us has escaped unscathed."

Meaning some of my students are injured. "And how many men have you lost?" I ask.

His jaw tightens. "Fourteen."

Fewer than I feared, but more than we can spare. "We will honor them as heroes. The city will rejoice at your return, Etricos."

He banishes the instinctive wistfulness that flashes through his eyes. "We stop only briefly, and then we leave again."

I'm not surprised. He has no reason to stay.

"I will instruct the people to prepare for your arrival. May you have swift travels to our gates."

"Thank you, Goddess Anjeni."

Demetrios opens his mouth to speak, but his brother spurs his horse with a cry to continue. As the host rushes upon my projected form, I wink to the shadowed confines of my tent on its hilltop above the city miles away. I open my eyes and allow them to adjust. On the other side of the fire, Huna chops carrots to add to the broth that bubbles over the pit.

"Etricos is coming."

Her hand stills. She observes me as I sit up, her expression frozen. "How soon?" she manages to ask.

I can't be too sure about distances, but I take a guess. "They're within twenty miles, I think. I will tell the tribal elders to prepare."

She sets the knife aside and starts to rise, intent upon running the errand for me.

I stand, waving her back to her task. "Stay here. I didn't overextend myself. The walk down to the city will do me good."

"How am I to face him, little goddess?" Her earnestness pierces through me. In the time since Tora's death, she has had too many opportunities to brood.

"He blames himself, Huna," I say, careful of her trampled emotions.

She shakes her head. "I kept them apart for so long. He must blame me for that, and he should."

"He blames himself." I harden my voice on that phrase. Too many of us carry this burden of responsibility. "Most likely, he expects you to blame him as well."

Huna looks up with watery, stricken eyes. Sudden tears prickle at the corners of my own. I cross to her and envelop her in a fierce hug. "I am sorry," I whisper. "If I had power to change it, I would."

She pats my head, for the moment accepting my sympathy, but her gruff exterior soon returns. She pushes me away. "Go to the tribal elders, little goddess. The city must properly receive its heroes."

I retreat, obedient to her command.

The news spreads from the tribal elders to the people, who abandon their usual tasks to prepare a celebration. Hours later, as the afternoon clouds roll across the sky, the guards in the watchtower blast a signal. People gather to the gates, anticipation thick upon them.

As Etricos and his company pass from the plains to the city, the throng roars with joyful welcome. The force of their ardor reverberates through the council hall where I wait.

Moru insists that a goddess does not descend to her warriors, but that they must ascend to her. He and the other tribal leaders clot the entrance to the hall. Huna and I sit within. For the sake of peace alone, I opt not to project my terrifying black-flamed image to the streets, but this blind anticipation might be the death of me.

I've already spoken with Etricos. Demetrios is more my concern. I cannot entirely banish the fear that nearly three weeks apart has irreversibly altered the relationship between us. It seems like eons have passed in that short span.

A stir of movement draws my attention. Tribal leaders back through the doorway to create a path, and Etricos ducks into the hall. Demetrios and Aitana come three paces behind him, together. My heart drops at how natural they look beside one another. I fix my gaze upon the leader of the Helenai, holding my emotions in tight check.

Etricos approaches my position at the head of the room but pauses halfway. He bows low, a sign of reverence. The council hall is a theater now, where onlookers crowd in the door to glimpse the interaction between their tragic hero and the goddess who favors him.

Demetrios and Aitana mirror their leader's action, though Demetrios chances to make eye contact with me as he bends. Simple though that gesture is, it eases the turmoil in my heart. If his concern for me is only pretend, he is a magnificent actor.

"Goddess Anjeni, we greet you upon our return," Etricos says. He and his two subordinates remain in their bent position, and I realize a split-second later that they await for my command to straighten again.

Because this is a theater.

"Rise, Etricos of the Helenai."

He obeys. Demetrios and Aitana each take this as cue to do the same.

Etricos steps away from them. "We bring you tidings of much success, Goddess, and of much yet to accomplish. By virtue of your name, we have rid ten settlements of the demons of the Bulokai and struck a decisive blow to Agoros and his brutal reign. Our newly liberated allies swear fealty to the goddess Anjeni of the Helenai and even now gather their strength to join us in further campaigns against our mutual enemy."

Were we supposed to prepare speeches? I wish someone had told me. "You have done well, Etricos," I say, feeling my own lack of eloquence next to his grandiose display.

"Thanks to you, Goddess." He bends his head in humble acknowledgement, which sets me wondering what new game he plays.

"And what yet lies ahead?" I ask.

"I desire to counsel with the goddess and the tribal leaders on that matter, if it please you."

As if I would tell him no, the manipulative goat. "Do you first require rest and refreshment, Etricos?"

"I do not. I trust that my men and your spark-bearers will receive according to their needs, but the war we wage presses upon me greater than any earthly comforts."

He wants to counsel immediately, then. I order it to be so. The tribal leaders assemble, and the onlookers retreat to the celebration that still flourishes in the streets. A trumpet sounds, and someone beyond the door announces that the goddess and her chosen servants meet together.

My legend writes itself before my very eyes.

Demetrios and Aitana remain for the council. They have acted as Etricos's seconds in battle and hold place at this meeting. Aitana seats herself between the pair of brothers, her expression defiant, as if she expects me to order her away.

I won't. If anything went wrong with my spark-bearers, I want her held accountable in front of an audience.

I half-expected Demetrios to resume his usual position as my guard. From the way Moru glances from me to the stoic warrior and back again, he expected it as well. No wonder Demetrios remains near his brother.

Or perhaps he remains for Aitana's sake.

The philandering cad.

I choke back a laugh at my heart's readiness to condemn him. We sit in tribal council to discuss a war. My petty jealousy can take a back seat for an hour.

On my direction, Etricos gives his further report. Though he does not sit at the head of the room, he commands the attention of all, a true leader in their midst.

"The Bulokai are in upheaval, Goddess. The demon soldiers cannot abide the spark. They flee before us without a fight, leaving only token garrisons of foot soldiers behind. Our first battles were hard won, but as word spread that a goddess had granted spark-bearers to the Helenai, our enemies' fear undermined their prowess. A week ago, we took three settlements in two days, with not a man lost in those skirmishes."

"The demons fear the spark to that degree?" Moru asks, his gaze intent.

"Even the feeblest attack can fell them," says Etricos. "We know that Agoros and his predecessors rooted out spark-bearers for decades. These demon soldiers appeared only after they would face no threat of enemy magicians, and they refuse to fight in a battle where such enemies exist. It was thus when the goddess first arrived: those demons that she did not slay fled from her sight, though they still numbered in the hundreds."

"Had we known their fear of magic to run so deep, we might have struck the Bulokai sooner," one of the tribal leaders says.

Etricos nods. "Truly the presence of a goddess within this city keeps these demons far from us. Agoros has sent only human agents against us since that first battle, but this was by necessity rather than stratagem. The demons will not fight. Even now, they rebel. The Bulokai soldiers we captured confirmed as much. The demons believed our goddess's influence to be contained to our territory here at the ends of the earth. They consider the existence of additional spark-bearers a betrayal of a covenant between them and Agoros."

"The demons and the magicians of the Bulokai never mingled," Moru says, a frown upon his face as he muses upon this revelation. "I cannot think that I ever saw them work together."

"We always assumed unity in the ranks of the Bulokai," one of his peers adds, equally bewildered.

Etricos leans into the circle, eagerness on his face. "We assumed what does not exist. Agoros has knit together forces that refuse to mix, and it appears that he did so on the pretext that they would never have to deal with one another, or with enemies of the same skill. With magicians on our side, we have an opportunity to strike and to strike hard."

Moru stiffens, wary. "What is your plan?"

Because we all know Etricos has one.

"In three days' time, I meet our newly freed allies at the Red Cliffs, to the north. I have promised to bring them weapons and armor. If rumor is true, Agoros himself marches with a horde of Bulokai warriors to squash our uprising. We will meet him and destroy him."

"Our numbers are yet too few to meet the Bulokai," says Moru. "Even without their demon fighters, they are many. Agoros will have spark-bearers in his company."

"He is a spark-bearer himself," I say. All eyes in the room turn to me, but I fix my gaze upon Etricos. I'm fairly sure I know what he plans to do, but I will allow him to ask rather than volunteering for the role I must play.

Etricos tips his head. "If we have a goddess in our company, even the legions of Agoros stand no chance."

Voices ring out, protests of alarm. They clamor roughly the same question:

"If the goddess Anjeni leaves us to meet the Bulokai, what protection will we have?"

Etricos raises his hands for everyone to remain calm. He pitches his words above the din. "If we destroy Agoros upon the plains, we will have no need of divine protection here. If we fail, he marches for the city anyway. It is better to keep the conflict away from our people, away from our women and children."

Their alarm does not dissipate. Moru adds fuel to the fire with a quiet observation.

"It seems the best choice. If our goddess cannot defeat Agoros of the Bulokai in battle, she would also fail to protect this city should he come upon it in the fullness of his wrath."

A stricken silence possesses the room as, again, all eyes fix upon me.

This weight of responsibility might kill me before I come anywhere near Agoros. My throat, tight with sudden panic, refuses to work any words. I breathe a deep inhale.

The legends say that the goddess aided Etricos in his quest to defeat the demon hordes, and I know from my time that his campaign succeeds.

But I *am* the goddess, and the possibility for failure wracks my nerves.

Even so, I swallow my apprehension and replace it with pretended confidence. "You speak wisdom, Etricos of the Helenai. I will go with you. Together we will eliminate Agoros and his Bulokai warriors from the face of the earth."

I sound so much more arrogant than I feel. Etricos dips his head in approval, and my anxiety eats me alive from the inside out.

CHAPTER THIRTY-THREE

—⁂—

My spark-bearers have injuries, more than simple scrapes and bruises. By the time I arrive in the dormitory where they congregate, their fellows already treat their wounds with herbs and fresh bandages. I come alone: Etricos will want to speak with me in private, but he cannot request such an audience without raising suspicions, and right now the tribal leaders waylay him with questions and concerns. Demetrios remains with him, which means that Aitana lingers there as well.

I survey the eleven newly returned spark-bearers before me. They bow their heads in reverence, even in the midst of their treatments. From Etricos's report, I expected cuts and gashes, but most of the injuries I can see are burns, evidence of magic encountered. Or mishandled.

And I can guess who to hold accountable for that, but she's not here for me to scold.

I frown upon Ria and Ineri as they bind the blistered arm of one of the youngest who traveled among them. Ria refuses to meet my gaze. Ineri glances up, contrition written on her face.

"Etricos reports that you did not engage with any Bulokai magicians," I say. "How, then, came my spark-bearers to receive such wounds?"

Ria shoots a warning glance to her peer, but Ineri lifts her chin in defiance. "Goddess, Aitana insisted on instructing in the superlatives as we traveled."

"The younger spark-bearers *begged* her," Ria says, but she speaks to Ineri rather than to me.

"And *I* told her they were not ready," Ineri retorts, her low voice simmering with anger.

Meaning that Aitana took the position of leadership after all. I knew that Etricos would elevate her above the others, but irritation lances through me anyway. "Did I not send you three as equals?"

Resentment dances across Ineri's face. "Aitana is of the Helenai. Ria and I are not."

I wave aside her words. "Aitana is no more Helenai than you are. The tribe took her under their protection as they did you."

"She is the strongest of all your spark-bearers, goddess," Ria says.

I wonder at her willingness to defend her perceived superior. "Strength and wisdom do not travel hand in hand. She does not understand how to teach because she does not struggle enough to learn. I made you her equals to keep her folly in check."

"She would not listen," says Ineri, her brows drawn together in a frown.

The beast within me prowls its cage. "And the weakest among you paid the price."

Between them, the injured spark-bearer chokes back a sob, tears welling in her eyes. I crouch to her level, drawing upon one of the worst manipulative tactics that my father's example taught me.

With a gentle hand on the girl's shoulder, I meet her gaze and ask in all compassion, "Do you understand now why patience is so necessary?"

Kindness is a weapon of the very worst order. It drives its point into the soul.

My pupil bursts into tears with a gibbered nod. I gather her up in my arms and drop a kiss on her forehead, considering what more to say. I care about my spark-bearers—so much so that it surprises me. They delight in their talents, eager to study and to improve. I don't want to kill that fervor, but it does require corralling.

"It is good that you want to learn. The order of the principles is not to hold you back, but to keep you safe."

She nods again, murmuring apologies. I withdraw from her and look to Ria and Ineri for any last words.

Ria hugs her arms to her chest, defensive. "Most of them were able to work the superlatives we taught, Goddess."

"But they had not the control they needed to work them properly."

A blush stains her cheeks. She looks away and mutters, "Even you have overextended your abilities at times."

Ineri hisses. "Ria!"

"She's correct," I say. My spark-bearers turn upon me a wondrous gaze, the room at a stricken hush. "I have overextended my abilities. But I have never allowed or encouraged those beneath me to do the same. If a goddess sacrifice herself for her people, that is her right. I know the boundaries of what is safe because I have walked their length."

Not to mention that I witnessed years upon years of magic students who tried to advance beyond their abilities, only to receive injuries similar to those before me now.

The rules exist for a reason. Rivers must always run their designated course.

And volcanos can forge what paths they see fit, but I'm not going to tell my students that.

The door behind me opens: Etricos, with Demetrios and Aitana at his heels. I straighten in a slow, controlled movement, favoring him with an unspoken question.

"The spark-bearers ensured our victory, Anjeni," he says, dispensing with all of the pomp and ceremony he stood upon less than half an hour ago. "They deserve your praise for their valiant efforts."

Aitana stands proudly rigid, ready for the rebuke she assumes I will give.

I oblige her. "They have done well. They would have done better had Aitana kept them safe within the bounds of their abilities."

Anger flushes her cheeks. She opens her mouth for a hot reply, but Etricos speaks ahead of her.

"Anjeni, I—"

"These are *my* spark-bearers, Etricos," I interrupt, my spine straight. "I only lent them to you. Their worst injuries come not from the enemy, but because one who I instructed to protect them willfully endangered them instead."

"I spoke with Aitana when the incident occurred. It will not happen again."

"No, it won't, because I go with you myself this time."

Etricos inclines his head, acknowledging my words. Beside him, Aitana trembles with rage. Tears shimmer in her eyes. She holds my gaze as she sidles nearer to Demetrios, seeking comfort from him.

Their arms touch, and he glances down. His expression remains aloof as she clutches his wrist in both her hands to draw even closer, but when he lifts his gaze to me, surprise flickers across his face. He tactfully extracts himself and says, "Goddess, Aitana understands her mistake. She deeply regrets it."

It's not regret that smolders in her eyes.

"I certainly hope so," I say, "for her sake as much as that of my other spark-bearers."

The corners of his mouth twitch with amusement. Aitana's brows descend in a glower, and she clamps her hands around his arm again.

Etricos clears his throat. "We will need more spark-bearers this time, Anjeni."

I choose my words carefully. "The demons may fear us, but Agoros and his magicians do not. They will twist the spark of any bearer who has not attained full control, to the destruction of your other warriors. Is that a risk you are willing to take?"

The Etricos of former days would brush off this remark with glib reassurance that nothing so dire will occur. This one nods, ever solemn. "It is a risk we must take for the strength that we need."

Gone is the cavalier belief that those beneath him are expendable to his cause. He is a warlord now, one who carries the burden of casualties that result from his decisions.

And I must support him in his campaign, but only to a degree that logic upholds. "I will bring with me those who have reached the fourth intermediate and above. Any who have not achieved that mark will be more hindrance than help. When do you depart?"

"Tomorrow, midday."

"Then I will assess my spark-bearers at dawn. Everyone should rest well tonight."

The trio in the doorway steps aside to allow my exit to the darkened road beyond. Further down the hill, firelight and music mark the celebration that yet continues, the scent of savory foods heavy on the air. My stomach churns with nervousness and I orient my steps instead to my isolated tent.

Etricos and Demetrios follow me in silence. So, too, does Aitana, who keeps close to the younger brother. My temper simmers. Apparently one rebuke wasn't enough for her tonight.

I pause at the entrance of my tent, looking back in time to catch Demetrios's disapproval at the lack of warriors to guard my fence.

Etricos gestures for me to proceed. "Anjeni, we must speak within, away from prying eyes."

I pass through the door. Huna stoops over the fire at the center of the tent, stirring her pot of soup. She glances up at our entrance but averts her gaze again. "Your people have left you offerings, little goddess."

A small, squat table holds dishes laden with foods from the celebration, including the Terasanai's dumplings and a bowl of heavily spiced curry. I have no appetite, but I smile nonetheless.

At the door, Demetrios barely contains a growl. He glares at the food like I want to glare at Aitana beside him. What does it say about me, that he sees food as his greatest rival for my affection? We make a ridiculous pair.

Etricos, within the relative privacy of the tent, launches straight into the heart of his concerns. "Can you defeat Agoros?"

My nerves flare anew. I indulge in a short sigh. "I don't know. I won't know until he and I come face to face in the flesh."

Aitana studies me. I meet her gaze and arch an eyebrow, challenging her to speak aloud whatever skeptical thoughts course through her head. For the moment, she refrains.

"If he dies, the Bulokai forces will scatter," says Etricos.

"As will we if Anjeni comes to harm," says Demetrios, his steady gaze upon me.

His brother claps a reassuring hand on his shoulder. "We have not come this far to fail, Dima."

"Your success depends not only on how potent a magician Agoros is," I say, "but also on how many magicians he has under his command. I suspect I can meet him as an equal in a battle, but if he has dozens of spark-bearers—or hundreds, heaven forbid—I cannot control all of them and him at the same time."

Agoros commands a greater distance than I do in his projection magic, but his reluctance to use the intermediates in that form speaks to his limitations—or to my folly for not exercising the same caution. Perhaps it is my inexperience that makes me hope I am not far behind him in ability.

"You don't have to control them," Aitana says, her voice stiff with umbrage. "You are not the only one who can use the superlatives."

I look to the fabric of the tent wall and ask, "How have you achieved all of the superlatives when I have only taught you the first five?" Silence meets my question. I turn to observe the fury in her renewing blush. "There are *nine*, Aitana. Agoros knows them all. His magicians—the ones we have encountered, at least—were proficient in the first eight."

Assuming that projection magic is the manifestation of the ninth superlative, I have no reason to believe that anyone under Agoros has acquired it. He would have sent his magicians to menace us in our very midst, were it otherwise.

She clenches her fists at her side. "So you put us all in danger by withholding those higher principles?"

I fling my hand out in the direction of my students' dormitories down the hill. "Have you not seen the result of teaching a principle before the pupil is ready? How many injuries might they have avoided if you had shown restraint?"

"Anjeni." Etricos steps forward, a shield between her and me. "She acted on behalf of the Helenai."

"As do I!" The fire flares, its flames encircling Huna's pot to lick the air, dangerously close to the ceiling. My audience jumps while my beast of magic rumbles within me.

Etricos raises defensive hands. "No one questions that. Aitana will not repeat her mistake. Your spark-bearers seek for victory as much as the rest of us. They will obey your command."

A strangled noise presses against the back of Aitana's throat, as though she smothers an instinctive protest.

The fire vents my wrath in another upward spiral. Aitana's shoulders hunch in the slightest degree and her chin drops. The subordinate grudgingly acknowledges her place. I shift my attention from her to Etricos. "I hope you are right. This battle will be difficult enough without mutiny in our ranks."

"Aitana knows the proper order," Demetrios says. Her gaze jerks up to him as he grips her arm. "She knows what is at stake. Anjeni, you must rely more on your spark-bearers. You cannot carry this burden alone."

My heart shrivels into itself. He is correct, and had anyone else spoken those words I would agree. His support of her right now only makes me wonder how close they became during their time away from the city.

And he has the audacity to growl at the Terasanai dumplings. I'd bean him with one in the head if it wasn't a complete waste.

Etricos eyes the roiling flames in my fire pit. They stay within their proper confines now, but their frenzied depths provide that bestial portion of me a fitting playground. "We will leave you to your rest for tonight, Goddess," he says. A wise decision. "Sleep well." He motions for Demetrios and

Aitana to exit the tent ahead of him. With a rustling of fabric, they are gone.

I huff in the aftermath. The fire calms from frenzy to quiet, licking flames. I face my attendant, who watches me with upraised brows, her mouth flat.

"Sorry about your cookware."

"There's no harm done. It's created to withstand flames."

True to her words, the fire-scorched pot appears none the worse for wear. The contents within bubble and steam. I force a steady breath to loosen my taut nerves.

"Are you truly that worried, little goddess?"

Fear crawls up my spine. I give it voice. "Agoros is strong—stronger than any of us knows."

She smiles, though wistfully. "You will triumph. The fates did not send you to us to fail."

The legends of my time agree with her, but they have proved wrong before, to disastrous ends. "I hope so, Huna."

I glare at the exit where Demetrios disappeared with his brother, and then I flop onto my bed, my back to it.

"Will you not eat?" Huna asks.

"I'm not hungry."

She clucks in mock sympathy. "It must be dire indeed if the little goddess has no appetite."

I favor her with a sour glare, but she only grins at me in return. Her toothy good cheer warms my soul: it is the first time I have seen such humor in her since Tora died. I change my mind and accept the food she offers me, though I manage no more than a few bites.

What will I do if Agoros is, like me, a volcano of magic? That he could spare a dozen magicians to send to our gates tells me he has many more. We will have twenty or fewer on our side, and most of them nowhere near proficient in all the intermediates, let alone the superlatives.

And their lack of preparation is my fault. Aitana's accusation rings in my ears. Have I truly put the Helenai in danger by withholding the higher principles? Should I have taught her, with Ria and Ineri, the words at least, so that they could ponder the concepts attached?

But then she may have taught them to the younger students, with worse results than their premature forays into the superlatives have already produced.

I heave another sigh. On the opposite side of the tent, Huna grunts at my melancholy.

A rustle at the door draws my attention. Demetrios enters, with neither Etricos nor Aitana behind him. I sit up in surprise, my heart leaping into an eager rhythm.

"Baba, I need—"

"Take her outside if you wish to be alone," Huna interrupts. "She could do with a long walk right now."

He opens and shuts his mouth, then looks to me in confusion. I suspect he had steeled himself for a rebuke for entering my tent unattended, and so late in the evening. I would have anticipated one as well. I glance to Huna, who tips her head to the exit.

"Go on, little goddess. Take your cloak and shoes and go."

My shoes are still on my feet. I sweep my cloak around my neck, my throat tight. Wordlessly Demetrios and I depart. We orient our steps away from the merriment and lights in the city below.

"I thought I would have to persuade her," he says. We descend the back of my hill, to the basin.

"She blames herself for keeping Etricos and Tora apart for so long. She doesn't approve, but she won't interfere." I surprise even myself with this observation, but the truthfulness of it thrums through me as the words roll off my tongue. My heart might beat itself right out of my ribcage, so torn between dread and anticipation for the cause of his visit. I pause in my descent to pin him with a stare. "What have you to say to me, Demetrios?"

His brows arch. "What if I didn't want to say anything?"

I laugh, but skeptically. The image of Aitana beside him this evening burns upon my mind. She sidled up to him every chance she got, and though he did not especially acknowledge her, he did not entirely rebuff her either. I pivot, my cloak swirling around me as I continue my descent. His footsteps rustle in the grass behind me, his presence close at my elbow.

The basin is damp. We cross it in silence.

As we start up the hill toward the Eternity Gate, he speaks. "You did well tonight."

I turn a bewildered look upon him. "In what respect?"

He takes my hand in his, contemplating it, running his rough larger thumb over my smaller knuckles. "In holding Aitana accountable in front of the younger spark-bearers. Cosi did as much as well, but it is good for them to see that you care for them. You keep yourself so distant most of the time."

I scoff and pull my hand from his grasp, but he snatches it again, his grip tight. The intensity of his gaze burns me all the way to my toes.

"It will be over soon," he says.

My breath leaves my lungs in a whoosh. The nerves I have quietly battled erupt anew within me. I swallow and nod.

"You will prevail."

Again I nod, though not because I believe his words. He tucks my hand in his arm and guides me to the crest of the hill. We continue onward, our steps directed toward the black ribbon of ocean on the horizon.

"Cosi doesn't fully trust the tribes we liberated," Demetrios says. "He won't allow them shelter here with us, not until

Agoros and the Bulokai vanish from the earth. *I* trust them, though."

I lift concerned eyes to him, and he smiles reassurance down upon me. "They have suffered, Anjeni, and they are eager for vengeance. We left behind what weapons and arms we could, and they continue the raids on the strength of our reputation."

"But they have no spark-bearers, do they?"

He shakes his head. "It doesn't matter. Word of the Helenai precedes them. The demons will flee before they ever glimpse their warriors, and the Bulokai foot soldiers make easy prey. The tribes we liberated will liberate others, and they will join us to defeat Agoros and his ilk. And all of this is thanks to you."

A denial perches on the edge of my tongue, but he drags me into his arms before I can speak it aloud. Demetrios cradles my head against his shoulder and leans in, his warmth encompassing me. Calm floods through my jittering nerves. I wrap my arms around him and revel in the comfort of his embrace.

Three weeks was too long a separation. How will I cope when I don't have him at all?

I push away on that thought, terror descending upon me anew. His arm around my waist won't allow me to withdraw more than a scant few inches.

"Don't go," he whispers. His eyes gleam fervid in the darkness that surrounds us.

I gaze upon him, my heart in my throat and grief puddling in my soul.

Demetrios repeats his plea. "Don't go, Anjeni. When it's all over, when the Bulokai are no more and peace comes to this land, don't go. There's no law that says you have to leave us."

A slow tingle works through me, raising goosebumps along my skin. I have always assumed my time here was finite, that I would leave the way I came, whether to my own era or another that awaited my arrival. In the months that I've lived among the Helenai, I have kept that inevitable end in my thoughts. This life is a difficult one. Even coddled as I am, I recognize the work that goes into daily living. I don't know how to accomplish even a fraction of it.

I don't belong here any more than I belonged in my native time, but for entirely different reasons.

Demetrios drops his forehead to rest against mine, his eyes shut, his arms still firm around me. I cannot speak the reassurance that he wants. Instead, I breathe deep to calm my racing pulse.

"What is my future, Anjeni?"

The question jars me. I recoil, staring up at him. He meets my gaze, his eyes steady.

"What is my future? What do the people of your time say of Demetrios, brother of Etricos?"

Emotion sticks in my throat like a lump of food. My quick, shallow breaths betray my inner turmoil.

He presses the issue. "You knew my name when you first arrived. You knew of me already. Tell me truthfully: am I to die in this final battle?"

Confusion tumbles over me. "What? No."

A measure of tension drains from his shoulders. "Then what becomes of me? What is it that makes you retreat behind this wall of yours? Whenever I think we have an equal understanding, something makes you withdraw from me again. What is my future?"

Philanderer. Faithless betrayer. The epithets I have always used for the Demetrios of legend bear no resemblance to the sincere and earnest man before me now. I seek refuge in the answer I gave him months ago.

"Your future is your own to choose."

He cups my cheek in one hand. "And I have chosen it."

And yet, another woman leaned upon him only an hour ago. "Have you?" I ask, my voice a touch more waspish than I would prefer. "Have you really chosen?"

The corners of his eyes wrinkle with amusement. "Yes."

I bristle. "Why are you laughing?"

"You're jealous of Aitana, and for no reason. You have the same expression on your face that you wore earlier, when we all stood in your tent. She's only playing games. Cosi is in mourning, but when enough time has passed, she will focus her attentions on him."

"And until then you'll let her hang upon your arm as much as she pleases?"

"I didn't know you could be so jealous," he says, fighting a laugh. He stoops to kiss my cheek.

I tip my head away. "Demetrios, it's not funny."

"I've always let her hang upon my arm, ever since we were young. It doesn't mean anything."

"It did once."

He pauses, assessing me in the darkness. His mirth settles into a more solemn expression. "I won't allow it anymore, if you don't like it."

"I don't."

"Is this your promise to stay with me? I am yours, and you are mine, and we live the rest of our lives as husband and wife?"

That fervid intensity has returned. My heart plunges into my stomach. If I demand faithfulness from him, why should he not require the same from me?

But still I deflect the question. "I would make a terrible wife, Demetrios."

He looks to the horizon with a laugh, his hold upon me loosening. "There's that wall again. Does it keep you safe? I hope it does."

A protest bubbles up in my throat, but he grabs me by the hand and pulls me back the way we came.

"You should rest," he says. "The Helenai need their goddess to be strong."

This can't be the end. I can't let this be the state of our relationship. "I love you," I blurt, stumbling in my steps as I try to keep pace beside him.

Demetrios stops on the hillside, his full attention upon me. He draws me in and kisses me with such dizzying passion that my head spins and my every nerve stands on end. But it's over almost as quickly as it began. "I know you do," he says, half-breathless. "And I love you. But somehow, it is not enough." He smiles, sorrowfully. Tucking my arm to his side, he leads me down the hill and across the muddy basin.

This wall between us, I have kept it as a refuge against heartache and abuse. I only meant to protect myself, to limit the emotional damage that seems to be my destiny. But the wall itself is now the threat: Demetrios has retreated behind it as well, on its opposite side, and this separation is worse than all the days we spent apart.

CHAPTER THIRTY-FOUR

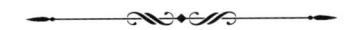

The Helenai warriors string out in a long line, their horses loping through the tall grass. Etricos rides at the head of our host. I bring up the rear with my spark-bearers, the goddess protected by hundreds who precede her. Demetrios keeps close, supposedly as a guard, but I suspect he's here more to ensure that my horse doesn't run away with me.

And I'm grateful to him for it.

"Is this the way to the Helenai homelands?" I ask.

He looks askance at me. "We came from further east, in the mountains."

"Do you wish to return there, someday?"

"No. The Bulokai have ravaged our lands. We cannot return to what we once had, because it no longer exists."

In this respect—among many—he differs from his brother. I study his profile, my heart in turmoil.

He favors me with a reassuring smile, though that imaginary wall between us remains strong. "Our past is gone. Only the future matters—now more than ever."

His speaking eyes trigger a blush up my neck. If I could safely jump from my horse to his and wrap my arms around him, I probably would. I suppress the irrational urge and train my gaze forward.

We follow the boundary of the river inland. The sun blazes through trailing clouds overhead. Close to dusk we pass beyond the terrain I have roamed in my projected form.

When we stop for the night, Etricos orders tents erected for me and my spark-bearers. The warriors have smaller, simpler shelters that will keep off any nighttime rain. I stride through their ranks, lighting campfires where needed and surveying the men as they prepare to rest.

They dare not meet my gaze. Huna insisted that I head into battle in my full goddess regalia: death paint, headdress, flowing attire. Over the past several weeks, she has traded out all of my masculine pants for more feminine counterparts, long and full, their silhouette almost mistakable for a dress. They're comfortable to wear, so I hadn't thought twice about the missing clothes until it came time to prepare for this journey.

"You are a goddess, not a warrior," Huna said when I confronted her. "I gave the other clothes to your spark-bearers. These are more suitable for you."

The sneaky old crone.

True to her word, my spark-bearers—all twenty that qualified to come—dress in pants, with banded-collar shirts beneath their cloaks. Death-paint motifs highlight their eyes, their hair pulled high in braids and topknots. They make a fearsome sight.

I share my tent with Aitana and half the younger girls. While I would have preferred Ineri as a roommate, I don't trust Aitana and Ria together. We recite the fundamentals and intermediates before we retire. I give brief instruction in the superlatives to those who can receive it, but with a strict charge that they should not attempt practice unsupervised.

My skull aches from the weight of the headdress when I finally remove it. I wash the paint from my face and settle back on my bedroll, listening to the sounds of the wilderness beyond the tent walls. Around me, my tired spark-bearers slip into steady, quiet breathing.

In contrast, restlessness eats at my soul.

We covered a lot of ground today. We have much more to cover tomorrow, but I cannot go into it blind. A whisper of energy projects me into the outside world. Amid swirling shadow and black flame I cross through the quiet campsite, a specter in the darkness. I pass beyond, to the path that lies ahead.

The clouds thicken above. I fly through foreign lands, bouncing from one point to the next until the unseen tether between my spirit and my body tugs. I stretch my limits and spring back into the quiet depths of the Helenai encampment. The sleep-rhythms of my spark-bearers press upon me, and I succumb to my exhaustion, satisfied with my progress for tonight.

In two days of travel we pass through forest and plains. I grow accustomed to stiff legs and sore muscles. The land rises gradually, and in the distance, a range of snow-capped mountains hovers against the horizon. Our army courses through low, scrubby trees like a river of horses and men. We encounter small villages, women and children only, the Bulokai expunged from their ranks. They peer at us from within their rudimentary homes, wide eyes seeking glimpse of the goddess who enabled their liberation.

When my gaze connects with any of them, they cringe and bow in reverence. My headdress steadily works a sore spot against my scalp.

On the third day, the land swells upward into deep trees. We pause at midday to rest and scout ahead. Etricos picks his way back through the ranks to where I stand with my clustered spark-bearers.

"We reach the Red Cliffs before dusk," he says. "Our allies should await us there, if they have not lost their courage."

Uncertainty bleeds through his usual confidence. Demetrios's warning near the Eternity Gate rings through my mind: Etricos does not trust the liberated tribes. For all he knows, we are riding straight into a trap that Agoros will gleefully spring.

"Shall I go into their midst from here?"

Demetrios stiffens, guarded as he waits upon his brother's response.

"Yes, Goddess," says Etricos. "I would be most grateful if you did."

I glance around at the overgrown woodland, seeking a secluded nook where I can rest unseen by the company.

Demetrios tugs my sleeve. "This way."

His unspoken promise calms my sudden anxiousness: he will watch over me. We start into low underbrush together. Aitana and Etricos both move to follow, but Demetrios halts them with a raised hand. "Stay here. Keep watch for scouts from the enemy, or from our allies. We will not be long."

Aitana bristles like a jilted bride. Etricos merely arches an eyebrow at his little brother. Demetrios gently prods me onward. I move, stiff-backed, among the trees, all too aware of the dozens upon dozens of eyes that watch my retreat.

The land here buckles and caves, with fallen trunks swathed in spider webs and moss. The more I look, the less I see a suitable place to sit, let alone leave my body unattended. I'm going to end up with a hundred ticks and chiggers if I crouch anywhere in this arboreal mess.

Demetrios, less concerned with parasitic pests, pulls me into an alcove where land and tree meet a jutting rock. "This should suffice," he says. Before I can voice approval or protest, he flops down upon a nest of leaves, dragging me with him.

"What—!"

He settles back against the rock and tucks me close, securing his hold upon me. "You know I hate this brand of magic, Anjeni. Do it quickly and return. I will keep you safe."

I could protest. I could insist upon lying flat as I usually do, but my heart sings at his warmth, at the deeply masculine scent that he exudes, at the assurance that he will protect me in my most vulnerable state. Among the warriors and spark-bearers, we guard against even the slightest touch, so this moment presents a luxury I will not reject. Heedless of my headdress, of the painted motif that decorates my face, I rest my cheek upon his chest and close my eyes.

My breath steadies and my muscles relax. I melt against him, secure in his arms, and shift my spirit beyond its physical constraints.

We make a strange picture, he and I. My cloak covers both of us as we lie against the jutting rocks. Were it not for the golden headdress and the extra pair of feet, an onlooker might mistake us for one person instead of two.

Demetrios looks up at my shadowed form, and the misery upon his face almost wrenches me back into myself. Do I cause him that much grief?

"Go, Anjeni," he says, the words echoing doubly in my ears.

I wink away through the trees, crossing miles in the blink of an eye.

When Etricos said we would travel to the Red Cliffs, I assumed that we traveled to their base. Instead, I emerge from the forest against a long, high ridge that overlooks a huge, rock-strewn canyon. The earth beneath my feet reflects vermillion in the afternoon sun. Below, the red rock gleams among scrubby trees and bushes.

A shout from my right draws my attention. Further up the line of the cliff, bodies cluster like ants upon a pile. I flash into their depths amid outcries and scuttling retreats.

The men create a circle around me, giving me wide berth. Wordlessly I scrutinize them, turning in a tight rotation as murmurs erupt in their ranks. They are old and young, with more of them at the extremes of age than in the middle. There are women, too, armed with swords and clubs. Their faces, coarse and brown and lined, speak of difficult lives.

Some of the people duck their heads. Others drop to their knees, their wide eyes fixed upon me. A bald warrior muscles through a cluster that quickly falls back to let him pass. He enters the open space and observes me, from the crown of my head to the shadowed flames that spill outward at my feet. Wonder marks his expression. When he speaks, it's with the accent of a different dialect. I'm grateful to understand him at all.

"You are the goddess of the Helenai?"

"I am."

More bodies drop to their knees. Some prostrate themselves upon the ground. As the line of the circle nearest me bends, so too do the people behind them. At the edge of the crowd they gather to glimpse their divine visitor and alert those warriors further down the cliff's rim of my arrival.

"I am Zahar, whom Etricos of the Helenai freed," says their leader, his head bowed. "My people have liberated many in your name, Goddess Anjeni. We will fight for you until death tears us breathless from this world. You come not a moment too soon."

"How so?" I ask. Some of the warriors have clasped their hands in prayer. Their worship of a false goddess rubs me wrong. If I am truly their salvation, they should worship the power that sent me here.

"Agoros and his army approach from the north," he says, and he points to the far-flung horizon, where a ribbon of dark haze shimmers low. "They will be upon us in another day. Though we occupy the higher ground, we have not the men nor the weapons to withstand the Bulokai in their fury without your support."

Fear tinges his words, as though he expects me to pull the rug out from beneath him, so to speak. He is as cagey of Etricos's promises as Etricos has been of his.

"How many warriors have you?" I ask.

He puffs his chest. "We number a thousand strong."

Strong might be a stretch. The Bulokai culled the ablest bodies from among them in their captivity. Those who remain exhibit more determination than strength.

But, their numbers are three times the number that travels with the Helenai. "You have done well," I say. "Etricos and his company arrive here at dusk. I come in their midst."

"We will prepare for your arrival and rejoice, Goddess Anjeni." He bends low, the afternoon sun shining on his head. Those in the circle around us take this as cue to press their foreheads to the ground, their voices vanishing into a silence that ripples back along the edge of the cliff.

Am I to offer a farewell? Who would have expected godly visitations to be so awkward?

I shift from their presence, back to the warmth of a protective embrace, curled against Demetrios so snugly that my first inclination is not to move. Reluctantly I crack open my eyes. The forest seems dull and drab around me.

"Well?" His breath ghosts over my ear, raising goosebumps along my spine.

I shift in his arms. "You were right. They await the support that Etricos promised to bring them."

His hold upon me loosens, signaling me to draw back and stand on my own power. Demetrios watches me through half-lidded eyes, never moving from his spot among the leaves.

I adjust my headdress. "Was I gone too long?"

"Your body grows cold when you use that power," he says.

"I've never noticed."

"Perhaps you're numb to its effects."

"Perhaps I should keep someone to warm me when I use it." I offer him a hand to rise, though I expect him to decline my help. To my surprise, he accepts, hoisting himself up. He doesn't immediately let me go, but first plants a kiss upon my palm, his gaze locked with mine.

"Thank you," I say, drawing my hand to my chest like a newly recovered treasure.

"Always," he replies, and my insides transform into a mass of twitter-pated goo.

CHAPTER THIRTY-FIVE

———⁂———

Our allies line the edge of their encampment to greet our arrival. They speak not a word, and the solemn silence sends a chill up my spine. Only the hoofbeats of our horses punctuate the darkening air. The waiting host bows in reverence as I come into view at the end of the company. We pass through them to the center of camp and the cluster of tents that poke toward the cloud-strewn sky.

The leader I spoke with, Zahar, waits with a collection of peers. Most of our warriors peel away and I move to the front of the host. Etricos dismounts. I do likewise, alongside Demetrios and my spark-bearers. Our reception committee greets us and guides us to the tent at the very center of the cluster, its doors open. Within are rudimentary fixtures—though probably among the finest that they possess—but no fire in the pit.

"We hope this offering suits the goddess of the Helenai," says Zahar. He bows deep. I survey the tidy cot with a nod of approval. When my gaze rests too long upon the empty pit, he bows again. "We have not dared light any fires today with the Bulokai so close."

"You may light them now," says Etricos, "but keep the flames beyond sight from the plains below."

The leader looks to me for confirmation, and I nod. The smoke may betray our presence, but Agoros already knows his enemy lies in wait. He comes for us whether we light campfires or not.

Messengers travel through the camp to give this command; my spark-bearers go with them to assist with the fire-lighting. It's unnecessary magic, but it allows them practice and gives occasion to display their sparks to the ragtag resistance that has sprung up with the hope their power inspires.

Aitana, Ineri, and Ria remain at my side as my seconds-in-command. Zahar shows the tents designated for Etricos and for my spark-bearers. The Helenai warriors will occupy the forest around us, which our allies have already cleared of underbrush.

Tents large and small mark the territory of the other tribes. They organize their company by kinship. Zahar points to each cluster in its turn: some tribes have as few as a dozen warriors to their name. This amalgamated host represents more communities than I can keep track of. I lose count at seventeen, and the list goes on. Etricos liberated ten settlements in his raids, and they have liberated at least that many more on the reputation of the Helenai.

Dusk falls. We move through the encampment, tracing the swell of land to the cliff's edge. Afar off, through the deepening shadows in the canyon below, firelight marks the presence of the Bulokai host. The incandescent spots extend toward the horizon like stars smoldering in the night sky.

"They will arrive at the base of the cliffs by tomorrow," Zahar says. "Their magicians will attack us from below, forcing us out and away from the cover of the forest. It is a method they have used to great success in the past."

He looks to me, fear and hope mingling in his gaze.

I'm supposed to give words of affirmation here, but the enormity of the task before me robs my confidence. Etricos comes to my rescue.

"We have a goddess in our midst. Agoros and his magicians will exercise more caution in their attacks. Our higher ground gives us the upper hand."

I hope he is correct. If I were Agoros under the circumstances, I would leave the campfires behind and sneak with my armies through the night to attack while my enemy was unaware. With magic no longer his exclusive advantage, he will call upon other nasty surprises.

A small crowd has followed us on our tour of the camp. A commotion rises within them as bodies press through their ranks. I turn, my heart in my throat, as a weathered man squeezes through the front line with a teenaged girl and an even younger boy on his heels. He does not look to me but beyond, and he shouts a single word.

"Aitana!"

A strangled noise escapes her lips. She pushes past me. "Papa? Papa!" She collides into his outstretched arms, tears glistening on her cheeks. Wide-eyed, I observe the reunion, barely able to follow the emotion-laden exchange. The girl and boy, Aitana's brother and sister, crowd close, but they do not touch her. Rather, they somehow keep their father between them and her. Their stares take in her high braid and the black motif that decorates her cheekbones.

Aitana, noticing their apprehension, tips her nose proudly in the air. She lifts her hand, the spark of magic on her fingers. Her sister and brother cringe away, terrified. The look on Aitana's face suggests that she revels in this reaction, in her superiority over them.

With a haughty tilt of her head, she swings her hand and the bright-burning ball upward.

Etricos and Demetrios cry out a warning, but lightning-quick I snatch her power and slam it into soft earth. I snuff the resulting flames as a stricken silence encumbers our onlookers.

Fury boils within me. It takes every ounce of my self-control not to scream. My rebuke emerges in a waspish accusation. "Did you seek to kill us all?"

"I—" Her voice catches in her throat. She looks past me, to Etricos and Demetrios, contrition on her face. "I only wanted to show—"

"We are at war. The Bulokai magicians might snatch any visible spark and turn it against us," I say.

For once she seems to recognize her mistake. "I am sorry, Goddess." Tears glimmer in her eyes. She drops her gaze to the ground and hugs her arms to her stomach. Her family, cowed as they were by her presence, look at me as though they await execution.

Like I'm a tyrant in their midst. And so I shall be.

"Save the higher principles for the enemy. You can show off without putting our entire encampment at risk. Do you understand?"

"Yes," she says woodenly.

"Good." I sweep past her, back toward the area designated for the Helenai. Ria and Ineri follow in my wake, with Etricos and Demetrios behind them. The gathered onlookers fall back, allowing me swift passage through their ranks. I arrive at my tent, where a small fire now burns in the central pit. My pair of acolytes shifts nervously, awaiting my command.

"You don't have to stay with me," I tell them. "You may seek out the others."

Ria ducks away with a murmured, "Yes, Goddess."

Ineri lingers. "Will you be all right?"

"Of course."

"Aitana was lucky you were there to stop her. We all were lucky."

Bitterness eats at me. "Yes," I say. If Agoros or his magicians in the canyon had seen that spark of light rise from the cliffs, they might have caught it, divided it, augmented the fragments, and slammed them back into our midst with the certainty of hitting an array of targets. My nerves, so taut over the past few days, stretch almost to their breaking point.

"Thank you, Goddess."

My attention jerks up from the ground. Ineri gazes back at me, all sincerity in her expression.

"Thank you," she says again. "Had you not been here, we might already be lost."

Words fail me. Her simple gratitude disarms my wrath. She bows and retreats before I can gather my wits. I look to Etricos and Demetrios, who hover in the doorway of my tent.

Etricos tips his head. "Once again, Anjeni, your quick reaction saves us."

This is getting ridiculous. "I did what anyone with a modicum of sense would have done in my place."

"You did what only you were capable of doing," Demetrios says. "Aitana acted without thinking."

My thoughts flit back to the mistakes I have made with my magic. I attacked Agoros, provoked him from afar, nearly killed myself in learning the ninth superlative—multiple times. Much as I despise Aitana, I'd rather drop this subject than dwell on her foolish misstep.

A throat clears from beyond, someone outside my tent. The pair of brothers turns, and between them I spy the subject of our conversation silhouetted against the bonfire behind her.

"Cosi, Dima, I'm sorry," she says. "In my joy at seeing my kinsmen, I acted on impulse. I only meant to show them what progress I had made with my spark."

Etricos kicks up one corner of his mouth. "If you understand your mistake, that's good. Thanks to our goddess, no harm befell anyone."

The shadows obscure her rising blush. She bites her lower lip and glances to one side. "My father wishes to meet you, to thank the Helenai for their many years of protection."

His mask of cordiality firmly in place, Etricos says, "Of course."

She beckons, and the man joins her from the far shadows. My position inside my tent allows me to spy the skittish sister and brother who remain at the edge of the firelight.

Aitana makes her introductions. "Cosi, this is my father, Marakush. Papa, this is Etricos, the leader of the Helenai. You might remember him from long ago."

Marakush bends. "Your father was a good man. I was sorry to hear of his passing."

"Many good people have died at the hands of the Bulokai," Etricos replies. The false politeness in his voice sets my nerves on edge. His icy smile might come from a dozen sources: does he reference Tora, or is he reluctant to speak of his deceased father? Or does this conversation with a member of another tribe signify obligations he does not wish to fulfill? Etricos is a many-layered enigma right now, but beneath that façade of geniality lies a serpent ready to strike.

Aitana recognizes the danger. She suppresses her instinctive alarm and shifts her focus to his brother. "And this is Dima, Papa. He was my guard and protector from the moment you left me with the Helenai."

Her father's face warms. "You have my thanks, young warrior. The Helenai have my eternal thanks, and that of my tribe. The Bulokai spared more of us because we had no spark-bearers in our midst. Had you not taken my daughter into your care—"

"Our father was a noble and trustworthy man," Etricos interrupts. "It was our honor to take up his mantle of protection over all who reside among the Helenai. Now if you'll excuse me, I have many matters to which I must attend." He starts toward his own tent nearby.

"Wait," Aitana blurts. He arrests his footsteps. She falters for words. "Please—Cosi, Dima, my father wishes to offer a sign of his thanks."

Her father adds, "Will you partake of our evening meal with us, as a show of our kinship and gratitude?"

Kinship. This is a power play after all. Tucked away in the background, I stand as awkward witness to this interchange, my existence seemingly forgotten.

Etricos glances to his brother, but whatever he conveys in that unspoken communication escapes me. "Thank you, but for my part of the offer I must decline. Too many other matters demand my attention tonight. Dima?"

Demetrios starts. Almost he glances at me over his shoulder. "I do not lead the Helenai. Receiving such tokens of thanks on their behalf is above my station."

Aitana's father remains undeterred. "As my daughter's guard and protector, you deserve such tokens of thanks on your own merits. We would be honored to have you as our guest."

This time Demetrios actually does glance back at me, meeting my gaze within the dimness of my tent. Anxiety squeezes my windpipe. Aitana's father exudes the same atmosphere as every politician and diplomat I once encountered in my native era. He will ramrod his way, intent upon giving and receiving favors, with timing that suits his purposes best. On the eve of a great battle, the Helenai can hardly afford to offend their allies.

Even so, Demetrios squares his shoulders and his expression stiffens with resolve.

But Aitana interjects before he can speak. "Will you not bring your evening meal here, Papa? We may partake of it together."

Mutiny flashes across her father's face, though he replaces it with a congenial smile. "Yes, my sweet girl." He kisses the side of her forehead. "We will return shortly. Again, my thanks to the Helenai."

Etricos disappears into his tent before the man even clears the ring of firelight. Aitana looks to Demetrios in desperation. "Please, Dima. He is in your debt. I know I made a mistake before, but please don't punish me for that now."

"He, and you, and all of us are in the debt of the goddess Anjeni," Demetrios replies, and the thorn of anger in his voice sends a jolt of surprise up my spine. He flings his hand toward me. "Why did he not invite *her* in thanks?"

Aitana scoffs. "You think my father is so bold as to ask a goddess to share his evening meal? We do not expect her to condescend to us!"

Briefly she glares past him to where I stand in the dim light of my tent's smaller fire. She averts her eyes again, but her jaw clenches with bitterness. Onlookers from among the Helenai step closer—warriors and spark-bearers alike—for a better view of the discordant scene.

"A goddess does not require an invitation," says Aitana grudgingly. "She may dine wherever it pleases her to dine, and she is always welcome."

Obviously I'm not welcome at her little dinner party, though. Not that I want to attend. I settle a reassuring hand on Demetrios's arm. "I should speak with your brother," I say quietly.

"You should eat and rest," he replies in the same low tones.

I shake my head. "I need to know his plans going forward. This might be a very long night."

He studies me, assessing. With visible reluctance, he steps aside to clear my exit. I offer him a wan smile as I pass. To Aitana, I spare only an arch tip of my head, *condescending* to acknowledge her existence. With utmost dignity I cross to Etricos's tent. Demetrios follows as my escort until I pass through the door.

I enter to find Etricos at a small table within. He sets down a stylus and angles his hand to hide the piece of paper upon which he has been writing. He forces a welcoming smile.

Suspicious.

"Did I intrude?" I ask.

"Of course not, Goddess. You are welcome anywhere at any time."

I doubt he intended to echo Aitana's accusation from a moment ago, or that he even heard the muttered remark, but it rankles me nonetheless. "That's not true. If I'm interrupting, you should tell me."

He waves aside my concern. "I was only writing a letter."

I nod, my brain turning this sentence over and over. His secretive nature makes me question the letter's content. Is it a treaty? A threat to another tribe?

"Does it have to do with the battle tomorrow?"

Again he waves my words aside, but he can't make eye contact. A slow blush crawls up his neck to his ears. "It is nothing, Anjeni."

A thought occurs—*Etricos, letter-writing*—and I blurt it without reasoning whether I should speak. "Do you write to Tora?" He jolts, wide-eyed. Tears blur the edges of my vision. "Etricos, I didn't mean to... I'm so sorry."

He sags back in his chair, no longer endeavoring to cover the page from my view. "I suppose it's foolish of me, writing to someone who is already beyond this world."

I shake my head. Caught in an onslaught of torturous emotions, I do not trust myself to speak. But he does not expect me to.

"I can see so much clearer now, Anjeni. She loved me. She was willing to die for me, beside me. And I loved her too, but I loved myself more."

I start to protest, but he doesn't give me the chance.

"Not in word, but in action. My power, my advantages—I put off my love for her because I thought we had time. I spent my efforts in securing a greater position among the people, convincing myself that it was for both of us, but it wasn't. Tora would have loved me even if I held the lowest rank in the tribe. I was the one who wanted more. I did it for myself, not for anyone else. I didn't deserve her love or her loyalty."

My heart breaks for him anew. His loss, still so fresh, burns within him.

He straightens in his chair and pins me with a determined gaze. "I will earn her love and loyalty. It is a debt I will hold until the day I die, and when I meet her in the next life, I hope to pay it in full. In the meantime, I will write to her."

The letters in the National Archives—this is their origin. I blink, and tears tumble down my cheeks. I catch a shuddering breath at the cause and effect manifested before me: Etricos becomes a national hero in honor of Tora, his lost beloved.

It is tragic and beautiful, and far too painful for words.

"Don't cry, Anjeni," he says, brushing off my sorrow by shoring his own behind heavy fortifications. "All is well. I will see her again."

Though I have no assurance of his words, I nod. There is a governing force in this universe greater than anyone can understand. If that force has any mercy whatsoever, Etricos will join his love when he passes from this life.

Gently he changes the subject. "You did not, I think, come to speak to me of my letters."

I wipe my cheeks, restraining my raw emotions with a sniffle. "What would you have me do tonight? The Bulokai fill the canyon. Would you have me scout their ranks? Would you have me attack?"

"Our allies have scouts observing them already, though no one in their midst. But unless you can kill Agoros tonight, we need your strength in battle tomorrow."

"You think he will wait until tomorrow to attack?"

Etricos looks down at his hands. "I don't know."

"Would you?"

"No. Darkness creates confusion. If we could attack tonight without losing our higher ground, I would order it."

I consider the options before me. "We can see their fires from the cliffside. My students can attack from here with their superlatives."

A corner of his mouth lifts in amusement. "Can they cause any damage from such a distance?"

"Distance is but an illusion," I reply with an airy wave of my hand. "The issue will be whether the Bulokai have enough magicians to guard their fires against our interference."

"Then perhaps you might scout among them before you engage your students in such attacks. They are your spark-bearers, Anjeni. You may command them as you please."

Surprise seeps through me. Etricos trusts me to decide our path without him. The weight of responsibility digs into me like the ornate headdress I yet wear. Wordless, I turn to leave.

"Anjeni," he says, and I pause at the exit of his tent. He draws his letter close to resume writing, his voice casual. "At some point, Aitana will understand that there is no room at my side for anyone but Tora. Dima is her second choice. He deserves to be someone's first."

To what degree does he know of my relationship with his brother?

"Demetrios will choose his own future," I say, unable to meet his gaze.

"Then I hope he chooses wisely."

This remark earns him a quick glance. Etricos smiles, as sincere as he can be under the circumstances. I nod and slip through the tent flap, into the night.

Voices around the campfire hush as a dozen or more gazes bore into me. Aitana and her father sit on either side of Demetrios, with the younger brother and sister nearby and half of my spark-bearers filling out the circle. I incline my head—*condescending*—and glide into the privacy of my own tent, where I pull the painful headdress from my skull and toss it to the ground.

CHAPTER THIRTY-SIX

THE GREASY SMOKE OF OIL-FUELED FIRES billows into the night air amid swirling embers. Warriors move in and out of the shadows. The spikes of their armor glint wicked in the dancing orange light. I skulk along the edge of the Bulokai camp, ever alert for signs of their magicians, or of Agoros himself.

Does he lead his armies, or do they nest around him as protection? I cannot venture into the camp without risk of someone glimpsing my shadow-form between the fires. If he is not at the edge, he is beyond my reach for now.

The Bulokai foot soldiers show no signs of bunking down for the night. Rather, they sharpen weapons and spar with one another. Their commanders stride through their ranks, eyes alert as they observe these activities.

A chittering sound draws my attention. Shadows move further down the encampment, huge hulking shapes. The churring shifts in volume to a screech that shoots a chill up my spine.

It's the screech of the scaly, monstrous creature I encountered when I first arrived through the Eternity Gate.

Meaning that demons cluster within this host, and their mutant horses with them. But the demon warriors were supposed to fear the spark to such a degree that they have fled on mere rumors of magic alone. Was it a ruse, a pretense to embolden the Helenai?

I move toward the sound, a moth drawn to the flame that may prove its demise. Four of the strange mounts hunch together in the dark. One spots me and bucks its long head. Its eyes roll back as another screech cuts from its throat. I blend into the shadows of a scrubby tree to observe.

A demon warrior lopes between the tents. The far, feeble fires highlight his bristled face, but dimly. I expect him to comfort the restive beasts. Instead he singles out the noisy one and tightens a muzzle around it. The creature chitters, and the demon utters what sounds like jumbled curses. He yanks on the strap around its mouth, eliciting a smothered yelp.

I never thought I would pity a mutant horse, but I do. Quickly I move on. If my unnatural presence upsets the creatures, they will only receive further punishment.

Ever watchful, I glide through the underbrush. Now that I know to look for them, I spy many more demons within the camp. They clump together in areas away from the fires, sometimes blending so closely into the dark that only their slight movements betray them. Their scaly mounts pepper the borders of the army. Another of the creatures spots my projection and shrieks its alarm.

"If you can't keep those wretched beasts quiet now, how will we possibly sneak up on the insurrectionists?"

A Bulokai warrior—human—stands arms akimbo by the closest bonfire. He addresses a mammoth shadow, a sneer upon his face.

The demon, in lieu of answering, hocks a loogie on the warrior's gleaming boots. A strangled cry erupts from the man. He jumps back and utters a string of insults as he wipes the top of his boot against a patch of scrubby grass. "You filthy *lug*. If Lord Agoros himself had not expressly forbid it, I would repay your insolence with flames."

In this manner, I pinpoint my first magician in the Bulokai army.

The demon lumbers to its feet, towering over the furious man. He speaks in a guttural voice. "If Agoros had not expressly forbid it, I would cleave your skull in two and eat your brains for dinner."

The magician doesn't flinch. "You'd be dead before you could heft your weapon, lummox."

They glare at one another, each refusing to allow the other to menace him. A shrill whistle from further within the camp slices through the palpable tension. Demon and magician alike step back, their attention flitting to the source of this interruption. A second man emerges from between the tents, his uniform similar to the magician's.

He eyes the pair. "Is everything here all right?"

"No." The demon growls and turns away in contempt. His hulking silhouette tromps toward the churring mounts. I keep him in my sight as I focus my ears on the pair of magicians he left behind.

"You know that Lord Agoros commanded us not to provoke them," the newcomer says.

His fellow snorts. "The cowards should know their place by now. We lost a dozen settlements on mere rumors of enemy magic? Pathetic."

A form crosses behind them, another demon who spits at their feet as he passes. The first magician twists to follow him, a blaze of fire on his fist, but the second grabs him by the arm and strips the magic from him.

"Don't—!"

Monstrous figures peel from the shadows, forming a circle around the pair, clubs and morning stars held at menacing angles. The first demon returns from attending his restless animals and joins his fellows.

"Stand down," says the second magician. "We're allies, not enemies."

No one moves. The hostility in the air is thick enough to strangle someone. The first magician narrows his eyes. His mouth curls upward in a sneer, and—

"What have we here?"

The question snaps everyone from their silent confrontation. Demons slink to one side to allow the speaker passage through their midst. The two magicians, meanwhile, bow their heads in obsequious greeting.

But I require none of these cues to identify this newcomer. I recognize his voice.

Agoros of the Bulokai addresses the first demon. "Why do you threaten those I have charged to protect you?"

"*Protect*," the demon repeats in a guttural sneer. "Protectors who will strike us when we turn our backs."

Though a head shorter than the hulking figure, Agoros does not cower in the least. His expression hardens, evidence of a short temper held in check. "My magicians keep you safe from the enemy spark-bearers. They stand ready to intercept the attacks you fear the most, to pave your pathway to battle and destruction."

"They summon flames to subject us, as though we are slaves or pack animals."

Agoros slides a glance to the pair behind him. They stand their ground, their shoulders stiff. "They will not attack you. I have given you my word."

The demon swipes the air with a massive hand. "Your word means nothing. We have seen you break it countless times."

"You question my honor?" Agoros's voice has turned deadly. The scene stills, every onlooker—including myself—hanging upon the tense interchange. The leader of the Bulokai waits until the demon before him starts to squirm. Only then does he deign to say, "We are all on the same side, Captain. When this last sliver of resistance dies, you and your kind will have free rein in these southern lands, as I promised you from the start."

Bristled lips curl to reveal sharp, pointed teeth. "And what will stop you from enslaving us as you have enslaved your human conquests?"

Agoros views him through half-lidded eyes. "What use have I for slaves who would consume more than they produce? You are creatures of war, not of industry. When this conflict ends, we go our separate ways."

He turns on his heel and strides past his pair of magicians. The demon captain glances speculatively to the weapon angled in his hand, as though he contemplates whether to strike down the leader of the Bulokai here and now. The spikes of his morning star glint from the far fire.

Lightning-quick, I wrench a spark from those flames and shoot it like an arrow through the demon's heart.

He keels back with a ghastly intake of breath. The demons nearest him lunge to catch him.

Agoros spins to confront his pair of underlings. "Who dares—?"

But it's too late. The area erupts in chaos. Demons howl and magic flares, and a war horn cracks through the night. Agoros cuts a flaming path through the bristle-faced beasts, his wild eyes seeking the darkness for the source of the errant superlative that felled his reluctant ally.

His gaze swivels my direction, but I wink away and surface in my tent with a deep, tight-throated gasp.

My head swims and my body shudders. I roll off my cot to the ground and retch, the whole world shaking around me.

What was I thinking? The upper intermediates in that projected form nearly killed me. The second superlative, simple though it was, has drained any sense of equilibrium. I labor for air; tears well in my eyes as prospective death by suffocation looms before me. Bile pushes up from my stomach, burning my esophagus and leaving an acrid taste at the back of my throat. I cough and heave, my cheek against the ground as my limbs flutter like leaves in the wind.

A commotion arises beyond my tent. Voices shout warnings I cannot discern. The entrance parts and Demetrios comes in.

"Anjeni—!" The rest of his words catch in his throat when he spies me lying in the dirt. He skids to his knees and gathers me into his arms, a dozen curses falling from his lips. "Get Cosi!" he barks, and I vaguely register the presence of a second figure in the door. The person retreats.

Demetrios smooths my hair back from my face. "Breathe, Anjeni. *Breathe.*"

I force an inhale, my lungs on fire. He tilts my chin up, and my airway loosens. Still my body trembles in the throes of its seizure.

The tent flap parts again, and Etricos enters.

His younger brother lights into him. "What did you do? What did you tell her to do?"

Etricos shakes his head. "I told her only to scout, to conserve her energy for battle. What has she done?"

"I don't know! I found her like this!"

"Keep her safe. Do everything you can. I'll engage our allies outside and keep them away from her for now. How long do these episodes last?"

"I don't know," Demetrios says again. "I've *told* her not to—! Cosi—!"

"Keep her safe, Dima. I'll return when we know what's happening in the Bulokai camp."

Etricos departs into the night. Demetrios, his hand gentle, wipes the corner of my mouth and the tears that pool in my eyes. My breath comes easier the longer he holds me, and the shuddering lessens. I grasp the buckle of his armor.

"D-didn't m-mean to..." I manage through wavering lips.

"Don't talk," Demetrios says, and his hold on me tightens. He cradles me in his lap, hunched protectively around me. "The Bulokai have sounded their war horns. Messengers from the cliffside came to warn us, and I came straight to you. Anjeni, what did you do?"

He tells me not to talk but asks me questions? I bury my face against his chest and focus on controlling the tremors within me. I'm as weak as a newborn; even holding up my head is a monumental task.

He adjusts his hold upon me and drops a kiss upon my cheek. The act startles me so that I instinctively open my eyes and look up at him.

The anguish I saw in him this afternoon has returned. I reach fingers up to touch his face, but he catches them. "Don't move. Don't talk. Just breathe, love."

A raspy chuckle erupts from my throat, and his expression darkens.

"Anjeni—"

"I won't die," I murmur. The world around me still trembles, but my body has settled closer to its usual rhythm.

"You'd better not," Demetrios says.

We sit in silence. Beyond the tent, voices shout orders to arm and assemble. I hope that my seconds-in-command have sense enough to corral the other spark-bearers. The longer I lie motionless, the more alert I feel, but when I try to sit up, Demetrios's grip on me tightens.

"You're not going anywhere."

I start to protest. "The Bulokai—"

"Cosi will handle it."

"I saw him, Demetrios. I saw Agoros."

He stills, his expression hard. "You attacked him?"

I shake my head, a minute movement that sends my vision spinning again. "I killed one of his demon captains."

"Why?"

"They were at odds—so much mistrust. Too perfect not to interfere." I squeeze my fingers around his and offer a faint smile. "Shouldn't have used a superlative. Didn't think. Sorry."

He breathes a frustrated sigh.

Upon this scene Etricos reappears. "The Bulokai are fighting among themselves. Magic flares in their midst, and the war horns echo across the canyon below without drawing nearer to us."

Nestled in his brother's arms, I meet his gaze. My words leave my throat in little better than a croak. "Take my spark-bearers to the cliff's edge. Spread them out. They can add to the chaos."

Etricos assesses me. "What risk will that bring to us?"

"If they use only superlatives, there should be none beyond the usual fatigue." I rub my forehead against Demetrios, my eyelids drooping. "I will join them when I'm better."

"You're not going," my caretaker says, his voice rumbling in his chest.

His concern, endearing as it is, cannot govern my actions. This is war. "I will come when I can," I reaffirm.

Etricos exchanges a glance with his brother and bows out of the tent. His voice rings from beyond as he issues orders to my waiting spark-bearers.

I turn my gaze upward. "I can't stay in here while everyone else fights."

The muscles along Demetrios's jaw tighten. "Know your limits, Anjeni. If you die, so will we all."

He exaggerates, I think, but I won't protest an extra half-hour cradled against him. I relax and focus on keeping my breath steady. His warmth provides comfort. As my senses level, my awareness of my situation heightens.

My limbs are like ice, stripped of energy. The warmth that returns by degrees sends goosebumps shivering up my arms. "Demetrios, thank you," I whisper. His presence has calmed the panic within me, and his nearness restores the heat I have lost. As the seconds and minutes course by, I feel more and more like myself.

Beyond the walls of my tent, the encampment has fallen into restive silence. I strain my ears for sounds of battle, for the far-off call of the enemy war horn, but I cannot hear anything. Tentatively I lift my head.

The world does not swim before my eyes. I meet Demetrios's wordless gaze. As though sensing my resolve to join my spark-bearers, he loosens his hold upon me.

Despite my best efforts, I list in my attempt to rise. Demetrios catches me before I can fall. "Anjeni—"

"I'm all right," I say, my head ducked low. My vision fizzles with one breath and returns with the next. "If I make no appearance, our allies may lose their confidence."

He does not argue, much to my surprise, but supports me as I stand. We trudge to the tent flap and exit to an abandoned campsite. Warriors dash among the shadows beyond the ring of fire, headed toward the cliffside and the commotion it overlooks. I orient my steps that direction as well, but a call from the gloom arrests me.

"Goddess Anjeni."

Adrenaline spikes into my blood. I whirl upon the familiar, insidious voice. From the darkness, Agoros emerges in his projected form, hatred in his eyes and a sneer upon his mouth. Demetrios grasps my upper arm as though to drag me away, but I dig in my heels.

"I should kill you right now," Agoros says. That gossamer thread that connects him to his physical form burns with menace of a building attack.

Yet he does not release it, and I think I now know why. The Bulokai do not follow him from love or loyalty but from the power he offers them.

"Your own men would slit your throat in the aftermath if you attack me in this form," I say.

His sneer intensifies, proof that my guess has struck its mark. "Ready yourself and your people, *goddess*. Death comes upon you this night."

"Only if you can quell the conflict in your own army first."

He barks a laugh. "I thought Etricos of the Helenai would drum up more than a few hundred warriors. I can destroy your pathetic uprising on my own power. Your interference tonight merely saves me the trouble of tidying up my followers when all is finished." On that mocking declaration, he vanishes into wisps of smoke and ash.

The far-off war horns carry on the wind. I glance toward the cliffs, my heart rising in my throat. "I need to find Agoros in the flesh. I should have aimed for him instead of the demon."

I stagger, and Demetrios reels me back by my elbow. "He goads you into another foolish attack, Anjeni."

"No. He spoke truth. He'll kill us all on his own power if he gets the chance."

My solemnity strikes a chord. Demetrios aids me to the cliff's edge, where the Helenai and their allies line the ridge that overlooks the canyon. Only a handful of my spark-bearers are proficient enough with the superlatives to influence the enemy camp afar. Nearest to me, Ineri strains amid a cluster of warriors.

She spots my approach from the corner of her eyes. The bodies between us fall away to cut me a path.

"Goddess, their magicians steal back control of the sparks almost as soon as I can grasp them. The conflict is dying, and we have accomplished so little against an army so great."

The enemy fires yet burn like pinpricks in the darkness. Flares spring up but die out just as quickly. Somewhere down there, Agoros found safety enough to project into our encampment. He is out and away from his army, that must mean, with however many magicians and foot soldiers he could rally around him.

If he comes against us on his own power, he has no need for the warring host he has left behind.

"Anjeni!" Demetrios grabs my shoulder, but he's too late to stop me.

The eighth superlative of magic is that it amplifies all discernible sparks. Unite and intensify power from afar.

Before my eyes, at my command, the pinpoints of light explode. They splatter outward to create an ocean of fire. A hush falls around me as some ten thousand enemy soldiers perish in one furious attack. My beast of magic roars into the darkness, and yet I push for more power, for more destruction, until the shaking of my limbs renews and the burning flames jitter in my vision. The fire resembles a lava plain. Its brightness illuminates ant-like figures that flee the enormous blaze. The eighth superlative falters on my fingertips.

And then I lose my hold upon it. The massive blaze winks out as swiftly as it ignited.

My knees strike rock. I catch myself on my palms, blinking in surprise, staring at the earth upon which I've unwittingly collapsed. Static rings in my ears, blocking all other sound.

Demetrios kneels beside me, but he does not touch me. In shock, I turn to view him. He regards me with apprehension. All others have backed away, giving me wide berth. Many lie in prone worship, oblivious to my tattered state or the exchange of power that just occurred. My mouth moves to utter a warning: another presence wicked away my attack. Agoros yet comes to destroy.

But I cannot form a single word.

Panic rises as my vision fades. I grasp at Demetrios, and he catches me before I can crumple to the ground.

CHAPTER THIRTY-SEVEN

MUSIC FLOATS UPON THE NIGHT. I awaken to the dimness of my tent and the sounds of merriment afar. My pulse quickens in my veins and I sit bolt upright.

"Goddess? What's wrong?"

The low fire casts Ineri in pale orange light, illuminating her alert expression.

"What time is it? How long have I slept?"

She untangles her legs and rises. "It is fourth watch. Dima instructed me—"

I tear from my bedding before she can finish her sentence. Ineri cries out a warning that I disregard. Instead, I summon my spark to quench the meager flames at the center of my tent. "Put out the fire. Put out all the fires in the encampment."

Darkness floods the enclosure, but I have already stumbled to the exit, with Ineri close behind me.

"Goddess—"

"Agoros yet lives," I say. The larger fire outside my tent lies low. The warriors who sleep around it lift their heads in groggy confusion as I intrude upon their space. The embers go black on my command—the third superlative, which diminishes an unconnected spark.

Through the trees, other areas dance with light and song. The star-strewn sky overhead fades with the first signs of a coming dawn.

Ineri has already darted to Etricos's tent. I follow her, entering on her heels as she announces that I am awake. Etricos stands from behind his table. Demetrios casts off the covers from his bed in the corner.

"Anjeni, you should not be up," Etricos says.

I extinguish the fire in their tent but leave a small oil lamp on the table burning. Its yellow flame throws us all into deep shadows. "Agoros may be upon us at any moment."

Etricos stiffens. "He lives?"

"Yes," I say, with all certainty. When my magic failed upon the cliff, the fiery plains should have burned until their fuel was spent. Their immediate extinction came at the hands of a powerful magician as a threat from afar: whatever I might set ablaze, he could snuff.

The destruction of the Bulokai army occurred before second watch. Agoros has had most of the night to skulk across the scrubby plains and up the Red Cliffs.

Etricos, thankfully, accepts my assertion without further question. "Ineri, gather the other spark-bearers. Send out a call to extinguish all fires and ready for an attack."

Ineri darts into the night. Etricos threads his sword through his belt and follows, but when I move behind him, Demetrios catches my elbow.

"Have you eaten?"

Is he serious right now? I goggle up at him, but he meets my incredulous stare with flat resolve.

"I told Ineri to feed you the moment you woke up. You need your strength." He presses a pair of wafers into my hand, the thin, hard bread that the Helenai warriors carry as provisions.

"I can't—"

"Eat," he says, in a tone that tells me I'm not going anywhere until I comply.

I break off a piece and put it in my mouth. "Agoros might come at any time," I say around it.

"Then eat quickly," Demetrios replies. He straps his sword and his knives in place. "We need you to be strong. Cosi instructed for everyone to remain on guard tonight, but the other tribes ignored his counsel and celebrated your victory instead. Their strength will be spent. Are you rested, Anjeni?"

The tremors that wracked my body last night have all but subsided, with only the faintest sense at the back of my mind that they yet linger. "Yes. You?"

He nods, his hand firm upon my elbow. "We watched over you in shifts. Before you collapsed, you looked at me with such alarm. I thought you were dying."

"I tried to tell you that Agoros was still out there."

He nods and guides me from the tent. The Helenai warriors have dispersed to other areas of the encampment. Commotion disrupts the music that dances upon the night breeze, revelers incensed at having their celebrations curtailed.

I exercise a third superlative on each of the blazes I can see, snuffing out their flames into darkness. More protests sound from the shadows. From further up the cliff, a shriek carries on the wind.

I whirl. A pillar of flames shoots into the air and explodes, rocketing fireballs back down into our midst. I deflect them into the trees. They crash in a spray of sparks, a dozen hungry infernos amid shouts and screams of terror.

"Let the forest burn," Demetrios says before I can summon the superlative that will quench the flames. He drags me into a run toward the source. "Save your energy for Agoros himself."

Bodies stream the opposite direction as we run. The revelers, unprepared, flee into the darkness of the woods as their encampment ignites. To my horror, warriors of the Bulokai follow them, weapons raised and battle cries upon their lips. Whatever army I may have destroyed, Agoros mustered enough of a remnants to mount a formidable attack. Ahead of me, Demetrios hews down those who block our path, his deadly sword precise.

I spy Ria and Aitana working to quell the blazes that have erupted and pause to call out to them. "Search out the enemy magicians! Go!"

They exchange a glance, but I can't linger to see whether they will obey. Demetrios backtracks two steps and grabs me by the wrist to urge me onward.

Fires blaze against the fading stars, erupting through the trees to lick the sky. Embers shimmer around us as we emerge from the forest to the cliff's edge, where inky blackness swathes the plains below. A rim of daylight glimmers on the far horizon. Smoke and the scent of charred wood fill my nostrils.

"Over there!" Demetrios points further up the cliff, where shadows stalk against a flickering backdrop.

I wrench at the flames behind them, but another presence tugs the spark in the opposite direction. The battle of wills lasts only a split-second before I drop my attempt. "He's there," I say, and I dart up the incline.

Silhouettes emerge from the darkness, their weapons raised. Demetrios whirls into their midst, his deadly thrusts rebuffing the attack. "Go," he shouts.

I press up the hill. A spark flares in the night, an enemy magician lurking along my path. Before I can snatch it away, the spark rebounds, consuming the man in flames as he shrieks in agony. Through the trees I glimpse Ineri ducking back into shadows in search of her next prey.

At the highest point of the cliff, an enormous, livid fire rages. It bathes me in vibrant white light as heat ripples the air. I move closer to the tree line, where searing flames consume the upper branches.

A ring of magicians surrounds a central figure, feeding their power to him. Agoros sees me coming. An arc of white-hot fire lashes toward me, but I catch it and fling it back upon his minions. The force of my reaction picks off two men and tosses them into the inferno.

Shock zips through me. They cannot defend themselves because their master controls their spark. This application of the eighth superlative creates a strong central figure but renders those who donate their power vulnerable to attack.

And Agoros knows it. His hard expression does not flinch at the loss of two magicians.

The blistering heat intensifies. It drowns out the frenzied noise of the encampment behind me. Agoros and I face, he in his cage of underlings and I on my own. When he speaks, his voice carries as though we stand alone in a silent room.

"The goddess of the Helenai looks so much smaller in the flesh."

I lift my chin. "As does the tyrant king of the Bulokai."

A sneer crosses his face. "I've come as promised to rain death upon you and your people."

Flames rush the space between us. I force them into the air to dissipate, still processing the best way to fight this fiend and his borrowed strength.

Agoros laughs. "No counter-attack? You must know you can't defeat me. I labored for this power, clawed my way into its depths, faced my own mortality before it would recognize me as its master. No upstart *child* can fathom its true capabilities."

Another wall of flames rips across the earth. I halt it with a superlative, but I cannot wrest full control of it away from the madman.

I am not strong enough. Agoros, like me, is a volcano among rivers.

A cry rips from my throat. I strain against the onslaught of power. To my left, something flits through the wall of white flames. A magician in the ring pitches to one side, and the strength of the magical attack falters in my favor. The blaze hurtles as a ball into the sky, casting the forest and the plains below in mock-daylight for a scant few seconds.

The fallen magician has a knife through his neck. A second knife—from my right this time—picks off another. Agoros screams and lashes fire toward the unseen attackers, only for yet another knife to fly from the left into his midst.

Magic bursts from the Bulokai formation, a fifth intermediate that cuts like an expanding circular blade through the air. I warp the radial attack but fail to deflect it. As I duck my head, it rakes across my arm and neck and slams me into the ground.

The beast within howls. I fling myself aside to dodge a third intermediate. Movement in my periphery catches my attention.

Through the flames, Etricos leaps, sword drawn, and cuts down one of the remaining magicians. Agoros spins, a spell on his fingertips. Demetrios ducks in from the opposite direction as white-hot power sends his brother airborne.

Dread envelops me. A warning cry wrenches from my throat. Demetrios fells another magician, but Agoros turns upon him. I lunge from the ground, my hands moving to protect against the tyrant's attack even as it forms. The magic curves and stabs the chest of one more Bulokai minion. The inferno around Agoros diminishes from white-blue to orange-red.

Even so, he hurtles Demetrios toward the cliff's edge in a fiery burst. I shriek, my feet pounding across the charred earth. A swipe of my wrist fells the last two magicians. Agoros whirls as I barrel into him. We land hard, and I rake my fingernails down his face.

His outrage multiplies. "You think you're a match for me, little girl?" He shoves me away in another explosion.

Stars dance before my eyes. My hair sticks to the side of my face, where sweat and bloodied flesh mingle. Power flares around me, and my focus narrows.

Control. I must control it.

Everything and nothing converged into one universal whole.

Agoros and I both crouch upon the ground, our eyes fixed upon one another as we wrest for command of the maelstrom around us.

He bares his teeth in a snarl. "Submit. You must submit. You *will* submit!"

But I am *stubborn, defiant, refusing to cooperate.* For once in my life, this is my strength instead of my weakness. Without his minions to siphon power from, Agoros and I are close enough to equal.

Two savage volcanos carving destruction in our paths.

But only one of us is willing to die for victory.

I scream. The beast within me screams. The universe itself screams, and the hateful eyes of Agoros bulge. Blazing whiteness overspreads us both, so vivid that my head might shatter.

All is white. A million stars collide, and I evaporate into the radiant aftermath.

CHAPTER THIRTY-EIGHT

BIRDS CHIRP. THEIR SICKENING JOY drags me from my blissful nothingness. My eyelids refuse to open even a crack.

But I *have* eyelids, which means that I'm probably not dead.

A groan tightens in my throat. There is scuffling, and then someone grips my hand. Cool fingers cradle the left side of my face.

"Anjeni? Are you awake?"

Oh, how I love the sound of his voice. It's worth the effort to pry my eyes open just to glimpse him.

"Don't move," Demetrios says, and he strokes my cheek. I squeeze his other hand in mine. He looks terrible—haggard and exhausted, with at least three days of growth on his chin and a bloodied scab across his forehead.

It's a burn mark. It glistens with a salve that smells of heavy herbs. They should have bandaged it, at least.

I try to speak, but my lingering fatigue weighs too heavy on me. Demetrios raises my knuckles to his lips and kisses them. His thumb rubs my cheekbone as his fingers thread into my hair.

I close my eyes and revel in the intimate touch. Sleep reclaims me in a gentle wave.

He is still beside me when I wake again. My eyes flutter open, and I look upon the circular vent above, where smoke curls out to a cloud-tufted sky. A sigh escapes my lungs. The world seems a tranquil place.

"What time is it?" I ask, my voice in a croak.

"Afternoon," he replies. He holds a cup near my mouth. "Can you sit up to drink?"

Rather than allow me my own attempt, he braces my back with his free arm and lifts me upright. The liquid—a watery, vinegary mix—slides down my throat and invigorates my limbs. I try to take the cup from him, but my right arm moves stiffly. Bandages envelop it all the way down to my fingers.

I stare in wonder at the linen strips.

"The burns should heal," Demetrios says.

"Burns?" I echo, catching on the plural. "Where else?"

His mouth tightens in a frank line. Gently he touches my neck from my collarbone up to my ear. Only I can't feel his fingers through the bandages there. Panic wells within me. Demetrios intercepts my hand before I can explore the area.

"They will heal, Anjeni," he says, his voice firm. "Ineri comes twice a day to change your dressing and apply the burn ointment. Baba sent a whole crock of it with us after all the accidents on Cosi's raids, and you have first priority."

His words fail to allay my anxiety. "How long have I slept?"

"Almost a week, love."

"And the others? Etricos? Aitana?"

"Alive and injured, both of them."

"Ria?" I ask.

He shakes his head, a carefully controlled movement.

Tears spring to my eyes. I squash my instinctive grief in pursuit of further information. "What of my other spark-bearers?"

Demetrios settles nearer to me. "The younger ones—those who could not work the superlatives—retreated into the forest. They fought off the wave of foot soldiers that Agoros brought with him and survived. The others..." He fixes me with a steady gaze and decides on a blunt response. "We lost seven spark-bearers to the attack."

My breath catches. With the fury that Agoros brought, seven is so few, but it is too many. These were my students. "And how many others?" I ask on a whisper.

He leans in and kisses my cheek. I tighten my grip on his hand before he can withdraw. "How many others died, Demetrios?"

Reluctance colors his voice. "Hundreds. Among the Helenai, a third of our warriors. Among our allies, more than two-thirds. Those who fled to the woods escaped the blazes that swept through the camp."

A sob works up my throat. Demetrios leans close again and whispers fervent words.

"Agoros is dead and the Bulokai scattered. Our sacrifice was not in vain."

He wipes my tears and gently takes me into his arms, so that I can cry my sorrow upon his shoulder.

Agoros brought death, as he promised he would. I am lucky not to be numbered among the fallen, but I don't deserve such luck when I failed to protect so many.

The Bulokai encampment is a patchwork of black against the scrubby plains. Etricos has pilfered from its ruins anything that survived my monstrous attack. He rides daily with the most able-bodied warriors to hunt down any remnants of the enemy, but by now they have fled this part of the land.

Our own encampment hardly fared better. Charred trees jut toward the sky like blackened sword-points. The inferno destroyed most of the tents, along with any who slept within. Our allied tribes suffered the higher loss because they refused to heed Etricos's warning for vigilance. Those who remain listen to him now.

Eight days after that final battle, he decrees it time to return to our own lands. "But only if you feel well enough to travel, Goddess Anjeni," he says to me in private.

He knows I will not protest.

His injuries, like his brother's, are less severe than mine. The burns have crusted over and the cuts mend. Aitana has a broken arm. Ineri escaped mostly unscathed and has the joy of tending us all as her reward.

We have fewer horses than people now and can travel only as fast as the slowest among us walk. Demetrios keeps close by me, as do my spark-bearers. Aitana's brother and sister remain near her, both of them on foot. Their father died in the battle, leaving the pair with no family other than the sister they yet fear.

Though we make a tattered, frightful group, Etricos rides at our head with his spine straight. One of his warriors cries out our victory to every village we pass. The inhabitants shout praises. Many of them gather their meager belongings and follow our company, until our numbers swell and straggle through the woods and plains in a long line.

After five days, we arrive at the familiar sloping hills of our safe haven. The waiting city greets us with festivities and feasts. The people bow in reverence to me, though they eye the bandages that yet cover my arm and neck. The raw skin beneath throbs, and I self-consciously toy with the edges of the linen strips.

"Your injuries are tokens of victory, Anjeni," says Etricos from beside me. "You above all others merit our praise."

My attention strays to Demetrios, who has resumed his position as a mere warrior before the crowds in the council hall. Our return to the city marks a return to the distance between us, for his brother's sake.

"You merit more praise than I do, Etricos," I say. "You have proven yourself a great leader."

He scoffs. "Leader? No. We have a goddess. What need have we of any other leader?"

I look to him sharply. On my other side, Moru angles his head. "You do not aspire to lead the Helenai?" he asks.

"To what end?" Etricos replies. "I will have no children to inherit. Let the people follow Goddess Anjeni and her chosen consort. The Helenai may establish their dynasty from her issue."

My voice lowers to a hiss. "I didn't come to establish a dynasty. I came to establish a republic. The voice of the people will choose you as the first leader of Helenia."

He favors me with a smile. "They will choose you, Goddess. They know to whom they owe their deliverance."

"I was never meant to stay among you, Etricos." The truth of those words—along with the absolute necessity of my eventual departure—thrums through me. Surprise flickers in his eyes. His brother never told him that I would one day leave through the same portal that brought me here.

He recovers his wits quick enough. "Wherever you go, the people will follow."

"They cannot follow me back through the Eternity Gate!"

A hush falls down the line of tribal elders. They turn from the celebration feast to fix their attention on me.

Etricos, well aware of his expanded audience, quirks a half-smile. "That may be so. But as long as you are here, Anjeni, you will be the only leader I or anyone else will recognize. You have earned that honor, and we give it to you freely."

Moru nods his agreement, along with the other elders on either side of me. My voice catches in disbelief, but what can I say to refute them? Instead I seethe with growing dismay.

As daylight bleeds into night and the festivities wane, Demetrios escorts me up the hill to my tent.

"I have to go back," I blurt. "When the Gate opens again, I have to go back."

He studies me, silent. My face burns with self-consciousness—more so beneath the bandage that runs along my neck. The injury disfigures me. I need no mirror to know that my right ear is mangled, and that the scar will encroach upon my cheek. Perhaps he will not lament my departure at all. Aitana's pretty face emerged from the conflict without a blemish to it.

"You would abandon me?" he asks.

My breath leaves my lungs in a whoosh. The strain of the day's celebrations—of the week's travels, of the month's battles, of all my existence in this era—cracks within me. "According to the legends of my time, Demetrios, you are the one who abandons me."

He recoils. "What? That's a lie."

I shake my head and resume my path up the hill, but he clamps a hand upon my shoulder and drags me back.

"Anjeni, it's a lie. I would never abandon you."

I can't meet his gaze. I shouldn't have spoken, but I cannot retract my words. He releases his hold upon me and steps back a pace.

"This is truly what your legends say? I thought I was to choose my own future."

Music floats up from the city, a merry tune that contrasts with the somber mood between us. I swallow my emotions and disclose the ugly truth.

"The warrior Demetrios, the goddess Anjeni's lover, abandons her for another woman. Anjeni vanishes into the Eternity Gate with a broken heart."

"What other woman?" he asks, his voice tight. "Did they give my paramour a name, or am I to run off with an unknown, unsung entity?"

At this point, I might as well reveal that final detail. I turn my gaze upon the city that glows bright against the darkness around it. "Our legends say that you abandon me for Aitana."

"Your legends are absolute rubbish." He is angry, and rightfully so.

I raise my hand to his face, though I am surprised that he allows the touch instead of bucking away. "I'm sorry. I should not have spoken. You are not the Demetrios of legends."

"But you have believed all this time that I was."

"I believed what I had been taught in my infancy, yes. I believed it when I first arrived, and for many weeks afterward. But as I came to know you better, I often thought it would be my fault rather than yours." My breath squeezes in my chest as I consider this possibility anew. "Perhaps it is my fault still."

He grasps my hand upon his cheek and kisses the palm with such ardor that it shoots a wave of goosebumps to my toes. Then, throwing caution to the wind, he wraps his arms around me and kisses me in full view of the celebrating city.

Fireworks, that's what this moment needs. They explode in my head, but they should be bursting in the starry sky above.

"So long as you are here, I will be by your side," Demetrios says, resting his forehead against mine.

I steady my breath and will my racing heart to calm. "So long as I am here, your brother will not ascend to his rightful place. Would you lead the Helenai in his stead?"

A frown wrinkles his brows. "Cosi is a fool. You should command him to play his proper part, and he should obey."

I chuckle at the simple solution, but we both know how well it would work. Etricos, having set his mind to a particular course, will not deviate from it.

Demetrios turns his attention elsewhere. "I am to be your lover but not your husband, then? I don't like that."

"You can be my husband, if you want—if you can find someone to marry us, and if you're willing to become the consort of a scarred and fraudulent goddess. But not until after the bandages come off, I think." I raise my right hand, where the linen binds my hidden wounds. What lies beneath that wrap is an unsightly mess.

"I see no cause to wait unless you wish it, Anjeni."

"I think I do." Uncertainty of the future still roils within me. I cannot rush into such a commitment while my mind is yet in such turmoil.

With a sigh, Demetrios drapes an arm around my shoulders and guides me toward my waiting tent.

I contemplate his earlier words as we walk. "The legends aren't rubbish, you know. They're only incomplete—fragments of fact woven together by fancy."

"I intend to prove them wrong, at least where my reputation is concerned," he says.

Really, I'd be more than grateful if he did.

CHAPTER THIRTY-NINE

THE CITY SPREADS QUICKLY. With the Bulokai vanquished, people flock to the fledgling nation of Helenia and the goddess who watches over it. Tents mushroom and buildings multiply. In council, Moru proposes that I move my dwelling to the hill above the Eternity Gate, where Etricos's pavilion stands.

"That is where the leader of Helenia will live," I say.

"And you are our leader," Etricos pipes up. Though the people hail him as a hero, he seems content to farm the plot of land alongside Tora's grave. He even builds a house there now.

I have discovered that there's no point arguing about my leadership. My tent moves from one hill to the other, and the council talks of erecting a permanent structure. I can't argue against that proposal either. Huna, my perpetual chaperone, deserves a solid roof over her head.

I fill my days with teaching my spark-bearers. More and more join our ranks from the incoming tribes, no longer in hiding now that the threat of certain death has vanished. Ineri and Aitana share in the responsibility. We feel of Ria's absence every day, along with the six others who perished in the Bulokai flames, but our younger students steadily progress. One day they will fill the gap their predecessors left behind.

The dry season looms before us. The afternoons grow hot and the storms ebb from downpours to spitting. On the day that Huna determines my bandages no longer necessary, I remove the dressings and study the scars left behind.

The mark upon my arm twists from my hand to my shoulder in an angry reddish pink that clashes with the natural earthy color of my skin. It is fire inscribed upon my very flesh, a lifelong reminder of the battle I fought. The mark upon my neck curves up and around toward the back of my head, into the hairline. My earlobe is gone and the shell above it crumpled. The surviving hair closest to it was shaved while I healed, but it will grow back to cover the disfigurement.

If I wish to cover it.

The rest of my hair falls past my shoulders now. I study my reflection in a polished disk of metal. I hardly know the woman who looks back at me.

Should I veil this face and arm from view, to maintain my dignity as a goddess of this people?

But these scars are tokens of victory, as Etricos said. They prove that I once faced a formidable monster and triumphed.

I set the mirror aside and bind my hair into a high ponytail. The ruined flesh upon my arm blazes bright as I cross from my tent into the outside world.

"We wish to return to our own lands, Goddess Anjeni."

I sit in counsel with the elders of Helenia. Twenty men, women, and children stand before me. They belong to one of the first tribes to seek refuge with the Helenai, but their elder on the council does not stand in their midst. Instead he shakes his head.

"There is safety here," he tells them.

"And we are grateful for it," the leader of this small group replies. "But we yearn for our home in the mountains. The snows there will soon melt. Spring and summer will allow us time to rebuild what we have lost. Goddess, please, we wish for your blessing to depart."

I look to the elder of their tribe, who shakes his head again. He has done all he can to persuade them, but if they will insist, we cannot force them to remain.

"The journey will be difficult," I say. "Your families and your flocks will face danger from marauders along the way." The remnants of the Bulokai, small bands of warriors who evaded destruction, now haunt the highlands, harassing travelers that pass through their domains. Etricos contends that, in time, we will hunt them to extinction. For now we must focus our efforts elsewhere.

The leader of this small faction remains undeterred. "We hope, with your blessing, to take ships up the coast and start our trek from there."

We have ships now—small, light vessels that bob upon the ocean to catch the fish so essential to this people's survival. "You wish for a ferry north, then?" I ask.

The spokesman nods. "Yes. And…" He twiddles his fingers together nervously. I wait for him to gather his courage. "And we invite any who may wish to come with us—farmers, hunters, warriors… spark-bearers."

The murmur in our daily crowd deadens to a hush. Everyone focuses on me to gauge my response.

But I refuse to make a spectacle. "Those who wish to join you may do so. This is a free nation."

He glances at the onlookers. Most of them frown, skeptical of the decision.

"Goddess, I would like to join them."

I turn curious eyes upon Aitana. She separates herself from the other spark-bearers that sit in attendance during this morning council. With a stiff neck she meets my gaze.

Does she expect me to challenge her? To beg her to stay?

But her attention flits to Etricos, and then to Demetrios at his post by the wall. It is not my reaction she seeks. If she desires opposition from either brother, their disinterest surely must cut her to the quick. Etricos spares her only a sidelong glance before returning his attention to the petitioners. Demetrios merely offers her a wooden smile.

Aitana's face flushes with chagrin. "May I join this group, Goddess?"

Yes, and good riddance.

"The choice is yours," I say. "Would your brother and sister go with you?"

She inclines her head. "They are unaccustomed to this climate. The lands further north would suit them better." As though she makes this decision on their behalf rather than her own. The strongest of my spark-bearers will hold a high position in this new community. She might even believe she punishes the Helenai for not valuing her more.

Pity she doesn't know that I am meant to leave this place. She would be my logical successor here.

A strong spark-bearer among our allies will ensure them protection on their journey. She can be a teacher should the spark manifest among them.

All the same, if Ineri were the one asking to go, I would do everything in my power to dissuade her.

The group leader looks as though he might cry for joy to have such a remarkable addition to his ranks. The word spreads through the city, and when all is decided, roughly eighty souls choose to leave our safe haven for this new destination. Preparations ensue, with an alliance established between this offshoot and the fledgling Helenia. These people will reclaim their lands under our banner. The nation expands through colonization rather than war.

As their departure nears, Aitana finds excuses to speak with Etricos and Demetrios. She talks of the opportunities, of the mountain homeland they left behind and how the climate of this new settlement might be similar. She hints with everything but words that they should come with her or insist that she remain.

Etricos has no desire to stray from his beloved Tora's grave. He ignores her hints outright. Demetrios, fiend that he is, listens and smiles, and when her back is turned he winks at me.

When the group's day of departure arrives, a crowd accompanies them to the shore. Etricos and Demetrios go to see them off. On Moru's advice, I remain behind. The council of Helenia does not wish to encourage others to leave this land; though the goddess might grant permission, she shows no special favor.

As sunset descends I exit my tent to trailing clouds upon the horizon. Earlier I could spy the little boats upon the ocean, mere specks against the ribbon of glittering waves, but they have moved beyond sight. Most of the farewell crowds have returned. Isolated on Monument Hill, I have encountered none of them, but I expect Demetrios will make his way over sometime this evening.

Unless Aitana clubbed him over the head and dragged him with her into a boat, that is.

My steps take me to the hillside where the Eternity Gate looms in its vigil above the city. Shadows stretch across the buildings as the fiery orange in the sky recedes into purpling darkness. I lie in the grass, as I did in days long past, and contemplate my existence among this people.

My nerves will calm once I know Aitana is gone. Talented as she is at magic, her sour attitude grates on me daily. Part of me still fears the fate I always believed would occur—particularly when I catch sight of my reflection and the mangled ear I refuse to hide.

I'm not sure at what point my mind registers the humming. It sounds at first like low white noise, as though it has always been there, but it grows stronger when I focus on it. In confusion, I sit up.

The air within the Eternity Gate shimmers.

"Oh." The syllable leaves my throat on a sigh. Dismay, regret, confusion pervade my thoughts. Is this the universe telling me my purpose here is complete? I glance around. Huna is in the city, Ineri with the younger spark-bearers. Etricos and Demetrios linger somewhere along the path from the ocean, I assume.

I would have liked to say goodbye.

A familiar cityscape flashes in the gap, and my heart quickens.

Home. And yet no longer home. My fear that the Eternity Gate might send me to another time and place dissipates, but a disconnect from the modern world before me lingers. How long has it been since Tana shoved me through? Minutes? Days? Years? How will the people of my era react to the Gate opening? Do they even know it opened a first time?

I push away from the ground and approach with caution. In wonder, I touch the rippling energy and receive the same electric shock I suffered almost a year ago. I jerk back my hand and hold it protectively to my chest. The cityscape interlaces with its primitive foundation, daytime skyscrapers overlaid upon nighttime huts.

The Gate may never give me another chance. It may connect elsewhere if it ever opens again. Whether I'm ready to pass through it is of little concern.

Etricos must ascend to his proper place. That legendary event at least I must honor.

If I go, I will stride through with triumph and dignity. The goddess Anjeni will return in a blaze of glory, her heart mended from wounds the legend did not know she bore.

"Anjeni! What are you doing?"

My breath spasms in my chest. I whirl to discover Demetrios bounding from the hilltop, alarm on his face. He stops several paces short of me, his huge eyes moving from me to the rippling portal and back again.

"It's open," I say—stupidly so. The Gate casts a daytime scene against the night around us. Obviously it's open.

Demetrios steps forward as though to intercept me, but he stops himself. A pained expression crosses his face. "You were going to leave without even saying goodbye?"

"No! I was here and it opened. I didn't know—"

"Don't go."

This plea strips my senses. "What?"

"Don't go, Anjeni. Stay here. Stay with me. Please."

An iron belt binds my lungs. My breath, shallow and constricted, comes in small gulps. "If I stay, Etricos cannot rise to his full potential."

He shakes his head. "I don't care."

"But I do," I reply.

"We can go elsewhere, you and I, just as Aitana and the others have today."

"You would leave your brother and your people?"

Demetrios waves aside this concern. "Cosi will understand."

But others would follow us, possibly more souls than left in this splinter group today. Wherever I go in this land, I will be the goddess Anjeni, and wherever the goddess dwells, that will be the recognized seat of power. Leaving would undermine the strength of Helenia in its infancy.

I look once more through the rippling membrane. The city of my upbringing flutters in and out of sight—the trees, the skyline. It's close enough for me to touch. I can step back through to the world I know, to the conveniences of a modern society where magic is a novelty instead of a necessity, to indoor plumbing and hot water on tap and telephones and electronics and everything easy.

I can return to my family.

Or, I can stay with Demetrios and seek another avenue to elevate Etricos from hero to leader.

Is it worth it? Is it worth the risk of failure, the sacrifice of a difficult life?

I must be crazy, because I think it is.

I brush tentative fingers against the portal's opening, a silent farewell to the world of my youth as my decision solidifies—

And a weight slams into me, propelling me through the gap. Light and flame erupt. Daylight envelopes me, and so, too, does a strong embrace. I tumble down the hill tucked against that second body, my senses jumbled.

Somewhere on the way down, the hold upon me releases, and one falling projectile becomes two. I slide to a stop at the base of Monument Hill, the ornamental fence looming above me, and the figure beside me lifting up on his elbows, bewildered.

Demetrios.

He tackled me.

Through the Eternity Gate.

"What... did... you... *do*?" I ask through gritted teeth. The sky above dazzles with blue behind a stretch of puffy white clouds. I arch my neck to view the Gate. The air within its gap has no shimmer.

Demetrios's breath heaves in his lungs. "If you will not stay, I must come with you. How can I live where you don't exist?"

That's incredibly sweet. And ridiculously stupid. He knows nothing of this world. He's just given up everything familiar to him to follow me. My insides roil and panic swells in my throat—

His hand clasps mine in the space between us. He lies flat, staring upward at the sky, at the clouds, at the fence and trees. "I was gone half a day and you were set to abandon me. What am I to think of that?"

"You shouldn't have done this." My voice quivers, my anxiety held at bay by the thinnest of restraints. "The Gate won't open again. You're stuck here."

"With you," he says.

I swallow a sob. "What if you regret it?"

"I won't."

"Demetrios, I was going to stay."

He turns his head, his gaze a caress upon me. "I know. But I realized I had no right to ask it of you. And because you have never thought to invite me to come with you, I made that choice on my own. The fates have aligned, Anjeni."

How am I going to handle the intensity of this man for the rest of my life? "They didn't align. You forced them into place."

"Then I have done well."

With a self-congratulating smile, he rolls over and kisses me—or I kiss him. Regardless of who instigated it, we tangle together at the base of Monument Hill like two shameless lovers who have jumped the fence to engage in a public display of affection on government land.

Which is how the security guards find us.

Their shouts strike my ears like a song played on an untuned violin. Demetrios, ever the warrior, bolts to his knees and grips the weapons he always keeps at his belt.

I forestall him from drawing them. "Don't panic. This is my world. Hold my hand, and whatever you do, don't let go of it."

He interlaces his fingers in mine. Together we rise. A circle of guards converges on us, handguns raised in warning. Recognition flashes across their faces as they meet my gaze. Weapons lower in wonder.

I smile an awkward, crooked smile, my native language rusty on my tongue.

"Hello. I'm back from my spiritual journey."

The guards quarantine Demetrios and me within a holding cell at the security base. They would have split us up, except that I persuaded them not to.

Like, with-a-threatening-fistful-of-magic persuaded them.

The quarantine is a precaution, but a good one. There's no telling what germs we've brought back with us, and Demetrios has never been inoculated against the diseases of this era. The less contact he has prior to vaccination, the better.

(How do I explain to a warrior from seven hundred years past that he needs to let someone stab him repeatedly with a series of needles? We'll manage, somehow.)

The Eternity Gate, as it turns out, shot out a magnetic flare both times I passed through it. In the ancient world, with no electronic devices to worry about, this occurred without notice or difficulty. Here in modern day, it has caused havoc. They're still trying to pull the security system fully back online. A glass wall separates us from the rest of the room in which we wait.

Demetrios has obeyed to the letter my instructions to keep hold of my hand. We sit together on a low couch facing the glass panel, his fingers still interlaced with mine. Twice I have tried to withdraw, but he only tightens his grip.

If he's content, I have no complaints.

He gapes at the room with its electric lights and unfamiliar materials. The most menial of modern technologies awe him. I rest my head on his shoulder as I watch him take in his surroundings. I half wait for the moment when regret will strike him full force.

Surely it will. I'm a mass of writhing insecurities over its impending advent.

As if sensing my fears, he squeezes my hand again. He dips his head to whisper, "Anjeni, I do not understand your world. Are you sorry I'm here?"

I straighten in my seat. "No."

"Good. Because you're stuck with me." He plants a kiss on my cheek.

Voices carry from another room. The door beyond the glass wall opens, and two security guards usher in on either side of it, followed closely by my grim-faced father. He looks like he has aged ten years since I last saw him, with gray hair at his temples and deep-set lines around his mouth. He stops short just within the threshold.

Will he scold me? Disown me?

Does he even recognize me? I am not the same jaded daughter who quarreled with him on that night so long ago.

"Anjeni." My name falls from his lips in a strangled whisper. In two steps he crosses the distance to the glass wall, and presses his palm flat against it.

Homesickness surges within me, but I remain on the couch, my hand clasped in my love's. "Hi, Daddy."

My father searches my face as though he cannot believe his own eyes. Perhaps he can't. Not only my scars but my clothes and my companion present a foreign picture. He glances questioningly at Demetrios and then back at me.

A breathy laugh escapes my throat. "I brought back a stowaway." I switch dialects and address Demetrios. "This is my father."

His eyes widen. "Tell him we ask his blessing to marry."

I almost choke. There's no way I can lead with that request.

"Anjeni," he says, his voice reproving, "we should have married already, long ago. Your honor and mine both demand it now."

His sense of honor is adorable. I can only imagine the massive culture shock that lies ahead for him. I turn back to my father, who has watched this interchange with fascinated attention.

"We're getting married as soon as we're out of quarantine," I say. "Or you could send for a priest now and we'll perform the rite here, since we'll be staying in this room together. How's Mom? Tana? How long have I been gone?"

The final question jars him from his critical inspection of my betrothed. "Eighteen months. Anjeni, where did you go?"

It was closer to ten months for me on the other side. Does that mean I'm younger than I should be? Did I lose more than half a year coming back? Am I that much nearer to Tana in age?

"Anjeni," he says, pulling me from my speculation, "*where* have you been?"

"I..." My voice falters. "I don't think you'd believe me."

He eyes Demetrios again. Perhaps, deep down, he knows the truth. Whether he can accept it is another story. Even I might wonder if I had dreamt the whole interlude were it not for the flesh-and-blood warrior at my side.

A commotion at the door draws our attention. My mother passes through, takes one look at me behind the glass wall, and promptly bursts into tears.

"My mother," I whisper to Demetrios, who nods his understanding. His grip on my fingers tightens.

"Jen," she sobs, her forehead and one hand against the glass. She stares at me in disbelief, tears tumbling from her cheeks to patter at her feet. "How could you vanish like that? Do you have any idea how sick with worry we've been?"

She too has aged, though not to the same degree as my father. Renado has kept any new gray hairs nicely hidden, at least.

"I'm sorry," I say. It's true, and at the same time, it isn't. If I hadn't quarreled with my parents, I would never have caused them such grief. But it had to happen. It put me where I needed to be. It brought me to this point with this man by my side.

Speaking of Demetrios, "She's complaining that I disappeared," I tell him under my breath. "She says they were worried."

He wears a studious expression, already contemplating the foreign dialect.

My mother catches my string of what, to her, must sound like gibberish. Her tear-streaked face agape, she examines us beyond the glass wall.

"She brought a man back with her," says my father in an audible aside. "She says they're getting married."

Mom's eyes grow rounder. I suppress an instinctive laugh, and she takes umbrage at my good humor. "Where have you been, Anjeni? How did you open the Eternity Gate?"

"I didn't open it. It opened itself."

Mom thumps her fist against the glass. "But what could have possibly induced you to pass through it?"

I start to reply, but the words strangle in my throat. They don't know the truth.

"Where's Tana?" I ask, an edge to my voice.

Dad glances toward the door behind him and looks quizzically to Mom. She shakes her head, a tiny movement. "She was right behind me," she whispers, and then she turns on me. "Your sister has worried herself into a terrible state over you, Jen."

"Is that so?" I can't say anything more. My emotions have thoroughly detached. My parents think I passed through the Eternity Gate by choice, which means that in my eighteen-month absence, Tana never confessed her part in my "spiritual journey."

A shadow moves in the open door. My sister sidles up to the jamb, one hand clutching it tight, her cheeks hollow and dark circles beneath her eyes. Across the gap, her gaze meets mine. She flinches and looks away.

I teeter halfway between rage and laughter.

In eighteen months, my sister has wasted from worry not for my welfare, but for her own. She pushed me through the Gate, but she never told anyone. She has borne the burden of her guilt alone.

For the first time in my life, I pity her—truly and surely pity her.

"That is my sister, Aitana," I say to Demetrios.

He studies Tana with a frown. "The goddess Aitana?"

"I sincerely hope so." If the Eternity Gate ever opens again and she's nearby, I'll certainly give her a shove. If she's lucky, her spiritual journey will yield as many blessings as mine has. "And if you abandon me for *her*," I add with a note of wry humor, "I'll curse you and your children to the seventh generation."

He spares me a sidelong glare, refusing to dignify my jest with a verbal response.

I laugh and settle closer to him. "Hey, golden child, are you coming in, or do you plan to skulk in the doorway?"

A spark lights her eyes. Perhaps she realizes that I'm not going to rat her out here. With a stir of confidence, she slinks into the room, but she cannot meet my gaze as she joins our parents.

"Eighteen months," I muse. "I guess you've graduated high school and started college, then. Just another place you've surpassed me, Tana."

She tips her head and sets her jaw in a defiant line.

"Jen, how can you be so flippant?" Mom asks. "I told you your sister has worried herself sick over you. She hasn't even been able to concentrate on her magic studies, let alone her schoolwork."

Surprise darts through me. Before I can utter any smart remarks, my father hits on a tangent.

"Speaking of magic, the security guards told me you threatened them with a fistful of flames. Is that true?"

"I don't know what you're talking about," I reply, all innocence.

"Anjeni," he says in a warning voice.

I plaster a smile on my face. "It's so nice to be home, to see my family again. None of you has changed a bit, and neither have I. 'Stubborn as a mule,' you might recall."

Dad glowers. I shouldn't stonewall him, but it's awkward to tell the people who always knew me best that their insistent training finally paid off. Magic is a novelty here, sure, but it was life or death in the past, and this quarantine room seems too trivial to summon it.

"Does this man of yours have a name?" my mother asks. She studies Demetrios with mingled apprehension and awe.

I start to answer, but on impulse I change directions. "His name is Dima." Demetrios looks to me in surprise. I can't explain it to him, but my time in the past is suddenly precious to me. The moment I disclose his full name, their speculation will multiply. The truth will worm its way out, and everything will change. Will my parents broadcast that their daughter is the legendary Anjeni? Would the citizens of Helenia even believe such a tale? All I can think of is endless news cycles, demands for interviews, panels of "experts" opining on things they know nothing about.

"His name is Dima," I say again, firmly. I squeeze his hand. "He is mine, and I am his."

My father bucks his head at the declaration. "You must know we can't just set someone from another world loose in ours, Anjeni. A doctor will examine you both, and you will be released, but he—"

"Where I go he goes," I interrupt. "We're a matching set now."

"Anjeni, we can't—"

"You're the president of Helenia. You can order his release alongside mine."

My father's mouth sets at a stubborn angle. They want to keep Demetrios for what? Inquiries? Testing? Dissection? Over my dead body.

So much for keeping my magic to myself. My eyes slide shut and my astral projection rises in a billow of blackened flames. I glide toward the glass wall—*through* the glass wall—and confront my swiftly retreating father face to face.

"Know this," I say. "We have submitted to this quarantine as a courtesy. I have earned every last battle scar on my body, and I can destroy this entire building with a flick of my wrist. Your stubborn, defiant daughter has returned, and she will have her way in this matter. Do you understand?"

I have backed my family up against the wall. My father gibbers, nodding quickly. If Mom and Tana gape any wider, their eyes will fall out of their sockets.

Demetrios summons me back to my body with a pinch on my arm. I open my eyes and look quizzically up at him.

"You menace your own father and mother? Shame on you."

"They want to separate us and keep you here," I reply.

His grip tightens on my hand, and he seems suddenly less condemning of my deed.

Across the room, my father huffs as he straightens his tie. "I'll see what I can arrange, Jen."

I offer him a smile and a sunny, "Thank you."

Modern clothes seem strange upon Demetrios, but he looks good. I pause in my walk to appreciate how well the crisp button-up shirt fits against his shoulders. A passing car honks and we both jump.

"Why is everything here so loud?" he asks.

I sigh. "I know. I'm sorry. I have just this one last errand, and then we can leave."

After a week of quarantine, my father arranged for our release, complete with an identification profile for Demetrios to use going forward—not that he has the first clue what to do with it. During our time cooped up in that glass room, I took the opportunity to reacquaint myself with this era and to make some decisions.

We're leaving the city. I miss the stars and the quiet tranquility that I took for granted. Demetrios, unaccustomed to this hectic alien lifestyle, yearns for simplicity. We might try our hands at farming or ranching. We might become vagabonds. Whatever we choose, it will be away from the hustle and lights and cacophony that surround us at present. And we will succeed because we have each other.

A security detail dogs our footsteps, just like old times. Word has spread that the president's oldest daughter, who disappeared under exceedingly mysterious circumstances, has returned. Reporters and photographers alike seek me out, hoping I'll grant them an exclusive. They can settle for taking pictures of my fire-scarred neck and arm.

The path at my feet, so familiar, seems short. I crest upon a hill and view my high school and the magic academy adjacent to it. At some point, I'll probably have to sit for a test to earn my diploma. Today my footsteps orient toward the second building, though.

The Dean of Magic waits for me at the entrance. He eyes the side of my face. Renado has provided me with a dramatic undercut to showcase my damaged flesh when I wear my hair up, like I do today.

"Jen, it's so nice to see you again," he says, as if we weren't archenemies for twelve long years.

I nod and gesture to Demetrios. "This is my husband, Dima."

The dean mumbles some awkward pleasantry, proof that rumors of Demetrios's origins have circulated despite my father's best efforts to keep them under wraps. Demetrios, still working on the modern dialect, only nods in response. Hands in my pockets, I proceed into the building.

It's smaller than I remember. The students at their tables pause in their lessons; their tutors regard me with open curiosity—Miss Corlan among them.

I focus on the dean. "I know you're busy, so I won't keep you long."

He spreads his hands in an artless gesture. "An audience with the enigmatic Anjeni Sigourna is a rarity these days. You have as much of my time as you desire."

I take this as proof that rumors of my magic abilities have circulated as well. But that suits me fine under the circumstances. It saves me the hassle of revealing them myself.

"I came to say thank you."

Surprise flickers across his face.

I continue. "It was difficult, all those years of coming here with nothing to show for my efforts. I'm sure it was more difficult for you to put up with me. I know my parents fought to keep me here and that you would have rather expelled me from ever entering your doors, but thank you. The knowledge I received—little though I appreciated it at the time—saved my life and countless others."

Again he eyes the scars that twist up my right side. "You will not, I suppose, indulge me with a demonstration?" He shifts his attention to the nearest table, where one of his dreaded candles presides.

"I'm not a riverbed."

My hands remain in my pockets, but a spark jumps from one of the other tables to the waiting wick.

The dean hisses an appreciative breath as the room goes completely still.

"You've had others like me in the past," I say, "students who tested positive but never manifested a spark. If you encounter any in the future, and if they truly want to learn, you can send them to me."

He acknowledges this offer but chooses to address a different point. "What do you mean, you're not a riverbed?"

"I mean that your first fundamental of magic is completely useless to me. But I won't complain about it, because it's my own fault that everyone learns it that way."

The goddess Anjeni restored the principles of magic to the people of Helenia. Much to my consternation, I began the very traditions I despised throughout my youth. The only explanation that assuages my feelings is that those traditions—and I, and Demetrios, and all the people in this world—belong to a greater whole than I can comprehend.

Everything and nothing converged.

My errand complete, I take my leave as the shell-shocked Dean of Magic digests my final remark. Demetrios and I fall in line with our waiting security detail outside.

The city stretches before me, teeming with millions of people on their daily errands. They have their lives and goals and ambitions. I have mine.

The universe doesn't make mistakes.

Had I been crafted any different, I would have failed in my purpose. Armed with such knowledge, I can nurture others in similar straits.

And, if the universe allows it, I surely will.

ACKNOWLEDGMENTS

I didn't intend for this book to be so long. But then, I never intended to write it at all. When I pulled it from my stockpile of ideas, it was solely for tinkering purposes, so that I could look like I was being productive without actually investing myself into the process.

It was supposed to be a novella, if I ever finished it. Ha.

My critique partners, Jill Burgoyne and Rachel Collett, saw more potential in the story than I did and demanded that I develop my plot and my characters properly. Without the candid analyses of these two friends, Anjeni would have been a mere shadow of what she is today.

So, Jill and Rachel, thank you. You were right, on many, many occasions. You have that in print now, so treasure it.

I'm grateful also to my mom, Edith, who hates first person narration but loves this story anyway, and to my sister, Kristen, who felt like it was her bygone teenaged angst I was channeling instead of my own. Their faithful encouragement throughout this project has been invaluable.

Lastly, I give thanks to my Heavenly Father, who told me I could quit writing if I wanted to and then provided all the support I could possibly need to continue. This book in particular has been a huge learning opportunity. I'm so blessed to have had the difficult, slogging experience of writing it.

Hard work is the best work.

(Much as I sometimes wish otherwise.)

K.S.
July 2017

ABOUT THE AUTHOR

Kate Stradling is the author of seven fantasy novels, including *Goldmayne: A Fairy Tale*, *Kingdom of Ruses*, *Tournament of Ruses*, and *The Legendary Inge*. She received her BA in English from Brigham Young University and her MA in English from Arizona State. She blogs about linguistics, language use, and literary tropes at katestradling.com. She currently lives in Mesa, Arizona.

Printed in Great
Britain
by Amazon